A Calamity of Souls

DAVID BALDACCI

A Calamity of Souls

MACMILLAN

First published 2024 by Grand Central Publishing, USA

First published in the UK 2024 by Macmillan
an imprint of Pan Macmillan
The Smithson, 6 Briset Street, London EC1M 5NR
EU representative: Macmillan Publishers Ireland Ltd, 1st Floor,
The Liffey Trust Centre, 117–126 Sheriff Street Upper,
Dublin 1, D01 YC43
Associated companies throughout the world
www.panmacmillan.com

ISBN 978-1-0350-3558-8 HB
ISBN 978-1-0350-3559-5 TPB

1 3 5 7 9 8 6 4 2

A CIP catalogue record for this book is available from the British Library.

Printed and bound by CPI Group (UK) Ltd, Croydon, CR0 4YY

Visit **www.panmacmillan.com** to read more about all our books
and to buy them. You will also find features, author interviews and
news of any author events, and you can sign up for e-newsletters
so that you're always first to hear about our new releases.

To librarians and teachers: The shining stars of my universe

AUTHOR'S NOTE

I started writing this novel well over a decade ago, by hand, in a journal like the one my mother gave me as a child to jot down my stories. Then I set the manuscript aside to work on other projects, but something kept pulling me back to the story, and it has to do with my past.

I grew up in the sixties and seventies in Richmond, Virginia, the old capital of the Confederacy, home to all those statues of rebel elites on Monument Avenue. I was not born into economic privilege, and I grew up with an ethnic surname in a world steeped in the history of the Old South, where the names Lee, Jackson, Stuart, and Davis were revered by many. Thinking back, I believe I would not have become a writer had I not been born in that place and at that time.

I was observant and curious, and I remember much from my youth. Where I grew up, the Black-white divide was so ingrained that despite the efforts of the Civil Rights movement and the Warren Court, life was not so very different from many decades before. The old ways were intractable, and accepted to such an extent that most people never even thought about it, at least people who looked like me. And while I was the observer of racial bigotry and hatred, I was never the target. To borrow a line from Mark Twain, that is truly the difference between the lightning bug and the lightning.

There are many autobiographical elements in this story, from how Jack Lee grew up—although decades earlier than I did—to the thoughts, questions, and misgivings he had about the world in which he lived, how books played an important role in forming his outlook on life, the sometimes confusing and conflicting relationships with family and friends, and the uneasy coexistence of Black and white worlds, for they were distinct, separate entities. Like Jack, I delivered the morning paper, and I grew up to be a trial lawyer. My mechanic father fixed up an old Fiat that I drove for a period of time. And there is a Tuxedo Boulevard in Richmond, and, yes, to the best of my recollection, the county dump was at the end of the all-Black neighborhood.

My sixth-grade class was one of the first in Virginia to be bused to a Black school, finally realizing *Brown v. Board*'s ruling, albeit nearly twenty years late. It was an emotionally and mentally bewildering time for all the students, which I looked back on for quite a while as traumatizing. However, as I grew older, I came to understand that it had been necessary to allow children from different walks of life to finally be together after having been separated for centuries for purely toxic reasons.

When writing a novel dealing with race in America, the subject of the N-word usually comes up. I cannot think of another term that even approaches the heinous connotations of hatred and evil that stand next to it. However, to create a story set in 1968 that takes on issues of race and fails to use it in some form would be criticized, and justly so, as inauthentic at best, cowardly at worst. Thus, I have deployed it sparingly and in a hybrid form that may not satisfy some, but was the one I chose after much deliberation.

Though distinct elements of self-governance date back as far as ancient Greece if not further, democracies were a thoroughly unproven and unpopular form of governance when America came into being. At that time, the most powerful nations were organized under autocratic systems, usually monarchies, and "individual freedom" was an oxymoron. Although there are other legitimate claimants to the title, the United States of America is arguably the world's oldest nation with a continuously surviving democratic government; it is certainly the best-known example. However, having only been around for less than 250 years, we are an infant in the annals of history, and our existence has been, at times, uncomfortably turbulent.

There were multiple instances in our past when we were at each other's throats, and where a decisive breakup seemed imminent. We ultimately fought a costly civil war to end slavery and keep the union intact. Clearly, enough people believed the American experiment of freedom and self-governance was worth the blood shed on all those battlefields. However, none of us should ever take that sentiment for granted, lest our system of elected representation disappears from under our distracted gaze, taking our hard-won rights along with it.

Finally, I wanted to make this a story of two people from divergent life experiences who come *together* to tackle a problem as difficult as any America has ever confronted. I wanted it to be an unwieldy, fractious partnership, like the one experienced by those sixth graders decades ago. I wanted each to learn from the other, and for them to eventually find mutual respect and empathy for one another.

In the end, what can we strive for that is more vital, for all of us?

Not in Utopia, subterranean fields,
Or some secreted island, Heaven
   knows where!
But in the very world, which is the
   world
Of all of us, — the place where in
   the end
We find our happiness, or not at all!

—William Wordsworth

A Calamity of Souls

CHAPTER 1

O N ANY OTHER DAY THE dead quiet coming from this room would have concerned no one, because the elderly couple usually napped peacefully, sat stationary as cats, or read their twin King James Bibles in silence, aged fingers turning pages replete with wisdom, tranquility, and violence.

The latter was on embellished display, for the man was sprawled on the floor on his back, while the woman was draped across a finely upholstered chair. Life had been rent from them with a grim certainty of purpose.

They were not remarkable in any way that mattered to most. What *was* memorable was the grand upheaval that would define and qualify the full measure of their deaths. It would fuel a calamitous surge of energy, like that of a sawed-off shotgun randomly discharged into an unsuspecting crowd.

Their violent end would be gossiped about in Freeman County, Virginia, for decades.

"You got the right to remain silent. You hear me, *boy*?" the first lawman said to the only suspect in the room.

That suspect was on his knees, his hands shackled behind him, the cuffs cutting deeply into flesh. The only signs of his granular fear were the trembling of fingers, and the quick exhalations of breath.

"This coon don't look like he can talk even if he wanted to," countered the second deputy. He was six feet, cattail-lean, with a soft jaw and eyes that resembled creased bullet holes. A policeman's hat was tipped far back on his head.

The debilitating humidity, wicked off the nearby McHenry River, spread everywhere, like mustard gas weaving through the war trenches. The sweat dripped off the deputies' faces, darkened their starched shirts, and, like gnats flitting around nostrils and eyes, added annoyance to their rage.

The first deputy continued to read off the little white card he'd drawn from his pocket. He was short, and squat as a tree stump. He had just arrived at the part about an attorney being provided if the accused couldn't afford one, when his partner, clearly troubled by these new legal rights, interrupted once more.

"You tell me what lawyer in his right mind would represent this here colored boy, LeRoy. 'Cause I sure as hell would like to know the answer."

Raymond LeRoy ignored this and continued to read off the card, because he hadn't yet memorized the words. He actually doubted he ever would; the will was just not in him. He had no idea who this Miranda fellow was, but LeRoy knew that the legal-ese upon the paper was designed to help *those* people, who had committed crimes, usually against white folks. And that trans-formed every word, which he was compelled to read by the deci-sion of nine robed men hundreds of miles away, into bleach on his tongue.

"You understand what I just read to you?" said LeRoy. "I appar-ently got to hear your answer accordin' to those sonsabitches in Washington, DC."

His partner gripped the butt of his holstered .38 Smith & Wes-son. "Why don't you just take off them iron cufflinks and tell him to run for it? Save the good folks of this fine county payin' for his trip down to Richmond and the chair."

"They ain't doin' executions no more, Gene. Say it's cruel and unusual."

Gene Taliaferro bristled. "And what the hell has he just done to *them*, LeRoy?"

In one corner an overturned table had upset the items that had long rested upon it, chiefly, a photograph taken over fifty years ago of the couple in their courting days. He with his slouch hat in hand, along with a pair of brooding eyes, she with a bonnet resting on her small, delicate head, the hair parted in the middle, making her resemble a child. They were framed by an arch of fragrant honeysuckle and jasmine that was hosting both bees and butterflies, tiny, whirring apparitions trapped by the flash pop and shutterbug.

Now the photo lay on the floor, its front glass shattered, a cut across the picture bisecting the woman's face and reaching to the man's left eye.

LeRoy said, "We ain't gonna shoot him, Gene. Boy's in custody."

"He's only a g-d n——!" exclaimed Gene.

"I *know*," bellowed an out-of-his-depth LeRoy. "Do I got me two eyes or what?"

"Well then?" demanded Gene. "Ain't be the first time we done it."

"Well, it's not like that no more, is it?" countered a disappointed LeRoy.

"A hundred years ago where was the capital of the Confederacy?" Gene pointed to the floor. "It was right chere in Virginia. And nuthin' can change that. Granddaddy four times removed owned boys just like this one." He stabbed his finger in the direction of the kneeling man. "Owned 'em! I got me a picture! They ought 'a fry his ass."

"Then let 'em," muttered LeRoy. "But I ain't havin' a bunch 'a Negro lawyers comin' after me. And now that that Dr. King got hisself killed down in Tennessee, coloreds are riotin' all over the damn country."

Gene snorted. "He weren't no real doctor!"

"Gonna let my son take up the cause. We got to keep fightin'. Hundred years, thousand years, it don't matter."

Gene sucked in a long breath and let it go. The gesture seemed to sap the core of his fury like cold mist on a candle's flame. But then the lawman's expression grew cagey. He squatted down on his haunches next to the only suspect in the room and slipped a wooden billy club from his belt. Along the wood were cut a dozen horizontal notches.

"I don't remember tellin' you to get on your knees, boy. Now stand up." Before the prisoner could move, Gene struck him full in the gut with the head of the billy club, propelling the man to the floor.

Gene rose. "I told you to get up, not fall on your damn face. Now get your ass up boy, right now. *Now*, or you get some more of the wood."

Slowly, the prisoner managed to come once more to rest on his haunches.

Gene knelt next to him and said in a near whisper, "Now who told you to get your ass off that floor?"

He battered the prisoner on the back of the head with the club, sending him down once more, now bleeding from his scalp.

Gene stood up and said, "Jesus, you ain't too smart, and here you wanna be equal to the white man. Now get up. Get up." He jabbed the prisoner fiercely in the ribs with the club. "I ain't tellin' you again, boy. Up!"

The prisoner, inch by tremulous inch, levered himself back onto his knees.

Gene knelt down again. "Good, good, boy." He grinned at his partner. "Who says you can't teach critters new tricks, LeRoy, huh?" He turned back to the bleeding, woozy prisoner and eyed the band on the man's finger. "Hey, now, you got yourself a woman?"

Gene walloped the suspect with the club on the side of his head. "I asked you a question. You ain't got no choice 'cept to answer me."

"Y-yes."

"Yes, what?"

"Yes...sir."

He leaned in closer. "Good, good. Bet she's pretty. She pretty, boy?"

The prisoner nodded, which got him another clubbing to the head.

"You speak, boy. You don't never nod at no white man. It's disrespectful."

His eyes closed, the man said, "She real pretty, *sir.*"

"Good, good. Now, you got you kids?"

"Y-yes sir."

"Fine, that's fine. How many babies you got?"

"Three, sir."

"Three!" Gene looked at his partner. "Boy say he got him three colored babies." He turned back to the prisoner. "Okay, now after they fry your ass over in Richmond I'm gonna go see your pretty wife and your babies with some friends of mine. Now let me tell you what we gonna do to all them after we finish havin' some fun with her."

He leaned close and whispered in the prisoner's ear.

The man roared in rage, knocking Gene down with his maddened, gyrating bulk.

The deputy slid across the floor, grinning. He took off his hat, swiped back his hair, and gripped his billy club extra firm. He rose and headed back to the only suspect in the room, who was now sprawled helplessly on the floor.

Gene said triumphantly, "Resistin' arrest plain as day. You seen it, LeRoy."

And he raised the club.

CHAPTER 2

JOHN ROBERT LEE, WHO WENT by Jack to all but his mother, finished pumping Esso gas into his ancient, four-door Fiat pillarless saloon car. The front doors opened regularly, back to front, but the rear doors opened front to back. It had a long hood terminating in a fancy grille with silver cased headlights that sprouted from the front slim fenders like incandescent daisies. Its four-cylinder engine could hit fifty-three miles an hour with a decent tailwind. He paid over a crisp single and two dull quarters to the attendant, who was studying the funny-looking car with interest.

"What the hell is that thang?" he asked.

"It's a Fiat," answered Jack.

"A fee-ought?"

"It's Italian made."

"I-talian? Ain't that where the pope's from?"

Jack nodded. "That's right."

"You Catholic?"

"No, I'm agnostic," said Jack.

The man screwed up his face. "What's that? Like Presbyterian or Methodist?"

"It's actually a skeptical man's faith," replied Jack.

He climbed into the Fiat that his father had gotten from a car cemetery and resurrected back to the road. It was a gift from his parents when he'd graduated from law school. It was not a prestigious law school, like the mighty University of Virginia, or Richmond's or William and Mary's illustrious legal institutions. However, he had passed the Virginia State Bar exam on his first attempt, while he knew some from the glorified universities who had failed to do so. They still got the jobs in the big firms because that was where their daddies labored, too, selling their professional lives in hour increments for handsome compensation, prestigious homes, and golf memberships at the country club. They also married lovely, elegant women with fine pedigrees and firm skin, who ended up drinking too much, or bedding the gardener or the pool boy because of all the extra time on their hands.

Jack was a white man, thirty-two years old, at least for a bit longer, and eight years out of law school he was just getting by, and still unmarried, much to his mother's chagrin. As the 1970s approached, men were wearing their hair far longer, but his was as short as when he'd been in the Boy Scouts, though he was starting to grow out his sideburns. He was two inches over six feet, broad shouldered and slim hipped and a bit too lean; he had never earned enough from his law practice to eat all that well. A six-pack of peanut butter crackers and an RC Cola was often his end-of-day repast.

The Second World War had made everyone underfed and overworked. Then the fifties had ushered in a roaring economy with a chicken in every pot and a Ford or GM loitering in every driveway. Then the sixties had come along and proceeded to upend all that dollars-and-cents progress. It had also foisted stark changes upon society at large that were far too swift for many.

He drove over to his parents' modest house in a working-class neighborhood where the husbands primarily used their muscle to earn their daily bread and their wives handled everything else. He had been born there in the main-floor bedroom, and he was fairly certain both his parents would die there, barring something unforeseen. No fuss and no muss, that was the Lee way.

He pulled into the gravel drive. All the homes here had been carved out of a plantation that more than a century ago had grown tobacco as a cash crop. Nearly all the residences looked the same: brittle asbestos siding, high-pitched roofs with black asphalt shingles, one front door and one in the rear, three bedrooms total along with one bath, set on a quarter acre of solid red clay with a grass veneer.

At his parents' house there was an aging weeping willow tree out front, and an apple tree in the back that had never been honestly pruned, and consequently sagged with the weight of the coming harvest. There was also a detached garage sitting where the gravel drive ceased. At the very rear of the property was the grave of the dog that had been Jack's faithful companion as a child: a black-and-white Belgian shepherd as loyal and good as God ever made canines. He'd toppled over one morning in his ninth year of life and hadn't lived the day. Jack and his younger brother had cried like they'd just lost their best friend, and, in some important ways of little boys, they had.

The Lees also had a second bathroom upstairs, thanks to their father, who was quite talented at creating useful things from castoffs. Then there was a galley-sized kitchen, an eight-by-ten dining space bleeding off that, a small living room, and a TV den containing a faux-wood Motorola with two dials big as saucers on its face.

Jack climbed out of the Fiat and put on his suit jacket.

He could smell through the front screen door chicken breasts and legs popping in a frying pan of sizzling Crisco. And he imagined the potato salad resting in the small almond-white Frigidaire, and the heated pots on the electric stove top, the coils red-hot and holding pans of simmering green beans and stewed tomatoes his mother had harvested and then preserved from the kitchen garden. The meal would be concluded with chocolate sheet cake and Maxwell House coffee purchased from the A&P.

The dinner tonight was to commemorate Jack's thirty-third year on earth. At 7:10 p.m. on this day in 1935 he had emerged headfirst into a world still devastated by an economic collapse. His birth had occurred in the downstairs bedroom, while his nervous father had prowled the hall outside smoking his American-blend Camels. After a spank on the ass Jack had given his first cry and hadn't stopped for four years, according to his mother.

He'd grown up to play myriad sports, loved to debate folks, and was an avid reader from a young age. And every morning from the age of twelve until his junior year of high school, he'd risen long before the crack of dawn to deliver the *Virginia Times Dispatch*.

Many of the parents from his childhood still lived in the neighborhood. Their children, like him, had moved on. Most, unlike him, had married and now had their own swelling broods. He'd see them occasionally disgorging a passel of kids from battered station wagons to go visit grandparents who were getting more fragile and forgetful by the day. Yet sometimes the natural cycle of life was broken and children remained closer than Mom and Dad might desire.

And didn't Jack's parents know that.

He opened the screen door.

"Hello?" he called out. "Birthday boy's here." He'd seen his father's tan GMC pickup by the garage. It was their only vehicle because his mother didn't drive.

"Hello?" he said again.

His sister edged around the corner from the dining room, where he could see the dinner plates laid out on the small table purchased years ago on layaway. There was a balloon tethered to a closet door handle, the words "Happy Birthday" stenciled upon it.

"Hey, Lucy girl," said Jack.

His elder sister rushed over and gave him a hug that nearly cracked his back. She'd always been strong, and he'd always believed it was nature's way of balancing out what was missing upstairs.

It had begun with his mother's trip to the dentist to remove a painfully impacted wisdom tooth. She'd been given laughing gas as a sedative, a term Jack had later learned was for the compound nitrous oxide. Only she hadn't known she was with child at the time. Eight months later his sister had been born. And a year after that, when Lucy was not developing as she should, some specialists had diagnosed her with "severe and irreversible mental retardation," or so his daddy had told him years later when Jack had questions about his sister.

She was now thirty-seven, a grown if physically stunted woman, with the innocent mind of a child. Her blond bangs hung right above eyes so extraordinarily blue it was the first thing folks noted about her. Jack had the same eyes that she did, only with something of a different sort behind them.

He kissed the top of Lucy's head and said her dress was very pretty. It was light brown with vivid blue dots that nearly matched her eye color and had puffy sleeves that hung down to the crooks of her delicate elbows. His birthday was probably the only thing that she had talked about all day.

"Momma, Daddy, it be Jack," Lucy bellowed over her shoulder.

She pulled him over to the balloon, poked it, and laughed as it oscillated on the end of its tether. Jack laughed, too, but there was a definite hollowness to it. The same gas that was holding the balloon aloft had made her what she was today. He'd often wondered what his sister would have grown up to be if the dental visit had never occurred. Perhaps Lucy Lee would have been the lawyer in the family.

His mother had never forgiven herself for her daughter's fate, though there was no fault in her ignorance. She had had two more children, Jack and his one-year-younger brother, Jefferson, who went by Jeff to all but his mother, who always referred to him by his full name. His mother had employed a midwife and taken no drugs for her sons' deliveries, preferring to endure the unique pain of childbirth as perhaps penance for the daughter who had never been allowed to truly grow up because of the mother's bad tooth. And ever since, she had refused any and all medication, including aspirin, though she was susceptible to migraines that sometimes forced her to lie in agony for hours in the dark.

"Momma?" he called out expectantly.

And he heard the woman coming.

CHAPTER 3

HILDA LEE, KNOWN TO ALL as Hilly, appeared, dressed in a crisp white T-shirt, faded Wrangler jeans, and flat canvas shoes, with an olive green apron tied around her middle. It was a tomboy foundation comfortably twined with a domestic facade.

She was quite tall and sinewy lean, and her short hair was light brown with a reddish tint attributable to her Scottish ancestry; it was also now liberally laced with gray. Her nose was straight as a razor blade. Her calm, pale green eyes gave the impression that no matter the challenge not only would she persevere, Hilly Lee would also conquer all comers, with grit to spare.

The woman's veined, wiry, tanned forearms were festooned with sunspots because she liked the outdoors. However, when she was outside, Hilly moved with force and had some purpose, tending the kitchen garden, mowing the grass, helping her husband to reshingle the roof, felling a dead tree, or repainting the backyard wire fence. She had been raised on a mountain ridge on the far western edge of the state that to this day had no electricity or running water. His mother rarely spoke of her hardscrabble time there, and that in itself articulated volumes.

Hilly wiped her hands on the apron and gave her oldest boy a hug. "Ten minutes to go, Robert." She had never called him anything other than Robert. *John was your father's idea, Robert was mine, so Robert it will be, at least for me.* And they had left it at that. With his mother he had left many things at *that*.

If she'd had her way he would have officially been Robert E. Lee, after the gallant Confederate general who had sacrificed all to carry the mantle of the Army of Northern Virginia against his birth country in defense of states' rights, or so the old story went.

But they were not *those* Lees. No First Families of Virginia lived on this street or even in this blue collar parcel of Freeman County. The homes weren't big enough, and neither were the opportunities.

"Yes, ma'am," he said back.

Her expression turned somber. "I still can't believe they killed JFK's brother."

"I know," he replied. A little over a week before, America had had another Kennedy running for president. Now they simply had another Kennedy to mourn.

"And Dr. King just two months ago. What is this durn country coming to where we have to settle things with guns?"

"World is a troubled place. Look at Vietnam."

He shouldn't have brought that up because of his brother, but perhaps it had slipped out intentionally, Jack thought. He'd had that sort of verbal sparring relationship with his mother from an early age. She usually seemed to relish the jousting.

And he had always found it bewildering that she venerated a long-dead Confederate general at the same time she shed tears for the recent deaths of two men who held views diametrically opposed to all the Confederacy had stood for. But then he had found much about his mother to be irreconcilable.

"Walter Cronkite said it was a man with the same two names who did it."

"Sirhan Sirhan," Jack told her.

She said, "What kinda name is that?"

"He's from Palestine."

"How did his kind get close to Bobby Kennedy of all people?"

"They say Kennedy was walking through the kitchen at a hotel in Los Angeles, and the man was waiting and shot him."

"This Sir-han will probably hire himself a fancy lawyer like you and get off."

He smiled at her. He would never be a fancy lawyer. "Doubtful."

"Well, you're the attorney in the family, Robert," she said. Hilly's gaze flitted to her daughter, who was still poking the balloon and giggling each time it moved in response to her jab. In his mother's eyes Jack could read the unspoken thought: *The family I have left*.

"You seeing any girls I don't know about?" she asked, turning back to him.

"You'd know. The gossip chain in Freeman is top-notch. Where's Daddy?"

"He'll be in shortly." She gripped his arm. "Miss Jessup came by today."

"Miss Jessup? What'd she want?"

"What she wanted was *you*, but didn't say why. She didn't look good at all, Robert." She added hastily, "Not that I ever had much contact with her, obviously."

"You think she's sick?"

"You're not a doctor."

"She have family around?" Jack asked.

"Yes. Her husband's long dead. But she has children and now grandchildren. Maybe great-grandchildren," she added ruefully, making Jack sense his mother was thinking that she had none of those future generations lined up.

Jack went over to the door and stared up the street to the only house in the neighborhood that didn't look like all the others. A retired lawyer by the name of Ashby owned it. And he'd added to it over the years, usually when he'd gotten a big client, or made a few bucks in the stock market. Thus, it was rambling and had oddly mitered wings and loose joints.

Jack had read that there had been nearly one hundred slaves on

the sprawling plantation once situated here. They and their prog-
eny had labored all their lives for not one penny in return to make
their wealthy owners richer still. Almost nothing had been recorded
about them other than their actual numbers. And that reportage was
apparently solely done for the benefit of their master's ego.

Ashby had six children, all long grown now and with their own
families to run. His wife had died many years ago, but not of illness. Well, Jack supposed it was a sickness to go to your garage, stuff
a towel in the tailpipe of your Plymouth, lie across the front seat
dressed in your finest cocktail dress, and, sipping on a Mason jar of
Old Fashioned, start the engine, and stay there until you were dead.
Ashby had reputedly focused his final years on imbibing as many
bottles of Rebel Yell bourbon whiskey as he possibly could.

Miss Jessup was Ashby's maid, cook, and nurse; Jack had never
known her first name. Years before Jack had been born, she had
gone to work for the lawyer and his family. Now she was probably
single-handedly keeping the old man alive.

Growing up, Jack and all the other children in the neighborhood
always called the woman Miss Jessup, the only sign of respect she
probably ever received on the western side of Freeman County, and
the only attention, too, unless items went missing and someone was
needed to blame or indict. She was the only Black person who ever
came around here, which lent her a certain novelty, at least in the
eyes of the white youngsters.

He flicked his gaze back to his mother. "What did she say other
than she wanted to talk to me?"

Hilly deftly pulled a heavy glass vase from Lucy's clutching fingers before saying, "Nothing. She walked right in the front door
without a by-your-leave and just asked for you. But she was upset,
so I made allowances."

"It's not like Miss Jessup's a stranger. We've known her a long
time."

"We don't really *know* her kind."

"Times are changing," he said, not really wanting to go there on his birthday.

She pursed her lips. "I'm sure she'd feel the same way if I barged into *her* house. Tell all her friends about that crazy white woman and how she came barging into her house."

"So what did you tell her then?"

"That you'd be here for dinner and that I didn't appreciate her intruding. Scared poor Lucy half to death. Took me forever to calm her down."

She reached out and hugged placid Lucy to her bosom.

"Okay, but how did you leave it with her?" Jack asked patiently.

"I didn't leave it any which way with her. I just asked her to *leave*."

"Just like that?" he said, clearly annoyed.

His mother checked her slim Timex. "You were born one minute ago, Robert. Happy birthday, son."

CHAPTER 4

COMING HOME FROM DELIVERING THE morning paper Jack would sometimes see Miss Jessup get off the bus that stopped at the corner. She always exited from the rear. He wondered why that was so until, as a teenager, he rode the bus one day into the city with his brother, and found that all the Blacks congregated in the back, while all the whites gathered in the front. Each group seemed to willingly accept this arrangement as fine, and thus so did he and his brother.

Jack would wave to her as he sailed past on his Schwinn bike, and she would wave back. Some mornings she looked tired and spent as though the mere act of living had done her in, while other times she looked full of fire, her eyes searching for a fight. He would think about this as he rode home and then his mind would turn to other things, and Miss Jessup's meager place there was always crowded out until next he saw her.

Occasionally she would call out to him. "How you doin', honey?" Or, as he got older, "You lookin' more like your daddy every day. Move like he do, too. With a *swagger*," she added, smiling, which made him smile in return.

Sometimes she would ask if he had a spare newspaper. She would tuck it away in her bag, and always thank him profusely.

"You're certainly welcome, Miss Jessup," he would say back because his parents had taught him to be unfailingly polite to all.

"Rich, poor, colored, white," his father would say. "We're all God's children. We all deserve kindness and respect. We may not break bread with colored folks, but we don't break bread with rich folks, either. Did little colored children have a say where they were born? No, they did not. You don't have to marry one or have a meal with them to respect the fact that they're people, too. You remember that, boys, and pass it on."

"Yes, sir, Daddy, I sure will," Jack and Jeff Lee had each dutifully said back, but now also starkly aware of differences between Blacks and whites, and rich and poor.

Miss Jessup would wear her maid's uniform, starched and crisp, on even the hottest summer days. Her wide feet were squeezed into uncomfortable black lace-ups. Her hips were broad and grew wider still over the years. He could remember going over to play with the youngest Ashby boy, and some other children from the neighborhood, and having Miss Jessup bring out glasses of lemonade with little chips of ice. She would also have some cookies and paper napkins with designs on them. This was how Jack knew the Ashbys were rich. They had napkins and lemonade and cookies on a platter in the afternoon, and a colored maid to carry it all right to them.

He would watch as Miss Jessup trudged back inside, her hand slipping to the cookies left on the platter and several of them would disappear into her apron pocket. He never begrudged the woman any of that. They weren't his cookies after all and the Ashbys had plenty more. The rich always had plenty more.

He hadn't really thought of the woman that much since he'd become an adult. That is until he had seen her about three months ago when he'd come to his parents' house early one morning to pick up some papers he needed for court and had mistakenly left there the previous night. She was just getting off the bus, her hair still wavy and abundant but also all gray now. The driver had closed the door so fast it clipped her in the rear end. And he sped off with such velocity that she got a lungful of exhaust fumes to start her workday.

Jack could imagine the driver thinking what a good deed he had done putting a Black woman in her place. Although ever since Rosa Parks and others had come along, Miss Jessup could ride anywhere on the bus she wanted. Yet Jack knew legal rulings were one thing, making folks live in accordance with them was quite another.

This made him remember something. When he was a little boy he had once heard Miss Jessup talking to Ashby's wife. There seemed to have been a disagreement between the two women, for Mrs. Ashby looked upset and Miss Jessup was saying, "I got me my place and you got you your place and they's oil and they's water and they just don't mix. Fo' sho' they do *not* mix, *ma'am*."

A flustered and teary-eyed Mrs. Ashby had quickly gone on her way, while Miss Jessup had just stood there, hands on hips, shaking her head and looking—at least to Jack—like she'd just finished dressing down a youngster for doing something foolish.

"Hello, son," said a familiar voice.

CHAPTER 5

JACK TURNED TO SEE HIS father wiping his hands off on a work rag. His daddy was a union mechanic at Old Dixie Transport. As a young boy Jack had little reason to dwell on what his father did for a living until an accident involving one of the company's trucks. A semi hauling Hostess products had overturned on a rain-slickened road. His father had gone out at near midnight to remedy the problem. In return he had been given first dibs on the ruined cargo. The Lees had, for years afterward, been knee-deep in cupcakes and Twinkies off that one doomed shipment. And during each of those years Jack had desperately wanted to grow up to be a union mechanic.

"Hey, Daddy," said Jack.

Francis Lee was known to everyone as Frank, except his wife, who thought the name too juvenile. She always called him Francis. He was an inch short of his oldest son's height, but he was more heavily built in the shoulders, arms, and chest. Pulling wrenches for a living had made his forearms as broad as the widest part of his Remington twelve-gauge's wooden stock. He still had on his work uniform: light blue long-sleeved shirt with a white T-shirt underneath, and dark blue pants. His salt-and-pepper hair was cut as close to his scalp as a soldier's, which he had once been, performing his patriotic duty in World War II, much of it in the Pacific Theater.

Frank Lee never talked about the war, but sometimes Jack had caught him sitting in the TV den, a beer in hand, just staring off, his unblinking gaze dead on the far wall. Maybe seeing through the cheap wood veneers directly back to Guadalcanal, Luzon, or the Battle of Okinawa, where the Americans suffered fifty thousand casualties in less than three months.

Jack had only learned about some of his father's military career when he'd discovered a cigar box in the back of a closet that contained medals and ribbons, photos, commendation letters, and official discharge papers. That was when he'd read the names of these Japanese outposts that American soldiers had had to take one by one with appalling losses at each island stop. He'd later been told by his mother that after a particularly vicious battle on Iwo Jima his father had been the only survivor of his rifle squad.

He'd heard his father screaming at night a few months after coming home. That was when his two Smith & Wesson revolvers and the Remington over-under shotgun had disappeared from his parents' bedroom.

"Happy birthday," Frank Lee said after crushing his boy's hand in his, and flicking his brown-eyed gaze over his son. "You're way older'n I was when we had you. Now you just go ahead and think about that." His father added a hard slap on the shoulder to the bruising handshake.

Preambles over, they sat down to their meal after saying grace, which was given by Lucy, who stumbled over some of the words but otherwise did fine. She slipped in an ad hoc prayer for her youngest brother and hoped he was okay, wherever he was, while her mother and father gazed stoically at their food. A half an hour later, the cake and coffee consumed, Jack looked at his father.

"Momma said Miss Jessup came by looking troubled."

His mother said sharply, "And I told her she never should have stepped foot in this house. I was very clear on that point with her."

"Nobody talkin' to you, Hilly, would ever come away not knowin' where they stood," observed her husband.

"Being wishy-washy never leads to a positive end, Francis."

"Miss Jessup's a good woman."

"She could be the queen of England and it'd be the same principle."

"Uh-huh," said her husband. "Only maybe the queen of England wouldn't want *you* to step foot in *her* house."

"Well, I can see this will get us nowhere fast," retorted Hilly.

It was a line she was using with increasing frequency, Jack had noted, especially with his father.

She started clearing the dishes. The Lees did not do presents anymore for celebrations like this. Money was tight and the meal was deemed sufficient.

His father put down his cup, pried at something between his teeth with his axle-greased fingernail, and then rubbed the freed bit of fried chicken skin onto the perimeter of his plate. A hunched Lucy rose and stood in front of the GE window air conditioner twirling her hair and letting the cool air waft over her.

Frank eyed her and said, "Let's head on out to the garage, son. Lucy, girl, you keep the air conditioner and your momma company, honey."

They walked out to the garage, where Jack leaned against a workbench he and his brother had built for their father nearly twenty years ago. Half the driven nails were bent, and where board met board the edges were so badly mitered they appeared not to even be joined together. It was so unlevel that if you put a marble on the workbench's top it would roll right off. But their daddy had thanked them for the honest, heartfelt effort, and he had begun virtually every task undertaken in his garage right there.

Frank took a socket wrench from his rolling toolbox and started loosening the bolts on a Ford straight-six engine block he was rebuilding for a neighbor for cash.

"Your sister thinks the air conditioner can talk to her. Did you know that?"

"No, I didn't," said Jack.

His father broke loose a stubborn bolt and nodded. "She stands in front of it and just jabbers away. And she likes the way it blows her hair. Apparently, General Electric and Lucy are good friends." He wiped some crud off the socket and leaned against the metal stand the engine block sat on. "When your momma and me are gone, she's gonna be your responsibility, Jack, you ready for that? We're not gettin' any younger and my lungs are gettin' worse every dang year."

As he said this Frank lighted up a Camel, sucked on it, and flicked ash into an old paint can, which hung on a nail half-driven into a wall stud. He held up the pack of smokes showing off the surgeon general's dire warning on the spine.

He grinned. "*Now* they tell me these damn things are no good for you. Day late and a dollar short, I say."

Jack drew a dirty penny from a coffee can full of nuts, bolts, and loose coins. "You can always quit."

"Don't smoke in the house, just out here or in the truck. Can't smoke at work. Too many flammable products around."

"You got some of those in here, too," said Jack, eyeing a shelf full of gas cans and a quart of forty-weight motor oil.

"Yeah, but it's my garage. So my rules." The words were uttered in a joking manner. Jack had long noted that his father's mood improved considerably when he removed himself from the tactical confines of the house. There was also an old recliner with its stuffing coming out set in the corner, and a boxy twelve-inch black-and-white TV with crooked rabbit ears perched on a stack of cinder blocks, its power plug spliced into an overhead light.

That setup was new, he noted. "You're not sleeping out here, are you, Daddy?"

His father flicked away more ash as he worked the socket wrench on another bolt with his free hand. He squinted at Jack through the Camel smoke. "Not yet, but tomorrow's a new day."

Jack stared down at the penny and gave it a flip. He caught the coin and turned it over. A grim-faced Abe Lincoln came up to greet him.

"Jacky, you ready for that, son? Your sister I'm talkin'?"

"How am I supposed to be ready for something like that?"

"You just do what you gotta. I love that girl, but it ain't been easy."

"I know that. I grew up with her."

His father shook his head. "She just flat wears you out. It's why we waited a few years before we had you, and then your brother. We wanted kids that…well, you know." He gave the wrench another hard tug and the bolt came free. "She was tryin' to stick the end of a hanger in the wall socket the other day. Sometimes I think I'll come home from work and find 'em both stretched out on the floor dead. Lucy from electrocution and your momma from the guilt of lettin' her do it."

"I know, Daddy. I know."

"No, I'm not sure you do. Legally, she's not your responsibility. Hell, you're a lawyer, you know that. Now, we can put her in a state-run nursin' home. But that's surely not your momma's first choice."

He drew all the remaining juice out of his cigarette and then crushed the remains on the concrete floor with the heel of his steel-toed work shoe.

Jack said, "Look, if I can take care of her I will. But some days it seems I can't even take care of myself."

"You're thirty-three today, Jack. Long past time you figured things out, son."

"Yes sir," said Jack because he could think of nothing else to say.

His father went back to his bolts and his features relaxed. Jack understood this change. Engines his old man knew intimately; but dealing with people on such sensitive subjects was probably like being back on Okinawa, all foreign and incomprehensible.

"Did you see Miss Jessup?" asked Jack.

"Saw the back of her. She didn't look so good."

"Maybe she has some legal trouble since she wanted to see me."

"Don't know what that might be. She's a God-fearin',

church-goin' woman. Those people sing up a storm. And dancin'! Seen 'em come out onto the street doin' it when I was headin' to work on the Sabbath. More fun than I ever had in church, which is why I stopped goin'. That and our preacher knockin' up the choir director's wife."

"I'd like to know what she wanted."

"So why don't you go ask her?"

"You think she's still at Ashby's?" asked Jack.

"No, and anyway Ashby won't let her talk to you on his dime. That man's got more money than anybody else around here, but he don't let one damn dollar get away without a fight. But you can go see Miss Jessup at her place."

"I don't know where she lives."

His father broke another bolt loose, winked at him, and grinned. "I do."

"How?"

"Because I've given her rides home when the bus wouldn't stop for her."

"But the bus *brings* her here."

"Different driver. One's fair, the other's a maggot. Now, I'm no fan of this integration crap chiefly because I don't like people tellin' me who I got to associate with. But you don't get in the way of anybody tryin' to earn an honest livin'. Somebody wouldn't pick my ass up 'cause my ancestors come from Africa? I'd pull him out that bus and beat the livin' shit outta him."

"So where does she live?"

His father went over to a mud sink and began washing off his hands. "Do you one better. I'll *show* you. Happy damn birthday, son."

CHAPTER 6

THEY DROVE OVER IN JACK'S Fiat. He had watched as his father had taken his .38 revolver from a locked drawer in his tool cabinet and placed it inside the car's glove box. Now Jack knew what had happened to at least one of his father's weapons.

"Where the hell is this place that you need a gun?"

"Where white people don't ever go less they're lost, or lost their mind, or they got stuff to get rid of," his father answered cryptically and refused to say more.

Jack knew that Freeman County was roughly divided into halves, with two quadrants in each half. Northwest and southwest were the white side and northeast and southeast the Black side. The rich whites primarily lived in the northwest sector and the rest of the whites lived in the southwest. Carter City was located like an egg in a nest in the southeastern part of the pie. It had been white-dominated until the Civil Rights era; then they had left it to the Blacks.

The McHenry River ran roughly north to south, serving as a stark geographic barrier between the races before it hooked east and eventually emptied into the Chesapeake Bay. The Stonewall Jackson Bridge bisected the racial worlds, though neither side used it to casually visit the other. Blacks, almost all women, would only cross it in a bus to get to their jobs on the white side and then back home. Otherwise the bridge was simply a means to get over the water and on to somewhere else, though the recently opened interstate highway the Lees were now on provided an alternative to the bridge route.

In the distance they saw the low-rise, blunt-faced skyline of downtown Carter City, where a bank building's neon sign would change color depending on the weather. They passed small acreages of peanut and soybean fields after exiting the interstate, rural remnants among the modern concrete and rebar. The sun was creeping away, with the horizon just about to swallow it whole when his father gave him final directions. They had to double back because the highway had been built right through the community they were now in, cutting off easy access to both the interstate and the surface streets.

Jack noted this and said, "How do these folks get anywhere?"

"Probably their own two feet, if they manage to get out. Some never do."

"Tuxedo Boulevard?" commented Jack a few minutes later, looking at the mangled street sign where his father had just told him to hang a left.

"Yep."

"What's that smell?" asked Jack. The foul odor had flooded the Fiat.

"County dump. It's at the end of the street."

"The county dump is at the end of *Tuxedo* Boulevard?"

"Somebody's idea of a joke, I guess," replied his unsmiling father.

Jack observed that the homes dated back to the previous century and were cheaply and poorly built. The street was also in wretched shape; the tiny Fiat encountered potholes that seemed capable of ingesting it. A skinny snow-white cat darted in front of them, followed eagerly by a mangy burly brown dog. Jack tapped the brakes to avoid striking them.

He observed that people were sitting on many of the porches no doubt trying to snag a breeze. And to a person they were watching the Fiat. They were mostly rigid-faced Black men, although there were some women in their midst who gazed at them suspiciously, as though this was an invasion of sorts into their small bit of the world. Shirtless boys ran up and down the small patches of brown, wiry grass, probably trying and failing to outrun the mosquitoes. But even they halted to watch them. It was obvious why: there were white men on Tuxedo Boulevard riding in a car that looked like one from which circus clowns would eventually emerge.

Frank Lee put one hand on the dash, near the glove box and the gun.

"It's that one up there, on the left with the brown shutters," he said tersely.

Jack glanced that way and saw a small square wood-clad house that had mismatched rocking chairs on the sagging porch. There were lights on inside.

"Pull on up there," said his father crisply.

Father and son unwound their long legs from the diminutive car and headed to the house. There were four beer-drinking men staring at them from the porch of the house next door. Two of them wore Army jackets. One of them had his sleeve pinned to his shoulder marking the location of his missing limb. The largest of them took a cigarette out of his mouth, and called out, "Y'all need sumthin'?"

"Here to see Miss Jessup," replied Frank, his voice tight, his demeanor the same.

Jack had noticed that his father had slipped the .38 into the back of his waistband.

"Why?" The man stood, showing that he was far bigger than either of the Lees.

"We're friends of hers," said Jack.

When the men confronted the Lees as they neared the house, the big fellow looked Jack up and down, taking in the suit, tie, and the froth of whiteness. "You look like the man. You the man?"

"I don't know what you mean by that," said Jack. "Miss Jessup came looking for me, but I wasn't there. So now I've come by to see her."

"What she want with you?"

Frank said, "We don't want no trouble. If Miss Jessup don't wanna see us, we'll just get back in our car and leave you to it."

The big man said, "Ain't no trouble on Tuxedo Boulevard, man. We a fancy-ass place. Ain't you see that?"

It might have been meant partially as a joke, Jack thought, but no one was laughing, least of all him.

Frank said, "I've been here before."

"To dump shit?" The big man pointed to his left at the end of the street where the road ended and the chain-link gate sat fronting the county dump. Beyond the gates were enormous humps of dirt, thin membranes over the catacombs of decaying husks below, the noxious smells of garbage wrapped in red clay hugging all their lungs.

"No, to give Miss Jessup a ride home when the bus wouldn't stop for her."

"Why you want that old woman in your car?" said another man, smaller, thinner, but with hard muscles showing through his T-shirt; his bearded face made no attempt to hide his contempt for Frank. He had a dead eye—creamy white wash with veins of red and a black, useless pinpoint in the middle. "You wanna mess with that old n——?"

"Your momma hear you talk like that, Louis Sherman, you gettin' a fryin' pan upside your thick head. And there ain't a durn thing you gonna do 'bout it 'cause your momma is three times your size and four times as tough as you ever thought of bein' even with that filthy mouth you got on you."

They turned to see Miss Jessup standing by her screen door. Jack had never seen the woman out of domestic uniform. She wore a long black skirt that hid both her thick, wrinkled knees and her swollen calves; soft bedroom slippers that allowed her pinched feet to spread as far as they wanted; and a white blouse, with sleeves that stopped right above her calcified elbows. Her hair was tied up in the back and off her shoulders like she wore it at Ashby's. She held a glass of iced tea in one hand and a look of deep disgust on her face. This was the enflamed Miss Jessup looking for a fight, conceding no ground, that Jack had witnessed before as a boy.

"You hear me, Louis Sherman?" she said, staring at the muscled one-eyed man with the beard and that world of contempt clutched tight in his features, like a squirrel with a nut it didn't know what to do with—hide, chuck, or eat.

Frank watched Sherman nervously, no doubt wondering whether the .38 would eventually be required.

Sherman turned and went back up on the porch and picked up his beer can, and stared off at the darkness with his one eye.

"Mr. Lees," said Miss Jessup. "What y'all be doin' here?"

"You know them?" said the big man.

"Whether I know them or don't know them ain't your business, is it, Daniel? Do I ask who these other fellers are sittin' on your daddy's porch tonight drinkin' his beer? No, I do not. Why? 'Cause it ain't *my* business. That's between you and your daddy when he finds out, which won't be from me. And God, too, when you headin' on out this world. And you ain't been goin' to church. So you need to sit down and have a good long talk with God 'bout where it is *you* headin'."

"What's God ever done for me?" countered Daniel.

"You still alive, ain't you? He didn't let a war or the white man take you, did he? *Yet.* You think on that."

After this cascade of blunt words, Daniel turned and went back to his porch. The other men followed and Frank removed his hand from the small of his back.

Miss Jessup beckoned to them. "Mr. Lees, come on in here. And y'all do it right quick."

Jack and his father sped up the steps, and she held open the screen door for them.

CHAPTER 7

SHE LED THEM TO A small front parlor, which held four wooden chairs and a small table in the middle, and faded gray carpet under it all. There were pictures of people from young to old affixed to a wall. And on another wall were two framed photos: one of Dr. Martin Luther King Jr. and the other of Robert Kennedy. Jack noted that both pictures had a gauzy black crepe around the perimeters as a show of respect after their deaths.

She indicated two chairs and they sat.

Miss Jessup said, "Y'all want some sweet tea? Just made it. Nice and cold."

Jack said no, but his father nodded yes and she hurried away to fetch it. While she was gone Jack noted the stacks of the *Virginia Times Dispatch* on the floor. He looked at the one on top. The date was recent. She might have the paperboy in the neighborhood giving her some of his extras. Or maybe she had her own subscription now, he thought.

He turned to his father. "How does she stand living here with that smell?"

"Live with somethin' long enough, you just forget it's even there."

"You really believe that?"

"Better'n that, I've done it, son," said his father offhandedly.

"Momma will be wondering where we are," he said.

"Depends."

"What do you mean by that?"

"You don't live there, Jacky. Things have changed."

"How?"

Miss Jessup came back into the room with a tall glass of sweet tea and handed it to Frank. She sat down across from them, picked up a dog-eared *Look* magazine, and started fanning herself. "Lord have mercy, heat and skeeters awful bad tonight."

Jack said, "Heard you came by looking for me, Miss Jessup." He thought for a moment to ask the woman what her Christian name was but decided to let it pass. She would always be Miss Jessup to him regardless.

She put the magazine in her lap and gazed at him. "Your momma was so mad. Why I'm surprised you two here."

"Hilly can be a little...sensitive." Frank sipped his tea and smacked his lips. "Mighty fine. Nice aftertaste."

She gazed impishly at him. "Now you know that there's the little splash of rye."

"You were looking for me?" Jack said again, while giving his father a curious glance.

Miss Jessup nodded. "My middle daughter, Maggie, she got a daughter Pearl. Now, Pearl got a husband named Jerome. He need a lawyer and I thought 'a you."

"What does he need a lawyer for?" asked Jack.

"Police arrested him for killin' some folks."

A startled Jack said, "Who did he kill?"

"*Allegedly* kill, that what Mr. Ashby said I should say. Asked him in the mornin'. After about eleven o'clock that man ain't good for nothin' 'cept a chaser." She held up her hands. "But, sweet Jesus, don't tell him I said so."

"Okay. So who did Jerome *allegedly* kill?" asked Jack.

"Some folks, like I said."

"So more than one?"

"Two," she said, holding up the requisite number of fingers. She looked him over in an appraising manner.

Jack suddenly felt like he was back in high school and the teacher had picked him to humiliate that day.

"You a good lawyer, ain't you?" she asked cautiously.

"He's the finest damn lawyer in all of Freeman County," answered his father.

"Now, Mr. Lee, every daddy and momma think they's child is the prettiest and sweetest and smartest in the whole wide world. But I got to know what I knows. This Pearl's young man." She turned back to Jack. "So is you good or not?"

"I'm a good lawyer. I've been practicing eight years."

"You win your law cases?"

"Most of them, yes. Nobody wins them all."

"And you take on folks been accused of killin' other folks?"

"Pretty much my entire practice is criminal law," replied Jack, without actually answering the question.

"Mr. Ashby said he done tax law before he retired."

"I've never been much good with numbers."

"You lawyered for colored folks?" she asked, her scrutinizing look deepening.

Jack swallowed nervously. "Um, no. But that...doesn't matter to me."

She snorted. "Well, it gonna sure matter to Jerome."

"Are you saying he doesn't want a white lawyer?"

"'Course he do. 'Sides, I ain't know any colored lawyers. But my point bein' *any* lawyer can get a white man off for anythin', 'specially if he got him some money, *and* he done somethin' to a colored man. But you got to be as good as the Lord God Above to get a colored man off, 'specially for killin' white folks. For that you need a white lawyer." She looked at him doubtfully. "Thought everybody knew that."

"So he's accused of killing *white* people?" Jack asked.

"Didn't I say that before?" she said, her eyes wide and probing.

"No, you somehow left that out."

"Well, it ain't important 'cause he didn't do it. But you got to make the *law* see that, and for folk with my skin that ain't easy to do, no sir."

"The law's supposed to be color-blind," Jack pointed out.

"Law *is* blind if you colored, honey. It don't see us, no how, no way. That's why Jerome need your help. Lord, he need it more than anybody you know, Mr. Lee."

Jack looked at his father, who was still sipping on the tea and splash of rye and following all of this closely.

"Okay. What can you tell me about Jerome?" Jack asked.

"He's never had a lick of trouble before this."

"So no prior arrests?"

"No. He a fine man. Been real good to Pearl and the children."

"Your great-grandchildren," Frank pointed out.

Her heavy face crinkled. "Sweet, sweet babies."

"Where is Jerome now?" Jack asked.

The crinkles transformed to a scowl. "In the county jail. With 'bout a dozen white deputies wantin' to kill him before he gets himself in front of a durn jury."

"When did the murders happen?"

"Last Friday."

"Where?"

"Madison Heights."

Jack and his father exchanged a worried glance. Madison Heights was in the northwest part of Freeman County and was home to the area's richest citizens.

"And why did they arrest Jerome?" asked Jack.

"'Cause he was there when the police come and found the dead white folks."

Jack flinched at the far-reaching possibilities of her statement. "Why was he there?"

She took a sip of tea and said, "You best hear all that from Jerome. Me tellin' it secondhand and all won't do you no good. Lawyerin' means being pre-cise. Judges? They like things just so. That what Mr. Ashby say. Juu-esst so."

"Well, I haven't decided to take the case yet," said Jack. "I came here to find out what you wanted me for."

"Well, now you know, honey. But Jerome needs your help, Mr. Lee. Real bad. Ain't that what lawyers do, help folks?"

His father nudged his arm. "Won't hurt to see what the man has to say. Then you can make up your mind." He finished off the tea. "That sound good, Miss Jessup?"

"Not as good if your boy had just said yes, but guess it'll have to do."

The Lees rose. Jack said, "Look, if I take the case, I can't do it pro bono."

"What's that mean?" she said fiercely, as though he had cursed at her.

"It means I can't do it for free."

"Jerome got a job. Well, he had one. And Pearl works herself to the bone. So they got money. And I can help out, too."

"I don't want to take your money, Miss Jessup."

She held up a finger and waggled it back and forth. "Good, 'cause I ain't offerin' you no money. But I can do your laundry." She pointed to his neck. "You got your shirt collars messed up with the iron 'cause you a man and don't know better. I can do some cookin'. You too skinny. Always have been. Deep fryer and Crisco take care 'a that. And cleanin'. Bet wherever you live ain't too clean. Not with no woman 'round to take care of it. *And* you."

"How do you know I'm not married?"

She gave him a patronizing look. "If there's a ring on that finger, it's gone invisible, Mr. Lee."

"I'll get back to you after I've seen Jerome."

"You go see him tonight?" she said eagerly, fanning herself with the magazine.

He glanced at his watch and said, "I thought maybe in the morning."

"Shoot, why waste time? He ain't got nothin' to do sittin' in that durn cell."

"Has he been arraigned?"

"Ask him, honey. Can't wrap my head 'round all that. But do it tonight. Please, Lord, please."

"All right, tonight then."

She graced him with a satisfied smile. "You a sweet boy. Always thought you might grow up to be somethin'. Just had that way with you when you was a little thing."

"Thank you for the libation, Miss Jessup," said his father.

A minute later, after they climbed back into the Fiat, Jack turned to his father. "One question, Daddy."

"Thought you'd have a lot mor'n that after all we just heard. Didn't expect a murder with Miss Jessup's kin. And Madison Heights? Holy Lord. The poorest man there is worth a hundred 'a me."

"I meant a question aimed squarely at *you*."

Frank looked over at his son and said, "Fire away."

"How does Miss Jessup know you like rye whisky in your iced tea?"

Now his father studied his watch. "Best get on, boy. Sounds like this Jerome needs himself one helluva lawyer."

As Jack drove he said, "I've never handled a murder case before. It's the ultimate challenge for a criminal defense attorney."

"Colored man accused of killin' rich white folks in Freeman County? I'd say that will be some challenge, all right. Some might say impossible."

"You don't think I'm up to it?"

"You *are* a damn good lawyer, Jacky. Now you don't know this, but I got off work and went to see you in court a few times. You got a nice style, handle yourself real good, seemed to me."

"Why didn't you tell me you were there?"

"Figured you'd get all tongue-tied with your old man in the crowd."

A suddenly panicked Jack looked at his father. "We need to call Miss Jessup. I can stop at a pay phone. You have her number? Or maybe she's in the phone book."

"You see any phone lines strung on her street? And why you need to talk to her?"

"She didn't tell me Jerome's last name. I'll need that to get in to see him."

His father gaped. "How many colored men named Jerome you reckon they got in a cell for killin' two white people in Madison Heights last Friday? If it's more'n one I'll give up my damn smokes."

"I guess you're right."

"Now, just calm down and let's go do this."

"You're coming?"

"Hell yes I am."

"Why?"

"'Cause it looks to me like you need somebody with you. *And* your momma will likely still be up."

CHAPTER 8

Jack and his father pulled up to the Freeman County jail, which had been built nearly a century before; there had been no notable improvements since that time. The walls were brick, tall and thick and topped by rolls of studded barbed wire, with guard towers set at the corners, where grim, uniformed riflemen perched with orders to shoot dead any prisoner trying to escape.

The far smaller building next door was the jail for women. There were no riflemen on the walls there. Jack knew the thinking was no woman would try to escape. But if they did, the sharpshooters at the men's prison could easily pick them off.

A guard leaned toward the Fiat's window and shined his light in the car. "What's your business here?" he asked.

"I'm a lawyer here to see a client," said Jack.

"Visiting hours over a long time ago."

"I'm not a visitor. I'm a *lawyer*. And the accused has a right to see his lawyer at any time of the day or night."

Jack knew this was not a hard-and-fast rule, but his voice was firm and his eyes held steady on the man's now-wavering gaze. He added, "And denying the right to counsel can damage the prosecution's case. You want to be responsible for that?"

The wavering look collapsed into a full retreat. "Let me see some ID. And your State Bar card."

Jack produced these while his father grinned appreciatively at his son's artful maneuvering. Jack saw this and whispered, "Save your applause. That was the easy part."

The guard handed back the ID and card and said, "Which prisoner?"

"He's accused of killing two people in Madison Heights last Friday. Jerome?"

"Hell, Jerome Washington, you mean?"

"That's right. Jerome *Washington*," said Jack, shooting another look at his father.

The guard sneered, "He don't need no lawyer. He needs Helen Keller."

"What?" said a confused Jack.

"A miracle worker, man." The guard gut-laughed.

"That was actually Helen Keller's *teacher*. *She* was the miracle worker."

The man stopped his laughing. "You think I give a shit? Go on in and see your *client*, what good it'll do you. Or him."

Jack passed through the front gate and parked the Fiat in an empty space near the main entrance. He grabbed his briefcase and looked at his father. "You can't come with me."

Frank Lee's jaw went slack. "Why the hell not?"

"I'll be speaking with a potential client. Anything he says to me is confidential, but if you're there it breaks the attorney-client privilege."

"Why didn't you tell me that before?"

"You never asked. And for God's sake keep your gun out of sight."

Inside, Jack was searched by a man with a few wisps of hair left on his head. His rolled-up uniform sleeves revealed a green mermaid tattoo on his right forearm.

"Navy?" asked Jack, pointing at the mark.

The man nodded. "Submariner. Pacific. The Big One."

"My father was there, too."

When Jack told the jailer which prisoner he wanted to see, the guard said, "Every colored comes in this place got Washington or Jefferson as their last name. Know why?"

"No, I don't," said Jack dully.

"'Cause they don't know who their daddy is and they just pick themselves a *president*." He grinned crookedly, showing off two teeth stuffed with gold.

"Just take me to him," Jack said brusquely. As they walked along, he asked, "Has he been in front of a judge yet?"

"Arraigned, formally charged, case turned over for trial, and no bail was set; your boy's here for the duration."

"Did the grand jury return an indictment?"

"Don't know nothin' about that."

They stopped at a cell door.

"There he is," said the jailer after opening the door with a dramatic flourish. "President Washington."

CHAPTER 9

IN THE CELL THERE WAS one barred window, a rickety wooden chair, a short, narrow bunk, a stained commode, a cracked porcelain sink. And him.

"What happened to you?" asked Jack as the door clanged shut behind him.

Jerome Washington was sitting on the bunk, staring at the wall. The fact that his head was wrapped in a blood-soaked bandage and his face was bruised had prompted Jack's question. Instead of a jail-issued garment, he apparently had on the same clothes he'd been arrested in. Denim, sweat-stained long-sleeved work shirt, worn dungarees, and old boots with the edges curled, like the man was melting from the bottom up. He was large and robustly built, and in his midtwenties. He was several inches taller than Jack and carried eighty more pounds. His hair was short, and a trim beard covered his jutting jaw and curved over his top lip.

Jack sat in the one chair and put his briefcase on his lap. "I'm Jack Lee," he said. "Miss Jessup asked me to see you. I'm an attorney."

Jerome moved slightly when Jack mentioned the woman, but he remained mute.

Jack unbuckled his briefcase straps and took out a legal pad and a pen. With his other clients, Jack had not taken notes during their first encounter. It could be intimidating, and he wanted the folks to tell their story in their own time and in their own way. But this was different, since he wasn't even sure he was going to take the case. Despite what he had told Miss Jessup, he had never represented a Black client.

"You up for a few questions, Mr. Washington?"

For that he got not even a glance or a twitch.

"I've been told that you were arrested for murdering two people in Madison Heights. And that you've been before a judge and that no bail was set. Is that right?" Jack waited a moment. "How did you plead before the judge?" When Jerome still didn't answer he said, "Did a lawyer go with you?"

All Jack heard was the screech of katydids outside the window. He glanced that way and saw the wink of a firefly right outside the bars, an insect far freer than this man.

"What you be doin' here?"

When Jack glanced back the prisoner had leveled a darkly suspicious gaze on him.

"Miss Jessup said you needed a lawyer. *Do* you need a lawyer, Mr. Washington?"

Jerome made a show of looking around his cell. "What you think?"

"What happened to your head?"

"Cop bust it open."

"Why? Were you resisting arrest?"

"Naw."

"Why did he beat you up then?" asked Jack.

"Bumped into him."

"Bumped? Why?"

"'Cause man say he gonna do things to my wife."

"What sort of things?" asked a puzzled Jack.

Jerome looked directly at him. "Ain't gonna say. But they all be bad. Real bad."

"So you *bumped* into a cop?"

"Before that, he kept hittin' me with that damn club when I ain't do nothin'. And they already done cuffed me and I was on my knees. So why they keep hittin' me?"

"So he *provoked* you into doing something and then beat you badly, while you were already in custody?" said Jack.

"Yes sir, he did."

"Okay, I'll make inquiries about that and see what I can do." He looked Jerome over. "Why has no one come to take your clothes and issue you a prisoner's outfit?"

"They say they ain't have my size. They still lookin'."

"I understand you were arrested by the officers because they had a reasonable belief that you had committed a crime?"

"Guess 'cause I be there."

"And I also understand that you went before a judge or magistrate and that no bail was granted. Did a lawyer go with you?"

He nodded. "Some white man. Don't 'member his name."

"Was he a public defender?"

Jerome shrugged. "Don't know."

"What did he say to you?"

"He say, 'You got money for a lawyer?' And I think he mean right then. So I says no. Then we went to the courthouse and they ask me how I…"

"How you plead?"

"Yeah. And I say I didn't do nothin' to nobody."

"Did your lawyer request bail?"

"He ain't say nothin' 'bout that. But the judge say I gotta go to jail."

"Did the commonwealth's attorney mention an *indictment*?"

Jerome shook his head. "I ain't never hear that word."

"What did the man who went with you to court look like?"

"Skinny, short. Got red hair. Loud voice."

"George Connelly? That ring any bells?"

"Yeah. You know him?"

"Yes. I'll talk to him to get more details. Has he been here to see you?"

"Naw."

Jack wrote down a few things. "Did they take any bodily fluids from you? Like a urine sample?"

Jerome looked offended. "Naw. Why they wanna do that?"

"To see if you might have been intoxicated or on drugs."

"I ain't either one."

"Have you ever used narcotics?"

Jerome fidgeted and glanced nervously away.

Jack said, "If I'm your lawyer, everything you tell me is confidential. I can't reveal it to anyone."

"Took drugs in 'Nam. Army give 'em to everybody."

Jack thought of his brother. "I've heard that."

"But I ain't never take nothin' since I been back."

"How long were you in Vietnam?" asked Jack.

"Two years. Feel like twenty."

"Were you questioned by the police after you were arrested?"

"Two white dudes in suits got me in a little room. Say I killed them people and if I don't want to die in the chair, I better tell 'em how and why I done it."

"And what did you say?"

"I ain't say nothin'. They started screamin' at me, pushin' me, smackin' me and such. But I just looked at the wall and pretend I ain't where I am. Finally, they got tired out and put me in here."

Jack noted how stiffly Jerome was keeping his left leg. "Did the police hurt your leg, too?"

"Happened in 'Nam. Got shot there. Ain't much good, hurts all the time, but least I'm alive."

"You got a Purple Heart then?"

He said, "I got me lots of medals. So what?"

"Now, why you were at that house when the people were killed?"

"I worked there," replied Jerome. "Drove 'em 'round in the car. Worked in the yard, the garage, the house, fixed stuff needed fixin'."

"So like a handyman. How long had you worked there?"

"'Bout a year now. Big property, got lots to do keepin' it goin'. But Mr. Leslie want to keep it all goin' good."

Jack glanced up sharply from his notes. "Mr. *Leslie*?"

"Yeah, Mr. Leslie and his wife, Miss Anne."

Jack felt his skin grow cold despite the stifling heat of the room. "Leslie and Anne *Randolph*?"

"Yes sir. Good people, least they was." He lowered his troubled gaze to the floor.

Jack didn't personally know the Randolphs, but he certainly knew of them. They were one of the most prominent families around. And he did know their youngest child, Christine. And this man was accused of ending their lives. It must have been in the local news. But he hadn't read a newspaper or watched TV because he'd been shut up in his office over the weekend working on various cases. His parents hadn't mentioned it and he wondered why not.

He composed himself and said, "Can you tell me what happened?"

Jerome lifted his gaze. "You *say* Miss Jessup send you? But maybe you with the cops gettin' me to say stuff so's I end up in the chair."

Jack handed his business card to Jerome. "I'm a lawyer in private practice. My office is on Marshall Street. And, despite what the police told you, Virginia has stopped executing people for now. There hasn't been one done in five years."

Jerome stared uncertainly at the card. "Where it say where you is?"

Jack pointed at the address. "Right there. Marshall Street." He paused, something occurring to him. "Um, can you read, Jerome?"

Jerome stuffed the card into his shirt pocket. "What you wanna know?"

"Let's get the big one out first. *Did* you kill them? You can tell me and I can never reveal it."

"No sir, I didn't."

"It would be helpful if we can provide evidence absolving you of the crime."

He frowned. "What that mean?"

"To show you couldn't have killed them and then they'll have to let you go."

Jerome snorted. "Let me go? What drugs *you* on?"

"The state has to prove your guilt."

"Uh-huh, sure they do," Jerome replied bitterly, looking away.

"You're a citizen with rights."

Jerome stared at Jack and his look was withering. "No, I'm a n—— to every white person walkin' down the street lookin' at me like I don't belong here. Did they fight for this country? Did they get shot up? I did. I was. And this still ain't my country for why I don't know." Finished, he dropped his gaze and studied the floor.

Jack waited for a few moments to break the silence. He knew every word Jerome had spoken was the absolute truth. And he also knew it would not help his case in the slightest. "So tell me about that day at the Randolphs."

His head slowly swinging back and forth Jerome said, "I was in the garage cleanin' the car. They got them a big old Buick. Mr. Leslie like it spic 'n' span."

"Okay, then what?"

"I done finished cleanin' it. Then time for me to get on home."

"What time was that?"

"Clock on the car say six. 'Member the hands pointin' up and down."

"So you finished up and then what?"

"Went to the house get my money. They pay on Friday. Forty dollars cash for the week. Good money. *Good* money."

"So you went to the house, and then what?" Jack asked patiently.

"I knocked on the back door, but ain't nobody answer. I knock again. Ain't hear nothin'. Then I see the door open a little bit. I poke my head in, and say it's me."

"And no answer?"

"Naw."

"Did they sometimes go out?"

"Just for a walk, but it real hot that day and they stay inside. But they real good 'bout payday. So I think maybe they ain't hear me."

"So you poked your head in and called out?"

"Yes sir. But nobody answer me. So's I walk on in. I don't like bein' in the house like that, but I don't know what else to do 'cause I need my money. Pearl be expectin' it. I look 'round for 'em in the kitchen, front room, and then the eatin' room."

"But you *did* find them? And they were…?"

Jerome looked up into Jack's face and his lips trembled. "He be on the floor. Miss Anne, too. Blood every damn place, and all over them."

Jack nodded. "What did you do?"

When Jerome next spoke, his voice cracked. "I pretty sure they dead, but I still wanna help 'em. I try to get Mr. Leslie off the floor. But he too heavy. I'm real strong, but I got the bad leg and Mr. Leslie is a big man who like his food all right." He stopped. "Leastways he did."

"And Miss Anne?"

"Oh, she right small. So I done set her upright in the chair. She a fine lady. She ain't got no use bein' on the floor like that."

"You did all that but you don't have any blood on your clothes?"

Jerome looked down. "No sir. Blood all dried up when I get there."

Jack made a note of this. "And when did the police arrive?"

"'Bout same time I puttin' Miss Anne in the chair. Got the guns out and tell me to get away from her and to get on the floor."

"Did they read you your rights? To remain silent, right to an attorney?"

"Man say stuff off a little card. I ain't unnerstand none 'a it."

"Did you give them a statement? Talk to them?"

He shook his head. "My momma always told me colored man

talk to the police they won't never find him again. That why I ain't talk to none of 'em."

"Do you know *what* killed them?"

"Knife, most likely. They all cut up."

"Did you see a knife?"

"No sir."

"Miss Jessup said you're married to Pearl?"

He nodded. "Got us three kids, two girls and a boy. Elijah, Kayla, and Darla Jean be the baby." A wobbly tear suddenly bloomed in his right eye. "I ain't never gonna see 'em again, am I?"

"You'll see them, Jerome. I can arrange a visit here if you want."

Jerome shook his head fiercely. "No. Not with me all locked up like some piece 'a trash. I don't want 'em to see me that way."

"Okay. We can talk about that later. Now, do you own the place where you live?"

Jerome looked at him funny. "Naw. Why?"

"Just for purposes of posting bail."

"What that do?"

"It means you might get out of jail pending your trial. I'll look into it even though the court initially denied it."

"Okay."

"You ever been arrested before?"

"No sir, never."

"Good. I'm also going to look at the arrest report and find out what I can. Then I'll be back to see you again, hopefully tomorrow. Now, I'll need a retainer."

"What's that?" he said suspiciously.

"My fee to represent you."

"You talk to Pearl. She handle the money. She real smart with all that."

"Okay, but I need to know how it was left with the other lawyer, George Connelly. You said he hasn't been here. Have you heard from him at all?"

"Last thing man say to me is I better get me 'nother lawyer 'cause he ain't mine no more."

Jack thought, *What the hell is going on?* "I'll talk to Pearl, but do you officially retain me as your attorney?"

"How much you cost?"

"My rate is five dollars an hour."

"Five dollars! An *hour*," he exclaimed.

"It's the going rate, Jerome. But I will pack a lot into those hours, I promise."

"How long you reckon it take?" asked Jerome anxiously.

"If I were a public defender, the rate for a felony trial for murder would be about two hundred and fifty dollars."

"Sweet Jesus!" exclaimed Jerome.

"And depending on the facts there may be nothing I can do for you, Jerome. I won't sugarcoat this. It wouldn't be fair to you."

"Damn," he said as tears formed in his reddened eyes. "Okay, if you wanna be my lawyer, I hire you, sir."

"You can call me Jack."

"What your last name again?"

"Lee."

"I'll call you Mr. Lee."

Jack nodded as he slipped a paper from his briefcase. "Okay. If that makes you more comfortable. I have this document for you to sign, saying that you agree that I'm to be your lawyer."

He handed the paper and a pen to Jerome.

"Where I gots to sign?" Jack indicated the line and Jerome carefully made an *X* on the signature line. Without looking at Jack he handed the pen and paper back.

"That's fine, Jerome, thank you. Now, you are to say nothing to anyone except me. Not the police or the jailers or another prisoner. Do you understand? Nothing."

Jerome nodded.

"My phone number is on that card I gave you. The police have to let you call me. Don't let them tell you that you can't. All right?"

"Okay, Mr. Lee."

Jack rose and Jerome stared at the wall again, the tears trickling down his face and his big hands balling and unballing, his huge chest swelling and then emptying of air.

The jailer came at Jack's call and led him back down the hall.

"You know the Randolphs?" asked the jailer.

"I certainly know of them."

"Old Virginia stock. Back to Jefferson himself," said the jailer proudly, as though the Randolphs were part of *his* family. "And that colored man killed 'em."

"He's *accused* of killing them. Nothing has been proven yet."

The jailer looked at him like Jack was speaking in tongues.

Outside Frank Lee was standing next to the Fiat, smoking. "How'd it go, Jacky?"

"Just get in the car, Daddy."

Frank Lee stamped out his Camel and climbed in.

Jack put the Fiat in gear and they drove off.

"Well?" said Frank.

"Why didn't you tell me that Leslie and Anne Randolph were murdered on Friday?"

"What?" exclaimed Frank.

"They're the ones Jerome is accused of killing. You say you didn't know?"

"No. Your momma and me took Lucy to that special doctor over in Richmond. Left Friday night after I got off work, and got back late Sunday night. Didn't see the TV or read a paper. Murdered? The Randolphs?"

"Yes. The Randolphs."

"So what do you think after meetin' with him?"

"I think I have a better chance of becoming president of the United States than Jerome Washington has of ever walking out a free man from this."

CHAPTER 10

IT WAS AFTER MIDNIGHT AND Jack was still not in bed. He
had just made the most critical decision in the thirty-three years he
had been alive, and now deep uncertainty had crept in. And with
that the desire for sleep had vanished.

He was in his office, which was also his home, with a bedroom and shower upstairs, and an office and a toilet downstairs,
along with a small kitchen. It was located in a one-and-a-half-story
clapboard dwelling in Carter City, the sovereign seat of Freeman
County. It was within walking distance of the county courthouse
where Jerome Washington would be tried for his alleged crimes,
and, in all probability, imprisoned for life for those crimes, whether
he had committed them or not.

The cavernous brick structure next to Jack's had once been used
as a tobacco warehouse, and his building was where the warehouse
manager had once lived; like Jack's setup, it had also served as the
manager's office. The residual smells of the curing leaves were still
pungent all these decades later. He didn't know how folks could
have endured working there when the place actually contained the
leafy plants, but tobacco growing was synonymous with Virginia.
All the majestic plantations around here could trace their origins to
that sole cash crop.

He stared out the open window onto the lighted street below.

Before the Supreme Court had recently changed the rules, most poor whites and all Blacks went through the legal system without the aid of counsel, which meant they represented themselves, or *pro se*. Jack knew that was a Latin term that basically meant, "You lose."

He didn't know any white lawyer who had ever represented a Black person in Freeman County for two simple reasons: You weren't going to win, and you weren't going to get paid much. He was actually stunned that George Connelly had stepped in to represent Jerome, even at his arraignment.

He continued to stare down onto the streets of Carter City hoping for a breeze that never came. The city was named after Robert "King" Carter, one of the wealthiest American colonists, mostly by virtue of being Englishman Lord Fairfax's land agent. When Carter died he had left behind three hundred thousand acres, an immense fortune in British pounds, and over a thousand slaves. Carter had also been one of the most successful slave brokers in the Colonies, making several fortunes off buying and selling men, women, and children.

When Lord Fairfax read of this enormous wealth in Carter's obituary, he had his cousin board a ship to Virginia to be his new colonial agent. Apparently, the exalted lord was shocked that his former representative had become so wealthy, and he didn't want a repeat performance by another ambitious Virginian.

Jack lived in a world that had been sliced into halves that were termed separate but equal. However, even to an ignorant or a shameless eye, those halves never came within shouting distance of parity. Whether it was buses or bathrooms or water fountains or places of learning or praying or where you'd raise your knife and fork, there was "us" and there was "them" and the lines were drawn starkly, if not in any way purely.

The U.S. Supreme Court had started to break those walls down in the 1950s. But justice ran slow when it had to churn through people. Many of the major changes were still percolating, like water bubbling up to a desert floor. What you often got was nothing more than a mouthful of damp, gritty sand, if not an outright illusion of transformation.

Because of the passage of the Civil Rights Act in 1964, the WHITES and COLOREDS ONLY signs on water fountains, bathrooms, shops, and eateries had now come down for the most part as a result of federal decrees and the presence of armed U.S. marshals in Southern climes. It had occurred at the cost of the Southern states fleeing the LBJ-led Democratic Party and hitching their allegiances to the Republican Grand Old Party of Lincoln, which was irony beyond irony, thought Jack.

However, despite the law, on a bus when a Black sat down in the front, the whites moved to the rear. When a Black came into a store that used to be off-limits to his race, the whites gawked until he left.

Jack wasn't speculating about this. He'd moved. He'd gawked. And he'd never once spoken out against others who had done so as well.

Yet his upbringing had been different, at least in some respects. His mother had taken her children to the library every Saturday, and he had read books that allowed him to see far beyond the stark boundaries of Freeman County. One day when he was thirteen and checking out his stack as usual, the librarian, a fussy old woman named Mrs. Gooch, had picked up one of the tomes and said, "What in the world are you doing reading this, Jack Lee? I didn't even know we had this trash on the shelves. We ought to ban lies like this. Or better yet, burn 'em."

The novel was *Uncle Tom's Cabin*. The thing was, Jack had not put it in his stack. He was about to tell her so when his mother had come up and said, "The more books read the better, right, Mrs. Gooch?"

And Jack had taken the book home, and read it. He hadn't found it particularly well written and the main characters seemed exaggerated in many respects: all good, or all evil, without nuance. But what bothered Jack the most about the novel was the fact that the principal reason it seemed to have been written was to warn people of the dangers and cruelty of slavery. Jack, even as a young teenager, wondered why anyone needed to be told that enslavement of humans was wrong.

When he'd later asked his mother why she had placed it in his book pile, she'd said, "The world does not all look like we do, Robert. And if you want to live in that world you need to understand what all of it looks like. Not just our piece of the pie."

Again, he had been mystified by the seeming incoherence in his mother's wanting him to read books like that, despite her firm belief that the races should be kept separate. But as a boy he did not have the maturity or intellectual development to muddle through to any particular conclusion. And he dared not push his mother on it. Even as an adult, it continued to puzzle him. And it wasn't just about books.

As a little boy he had gone with his mother and father to bring needed food and medicine to the families of the Black men that Frank Lee worked with at Old Dixie Transport. He had watched his mother dutifully nurse back to health men, women, and their children. She had done so with the skills and knowledge she had acquired surviving largely by herself on that remote mountain ridge in southwest Virginia, or so his father had told him. He would watch his mother concocting a strong smelling plaster to rub onto the chest of a wheezing baby, or spooning homemade soup into an ill mother's mouth, or cleverly breaking the fever of a man who was not paid if he was too sick to work.

When he had asked his mother about this she had said it was just folks helping other folks that needed it. There was never mention of the race of the people being helped, although Jack remembered the stares of people in neighboring homes as his father pulled his pickup truck to a stop and they all clambered out with their bulky bags and pale skin.

His extracurricular reading also prompted him to think about things he apparently wasn't to question during his formal schooling. American history had been taught a peculiar way in Virginia, Jack had found. They had reached the three-day battle of Gettysburg with the South mostly victorious up to that point, but the tide about to dramatically turn in favor of the Union, when the next thing Jack knew they were studying World War I. When he'd asked his teacher about the other years of the titanic American conflict, she had told him firmly that he had learned all he needed to about the War of Northern Aggression.

Later, in college, he read works that powerfully chronicled the struggles of nonwhites in a white-dominated society. Collectively, they had set Jack's mind to thinking in different ways and directions. And yet despite that enlightenment he had never protested against Jim Crow, or used his legal skills to do so, or sought political office where he could address racism head-on. Apparently, books alone did not inspire bravery, although they could certainly be a catalyst to action. Yet he believed that one day the equal treatment of all would be both the law of the land and the strong preference of its population.

And now? Could this be the moment when all that reading and reflection coupled with simply observing the unfair plight of others was transformed into his actually doing something to further the cause of racial equality?

But you're not a risk-taker, Jack Lee, not really.

But what if you were, just this once?

He picked up his pen and made a list on a piece of paper:

One, formalize his representation of Jerome with the court.

Two, obtain the police record.

Three, visit the crime scene.

Four, interview the arresting officers who had beaten his client.

Five, meet with the commonwealth's attorney prosecuting the case.

Six, go to church and pray.

Despite his agnosticism that last to-do item might be the most vital.

He stopped there, marshaling his thoughts. If Jerome was telling the truth and hadn't killed the Randolphs, then who had? They lived in affluent Madison Heights. It could have been a robbery. Were things missing? Had the police even checked? But why would they have? They had their man.

In Freeman County it didn't get much easier than convicting a Black man in a court of law, particularly one who had been so obliging as to be at the scene of the crime.

Jack went upstairs to his bathroom, put his head in the sink, and opened the tap. He let the cold water wash over him and then toweled his hair dry. He gripped the edges of the sink and stared in the mirror.

Thirty-three years old. Way older than his father when Jack had been born.

And now there was Lucy. And as they got older, Jack might have to care for his parents, too.

So maybe this is not the right time to be taking on a case like this.

And while Jerome said he wasn't guilty, he could easily be lying.

The Randolphs paid on Fridays. That meant they had cash in the house. Maybe Jerome wanted more than they were willing to pay him. His wife, Pearl, was expecting money. Maybe Jerome hadn't even worked that day, or possibly the entire week. But he still needed his money. Motive was right there.

But if he had stolen the money, why was he there when the police showed up?

And who had called the police in the first place? He mentally kicked himself. He hadn't asked Jerome about that. Had *he* called the police? If so, that would cut against Jerome being the killer.

Then his thoughts drifted to a splash of rye in the sweet tea. How had Miss Jessup known his father liked it that way?

He glanced out the bedroom window, where in the far distance the McHenry River flowed under the Penny Bridge, so named because that had once been the toll to pass over it. The Penny had closed over three decades before, its ancient and brittle supports crumbling too fast for saving. The regal Stonewall Jackson Bridge, about a quarter mile away from the Penny, had taken its place with great fanfare and a visit by the governor, who cut the ribbon and was driven across the span of concrete and steel before anyone else.

As young teens Jack and his brother would venture on their bikes at night to the closed Penny Bridge. They would lie on their backs on one of the little walking paths on either side of the bridge, and gaze at the stars. They always hoped to spy a shooter, but were also content with counting the ones that stayed motionless.

Back then Jack had wanted to be an Army Air Corps pilot, with the dream that, one day, when folks went into outer space, he would be one of the first to climb to the stars. His younger brother was content to keep his feet on the ground and travel the country by boxcar looking for adventure. Neither one had realized their childhood ambition.

One night they had seen some boys about their age at the Black end of the bridge. These boys had lit a stick fire on the span and grilled hot dogs over the flames. The smells of the cooking meat wafted over the Penny to the Lee boys.

Their bellies rumbling, Jack and his brother had looked over at the fire long enough that one of the Black boys brought over two dogs housed in fluffy white buns with mustard smeared on top. The Lees had thanked the boy, who said he was called Homer, named after a great poet from long ago. Jack had not learned who Homer was until college, but that hot dog was the best he'd ever had.

The two groups then came together and sat around swapping tales of adventure and other matters important to boys of all backgrounds until a police car had approached. The Black boys and all remnants of the fire were gone by the time the police car arrived and stopped at the white end of the span.

The Lee boys had glibly lied to the cop who asked if they'd seen a gang of young n——s. "They stole some hot dogs and buns from our side," he said.

The officer had admonished the Lees to stick to their side of the bridge and added, "You go over there you gonna catch some disease from Africa they all got. You hear me?"

Both boys said they did. Jack's heart was beating so fast he thought he might throw up the remains of his hot dog into the McHenry, which would be proof positive of his perjury.

Jack had not slept a wink that night, convinced that God would strike him deaf, dumb, and perhaps dead for committing the sin of lying to a lawman to protect colored boys with hot dogs stolen from white people.

The river held another, far more pleasant memory for him. When he and Jeff were in high school, their daddy would bring home truck tire inner tubes as big as a table when inflated. Father and sons would spend lazy summer weekends floating in them down the McHenry when the water level wasn't too low. They would push off the huge boulders that sat in the water like submerged hippos. The gentle current and soft eddies, which nibbled at the underbellies of the boulders like blue gills on toes, combined to propel one down-river at a pace that was good for daydreaming or dozing. And his father would always bring along a six-pack of Pabst, and Jack and his brother would have a bottle apiece and keep the secret from their mother, who remained on the shore downriver with Lucy preparing the simple feast that would follow.

Later, they would lie in the sun and dry off and eat sand-wiches filled with Smithfield ham and fat tomato slices, and chew bread-and-butter pickles and devour homemade potato salad with thick slices of onion. The cold lemonade would soothe the parch-ing of their throats caused by the summer sun. They would lift up Lucy and take her to the McHenry and dip her feet in the water until she became more scared than amused. The ride home would have the exhausted children dead asleep in the back, and the mother in the front seat the same, while Frank Lee thoughtfully puffed on his Camels and watched the summer sun smolder into the vast cradle of the western horizon.

Those were fine times, Jack knew, that had now drifted away like a tide that had no intention of ever returning.

He made up his mind. Someone else would have to represent Jerome, although he doubted there was a white lawyer within a hundred miles that would touch it.

He heard the phone ringing from his downstairs office. He checked his watch. At this late hour it was most likely his parents, and that was not good. He took the steps two at a time and snatched up the receiver.

"Hello?"

The screech he heard on the other end of the line momentarily deafened him.

"Who the hell is this?" he yelled into the phone, his ear still smarting.

He heard the two words, drawn out and ugly.

He put the receiver down, went over to his file cabinet, and took out the .32 Colt revolver he kept there. It didn't have a lot of power, but if Jack shot someone, they would know it. And Jack was an excellent marksman, having been taught by his late grandfather and then his veteran father. And he and his brother had fired hundreds of rounds over the years working on their aim, especially after Jeff Lee had joined the Army.

He went back upstairs and stared out the window.

N——Lover.

Those had been the two spoken words on the phone. Drawn out so long that the caller had run out of breath and coughed with the effort. It had to be one of the prison guards, he figured. Maybe the one with the mermaid tattoo, who thought the Randolphs were Southern royalty.

During Jack's childhood, when bullies had come after him and his brother they had absorbed a beating, afraid to hit back. Or else run like rabbits while the older boys laughed their guts out. The reason for the bullying had been Lucy Lee. The boys had called her names, cruel, awful names, and Jack's father had hollered at them and complained to their parents. These boys had subsequently decided to exact their revenge on the man's sons.

One day Hilly Lee had intervened in one of these tense encounters and told her oldest son exactly what he needed to do to break the grip of such an adversary. So while his mother silently watched, Jack had marched right up to the biggest of the bullies and punched him as hard as he could right in the nose. It had nearly broken his hand, but blood had burst from both of the boy's nostrils like the violent discharge from a double barrel. And they had never been bothered again, as word had spread that Jack Lee did not take shit from anyone, and would break your damn face if you messed with him or his brother.

Jack breathed in the moist, humid air that had collected all around him. And that was when he decided that bullies over the phone were worse than the variety that stood in front of you. They tried to scare and intimidate from a perch of anonymity with no guts and no accountability. He was ready to break another nose and watch the blood gush.

Jerome Washington needed a legal advocate more than anyone he knew.

I guess it might as well be me. And after thirty-three years plus around five hours it's probably about damn time.

CHAPTER 11

THE NEXT DAY JACK WALKED over to the Mathias W. Bedford Courthouse, which had been built around 1800 and originally named for a judge from that era. In 1880 it had been renamed for Bedford, a major general who had fought in the Civil War. He had not worn Union blue.

On the other side of the courthouse stood the bronze statue of a solitary Confederate soldier resolutely facing due south. Jack had always been told this was because the silent sentry did not want to miss the Confederacy rising again.

"Mornin', Jack," said Sally Reeves. She was the clerk of the court for Freeman County. In her early forties, Reeves wore her brunette hair long, letting the row of curls drape her shoulders. Her face was pleasantly angular, and the cheeks rode high on it. Her black glasses were settled right at the center of her slender nose. She was always polite and professional and, as an assistant clerk, had been helpful to Jack when he was just starting out and learning the ropes. Back then she knew far more about the legal process than he had. Maybe she still did, he thought.

"Morning, Sally."

She shuffled some papers on her desk and slid her gaze down her official ledger. "Don't see you on the court docket today."

"Just filing an appearance. And here to pick up some documents."

He handed her the legal form in triplicate that he had typed up earlier.

She read down it. "Jerome Washington?"

"Yes. I also need a copy of his arraignment. It seems no bail request was made. And I need to think about asking for a preliminary hearing as well, of course. Don't want to waive that by not timely raising it."

"He's already been *indicted*, Jack. That preempts the accused's right to a prelim."

"He's already been indicted? When?"

"Monday mornin'," she replied.

"But wasn't he arrested *before* the indictment was handed down?"

"They didn't have much choice since he was found with two dead people."

"But if he was arrested before an indictment was returned, I still get to ask for a preliminary hearing."

"George Connelly waived it at the arraignment. And he didn't request bail."

"He isn't representing Mr. Washington any longer. I am."

"Which apparently makes him smarter than you."

"Well, I'm gonna find Connelly and chew his ass out."

"You can't. He went on vacation. Mexico, so's I heard."

"It was malpractice for him to waive the prelim."

"That would have just pissed Justin Reed off. You'll need to stay in his good graces, if he'll even listen to a plea deal. So you're really filin' to be his lawyer?" Her deliberate speech made the question seem twice as long as it actually was.

"Otherwise, I'd be wasting your time, wouldn't I?"

She closed the ledger and looked at him. "Have you talked to anybody about this?" Her tone was now cool and distantly judgmental.

"Who exactly would I talk to?"

"Anybody who would tell you not to do this, which would be pretty much everybody you and I know."

"Folks are entitled to representation, Sally. Law says that now."

"*Their* law. Not ours."

"Well, actually, it's just one big law that stretches from sea to shining sea."

"You won that burglary case just last week. I watched some of it. You were real good in front of the jury. A natural."

"I've currently got four clients to do work for, and the most challenging one involves a bar fight resulting in a simple assault charge."

"And you think representin' that animal will help your career?"

"Can you just stamp the form and enter me as his counsel? I'd appreciate it. And I'll need a copy of the indictment. And do you have a record of his arraignment?"

She looked through the files and made copies of the documents, and she handed them, along with a stamped copy of his appearance filing, to Jack.

"It's your funeral," she said.

He shot her a glance. "Figuratively speaking, you mean?"

She didn't answer him.

He walked out of the courthouse with the documents in his briefcase. It felt as though it now equaled the weight of the world. Jack knew he had crossed the Rubicon with this exchange of official paper. In college he had learned that Julius Caesar had done this very thing by leading a single legion of soldiers into Rome. This broke the law of imperium and subjected Caesar and all his legionnaires to a capital punishment.

Well, Jerome Washington had pierced the rule of imperium perhaps by virtue of being a Black man in a white world. Whatever the truth, *alea jacta est*, the die was indeed cast, for both of them.

Jack sat on the Fiat's thin seat, which was already starting to bake with the rising temperature, and looked at the other documents Reeves had given him.

An indictment for the first-degree murder of two people had been handed down by the sitting grand jury of Freeman County.

Connelly had not asked for bail and the commonwealth's attorney on the case, Justin Reed, had argued against any being set.

Jerome had pled not guilty, and that had been duly entered into the record.

Jack looked at the last piece of paper. Connelly had submitted his withdrawal from the case right after the arraignment, citing a conflict in schedule and doubt as to whether Jerome was truly indigent and thus entitled to a public defender.

Right, thought Jack. *The man just didn't want to get shot.*

He looked at his watch and pondered next steps. The law did not move slowly in Freeman County, especially when a Black man accused of a violent crime against the white race was attached to one end of it.

Which means I don't have much time, either.

CHAPTER 12

THE FREEMAN COUNTY SHERIFF'S OFFICE was housed in a dully painted cinder block building that rose three stories toward a heat-filled sky starting to cloud over, with the prospect of rain.

Jack parked next to a deputy sheriff's patrol car. A racked shotgun pointed vertically rested in the rear, caged seat, like a single finger lifted in warning.

He entered the building, where he was immediately greeted by the comingling of sweat, cigarette smoke, and gun oil. A sign on the wall indicated the Colored waiting room was in the rear. He pulled down the now-illegal placard and threw it in the trash. Before last night he would have never thought to do such a thing.

He checked in with the front desk sergeant. "I need to pick up an arrest report."

"You already got the one for the assault at the bar, Jack."

"Got a new client."

The man hooked his callused thumb to the left. "Then have at it."

In Room 103 Jack found a uniformed man with black specs whom he didn't know. He produced his bar card and the copy of his stamped appearance filing.

"Washington, Jerome?" the man said.

"That's right."

The man consulted a metal cabinet from which he pulled out

a slender file. Inside were four pages of indifferent looking official paper in the requisite triplicate.

"Defense counsel gets the pink copy," said the man.

"It's also the least legible. Doesn't seem fair when a man's liberty's at stake," noted Jack.

"I don't make the rules, son. I just do the filin' and the fetchin'."

He had Jack sign for them and then handed the pink pages over.

"And the arresting officers? Gene Taliaferro and Raymond LeRoy? I'll need to speak with them."

"Leave me your business card and I'll tell them you need to talk."

Jack did so and drove back to the courthouse, where the commonwealth attorney's office was located on the second floor.

He made his inquiry, and the woman at the front desk had him wait while she made a call. "It'll just be a moment, Mr. Lee," she said after cradling the phone.

A half hour later a door opened and Justin Reed, the commonwealth's attorney for Freeman County, dressed in a seersucker suit with a yellow bowtie, appeared. A smoky cigarette was clenched between two beefy knuckles. The man's stern expression and stiffened posture gave Jack pause, for while the men were legal adversaries, they had known each other for years.

"This way, Jack," said Reed.

Jack was led into a cluttered office reeking of smoke and sat down opposite the man he would likely be facing in court.

"What's your business with Jerome Washington?" said Reed, flicking ash into a bowl engraved with the state's motto: SIC SEMPER TYRANNIS—thus always to tyrants.

"I'm his lawyer."

"Connelly withdrew, I understand."

"And then fled the country, apparently."

"Maybe you should, too."

"I'm not going to do that. And don't ask me why," said Jack. "So you're handling the case for the commonwealth?"

Reed jabbed out his cigarette with two hard strikes into the bowl. "There's actually some debate going on about who the prosecutor will be on this."

"You fellows fighting over what looks to be an easy win?"

Reed lit up another smoke. "Fact is, we might be talking Richmond."

Jack felt his gut seize. "Heavyweights coming in?"

"Gotta make a stand somewhere. Hell, they're right now trying to integrate our schools."

"Which the Supreme Court ordered take place fourteen years ago."

Reed chuckled. "That's right, isn't it?"

"Wheels of justice move slow. But they are moving now."

"Look, what the hell are you trying to do here, Jack? Kiss a colored's ass?"

"I'm just a lawyer with a client charged with two murders. Now, walk me through the arraignment. Why no bail? And why did Connelly waive the preliminary hearing?"

"I'm not letting a cold-blooded killer loose on the streets. The magistrate agreed. And so did George."

"Funny that George even signed on for this."

"Magistrate appointed him when we thought Washington was indigent. George just happened to be around."

"Did anyone ask Mr. Washington if he was indigent? There is a procedure for that."

Reed said disdainfully, "Come on, how many coloreds have any money?"

"So you're telling me that George didn't really want to represent him, and pissed away valuable rights of Mr. Washington that he could have asserted—"

"*Mr.* Washington," sneered Reed. "Listen to yourself for Chrissakes."

"What would you call him?"

"You probably don't want to hear."

"So George didn't raise legal issues he should have. But I can tell you that *I* will. And I'm going to fight for every last one of them so long as I'm on this case."

"Might be your last case. Who can say?"

The two lawyers eyeballed each other across the span of the desk.

"Is that a threat, Justin?"

"Parts of this country started out different and stayed that way. Got an election coming up that could be the deciding factor. Might end up with two countries."

"Well, for some that *would* be the *easy* way out. But what does that have to do with my case?"

Reed looked at him quizzically. "Do you really have no clue as to the hurricane you're walking right into?"

Jack sat back. "Maybe not."

"Well, you sure as hell will. And sooner than you probably want."

CHAPTER 13

TWO BOXES WERE CHECKED. NOW Jack headed on to the third—the crime scene, and for good reason. He had as much faith in the lawmen of Freeman County to conduct a fair and thorough investigation with a Black man standing accused of killing two white people as he did in medicine's ability to make his sister whole again.

He drove toward the northwest part of the county, where the air held none of the stench of Tuxedo Boulevard, and the lifestyles of the privileged few were enviable, and emphatically cloistered.

Stately manors carved from the dirt hides of once far-flung tobacco plantations sat on substantial property and represented the monied class that always seemed to land on its feet. Jack glimpsed Black maids and nannies watching over their white wards in front yards, or else pushing them down the sidewalks in elegant perambulators passed down from generation to generation. White men with rakes, wheelbarrows, and pruning shears labored over immaculate landscapes. Jack knew Black men were routinely considered unpredictably dangerous and thus unwelcome here in any occupation, which consequently made Jerome's presence stand out.

Compact Mercedes-Benzes and lengthy Cadillacs sat in pristine driveways. The quiet was broken when a lovely woman, her hair done up and her costly dress tailored to her slim figure, fired up a convertible to travel perhaps to a luncheon, or tennis.

There was a deputy sheriff looking hot and riled as he fended off reporters at the impressive gates leading up to the Randolphs' home. Jack saw a news truck and a TV anchor he recognized confronting the deputy, while two other men, probably from the local papers, peppered the lawman, like pecking crows, with their own queries about the crime. A sulky-looking photographer stood by idly popping pictures of the scene.

A bored TV cameraman, his bulky machine dangling in front of him like a dormant mechanical arm, watched all of this while he listlessly smoked a cigarette.

When Jack pulled up, the deputy wheeled around to the Fiat, spoiling for a fight.

He bellowed hoarsely, "Now you just turn whatever the hell that thing is around and head right on outta here."

Jack held up his bar card and official court document. "Jack Lee for the defense. I'm here to examine the crime scene."

"You can't do that," said the deputy, barely looking at the card or paper, so intent was his angry focus.

"Go check with your boss. You don't want this case dismissed because you wouldn't let defense counsel exercise the accused's constitutional rights, do you?"

That remark hit the target, just as Jack knew it would. The flustered deputy called in another lawman to guard the gate and then stormed to the house on foot.

The TV anchor and newspaper reporters swarmed the Fiat. Jack locked the door and rolled up the window. Although sweating, he stared placidly out the windshield while ignoring their shouts and poundings on the car's metal.

The deputy came back a minute later and said, "Okay, you can go on up."

Jack headed along the wide pea-gravel drive to the house. The lawn was bracketed by robust flower beds, and punctured by stands of mature oaks, pines, maples, and multitudes of dogwoods, the state tree. In the spring bloom, legend had it, the dogwood carried

the blood of Jesus' crucifixion wounds on each of its four white pet-
als, representing the four sides of the cross. Jack had never believed
that, even when he'd been a churchgoer.

Two sheriff's cars were parked out in front. The cruisers faced
each other like two rams about to duel. There was also a black sedan
with official commonwealth plates. This captured Jack's full attention, and now he knew that the decision on the prosecutor who
would oppose him in court had been made. And with that revelation
he felt his anxiety spiking.

He got out and looked around. The Randolph estate was two
streets over from the Willow Oaks Country Club, which rivaled
Richmond's storied Country Club of Virginia in its pedigreed
members' list. It was all white and Gentiles only, and women were
allowed when accompanied by their husbands. Other than that, all
were welcome there.

"You look like you got a lot on your mind, son," said the smiling
man waiting for him at the front door.

He was tall and well-nourished, his skin thin as an onion's, his
head mostly bald on top, his age difficult to tell. His suit was coro-
ner black and somber, but with a tie that was blood red.

Jack held out his hand. "I'm Jack Lee, counsel for Jerome Washington, Mr. Battle."

"So I heard, so I heard," said Battle, shaking Jack's hand a bit
too energetically. Up close the man's aftershave got in Jack's nostrils
and made them twitch. Battle glanced at the black sedan. "Guess my
official state license plate gave me away."

"It did."

Edmund Battle was the attorney general of Virginia, the
third-ranking politician in all the commonwealth. A native of
Richmond, he'd been a litigation partner in a suitably prestigious
law firm and then became a circuit judge before throwing his hat
in the ring for the AG slot, which he won by a country mile. And
then, to add insult to injury to the same foe, he did it all over again
four years later.

"Come on in, see what you need to see. There's not much, I'll warn you. Medical examiner has the bodies." He shook his head. "So tragic."

Jack walked in and looked around at an opulence one would have imagined being in a place such as this, but very little that was to his taste, and not much that dated after 1940.

Battle led him down a long hall. Arriving in the room in question the man said, "Mrs. Anne Randolph was in the chair over there with all the blood, and Mr. Leslie Randolph on the floor right there. Can tell by the blood as well. Looks more like a damn butcher shop than a home."

"How did they die?"

"Waiting on the report."

"Surely you can tell that without a medical examiner's official tally."

Battle pulled out a cigarette pack, lit up a Pall Mall, and studied Jack through the haze. "How many murder cases have you handled, Mr. Lee? Be honest now."

"Counting this one, one. But as a lawyer, I've tried just about everything else. And every defense lawyer has a first murder case, don't they?"

Battle shook his broad head. "Not as *sole* counsel they don't. And 'everything else' doesn't come close when you're talking a man's life. There are public defenders in Freeman who have a lot of experience in such matters."

"He has money and doesn't need a public defender. And you said a 'man's life'? Virginia doesn't execute people anymore."

"Virginia still has its death penalty statute intact and, legally, there is no reason it cannot be immediately reinstated. And I can tell you, firsthand, there is talk in Richmond of the government doing exactly that." He paused and eyed Jack in a tactical manner. "And if it is reinstated, the commonwealth will seek it against Mr. Washington."

"Good to know. You got the murder weapon? Anything taken? Anybody break in?"

"Whoa, son, you're firing off questions like a machine gun does bullets."

"Just trying to get the facts right."

Battle sucked on his smoke. "Oh, we got the facts all right. And we'll give you what's required under the law, but focus on the *fact* that your client was found right here with two dead bodies."

"He worked here. So no surprise about that."

"Granted, he did, but that gives him no right to come in the house and kill his employers." He tapped ash into a glass ashtray set on a table and said, "Hell, people around here were already on edge."

"Why was that?"

"You heard about that colored man in Faulkner's Woods, right next to here?"

"Somebody shot him while he was walking down the street."

"He was up to no good."

"On the contrary, there was no proof he was doing anything other than walking."

"There was no lawful reason for that man to be there. Only coloreds around there are the maids, nannies, and cooks. He was clearly casing homes, looking for wives without their husbands, or children without their parents, a back door ajar, keys in a car. Somebody stopped him before he could set out to do what he was certainly going to do. Rape, robbery, kidnapping, who the hell knows."

"I take it there will be no investigation or criminal charges filed," said Jack.

"The Negro's dead. How would prosecuting him make sense?"

"I was referring to the man who killed him."

"You being funny? Might give him a medal." Battle looked around the room. "Too bad somebody didn't stop your client before he did what he did here."

"Now, I understand that there was no bail asked for."

"Oh, you don't want bail for your client, Mr. Lee. He's safer in jail. You let that man out, someone's liable to do him harm."

"I'll take that under advisement. The indictment was handed down very quickly."

"You have a problem with the law acting with alacrity?" retorted Battle.

"I just don't want it to act so fast that an innocent man gets railroaded."

"No chance of that here, since there's no innocent man involved."

"And he was arrested before the indictment was handed down, so I still have the right to request a preliminary hearing."

Battle shook his head. "That right was waived at the arraignment."

"By prior counsel who I believe acted without regard for my client's interests."

"A preliminary hearing? You just want a peek at the prosecution's case, right? Well, let me tell you something. We have uncovered so much evidence and built such a strong case that the grand jury had no problem returning that indictment. Hell, I'm ready to go to trial pretty much right now. I hope you are, too. So what use will a hearing be?"

"Lot of firepower for this one case. I wonder why?"

"And you can keep right on wondering."

"Who called the police?" Jack asked.

"Good Samaritan, I imagine. Seeing a colored man around here, what was he supposed to do?"

"He worked here, as I said, and you conceded. And I imagine the neighbors were used to seeing him around and thus would have had no cause to call the police."

"I know what a jury will think about a Negro man being *in* this house," retorted Battle. He pointed at the blood on the rug. "And your boy was a real monster."

"So he murdered two people and then hung around until the deputies showed up?"

"No, no, son, they got here in time to prevent his *escape*." He gave Jack another empathetic look. "You real sure about this?"

Jack pulled a small Brownie camera from his pocket. "You mind?"

"Snap away."

Jack took pictures of the blood marks, the overturned furniture, the damaged photo of the Randolphs, and anything else that looked important. He noted the footprints in the blood. There were a few that looked like they could be Jerome's. He saw something curious by the chair where Anne Randolph had been found, and took multiple pictures of the carpet while Battle looked on without a lick of interest.

After Jack finished, Battle tapped him on the arm. "Can I make an observation?"

"Help yourself," said Jack as he placed the camera back in his pocket.

"You are scared to death."

"Oh, you believe so?" replied Jack.

"You're wondering why the hell you pulled the trigger on this. And you're hoping there's a way out. Well, there is. You just say the magic words, 'I withdraw as counsel.'"

"For never having met me, you seem to think you know me better than my momma and daddy do."

"I've seen an army of fresh-faced lawyers just itching to take their shot. And do you know what usually happens to them?"

"I'm sure you'll tell me."

"They lose everything they care about. And you got a lot to lose. Like your whole damn race, son." He paused for dramatic effect. "You think on that."

"Can I look around while I think on that?"

"Sure. I'll have a deputy go with you while you're thinking on it. But don't take too long, Mr. Lee. I'm *thinking* this whole case is gonna go real quick. And it's gonna end with a barbeque in the electric chair at the state pen in Richmond, if the governor and the General Assembly do their damn jobs."

CHAPTER 14

LATER, AS JACK WAS LEAVING the house, a couple walked up to the front entrance. The woman was around Jack's age and the man with her a few years older. She was blond, lovely, seemed fragile as ice chips in August, and was dressed all in mourning black. The man was around five ten, trim, and wore a tailored light beige summer suit. His expression was a comingling of confidence and concern.

The woman was pressing a tissue against her reddened eyes, while the man had his arm draped protectively around her.

"Are you with the police?" the man asked in a voice well used to obedience.

Jack said, "No, I'm not. But Mr. Battle is inside with some deputies."

"I'm Gordon Hanover. This is my wife, Christine Hanover."

Damn, thought Jack. The Randolphs' youngest child, Christine. He knew there had been four children. The oldest was Sam Randolph. The two middle children had died decades ago, he recalled. He hadn't seen Christine in nearly fifteen years.

She focused on him with a pair of light gray eyes that matched a bundle of somber clouds directly overhead. A sense of revelation spread over her features. "Jack Lee, is that really you?"

"Yes, it is." He looked at her husband. "My brother, Jeff, used to…date Christine. In high school," he quickly added.

Christine had attended a private school, but that had not stopped her from asking out Jeff Lee after a football game where the Lee brothers had led Jeb Stuart High School to a thorough trouncing of the team from her elite institution. They had dated until Jeff had joined the Army and Christine headed off to a women's college.

"It's been ages since I've seen you. What are you doing here?" she asked.

"I...I was just meeting with Mr. Battle and seeing things. I'm a lawyer now."

"Oh, that's right. I knew that."

"I'm so very sorry for your loss, Christine," he said.

"Thank you."

He stood aside so they could pass by.

Gordon looked at him and said in a low voice. "Is...is it as bad as..."

"No need to let her into the room where it happened."

He gave Jack an appreciative pat on the shoulder, and they headed into the house.

Jack was heading back to his Fiat when a brand-new four-door Lincoln Continental pulled up at the gate. The capped and uniformed Black driver got out and held open the door for the sole passenger: a tall, pale man wearing an expensive suit and fingering a half-smoked chunky cigar. He was around fifty with graying hair, a long, full face, and a pair of dark, analytical eyes. Unlike Gordon Hanover, there was no concern in his features, only reams of confidence.

As Jack watched, the TV anchor and the other reporters hurried over and began assaulting the man with questions. He started talking animatedly, seemingly taking control of the media with a well-rehearsed performance. The clearly engaged photographer snapped away and the cameraman did likewise on film.

Jack noted that the man's driver stood next to the Lincoln staring off at a bird fluttering around.

He heard the crunch of gravel and turned to see Battle striding up to him.

"Who is that man?" Jack asked, pointing at the gate.

Battle took a look and came away obviously impressed. "*That* is Howard Pickett. Heard he might show up today."

"And who is Howard Pickett?"

"You don't follow politics?"

"Not if I can help it," replied Jack.

"Howard Pickett is a millionaire many times over. He built up a highly successful coal mining business over in West Virginia."

"Okay, but what is he doing *here*?"

"He is one of George Wallace's principal backers. Been raising support and dollars for him all over the country. Flies him around on his private plane. Badly wants to see him in the White House."

"Lord help us if George Wallace ever sees the inside of that place," said Jack.

"I disagree. He's a man of the people, of the working class. They get a raw deal from all those high-and-mighty elites with all their fancy education."

"If I remember correctly, you went to Dartmouth for college and Harvard Law, Mr. Battle. So *you're* one of those high-and-mighty elites you just denounced."

"Well, I sure don't see myself that way, son. I came up middle class."

"Uh-huh, and, again, why is that man here, do you think?"

"I believe Mr. Pickett senses an opportunity with this case."

"What sort of opportunity?"

"Oh, I guess we'll have to wait and see. Now, I got to get back inside and comfort Mrs. Hanover. Terrible thing your client did. Robbing the lady of her parents."

Battle hurried back into the house, while Jack drove toward the gate.

As he approached, the TV anchor saw him and the man said

something to Pickett. The coal millionaire turned and stood in the way, forcing Jack to stop the Fiat.

Pickett came around to the driver's side and motioned Jack to roll down his window. He smiled and said, "I'm Howard Pickett, Mr. Lee. Nice to meet you."

"Hello," said Jack as he looked at the cameraman filming this encounter.

"You're a nice-looking white man, law degree and everything, I've been told. So what the hell are you doing representing a Negro who killed some fine elderly white people in their own home?"

"And you're a millionaire many times over. And you get chauffeured around in a big, fancy car. You have your own plane that you fly George Wallace around in, and have somehow convinced the common man you're just like him."

The smile grew wider. "I grew up with nothing, son."

"So did I, and that's pretty much what I still have."

"Maybe it's because you associate with the wrong color of folks."

"Or maybe it's because I don't have any coal mines," retorted Jack.

"I like your attitude, son. I think we'll be seeing a lot of each other."

"Really? Are you a lawyer, too?"

"No, but I hire 'em by the dozen," said Pickett.

"Would that include Mr. Battle, by chance?"

"Oh, you best not go there, son. That could be considered slander."

"I'll be heading on. Got a lot of work to do," noted Jack.

"You got a lot of *thinking* to do. Make sure you come to the right conclusion."

"Which is?" asked Jack.

"Be loyal to your race. And don't be no longhair, either."

"Longhair?" said Jack.

"Hippies, potheads. And don't be no pointy head," added Pickett.

"You'll have to define that one for me too."

"Academic types. You know, Ivy Leaguers who don't know their ass from a hole in the ground and look down on ordinary folks."

"So you didn't go to college, then?"

For the first time the smile disappeared and Pickett glanced at the reporters gathered around, pens poised over paper. "What the hell does that matter?"

"I thought that was sort of the point of your argument. But I'm a sworn officer of the court. Everyone, regardless of race, deserves a proper defense."

"Well, that thinking is only gonna get you so far."

"How far do you reckon?" asked Jack.

"Six feet, but not in a direction you want to go," replied Pickett.

"Let's forget about slander and go directly to the law against death threats."

"I never make threats. Threats mean nothing."

"As opposed to what, exactly?"

Pickett waved at the cameraman, did a thumbs-up to the lens, and said, "Come November, vote for George Wallace, the only man capable of taking this country *back* to where it belongs." He walked off, got into his big Lincoln, and was driven away by a Black man who had never once looked at his employer.

Jack watched them go, while all the reporters stared at him like Jack had only a few breaths of life left.

CHAPTER 15

JACK DROVE BACK TO HIS office and was just closing the car door when two women approached, one Jack knew and one he didn't, though she seemed familiar to him.

Miss Jessup said, "We seen Jerome and he showed us this here address on your card. This is Pearl, my granddaughter."

"Jerome's wife, yes. You two favor each other."

Pearl was petite and appeared to Jack to be tightly wound. Her sharply edged features held pain, no doubt due to her husband's dire situation.

He led them to his office and got them seated at his small worktable. Pearl looked around the unimpressive space before her shrewd gaze settled on him.

"You ain't got you no secretary or nothin'? And no law books on the shelf? How you get your work done, Mr. Lee?"

He tried to smile reassuringly. "I'm a good typist, and I have an answering service. When I need help I can get it. And the court's law library has all the books I need. Saves me space, and money."

He noted that Miss Jessup held her purse on her lap with both hands and gazed at him with a sharpness that he could feel against his chest. Pearl sat straight and compact and formidable. He noted the etched lines around her eyes and mouth, each probably with a history all its own to recount. The woman's brown eyes did not seem to miss a single thing going on around her. He guessed her age to be around twenty-five, but in her hardened features there was a tale of a challenging life that likely doubled that number of natural years.

"Jerome say you his lawyer now," she said.

"Yes. I've filed my appearance as his counsel and I've also been to the Randolphs' home." He chose not to tell them that the state's top prosecutor would be personally handling this case.

"And?" said Miss Jessup. "How does it look?"

"The commonwealth believes they have their man."

He was watching Pearl closely as he said this. Her face did not crumple; the large eyes did not fill with tears. But the woman looked like she might be sick.

"Um…" she began. One hand went to her mouth. "Oh, my." She shuddered.

"Do you need the bathroom?" Jack said quickly. "It's right over there."

"No, Mr. Lee, but maybe…some water?"

He hurried over to a credenza that held a pitcher of water and some glasses. He poured her out one and rushed back with it. She drank it down thirstily and then handed back the glass, looking embarrassed.

"Thank you. So hot today. But I'm better now."

"So what you gonna do about the *situation*?" Miss Jessup asked Jack firmly.

"I've taken some pictures of the scene, and made notes. I'll interview the arresting officers. I have to find out who called the police because they might have seen something helpful for us. And I need to know who benefited from the Randolphs' deaths."

"You think it might be one of their own that done it?" suggested Miss Jessup.

His mind's eye held the image of the grieving Christine Hanover. "Children have killed their parents for money as long as there have been families," replied Jack. "But we would have to find some evidence." He turned to Pearl. "Jerome said he'd worked for the Randolphs for about a year? But he was in Vietnam before that?"

"He got drafted. Then with his leg all shot up they said he couldn't fight no more. I real glad. Jerome stay in the Army, he gonna die for sure."

"He got drafted even though he has young children?" said Jack.

"Yeah. They say you ain't in no college, you got to go, kids or no kids. And they say if we want to fight it we need a lawyer and it'll cost a bunch of money. So's Jerome went."

Jack shook his head, knowing that none of that was true.

"And how did he end up working for the Randolphs?"

"My uncle used to work for them. He told the Randolphs Jerome could do just as good as he had done."

"Did Jerome ever go inside the house?"

"Not unless they needed somethin' fixed. Jerome can fix just about anythin'. He just got that way about him."

"Like *your* daddy, Mr. Lee," interjected Miss Jessup.

The image of the sweet tea and rye whisky briefly entered his thoughts. "Do you know if the Randolphs kept money in the house?" he asked.

Pearl nodded. "They must 'cause they pay Jerome cash. Why? They sayin' Jerome took some money don't belong to him?"

"No, but if money does turn up missing they might claim he took it."

"I can tell you right now he ain't have no money. I feed him his breakfast and make him his lunch. And he liked the Randolphs. They treat him real good."

"And now they dead Jerome ain't got no job," added Miss Jessup. "How's that make any sense, I ask you?"

"I might have you help me write out my closing argument," said a smiling Jack.

"This ain't no joke," jabbed Pearl. "They gonna try and kill my husband."

Jack pressed his palms against the warm table where the sunlight hit it, and said, "I know this is no joke. And at least right now Virginia does not use the death penalty, so Jerome would be looking at life in prison."

Pearl said, "No way they gonna let a colored man who they say killed two white people stay alive in prison."

"You may be right. And I checked the list of items he was arrested with. He had no money on him."

She took out an envelope from her pocket and slipped some bills from it. "Speakin' of money, how much you need? Jerome said you need money to do the work."

"Yes, a retainer. But I know Jerome didn't get paid last week."

"I got a good job durin' the week, and I work a second one on the weekends."

"But you have three young children."

"My momma helps out a lot. And some of my aunts. And my granny here when she ain't at Ashby's. Now, how much?"

"Two hundred dollars for now. I have no idea how long this will go on, you understand? But I promise I'll make the money go as far as possible."

She carefully counted out nine twenties and two tens and slid them across. "You just tell me when you need more."

"I will, thank you." He wrote her out a receipt and handed it to her. The paper went into her purse with the rest of her money. "I will need to come out to your house to talk to you about the case."

Pearl looked at her grandmother with a surprised expression. "I just come and meet you here," she said hastily. "When you need me to."

"Do you have a car?"

"No. But it only a couple of bus rides."

"But it would be far easier for me to visit you. Wait, do you have a phone?"

She shook her head.

"Okay." He handed her a piece of paper and a pencil. "Just write your address down for me. I'll be glad to come and meet with you there."

She slowly wrapped her strong, callused fingers around the pencil in a way unfamiliar and almost fearful, at least to Jack's mind. As though he had asked her to handle a viper and not an instrument of writing.

Glancing nervously at Miss Jessup from time to time, Pearl slowly formed the letters and numbers like a clumsy novice skater stumbling fretfully over the ice. Finished, she set the pencil down and slowly moved the paper across to Jack.

He glanced at the writing and his brow wrinkled in confusion.

Miss Jessup said crisply, "Her address is Sixteen Old Anna Street. No signpost, but you turn right at the big oak that's split in half after you get off the bypass where the old fairgrounds was. House at the end of the road. Got blue shutters and a lean-to on the side. Can't miss it. Only one other house down there."

"I'm sure I can find it," said Jack. "Thank you."

Pearl rose and Miss Jessup mirrored this movement. Pearl said, "We got to get back to work."

"I can drive you where you need to go."

Pearl shook her head. "You got enough trouble comin' your way as it is, without havin' two colored women in your car."

Jack watched them walk down the street until they turned a corner and vanished from sight.

Are you up to this, Jack Lee? Taking on the whole commonwealth of Virginia, a coal millionaire, and George Wallace? For two hundred bucks?

CHAPTER 16

THE KNOCK ON HIS OFFICE door came at just past six p.m.
When Jack opened it he was gazing at two uniformed deputies, who
stared cautiously back at him.

The tall, lean one had his hands on his narrow hips and had
puffed out his shallow chest. The short, wide-hipped one allowed
his right hand to dangle enticingly close to his holstered .38.

Sweat lacquered both their brows and fouled their shirts. The tall
deputy pointed to the sign on the wall. "John Robert Lee, Esquire,
Attorney-at-Law. That you, mister?"

"I'm Jack Lee, yes. And you?"

"Deputy Gene Taliaferro," he said, tapping his chest. "And this
here's Deputy Raymond LeRoy. We the ones caught your boy after
he butchered the Randolphs." He rubbed his shoulder. "That sum-
bitch knocked me to the floor. He's like an animal, but most of them
are. Even the women."

"*Especially* the women," volunteered LeRoy. "You called at the
station for us?"

"I wanted to speak with you as part of my investigation. Come
on in."

The men did so, wiping their boots on the doormat, and taking
off their hats.

"What *investigation*?" said Gene. "We got the sucker. Folks rightly expect the chair for somethin' like this, though I guess they don't use that no more. Hope they start back up and let that boy be the first one on the hot seat. Hell, I wish they still hung 'em."

"Have *you* ever done that?" asked Jack. "Hung someone for being Black?"

Gene smiled. "Hell, lawyer, that'd be illegal. And I'm a man of the law."

Jack motioned them to the same chairs Pearl and Miss Jessup had occupied, and wondered what either man would think about sitting in chairs the women had used.

Gene said, "Hey now, ain't they got colored lawyers for colored killers?"

Jack drew a legal pad close and picked up a ballpoint pen. "So if you could tell me what happened the evening you made the arrest?"

Gene glanced sharply at LeRoy before saying, "We found him in the room with two butchered bodies. And then we arrested the n—that done it."

Jack glanced up. "There's no cause to use that word."

"What word?" asked Gene with genuine confusion.

"Call him Black. Like we're white."

"We ain't nuthin' like their kind," sputtered Gene.

"You know, the judge could look at your obvious bias and use it as an excuse to throw out your testimony, or even declare a mistrial. Do you want your boss to look upon *you* as the reason for that waste of time and unnecessary expense?"

Gene looked at LeRoy, who only had hateful eyes for Jack. Then he sat back and ran his fingers along the row of bullets on his gun belt. He eyed Jack shrewdly. "Okay. We arrested the...*Negro* and brung him in."

"You said he was resisting arrest?"

Before Gene could reply LeRoy spoke up. "We had our guns drawn and told him to kneel on the floor, which he done. Gene cuffed him."

"And the resisting part?" asked Jack as he wrote this down.

"Gene had a little chat with the colored boy, and he got all riled for some reason. Knocked Gene down. So naturally he had to get the situation back under control."

Gene grinned. "Boy was strong as a gorilla. Way I see it, the problem is we coddle the negroes. They don't know how to behave 'round white folks."

"And how should they behave?" asked Jack.

"Well, with respect, and knowin' they're around their betters," answered Gene, eyeing LeRoy. "Hell, everybody knows that."

"And who told you to go to the Randolphs' home?" asked Jack. "And what was the time?"

"Dispatcher," said LeRoy. "Around six or so."

"What did the dispatcher say exactly?"

"That two people were dead and the killer was still there. We got there real fast."

"How fast?"

"Hell, three-four minutes," replied LeRoy.

"You went in the front door? And you found the accused doing what?"

Gene said, "He had his arms 'round the old woman. Maybe doing somethin' sexual. You know how those boys are 'round our women."

"Perhaps he was lifting Mrs. Randolph into the chair?"

Gene snorted. "What for? She was dead!"

"Maybe out of respect?"

LeRoy exclaimed, "How in the hell is it respectful to kill somebody?"

"You're presuming it was him that did it," answered Jack.

"I got eyes that I see things with," countered LeRoy. "And I seen him and only him in the room with two dead folks."

"The actual killer could have already escaped."

LeRoy smiled maliciously. "Good luck provin' that."

"Did the dispatcher say who had called them?"

"Why's that matter?" said LeRoy.

"Well, how did the person know that two people were dead and the killer was still in the house? Did you see anybody else?"

They both shook their heads.

"Did you search the house to make sure no one else was there?"

"No need to," said Gene. "We got the bastard who done it."

"On your way there did you see anyone else? In a car? On foot?"

Gene snapped, "Just the *Negro*. Who was resistin' arrest real bad."

Jack put his pen down. "That's all I have for now. I'll take formal statements from you both later."

The deputies rose and put their hats back on.

Jack stood, glanced at Gene's gun belt, and said, "That billy club of yours. What are the notches for? One looks new."

Gene grinned and tapped the wood. "You know how some fellers mark the bedpost with their women? Well, this is sort of like that, only different."

"Uh-huh."

Gene drew chin to chin with Jack and said, "Now, look here, lawyer, you know your boy done it. In your heart, you do."

"He's not my boy. He's my *client*. And you must have a very different heart from me, Deputy."

"You just get paid to say that," replied Gene, grinning and stepping back. "You know how things stand. You let coloreds start thinkin' they're equal to us, then where are we white folks?"

LeRoy said, "Not in America no more, that's for damn sure. Even Abe Lincoln himself wanted to ship 'em all back to Africa. God's honest truth. Read it in a book."

As they were leaving, LeRoy added, "We're in this fight together, mister. You know that and I know that. We need folks like you who know the law real good and how it should be done proper and all. If we're going to win this."

"And Lord help us if we don't," added his partner.

CHAPTER 17

"HOW ANY SON OF MINE," began his mother.

Jack stared dully at her from the other side of the dining room table with the space between them resembling a potential no-man's-land of risky engagement.

"When I saw that on Channel Six, I almost had a heart attack. And the *Randolphs*, of all people. And then they had you talking to that man from George Wallace's campaign. The things you said to him. He's a millionaire, the TV said."

"He's a horse's ass, and I know for a fact you can't stand George Wallace. If it had been you there instead of me, you would have put that man in his place so fast it would have made my efforts look downright feeble."

Hilly glanced at her husband, who sat worrying at a grease spot on his thumb. "Why do I think this has something to do with Miss Jessup coming around, Francis? And you and Robert drove off somewhere last night. Well, now I know where you went. You put him up to this, didn't you?"

"*I* made the decision to represent the man, Momma. I think he's innocent."

"Innocent or guilty, this is going to ruin our reputation."

Frank said, "I wasn't aware we had any particular reputation, Hilly."

"And you always taught me to stand up for what I believed in," added Jack.

"So what are you going to get out of this? No white woman will ever want to walk down the aisle with you," she added.

"Momma, that era is over, and the sooner you accept that the better."

She retorted, "I've seen and experienced things you never will, John Robert Lee. So don't preach to me about the end of eras. And why are you all of a sudden so interested in all this racial business?"

"You taught me to be kind and respectful to people. *All* people. You and Daddy take care of Black folks at his work, and their families, when they get sick or injured, or need food."

"Oh, that was just helping someone in need. I told you that. But different races are not meant to associate outside of situations like that."

"Then why encourage me to read all those books that said the exact opposite?"

He watched her strong, nimble fingers, which had nursed his childhood injuries and dried his little-boy tears, play erratically over the tabletop.

Jack continued calmly, "And when I became a member of the bar I took an oath to fight for what was right, not for what was easy."

"So does an oath to a colored man mean more than your own family, Robert?"

"Black lawyers represent whites and whites represent Blacks every day."

She said, "Not in Virginia. Certainly not in Freeman County. I neither have nor want any colored friends, and I'm certain they're of the same mind."

"Well, last year a Virginia case went all the way to the Supreme Court. And in a unanimous opinion the court said miscegenation laws violated the Equal Protection Clause of the Constitution, and a Black can marry a white and vice versa. Now Mr. and Mrs. Loving are happily married and living right here in the Old Dominion."

"I don't know how *happy* they are," his mother retorted fiercely. "I bet both their families disowned them."

Jack was surprised at his mother's angry tone, which seemed overblown for the situation. As he stared at her quizzically, she looked away, her face full of heightened anxiety that Jack was not convinced was coming only from their debate. And it made him think of a long-ago memory.

When he was five years old, Jack had snuck into his parents' bedroom while they were out, just to look around. He had found one of his father's pistols in a sock drawer, but luckily it was unloaded. Then, underneath a compartment in his mother's small jewelry case, he had discovered something else. It had been a picture of what looked to be his mother as a young woman and, well, Jack wasn't sure what else the picture contained because his mother had come in at that moment and snatched it away from him. Then she had tanned his hide. For weeks after she had looked at him with fury. And for years Jack had half-convinced himself he had somehow dreamt the whole thing. Now, as he looked at his mother, he wasn't so sure. And the tanning had certainly been real; he well remembered *that*.

He said, "So if a Black woman and a white man can be husband and wife, why can't I, as a white man, represent a Black person?"

His mother looked back at him, her features now calmer, her tone less strident. "This has nothing to do with what a court says and everything to do with just the way things are. God put the Blacks in Africa and the whites elsewhere and if he had wanted them to mix, he would not have done that. I know you learned that in church when you were little."

"Indeed I did, but I don't find the Baptist church a reliable steward when it comes to parsing such issues. And, the races got *mixed* because whites brought them here to be slaves. You think that was God's will?"

The calmness in her look vanished. "I do not need a history lesson from you, Robert. What I'm saying to you is: That is not the world we live in. And the sooner *you* accept that, the better."

"Then maybe we need to change the world. In fact, people are."

"Oh for God's sake, I can see I'm getting nowhere fast with this."

"I did see Christine Randolph. Well, now Christine Hanover," he said.

Hilly's expression immediately softened. "I thought Jefferson and Christine might get married. But then your brother joined the Army instead of going to college like you did. Where'd you see her?"

"She was coming to her parents' house while I was there."

"Did she know...what you're doing?" Hilly asked anxiously.

"No. I just gave her my condolences. Her husband seems like a nice man."

"So you're still going to represent her parents' killer?"

"Their *alleged* killer. Yes, I am."

Mother and son engaged in a drawn-out staring contest, her resolute green eyes versus his determined blue ones.

Hilly finally looked away, stood, and declared, "Then I'm going to make sure Lucy is still breathing." She glided from the room.

Jack glanced at his father, who was still worrying at his thumb.

Without looking at him Frank said, "Your momma's a good person, Jacky, with a big heart despite how she comes across sometimes. Now, she has her beliefs. You may not agree with them, but they're what she believes because she's never known anythin' else. And she *has* seen more than you ever will. Hell, she had to learn to take care of herself at a young age because her folks would just leave her alone up on that mountain for months at a time. Guess after nine kids before your momma came along they were just tired of bein' parents. Gettin' coal in the dead of night, shootin' critters for food and plantin' and tendin' a garden, and looking after the laying hens so she'd have somethin' to eat, outrunnin' bears and mountain lions, goin' without, pretty much every day of her life, that was what your momma endured up on that mountain.

"And she was the best natural athlete I ever saw, man or woman. She'd bet the boys she could outrun them, speed or distance, and then she would. Way she earned money to clothe herself. When she was in school she could put the ball in the hoop, and knock it over the fence. I seen all the ribbons and trophies she won; she was proud of them. Then, after Lucy was born the way she was, your ma threw them all away."

Jack said, "I never knew it was that bad. She never talks about any of it."

"What that woman carries, she carries about as deep inside her as a person can. She shoulda gone to college. Become a doctor or a teacher; she has the mind for it. But she never had the chance, and that eats at a person. She was real proud when you went on to law school. I think she saw a bit of herself in you. At least what she coulda been."

"And what do *you* think about me representing a Black man?"

"I work with them folks all day long. Good solid people. Honest and likable. Do their job and go about their business and never bother nobody. Do I think any of them will be my best friend? No, I don't think so because I've never done that and neither have they. They stick to their own kind and so do we. I don't know if it's right or wrong, but it's just the way things have always been. But truth be known, it *will* change, least I believe so. But I'll be long gone by then. Hell, maybe you will too."

"But you *wanted* me to represent Jerome."

His father leaned forward. "What I wanted, Jacky, was for you to do somethin', I don't know, *important*, with your life. I know how smart you are and so does your ma. All you needed was a chance. And despite what your momma said, when she was watchin' you on the TV give back to that ass Pickett as good as you got, she was smilin' a mile wide. Proud as a peacock."

"So this is all about *me* and *my* path to shine? What about Jerome?"

"I got nothin' against him, 'cept if he did kill those folks he needs to pay for his crime. But is that so wrong, a father wantin' the best for his son?"

"Like you did Jeff?"

His father leaned back and his engaged look faded to nothing. "I'm a veteran. Got the scars on my skin and the memories burned into my head to show for it."

"So does he. But his situation was different."

"I don't see it that way. You wear the uniform, you don't get to choose who you take up the sword against."

"And Miss Jessup? She makes a nice iced tea with a splash of rye, just like you like it. But you don't socialize with their kind, so it must be a coincidence she knew that."

"Like I said, I drove her home a few times and she made me tea as a thank-you, and I mentioned that I like it with a splash of rye."

Jack rose. "So why don't you go see Miss Jessup then? She and Pearl Washington came to see me, but I'm not sure they told me all they could. Find out what you can."

"What, you mean right this minute?"

"Well, I don't think Momma will be especially good company, do you?"

CHAPTER 18

THE JAIL'S DENSE HUMIDITY COMPRESSED Jack's chest and made his throat swell. Somewhere nearby, a dull drumming was emanating from a fan. Jack didn't think it was anywhere near where the prisoners were. He'd represented clients who'd had the life nearly beaten out of them while awaiting trial. When he'd asked what had happened, it was always the same story from the guards: "Fool slipped and fell in the shower."

And Jack had nearly always answered back, "What, six damn times?"

The guard leading him now said, "Your boy's been bellyachin' 'bout headaches. Doc went to see him. Give him some aspirin. Still bellyachin'. But that's what their kind does, I guess." He laughed.

"He might have a concussion or a skull fracture."

The guard glanced at him, supremely unconcerned. "So?"

Once inside the cell, Jack noted that they had finally taken Jerome's clothes and issued him a pair of faded jeans and a light blue shirt that was too restricted in every place that mattered for comfort.

Jack pulled up a chair and sat down. "How's your head? I hear you're in pain."

Jerome shrugged. "I be fine, I guess."

Jack looked at the bloody bandage. "Hold on, that looks the

same as last night. Didn't the doctor clean your wound and change your dressing when he saw you?"

Jerome shook his head. "They come took my clothes and give me these to wear. Then a man give me two pills and no water to take 'em. He say use my spit."

Jack could now see that Jerome was sweating and shaking, and he didn't think it was just the heat. He felt the man's forehead. "You have the chills *and* a fever."

Jack went over to the door and pounded on it. The guard slid the peek window back. "Already finished with the monkey?"

"Tell the doctor to get back down here and bring his medical bag."

"Why? He just seen him!"

"Tell him to come now or I go to court and file charges against him and *you* and everybody else in this damn place for grossly negligent treatment of a prisoner entrusted to your care. And you can go to jail for that. You think you'll like the view from this side of the door? Go do it. Now."

The man trudged off, cursing Jack under his breath, and came back presently with the prison doc, a stout, barrel-chested man with a fringe of white hair and a cloth dinner napkin tucked in his shirt and spread over his chest, and an angry expression layered over his features.

"What the hell do you want? I was just sitting down to my supper."

"Has his head been x-rayed? Has his wound been cleaned and redressed?"

"You telling me how to be a doctor?"

"He's running a fever, so why do I think his wound is infected?"

The man waggled his head. "That's not your call to make. It's mine. Now, you get outta my business, lawyer."

"Well, let me tell you what *is* my business. If he takes seriously ill or dies before the trial, I can tell you that Mr. Edmund Battle will be one upset attorney general. Wonder who he'll take that anger out on? And I will file a lawsuit against this prison and *you* so fast it'll make what little hair you have left fall right off. I thought you doctors took a damn oath to do no harm? So what's it gonna be?"

The man glanced over at the clearly feverish Jerome.

"Well?" said Jack.

The two men stared at each other until the doctor coughed, glanced at the guard, and said, "Bring my bag, son, and tell the nurse to roll the X-ray machine down here."

"But—"

"Look here, we want this colored boy ready for his trial. He don't get off easy."

With a glare thrown at Jack, the guard stomped off.

The X-ray was completed and showed no fracture, but Jerome had likely suffered a severe concussion, the doctor conceded. The wound was thoroughly cleaned and redressed, and Jerome was given shots of penicillin and some other medication to help with the concussion, infection, and fever, along with two bags of fluids. Jack stood right next to the doctor and his nurse to make sure it was all done properly.

Then, noting how stiffly Jerome was holding himself, he told the doctor to check under his shirt.

Jack felt stomach bile flow into his throat at the sight of the livid purplish bruises that covered most of Jerome's torso and arms.

"What in the hell?" he exclaimed, looking furiously at the guard.

The man blanched. "Hey, hold on, man, we didn't do none 'a that."

Jerome said, "He tellin' the truth. This be from the cop beatin' me."

Jack said to the doctor, "You need to do something about that, too. Right now."

The man grudgingly ordered ice packs and a hot water bottle.

"You satisfied, lawyer?" said the doctor after this was done.

"Just make sure that dressing is changed every day and that his fever is gone by the morning. Now I need to meet with my client. In private."

After they left, Jack sat back down across from Jerome and opened his briefcase. He told Jerome what he'd done so far.

"The indictment is for first-degree murder. The penalty for that is life in prison. But I spoke with the prosecutor and he said if the death penalty is revived he will seek it. I know you don't want to hear any of this, but it's my job to tell you. Okay?"

Jerome nodded.

"You haven't talked to anyone, have you?"

"Ain't said a word to nobody, like you told me."

"Good, keep it that way. Are you from Virginia, Jerome?"

"Naw. I was born outside Jackson, Mississippi. Moved up here with my momma when I was a little boy."

"And your father?"

"Dead, long time ago."

"What happened to him?"

Jerome shrugged. "He went out to his job one mornin' and they find him in a ditch with his eyeballs cut out that night. Some say he was lookin' at a white woman on the street so they done what they done. Right after we buried him, Momma say we gettin' the hell outta Mississippi. These white folks crazy, she say. We took us a bus to Tennessee the very next day and then ended up here."

"Is your mother still alive?"

"Naw. Her heart stopped three years ago."

"I'm very sorry all that happened to your family."

Jerome shrugged. "Not just us, that's for durn sure."

Jack flipped through some pages and said, "Okay, let's get down to details. First, did you call the police when you found the Randolphs?"

"No sir. I just got to 'em when the police come in."

"Did you see or hear anyone else at the house that day?"

Jerome bowed his head as he rubbed his hands together. "They got a man that does the yard work and such. Name's Tyler Dobbs. He get there 'bout eight and leaves 'bout the time I havin' my lunch."

"So around one or so?"

Jerome nodded. "Yeah, 'bout that."

"Does he come every day?"

"Every other day."

"Was he there that day?" Jack asked.

"Yeah."

"Did you see him leave?"

Jerome nodded. "I had my lunch early and was workin' on the light where you come up the drive. Wire gone bad. He flipped me off when he was leavin'."

"Nice guy," said Jack. "What time do you get there?"

"Round 'bout seven."

"How do you get there?" asked Jack.

"My bike."

Jack thought about where he now knew the Washingtons lived versus the Randolphs' address. "That's about ten miles or so, isn't it?"

"Closer to fifteen."

"Can't you take a bus?"

"Take too long. Got to change 'bout three times. And bus costs money. And I like to ride my bike. That way I ain't have to count on nobody else and I get to where I'm goin' when I want to."

"How early do you have to leave to get there at seven?"

"I ain't real fast on a bike, and got some hills on the way, then across the Jackson Bridge, so's I leave 'bout five in the mornin'. I like to get there before folks 'round there are up, so they don't get all curious seein' me."

By *curious* Jack knew he meant *suspicious*. "Anyone else at the Randolphs'?"

"They got a woman come clean the house and such. Her name's Cora Robinson. She come every day 'round nine, leaves 'round two."

"Did you see her leave that day?"

Jerome flexed his brow. "Naw. I was in the garage cleanin' the spark plugs on the Buick 'round 'bout that time. It way back from the house."

"Did she drive there?"

Jerome shook his head. "She walk to a bus stop way, way down the road. She colored," he added, as though that would explain all.

Jack wrote this down and said, "Anybody else?"

"Yeah, I seen the mailman leave somethin' on the front porch that mornin'."

"What was it?"

"White package. Oh, I did see a car out front in the afternoon."

Jack perked up. "Do you remember the time?"

"Oh, be 'round four or so."

Jack looked at the man's naked wrist. "You normally wear a watch?"

"Tell by the sun. Got real good at that in the Army."

"So a couple hours before you went to the house to get your pay?" said Jack.

"That's right."

"Did you see who had driven it there?"

"No sir."

"Did you recognize the car?" asked Jack, writing some things down.

"Look, why you askin' me all this stuff?"

Jack looked up to see his client scowling at him. "Because, Jerome, if you didn't kill them, someone else came that day, while *you* were there, and did."

"I know *that*. I didn't kill Mr. Leslie and Miss Anne, but they ain't care. So I don't see what we doin' here 'cept wastin' time. And you makin' money," he added sullenly. Then he went back to rubbing his hands together.

"Speaking of money, Pearl paid me two hundred dollars."

Jerome stared up in shock. "That be five weeks' pay!"

"She paid it so I can get you out of here, and I need your help to do that. So *did* you recognize the car?"

"No, Mr. Lee, I ain't never seen it before," replied Jerome, sitting up straighter.

"What kind of car was it?"

"Little blue thing. Got the top that comes down."

"A convertible?" said Jack.

"Yeah."

"You see the license plate?" asked Jack. "Virginia or out-of-state?"

"I think Virginia, by the color, but I can't swear to it," replied Jerome.

"But the car was gone when you went to the house around six?"

"Yes sir, it was," replied Jerome firmly.

"Do you know the Randolphs' children by sight?"

"I know Miss Christine. She come by right often. And Mr. Sam, he come by a couple times. But he ain't been by for a long time now, least not when I been there."

Jack glanced at Jerome's head. "How do you feel?"

"Better." He had placed the ice packs under his shirt and the hot water bottle against his lower back. "Thank you for gettin' the doc back in here."

"I'll be meeting with Pearl again. Anything you want me to tell her?"

"Just that my head don't hurt no more and…that…" He faltered.

"You love her and the kids?" Jack quietly suggested.

Jerome glanced up at him, seeming to take all of Jack in for the first time. "Yes sir, Mr. Lee. I do. But don't tell her this."

"What?"

"That…that I be scared. Like bein' in 'Nam, but I ain't got nothin' to fight with."

"Well, Jerome, for what it's worth, you have me."

But I'm not sure I'm enough, thought Jack.

CHAPTER 19

FRANK LEE SLOWED HIS TRUCK as he turned onto Tuxedo Boulevard.

The same large man was sitting alone on the porch next to Miss Jessup's place.

What was the name again? Frank thought. *Right, Daniel.*

There were lights on in Miss Jessup's house. The humidity was dense enough to make Frank take extra breaths with his Camel-infused lungs.

Daniel lifted his can of beer in Frank's direction as he got out of his truck.

"Come to see your lady again?" said Daniel.

"Just come to talk to Miss Jessup."

"Your kind ain't need to be here. You unnerstand what I'm sayin'?"

Frank knew if it had been even five years ago, the man would not have dared talk to a white man that way, even on his own doorstep. But the Blacks were getting more impatient, and the whites more desperate. Or so his son kept telling him. But he watched the TV, too. If Walter Cronkite said it, he believed it.

"I understand. But my son is a lawyer and he's helpin' out Miss Jessup's kin, and I just need to ask her some questions."

"Uh-huh, sure you do." Daniel rose and took a step toward Frank.

Thinking quickly for some topic to calm things, Frank said, "I saw one of your buddies had on an Army jacket. He fight in Vietnam? I fought in the Big One."

"We *all* fought in 'Nam. And we all come back here and it all the same as when we left. You come back to parades, old man. We come back to shit. And not just the shit the white boys did."

"I hear you."

"I don't like it. I don't like *you*."

Frank didn't know if it was the fact that Daniel had not been able to say his piece the last time he had been here, but he seemed determined to voice it now.

"Any man fights for his country deserves respect. And you got mine, Daniel."

Daniel abruptly sat back down and sipped his beer.

Frank pulled his hand away from the gun in his rear waistband and headed up to Miss Jessup's.

They sat in rocking chairs on the front porch to catch what little breeze there was. In the moistened heat the smell of the dump was so strong that Frank started breathing through his mouth. Jessup seemed unfazed by the stench, but then Frank knew she had lived in this house for many decades, because she had told him so.

"I don't own it, Mr. Lee," she had said. "No bank loan me no money. One colored man own all these homes here. Charges rent three times what they worth. He takes my money with a smile on the first of every month when he drives here in his fine car. Only difference now from ten years ago? He come with a man who got him a gun. But I don't have a lot of other choices where I can live."

Frank had felt bad for her, but what could he do.

"Your boy seems to be workin' hard on things," said Miss Jessup.

"He'll do his best. Now, he wanted me to find out more about Jerome."

She stopped rocking. "Well, what you want to know?"

"Whatever you can tell me about him."

"He a good man. Fought in the war. He a good daddy to his babies."

Jessup rocked away, cooling herself with a green church fan.

"How was he when he got back from Vietnam? Anythin'... funny?"

She stopped rocking again. "He got him some nightmares, guess you'd call 'em."

Frank shifted in his seat and said, "Nightmares?"

"Yeah. Pearl say they was some bad ones. He sit up in the bed screamin' and punchin' like he still fightin'. Or sometimes she'd wake up and they be tears runnin' down his face and the poor man not even awake."

Frank closed his eyes for a few moments. He was instantly back on Guadalcanal with dead and dying men lying all around him, even as the enemy drew ever closer. Frank had never fought anything close to the Japanese. It got to be whenever he killed one, he shot the man six more times, because he never wanted to have to face him again. His face started trembling at the memory. Nightmares? How many times had he woken up screaming, reaching for a weapon, looking for someone to kill? That was when he'd had Hilly hide his guns.

"Mr. Lee, you okay?"

He opened his eyes to find her staring worriedly at him. "I'm fine, just probably somethin' I ate."

"I got bicarbonate."

"It's already passed. Look, does he, I mean, does Jerome get violent?"

"What you tryin' to say, Mr. Lee? He only done that asleep."

"I know. But they might say that Jerome might be out of his head sometimes."

She started rocking faster. "He done fought for his country. That's why he got him nightmares."

"I'm not sayin' they'll bring it up, but Jack just has to be ready if they do."

"Well, I don't know more than what I told you. When he awake Jerome is the most gentle person I know. Helps me whenever I need it."

"A good soldier and a good man."

"Speakin' of, how is Mr. Jeff doin'? You ever hear from him?"

"No," said Frank. "Look, is there anythin' else you can think of that might help?"

"Like what?"

Frank searched around in his head. "Does Jerome know anybody that might want to hurt the Randolphs? Anybody they didn't get along with?"

"No, least not that he told me. Pearl might know."

"So nothin' *you* can think of?"

"Well, now that you mention it, Jerome did say somethin' strange had happened."

"What was that?"

"Man come 'round to talk to the Randolphs one day."

"What man? What did he want?" asked Frank.

"Jerome said he was a white man in a fancy car and carryin' a black bag. He was workin' near the house and heard some noise, like folks arguin'. Then the man, he come runnin' out and scoot off in his car. Then Mr. Randolph come out the house and shake his fist at the car. Jerome asked Mr. Randolph if everythin' was okay and Mr. Randolph said somethin' like 'Nobody's makin' me leave my home.'"

"When was this?"

"Oh, a few months back."

"What do you think it was about?"

"Got no idea. Randolphs lived in that house fifty years or more. I can't see nobody makin' 'em leave. You think that man might have come back and killed 'em?"

"I don't know. But I'll sure let Jack know about it."

She gave him a calculating, sideways glance. "*And* about Jerome's nightmares?"

"Jack needs to know if he's goin' to defend Jerome real good."

He took his leave as Miss Jessup went back inside.

Frank had just reached his truck when Daniel appeared out of the darkness. He had no time to reach to his rear waistband before the man slammed him against the truck, knocking him down. He felt his back screaming in protest with the impact.

"You still here, mistuh, and I told you to get on with yourself," said Daniel. "You disrespectin' me or what?"

Frank slowly and painfully got back on his feet. "I'm just now leavin'."

Daniel pushed him up against the truck again and Frank felt the side mirror dig into his back. He cried out in pain. "Look, I got no quarrel with you."

"Well, I got a 'quarrel' with *you*." He undid the top buttons on his shirt and pulled the fabric away.

Frank saw what he knew to be a bayonet wound, sharp, brutish, and angry in the man's chest near his armpit. He knew this because Frank had one on his leg courtesy of a Japanese soldier on the island of Saipan.

"Got this defendin' *my* country, or *a* country, not sure which. Come back here and it all the same shit."

"It ain't fair, that's for damn sure."

But even as he said it, everything Frank had been taught and seen over his life rebelled at these words, could not accept them even as they left his mouth. And then he felt a measure of visceral shame about that for perhaps the first time in his life.

"Yeah, old man, it ain't *fair*."

Now Daniel looked like he was going to kill Frank.

"You know Jerome Washington?" Frank exclaimed, because the old Army vet could see this mortal threat plainly in the other man's eyes.

"Yeah, so what?" said Daniel, curling his hand into a massive fist.

"He's been charged with murder."

"He ain't kill nobody."

"I believe that."

"Sure you do, old man."

"My son's a lawyer and he's representin' Jerome. He's gonna do his almighty best to see that Jerome goes free."

"Your son the other white man that was here last night?" said Daniel, taking a step back as he asked the question.

"Yes, Jack Lee. I was here askin' Miss Jessup some questions to help with Jerome's defense."

Daniel seemed to take all this in and then shook his head and stared down at his shoes, his expression as weary as it was hopeless. "Get in your truck, and you get outta here. And don't you never come back, you hear me? You come back again, son or no son helpin' Jerome, you ain't leavin' here breathin', you got that?"

"Yes, Daniel," said Frank.

"It's *Mistuh* Daniel to you." His look was as grave as Frank had ever seen, in peace or wartime.

"Okay, Mr. Daniel." Frank climbed into his truck and drove off, every limb he had shaking like he was right back fighting for his life on foreign soil.

CHAPTER 20

WHERE HAVE YOU BEEN, FRANCIS?" said Hilly Lee as her husband walked in the back door rubbing at his spine.

"Ran out of smokes, Hilly, went to get a pack."

"The store is five minutes from here. You've been gone well over two hours."

"They didn't have my brand."

"They didn't have *Camels*?" she said incredulously.

"Where's Lucy?" he asked.

"She looked tired, so I sent her to bed."

"Okay."

"So you're not going to tell me where you've really been?" Hilly folded her arms over her chest and stared resolutely at her husband.

"If you got to know, I was runnin' an errand for Jack."

"What sort of errand?"

"It's covered by the attorney-client privilege. If I tell you, it won't be secret anymore."

"If that isn't a load of horseshit."

"Never thought I'd hear coarse words come out your mouth," he admonished.

"Like our son said, times are changing…But I…I don't like using that sort of language, Francis. I'm sorry."

"Look, I got to work on that engine. Dick Overton wants it by the end of next week. You were talkin' about gettin' one of them new dishwashers that hook up to the faucet? Save you a lot of time."

"We'll discuss that when you have the money. I've never trusted Dick Overton farther than I could throw him, and that durn wife of his gets on my last nerve."

"Well, he's not gettin' the engine back 'less that cash hits my palm."

She eyed him cagily. "What did you think about Robert running into Christine?"

"I didn't really think anythin' about it."

"Things could have turned out different for Jefferson, if…if he and Christine…"

"That was never goin' to happen, Hilly. They had fun, but somethin' permanent was not in the cards. Jeff always wanted to enlist. And we just ain't the right society for someone like that gal."

"I can't believe she was part of our lives for over a year. Came here all the time. Had meals with us. Sat and talked with us."

"But we never got invited over there, did we? To *her* house, did we?"

"I'm sure back then the Randolphs were very busy."

"Right. They just didn't want us riffraff in their fine home."

"We're not riffraff, Francis," she replied heatedly.

"I fix trucks for a livin'. Folks like the Randolphs hire people like me. They don't marry them. Hell, it would be like a white and a colored gettin' married."

"Well, as our son pointed out, people can legally do that now," retorted Hilly.

"Okay, I'm all talked out." He turned to leave, grabbing at his lower back.

"What's wrong?" she said.

"I've pulled too many wrenches in my time, Hilly. All adds up."

"And you're okay with your son doing what he's doing? People are talking. They think we're just fine with Robert representing that man."

"I don't care what anybody thinks of him or me."

"Easy for you to say. You're at work all day. I have to deal with the neighbors."

"Hell, you don't even *like* the neighbors, Hilly."

"He's going to ruin his career in Freeman County."

"Well, then maybe he'll have to move to a new place. Fresh start."

Hilly looked shocked. "What about us? What about Lucy?"

He drew closer to his wife. "I actually talked to him about takin' over her care when we can't do it anymore."

"And?"

"And now that I think about it, why is that his concern? She's *our* child."

"Lucy is his flesh and blood, too," countered Hilly.

"He didn't bring Lucy into this world. We did. It's our responsibility, not his. And I regret tellin' the boy that it was his burden."

"I don't understand you, Francis. Does family mean nothing to you?"

"The fact that family means somethin' to me is *why* I'm tellin' you this."

"You're making no sense whatsoever," she replied.

"Havin' Lucy changed our lives. I'm not sayin' I'm upset that we had her. I'm not. I love that sweet girl. We made her together. But it broke the natural cycle of things. We have kids, we raise our kids, our kids go off and make their own way and raise their own children. Lucy can't do that. And just because she can't, why is it Jack's job to step in? Because if he has her to take care of, his life will be completely changed, too. There ain't many women who'll marry a fellow if they know they're goin' to have to take care of a grown woman, and maybe not have her own kids because of that. Life is complicated enough without addin' that to his plate."

"And when you talked to him, what did he say about caring for his sister?"

"He didn't have many answers or opinions, and why would he?"

He edged closer. "Is really none of what I'm sayin' makin' sense to you?"

She glanced down. "I suppose it really isn't fair to him."

"Lucy will be taken care of, Hilly, one way or another."

"You mean a nursing home? You know we put my mother in one for a single week. When I saw how they were treating her—"

"You took her out of there and nursed her yourself in addition to takin' care of three kids right up until the day she died years later. No child could have done more than you did, even though Lord knows your momma wasn't always there for you. When your time comes you can rest easy on that."

Hilly looked away, her mouth twitching, which Frank didn't quite know how to take. Then she walked off. He heard the door to their bedroom open and then close, with finality.

CHAPTER 21

FRANK LEE WALKED OUT THE back door and trod the short dirt path to his garage. He glanced at the Ford engine block he was rebuilding. He hoped that Hilly would agree to use the money to buy that dishwasher. Several of the neighbors had bought one and the husbands had been uniform in their opinion that the appliance was a godsend.

"Happy wife, happy life," said one of them.

Lord, let me get there.

He slid open the bottom drawer of his rolling toolbox and took out the folded-up paper. Jeff Lee had always had extraordinary penmanship and Frank enjoyed reading the book reports that his youngest child did for school. However, this letter was from a grown man with significant issues weighing on him.

Jefferson Lee had served gallantly in the Army, a decorated soldier, a Green Beret. He had talked about wearing the uniform ever since as a teenager he'd seen a picture of his father in his military attire and held some of Frank Lee's old medals. He had been part of the first wave of seasoned warriors to go to Vietnam after the Gulf of Tonkin. Jeff Lee had fought hard and been wounded twice, and kept right on fighting. But when he'd come back stateside for a little R and R, he had instead gone to Canada and never returned.

His son a deserter. It had hit the veteran Frank Lee like a tank round to the heart.

Folks didn't mention his younger son anymore. But it was the glances they gave him, the pitying expressions that said, *I'm so sorry you raised a coward, Frank.*

But his son had not been a coward. He'd been brave, earned medals, been shot up. Far more than the sons of the men who looked at him funny had ever done.

This letter had come shortly after Jeff had left for Canada. In it he explained his reasons for doing what he did. He wrote that he didn't expect his father to agree or approve, but he needed him to know.

Frank hadn't cared about those reasons the first time he read the letter. Or the second or the tenth.

He sat down in his recliner, lit a Camel, and took up reading the fine handwriting again. And as he did so a part of him began to glimpse reason behind the words, and even eloquence, justifying the drastic action his youngest boy had undertaken in the face of a war in Southeast Asia with dubious origins and intents emerging on a daily basis.

He finished and lay the letter on his slack belly. He thought about the bayoneted Daniel coming back to the States after fighting for a country that clearly didn't care about the likes of him, which laid insult on top of injury on top of unjust damnation. He could understand Daniel not wanting him to come around. Tuxedo Boulevard was all he had. Folks like Frank had everything else. Why should they get that, too? Because if a man didn't have one damn thing to really call his own, then what the hell was the point of being a man at all?

He lay fully back in his recliner and let the oppressive heat wash over him. And even with that, Frank Lee felt oddly cold. As though he had no blood left in his body.

* * *

Hilly Lee sat in front of her small vanity and stared at her reflection in the mirror that held a large crack at the right top corner. That had happened the day she had come home from a hospital she had gone to for a lengthy stay after finding out what was wrong with her daughter. And why. She had stared at herself in the glass just like she was doing now. Then she had slammed her fist into the mirror, breaking it and deeply cutting her flesh. Frank had found her sitting here trancelike with blood pouring out of her. He had called the ambulance and doctored her wound until help arrived.

She eased her finger along the crevices scored deeply around her eyes, chin, and mouth. She was old, she thought, and looked it. It wasn't just the years gone by, it was what each of those years contained that had left its marks: A life with challenges that were often far beyond her abilities.

But I'm still here. I made it this far.

As she thought of Lucy, her eyes closed and her lips trembled. She self-consciously rubbed at where the tooth had been that had caused all that pain, all that sorrow. The robbing of the life her daughter should have had.

Hilly had been a churchgoer, even up in the mountains, when she'd often shown up alone for the Sunday service because she had no one to go with her. She'd take a seat in the back and listen to the preacher say that God was always with you. For the longest time it seemed God was the only friend she had. And then she had moved here, had Lucy, and then had endured a difficult talk with another official representative of the Lord.

And Hilly had stopped regularly going to church after that, making excuses to folks for her absence that simply deepened her guilt.

Her son Jefferson was now lost to her, she believed. He had made his decision, and after what Hilly had read about the war, she agreed with him.

And then there was Robert. She unlocked a little box she kept in the vanity drawer and took out the photo. Seeing this had cost her oldest boy the fiercest spanking she had ever meted out. And yet he had done nothing really to warrant that level of punishment. The reason, the culpability, lay solely with her.

She gazed at the two people in the photo, and memories from more than forty years ago trickled back to her, like slow water over a faded dam. It was her in the photo, though she looked nothing like that now. And the other person...

Her eldest son had represented Hilly's hope for something... different. And yet now, when he was seeking to do just that?

I've turned my back on him. I've said things to him that I never used to believe. I've taken the road all the rest did. And I don't think there's any going back now. For me.

She locked the photo back up as she felt the migraine coming on.

She soaked a washcloth and turned out the light. Placing the cloth over her eyes, Hilly lay down on the bed and prepared herself to suffer.

CHAPTER 22

THE NEXT MORNING JACK MARCHED with strident purpose up the steps of the Freeman County Courthouse. As he was passing by the clerk's office Sally Reeves stepped out to confront him with a triumphant smile and blue-backed legal filing in hand.

"You need to read this." She handed it over and Jack quickly ran his gaze down it. "Hearing's on Friday," she added.

He finished and looked up. "The commonwealth is seeking to have me removed as Jerome's lawyer, because I cannot be considered *adequate* counsel?"

"Now you don't have to tuck your tail between your legs and slink off to Mexico like poor George Connelly. You can just bow gracefully out."

"Come on, the judges here know I'm more than capable of trying this case."

"If you really believe this is about legal competence, Jack, you're not as smart as I think you are. And I watched Howard Pickett on TV. You know who he is, of course."

"I do now."

"Well, he said that any white man who represents a Negro for killin' white people should have his head examined."

"Is that right?"

"And he also said that if this case doesn't wake us up nothin' will. The truth is we've had it with all this Civil Rights crap comin' out of Washington. The government can't tell us what to do. It's why I'm votin' for George Wallace. He's the only candidate addressin' the colored issue. They need to find their own country."

"Sally, Black people helped *build* this *country*, including the damn courthouse we're standing in."

She waved her hand dismissively. "Only because we showed 'em how. And we saved them from runnin' around naked in the jungle and gettin' eaten by lions and such. *And* taught them how to speak English."

"They were *slaves*, Sally. Are you really saying slavery is okay?"

"But that was just a little blip in our history, and I hate that people are tryin' to make it some big deal. I never owned slaves and neither did my daddy or my granddaddy. And I've never done any harm to a colored person in my life. And we freed them."

"No, this country fought a war over that and the South lost."

"But my point is now they *are* free. And with all that, they want to go to our schools, eat in our restaurants, ride next to us on trains and buses, pray in *our* churches. Well, nobody's tellin' me who I got to associate with. They stay over there and we stay over here. Fair is fair."

"So they only get to live in part of this big country they helped to build? How the hell is that fair?"

Reeves leaned in and said in a hushed voice, "You have to pick a side, Jack, because there is no middle ground. Just make sure you pick the right one." She walked off.

After his father returned from the war Jack vividly recalled as a child driving with his parents in their old Ford station wagon when their route took them through one of the Black areas around the county. Their mother instructed her children to lock their doors and "not make eye contact with those people."

He and his brother had followed their mother's command, while a smiling, happy teenage Lucy simply gazed out the window at everybody and everything.

Then a curious Jack had decided to have a look of his own. The shirtless Black boy on the sidewalk was lean with every rib and muscle showing. Jack had been blowing bubbles with his gum, and he had used his tongue to get some of the residue off his chin.

The Black boy, obviously thinking that Jack had stuck his tongue out at him, angrily raised a fist at him and yelled out something. The hand and the angry words were only in the air for a second, though, before a man appeared, probably the boy's father, and grabbed the child's hand and yanked it down. As Jack craned his neck around to see, the man scolded the boy for his dangerous reaction to the perceived slight from a white person.

Jack had turned back around to see his mother also watching this stark, familial confrontation. Jack thought he saw a tear trembling at the woman's right eye.

When she saw her son staring, Hilly Lee said in a hoarse voice, "You see, son, even *they* know." She didn't speak for the rest of the trip. And that episode added yet another bewildering element to the puzzling picture that was Hilly Lee.

CHAPTER 23

THE KNOCK ON THE DOOR came right when darkness had overtaken the light.

Jack stared up at the tall, heavily built man with a broken nose that had been badly reset and hung crookedly to the left.

"Can I help you?" Jack said.

"I sure hope so, friend."

The man pushed his way in and was followed by three other men, nearly as large as he was. They were all dressed in black slacks and white short-sleeved shirts showing off defined muscles. One held a blackjack in his hand. The others just made fists.

Jack backed up to the wall as the men made a fluid and purposeful semicircle around him.

"Y'all need to leave here right now, before I call the cops," barked Jack.

The first man said, "They know we're here and they ain't comin'. We're here to convince one of our own to be loyal to his kind."

"And I got your message loud and clear. So y'all can leave now."

"No, I think you need some persuadin'."

Jack put up his hands as two of the man charged him. He ducked a wild swing and caught his attacker with a punishing right flush to the jaw that knocked him off his feet. But the other man pinned Jack's arms to his sides, while a third attacker whaled away at his midsection, driving the air out of Jack's gut with his rapid punches.

When the man let go of his arms, Jack fell to the floor. When he tried to get back up, the man with the blackjack leveled him with a blow to the jaw.

The first man said, "Okay, now repeat after me: 'I am no n——'s lawyer.' Say it now or you're gonna get some more ass kickin'."

Jack wiped the blood off his mouth and stood unsteadily.

"Say it!"

When Jack remained silent, one of the men kicked him in the side while another punched him in the face.

Jack staggered over to his desk and toppled against it.

"Okay, now you ready to repeat after me? 'I am no—'"

The man froze when Jack pulled the revolver out of the drawer, took careful aim, and shot off the top part of the man's right ear. He screamed and grabbed at the gaping wound, blood streaming down the side of his head.

Jack pointed the gun at the other men and declared, "Who's next?"

They tumbled over each other to get out the door. After they were gone, Jack limped over and locked it. He used a tissue to scoop the remains of the man's upper ear off the floor and threw it out the window. He next grabbed some ice from the small fridge, wrapped it in a handkerchief, and held it alternately against his ribs and his face.

He phoned the Carter City Police Department and reported the incident. They sent over an officer whom Jack had gone to high school with.

"Didn't recognize any of 'em?" asked the officer.

"I will if I see them again, Ben."

"Well, we'd have to find 'em."

"Shouldn't be too hard. One's a big man missing half an ear. He's probably over at the hospital right now getting it seen to."

Ben put away his notepad and gazed at Jack.

"You need to say something?" Jack asked.

"We were good friends in school, played ball together. And I know your momma and daddy and they're fine people. And I do not want to see you get hurt." He glanced at Jack's battered face. "Hurt *anymore*. You need to let this drop, man."

"Your momma and daddy are like my momma and daddy. Fine people, but *not* in every way. So are we gonna be that way, too? Go right up to the line of doing the right thing but never, ever cross it?"

"It's all I was ever taught. You want me to just flip that on its head?"

"What I want you to do, Ben, is ask yourself if the shoe was on the other foot, what then? How would you feel? What would *you* do about it?"

"But the shoe ain't on the other foot, is it, Jack? And I can't just close my eyes and imagine somethin' that ain't real, can I? You're askin' the impossible."

"You remember when we played those boys from York County? Everybody said they were too damn big and too damn strong. Everybody said just lay down in front of them and don't get hurt. And what did we do?"

"We played our butts off and beat 'em bad. You threw three touchdown passes and your brother ran for two more."

"And you sacked their QB in the end zone on the very last play of the game."

Ben smiled briefly at this memory and then he drew closer, his expression sliding to somber. "But we ain't kids anymore, Jack, and this ain't no game. You're a good lawyer. Don't throw it away over this."

"If I can't throw it away over this, what the hell else is worth fighting for?"

Ben shook his head, turned, and left. Jack locked the door after him.

About ten minutes later another knock came at the door.

He stood and readied his gun. "Who the hell is it?" he said sharply, half expecting it to be the police coming to arrest him for shooting the ear off a man who was trying to kill him in his own home.

"Desiree DuBose," said a voice.

Jack slowly opened the door, revealing a tall, slender Black woman in her late thirties standing there, professionally attired, and clutching a leather satchel along with a pocketbook over her shoulder.

"Are you Jack Lee?" she said politely.

He eyed her curiously and nodded. "Yes, ma'am, I am."

She studied the injuries to his face and then saw one hand pressed against his side, and the other one holding the gun. "I see they've already been by to see you."

"Who has?"

She hiked her slim, dark eyebrows and said nothing.

He took a step back and lowered the gun. "And who are you exactly?"

"I might be the answer to your prayers, Mr. Lee. May I come in?"

CHAPTER 24

DUBOSE INSISTED ON SEEING TO his wounds using a small medical kit that she took from her satchel. When he asked her about it, DuBose said, "I never go anywhere without essentials, especially south of the Mason-Dixon."

He eyed the deep, hook-shaped scar perilously close to her right eye.

She noted him staring and said, "One of several, Mr. Lee, though that is the only one that shows. And I have to say I'm proud of every single one."

DuBose had him take off his shirt and undershirt, and she delicately probed his ribs with her fingers, causing him to flinch and gasp.

"Badly bruised, but not cracked or broken," she concluded.

"You a doctor?"

"No, but I have a lot of experience with beatings."

She cleaned his cuts, applied topical medicine to the abrasions, bandaged them, and then wound some tape around his bruised middle and secured it.

"Keep using the ice. Takes down the swelling."

She put her kit away, and they sat on either side of his desk after he put his clothes back on.

"You said you were the answer to my prayers?"

She took a copy of *Time* magazine out of her satchel and handed it across.

On the cover was her.

He glanced up in surprise.

"Start on page fourteen. I'm not being vain. It'll just save a lot of explaining."

He dutifully read the four-page story on one Desiree Evelyn DuBose. She had gone to Howard University and then Yale Law School, where she had been an editor of the *Law School Review*. Remarkably she had entered Howard at age sixteen and finished college and law school in six years.

Jack looked up. "Impressive academic pedigree, Miss DuBose."

"I wanted to go to Yale undergrad as well but they didn't deign to admit women of any color until this year."

"I didn't know that."

"I graduated from law school the year the Supreme Court handed down *Brown v. Board of Education*."

"Did you clerk at the Court?"

She looked surprised. "There has never been a Black female law clerk on the Supreme Court, Mr. Lee. Bill Coleman was the first Black man to clerk there, under Justice Frankfurter in 1948. But I had a friend from Yale who clerked on the court for Justice Douglas when *Brown* was decided. Eisenhower later said picking Earl Warren as his chief justice was the biggest mistake he ever made. But if Chief Justice Vinson hadn't suddenly died of a heart attack, Warren would never have been on the court and *Plessy*'s separate but equal doctrine would still be the law of the land. I'm not really speculating, because my friend told me that Justice Douglas had taken an informal count that had it five to four to uphold *Plessy*."

"That would have changed a lot," noted Jack.

"That would have changed *everything*."

Jack read some more and said, "You were born and live in Chicago and you work for the Legal Defense Fund?"

"It originated with the NAACP's legal department, but Thurgood Marshall founded the LDF as a separate entity in 1940."

He kept reading and learned that DuBose had won a case before the Supreme Court the previous year. And then she had done legal business in his neck of the woods.

"You helped take on the Byrd machine here in Virginia?"

"The state closed all schools that desegrated, and provided public funding for private schools that promised never to admit a Black student."

"But the Virginia Supreme Court ultimately ruled that was unconstitutional."

"I'm impressed. Most white lawyers I know hardly keep up on such matters except to bitch about them."

"White folks can be pigeonholed, too, I suppose."

She compressed her lips. "I'm sorry if that's how you interpreted my remark."

Jack looked back at the article. "You marched at Selma."

She rose and walked around his office, keeping her gaze roaming.

"I never thought anyone could be meaner or crazier than Bull Connor in Birmingham, but I hadn't yet run into Jim Clark in Selma on Bloody Sunday. When we came over that bridge Clark ordered his state troopers to charge and they came at us with batons and bullwhips and tear gas and anything else they could get their hands on."

"Is that where you got that scar on your face?"

"A policeman hit me there. I woke up in a hospital the next day. But two weeks later Dr. King led us across the Pettus Bridge with thousands of supporters, all under federal protection. It was a glorious sight."

"I'm sure."

A few seconds of silence followed until DuBose sat back down and assumed a businesslike tone. "And, more pertinent to your situation, I've handled over two dozen capital murder cases, and I've won more than I lost."

"And now you're here in Freeman County. Why?"

"I go where I'm needed. And Virginia seems to be calling me once again."

"Would that be because Howard Pickett and George Wallace are focused on my case?"

"I *do* know of their involvement and that *is* one reason I'm here."

"And the other reasons?"

"Jim Crow is finally, finally, on his last damn legs, Mr. Lee."

"Make it Jack. And I wouldn't be too sure about that. Laws are laws, but people are people, Miss DuBose."

"Please call me Desiree. And laws shape people and their behavior, otherwise too many folks would be thieves and murderers. So my job is to keep driving the stake into that son of a bitch's heart until it beats no more." She crossed her legs, smoothing down her skirt and resettling her canny gaze on him. "And this case was made known to me. And then I was told that Edmund Battle is to lead the prosecution."

"You know him?"

"We last butted heads in the *Loving* case, when he was representing the commonwealth before the United States Supreme Court. It was the battle of constitutional amendments. Virginia relied on the Tenth, while we went with the due process and equal protection clauses under the Fourteenth Amendment. And our argument prevailed." Excitement danced in her expression. "And now if I can win this case, we might have Virginia solidly in our column."

"If *you* win it?"

"I've devoted my life to this, Jack. I can find a Virginia attorney engaged in the cause to be my local counsel. Then you can step away."

"Jerome has already retained me as his attorney and his wife has paid me money."

"You can return the money less what you've billed, and they can retain me."

"And what if *I* don't want that?"

"Have you ever represented a Black person before?" she asked.

"There's a first time for everything."

She said, "You've already been beaten up. The next time might be far worse."

"*If* you get to know me you'll find that just makes me try harder. And I grew up here. I know things about Freeman you never will."

"Are you absolutely sure you understand the risks?"

He touched his battered face. "Pretty damn sure, yeah."

"How about if I'm lead counsel and you're second chair? If Mr. Washington is okay with that. And if we win, I can move on to other campaigns that need my attention."

"You make it sound like a battle plan."

"That's exactly what it is, because we're at war. We have the enemy on the run. One enormous change is that they no longer have the law on their side. So they come to rely on people like Howard Pickett and George Wallace, and their money and their connections and their lies, and their vitriol used to rile up the public." She ran her gaze over him. "Why don't we have a drink and discuss this further? I passed a place. They didn't wash all the paint off, so I can still see the NO COLOREDS ALLOWED. But I assume it's okay now?"

With her help, he struggled into his jacket and put his gun in his pocket.

She said, "Think you're going to need that?"

"The night's still young."

CHAPTER 25

THE GOLDEN LEAF?" SAID DUBOSE, staring up at the sign on the building.

"Tobacco, the cash crop that built Freeman County," answered Jack.

"Of course."

The NO COLOREDS ALLOWED was, as she had said, still visible, like a knife wound semihealed to a blistered scar that might never fully vanish.

There were about twenty people in the bar, one bald, tattooed man tending to the drink orders, two waitresses housed in slinky outfits serving those drinks, and a mustached, cowboy-hatted man and his guitar, strumming well but singing poorly.

Jack and DuBose took their seats at a table and the stares commenced.

"You get these looks in Chicago?" asked Jack, noting the gawkers.

"I don't really have experience being out with a white man. But there are a lot of mixed-race couples in the Windy City, so most people don't take much notice anymore."

A waitress with frizzy blond hair and thick eyeliner came hurrying over.

"My God. Jack? Jack Lee?" she exclaimed.

He looked up at her, recognition dawning. "Hey, Amy, is that you?"

She smiled. "Good Lord, I haven't seen you in forever. And you haven't changed a bit, still the same tall, good-looking Jack Lee. Give me a hug, you handsome thing."

He stood and did so. She squeezed him so tight that Jack's bruised ribs ached like someone had hit him again. She must have had eyes only for Jack, because when Amy finally noticed DuBose sitting there, the smile vanished like someone had shot it off her face.

She snatched a glance at Jack as he sat back down. "You with *her*?"

"She's a professional colleague."

DuBose said, "Nice to meet you, Amy."

Amy looked around at all the people staring. Even the singing guitar player had ceased his vocals to ogle.

When Amy looked back at Jack she said, "What happened to your face?"

"Just a disagreement among some folks."

Amy eyed DuBose. "Jack was quarterback on the football team and also president of the debate club. All the girls were crazy about him, *and* his brother, Jeff. The Lee brothers were pretty famous around here. And then Jeff became a Green Beret, and now Jack's a lawyer and all." She looked at his empty ring finger. "And never found himself a wife, if you can believe that." Amy gave Jack a bewildered look as if to say, *And now you're here with* her?

DuBose said politely, "Well, some people just aren't the marrying kind."

Jack interjected, "How have you been, Amy?"

She gave him a sour look. "I'm divorced with twelve-year-old twins. I live with my parents right now. Sort of in between…things."

"I'm sorry to hear about your divorce," he commented.

"I'm not. He was an asshole."

This remark drew a smile from DuBose, which Amy picked

up on. She smiled too, but then she seemed to catch herself and the frown returned.

"What are y'all having?" she said irritably.

"Do you have white wine?" asked DuBose.

"I think so," Amy said curtly.

"Rum and Coke for me," said Jack. "And can you bring me a glass of ice?"

"With water?"

He pointed to his bruised face. "Nope, just the ice. Thanks."

She went off to get their orders, and DuBose turned to Jack. "How does it feel to be famous around here?"

"Right now, I'm *infamous* and I don't see that changing."

"So you met with Mr. Washington?"

"Twice."

"I've heard some of the facts. Give me your version."

Jack did so, although he paused about halfway through when Amy came back with their drinks and the glass of ice.

DuBose looked down at her glass of white wine. Floating on the surface was what looked to be a mouthful of spit.

Jack saw the blob. "For God's sake." He stared angrily up at Amy.

Amy's cheeks flushed. "I...I didn't do that."

DuBose said, "I'm sure you didn't, Amy. Please give the bartender my thanks for so *personally* attending to my wine."

Amy turned and hurried off.

Jack said, "I'm sorry, Desiree. You want mine?"

"He probably put poison in yours."

Jack pushed his drink away. "Saying thank you to the man who did that? Is that Dr. King's pacifism coming through?"

"Nonviolence is not the same as pacifism. It's done to flush out the other side, make them *show* their true colors."

"How so?"

"In Montgomery, when Rosa Parks wouldn't give up her bus seat, the boycotts started. That involved deciding *not* to partake of services. In Nashville, with the sit-ins, we were demanding service, just like whites, *not* withholding patronage. That was peaceful but directly confrontational. In Selma, we marched. And were beaten, while the whole world watched. You see, protest makes change occur, but attitudes are slow to come along for the ride. But real change transforms attitudes. And with that you have *sustained* change."

"I never really thought about it along those lines."

"That's because you never had to," she replied. "Now, let's get back to the case."

He picked up the glass of ice and held it against his jaw. "Jerome didn't have a drop of blood on him even though he had tried to lift Mr. Randolph off the floor and did put Mrs. Randolph into a chair. *If* he had cut those two people up, there is no way he doesn't have blood all over him. He said it was all dried up when he found them."

"And you said the maid usually left at two but he didn't see her leave that day. And Jerome saw the blue convertible there at four but it could have been there earlier?"

"That's right."

"Do you have a time of death yet?"

"No. Battle said he would get it to me, only he didn't say when."

"Battle actually said he would provide it to you?"

"Yeah, why?"

"As you know, Virginia is an ambush state when it comes to criminal pretrial discovery. They now have to adhere to the *Brady* rule because the Supreme Court said so, but *Brady* only covers exculpatory evidence."

"Right, any evidence that might help the defendant. Funny thing, though, I've never once gotten any exculpatory evidence from a commonwealth's attorney."

"Everything else they can withhold until trial. But that sword cuts both ways because we can surprise them, too. So no money found on him. No murder weapon. Thus, no motive, no means."

"But he had the opportunity. That may be all the commonwealth needs."

"Jerome said a package was delivered that day by the mailman. Did anyone find it inside?"

"Not that I know of. I looked around some but I didn't do a thorough search. Okay, if you want in on this case, you can be my co-counsel."

"So you see Jerome as what, your springboard to a partnership in a big firm?"

"Taking this case will ensure I *never* get that, at least not in Virginia."

"Why are you doing this, then?"

"Well, maybe I can aspire to be a lawyer like you."

"Is that what you really want?" she said skeptically.

"You can find out. As my *co-counsel*."

"It can get very dangerous, Jack. As in life-threatening."

"I already told you, I don't run from a fight."

"So long as you're sure. Now, any way to track the blue convertible?"

Jack said, "I have an investigator I use, Donny Peppers." He also told her about the former counsel, George Connelly, waiving Jerome's right to a preliminary hearing.

"We can always threaten to raise the issue to get an advantage elsewhere," she noted.

"The formal charges from the indictment were read at the arraignment."

"Should request a bill of particulars?" DuBose asked.

"I looked at the transcript. It was pretty clear. And Battle wants to take this sucker to trial as fast as possible. What about a change of venue motion?"

"Where else in this state would we take the case?" she said. "Richmond? Danville? How about *Lynchburg*? No, we plant our flag and make our stand here. Now, what about bail?"

"The commonwealth objected to any being requested. I talked

to a couple of bail bondsmen I know. It's doubtful the Washingtons have the money to post their share, or that a bondsman would even agree to put up the rest. They don't own their home, so a surety bond is out of the question."

"But we'll also hold that in our back pocket."

"There's also a motion on the docket for Friday to replace me as counsel because I've never done a murder case before."

"Really? Any thoughts on the lawyer Battle will want to replace you with?"

"Hey, Jack, buddy? Who's your friend?"

They looked up to see a stocky man Jack's age, dressed in a seersucker suit and carrying a martini, as he appeared next to their table. His slurred speech and unfocused eyes evidenced that he had imbibed more than he should have.

Jack began, "This is—"

DuBose held out a hand. "DeeDee. Nice to meet you…?"

"*Mr.* Douglas Rawlins," he said, not shaking her hand. "Jack, don't tell me this is the wife of the Randolphs' colored errand-boy killer I hear you're representing. Can't be. She's dressed too nice."

Jack stood, towering over Rawlins, and said, "Doug, call a taxi, go home, and take a cold shower before you get yourself in trouble."

"Oh, what a big man you think you are showing off for this colored chick."

"Go home, Doug, now," said Jack as he put a hand on Rawlins's shoulder.

Rawlins leered at DuBose as he walked off.

DuBose said, "You showed more self-restraint than I imagined you would."

"I shot a fella's ear off tonight. I doubt Dr. King would have condoned that."

"No one has the right to take your life without a fight."

Jack sat back down. "I was horrified when I heard about Dr. King's assassination. And my mother, who, to tell you the

God's honest truth, would be *horrified* that I'm here with you, was even more upset than I was about it."

"Interesting. I just presumed the state that once held the capital of the Confederacy would be jumping for joy at his death."

"My mother came from dirt-poor in the mountains. Small farms, no plantations. Lots of coal mines and just a damn rough life. She could have been a doctor, or hell, a fine lawyer. But people like her were just considered hicks who talked funny, not worth the trouble. My daddy told me she worked for years to get rid of the accent and work on her elocution so people wouldn't look down on her. But she just can't seem to bring herself to—" He shook his head, unable to finish.

"—to understand that maybe she has more in common with Black folks than she has with the likes of Douglas Rawlins or Howard Pickett?"

"Yeah, something like that."

"People with money and power in this country have pitted white and Black workers against each other for centuries. That exploitation has made a very few very rich, with everyone else barely keeping their heads above water."

Jack nodded. "W. E. B. Du Bois made that point clear in his works. The powers that be promise one thing to the whites at the bottom of the ladder."

DuBose said, "That they will always be above the Blacks. So, W. E. B. Du Bois? Is that how you came to be the way you are, then? By reading books?"

"You wouldn't think it would take cracking open a single volume. Just looking around at how people are being treated should have been enough. But don't mistake me for someone I'm not, Desiree. I'd be staring just like the people here are."

"So long as we're making confessions, I've looked at white people as the enemy all my life. I'm not sure I'll ever be able to see them any other way."

"I can understand that, but we need to commit to each other for this case."

"I wouldn't be here if I hadn't already made that commitment," she said curtly. "And after this, I will go on to the next case. And I will continue to do so until..."

"Until when?"

She looked at her spit-upon wine. "Until *that* stops happening, I suppose."

"I hope you have the patience of Job."

"Oh, I left Job in the dust a long time ago," she replied.

CHAPTER 26

ON THE WALK BACK TO his office, Jack asked DuBose if she wanted to accompany him to see Pearl Washington.

"I don't want to take you to see Jerome just yet. You'll need to show ID at the jail and they'll be sure to tell Battle all about it. I know when you told Doug your name was DeeDee, you wanted to keep your being here a secret for now."

"Yes. Do you have a car?"

"I do."

"Let me guess—a big old pickup truck?"

"How'd you know?"

When he escorted her to his Fiat, she said, "You going to keep surprising me?"

"I don't know, Desiree. This is all new for me."

As they drove off DuBose said, "What was your impression of Pearl?"

"Sharp as a tack and she minces no words." He glanced at her. "But—"

"But what?"

"I'm not sure she can write. Pretty certain Jerome can't read."

"They're in their midtwenties?"

"That's right."

"Separate but *unequal* was in *full* flourishing bloom when they were in school. And that, unfortunately, is the result."

Pearl came to the door when they drove up and she shone a flashlight at them. "Who y'all? What you want here?"

"It's Jack Lee. I've brought another lawyer with me to help."

Pearl pointed her beam at DuBose. "Her?"

They approached the house and Jack said, "Yes. Pearl Washington, this is Desiree DuBose. She's come down from Chicago."

"Chicago!" said Pearl. "She a lawyer?"

DuBose answered, "I *am* a lawyer, Mrs. Washington."

"And she won a case before the United States Supreme Court. We're lucky to have her help us."

"What happened to your face, and why you look all stiff?" This query came from Miss Jessup, who had walked out with a plump-cheeked baby girl fixed onto her hip.

"It's nothing, Miss Jessup," said Jack. "Just being clumsy and fell down."

"Uh-huh," said Miss Jessup, shaking her head.

"He brought us a woman lawyer," said Pearl.

"She must be better'n good," noted Miss Jessup.

"And why do you say that?" asked DuBose politely.

"'Cause, honey, they must have put up every roadblock there is to keep you from bein' one. So you must be somethin' special, all right."

Pearl said, "What y'all be doing here?"

"We wanted to ask you some more questions," said Jack. "If you have time."

"Baby got to go down," said Pearl, looking at the little girl on Miss Jessup's hip.

"I can take care 'a Darla Jean," said Miss Jessup. "You pour out some iced teas and get out those cookies I made and get down to it. This is for Jerome. Ain't nothin' more important than that."

They all went inside. The space was half the size of Jack's place.

At least five people lived here, he knew, and, unlike his home, it was spotless. He saw all the crocheted pillows with little sayings that looked hand-sewn by talented fingers.

Pearl led them to the kitchen and asked them to sit, while Miss Jessup put Darla Jean to bed. Pearl bustled around getting the iced teas and cookies.

"I think I heard you was from Chicago?" Miss Jessup said as she rejoined them.

"Yes. My parents were from Shreveport, Louisiana, originally, but they left two years before I was born to find work in Illinois."

"Lotta Black folk headed north, or west," said Miss Jessup. "I was born in Alabama. Had three of my children there. We were sharecroppers, all colored people around there were. I could pick my weight in cotton by the time I was ten. Penny a pound and the white man took the rest. Lord, you know how much cotton you got to pick to make a pound? Fingers all cut up, back bent, knees hollowed out." She shook her head. "Field of cotton looks right pretty from a distance. Close up it's ugly. It is *ugly*. But we made do. We got by."

Jack stared blankly at her. He knew none of this. Granted, she had never offered, but then again he had never asked.

Pearl set a plate of cookies down on the table along with two iced teas.

"Thank you, these look wonderful." DuBose picked one up and bit into it. "And they taste even better than they look."

Pearl said hesitantly, "Thank you, ma'am."

"It's just Desiree. May I call you Pearl, or would you prefer Mrs. Washington?"

Pearl's gaze now lifted to DuBose's and her features brightened. "Oh...you can call me Pearl, Desiree."

Miss Jessup turned her gaze to Jack. "Your daddy come by to see me last night."

"I know. I asked him to."

"I told him 'bout a man that come to see Mr. Leslie a while back.

Mr. Leslie got real mad. Run that man off and told Jerome nobody gonna make him leave his house."

"Who was the man?" asked Jack.

"Don't know."

Pearl added, "Jerome say he ain't never, never, never seen Mr. Leslie that mad."

"Did he mention anything else that Mr. Leslie might have said?" asked DuBose. "Like why he thought someone was trying to make him leave his house?"

Miss Jessup shook her head. "No. Jerome might remember somethin' more."

"Have you ever met the Randolphs' children, Pearl?" Jack asked.

"I met Miss Christine. The Randolphs asked us to come over one day. We got all dressed up and, Miss Anne, she made us this delicious lunch we had out by the pool." She paused and hunched forward. "She told Jerome to bring some swimsuits, so's we did and they let the children swim. Now, my kids ain't know how to swim so I didn't think I wanted them in the water. But Jerome say Miss Anne got these floaty things they wear to keep 'em up. And we just stayed in the part where it weren't too deep anyways."

DuBose glanced at Jack for a moment. "The Randolphs had you to lunch *and* a swim in their pool?"

Miss Jessup cleared her throat. "Surprised me too. Mr. Randolph ain't known for bein' like that with colored folks. I mean, who is 'round here?"

"So why?" persisted DuBose.

Pearl answered. "Jerome say Miss Anne told her husband that *she* want to do it."

"Now, I believe that with Miss Anne," said Miss Jessup. "I worked for them some, long time ago, cookin' and cleanin'. She come from Boston, I believe; so she might think different 'bout people like us."

DuBose nodded and looked at Pearl. "Go ahead with your story, Pearl."

"We were fixin' to leave when Miss Christine and her family showed up."

"And were they friendly toward you?" asked DuBose pointedly.

"Oh, yeah, they seemed fine."

"And when did the luncheon happen?" asked DuBose.

"First day 'a June. I know 'cause it was Darla Jean's birthday the next day."

"Okay, anything else that we might need to know about that day?" asked DuBose.

Pearl shook her head. "No, I don't think so."

Jack glanced at DuBose and said, "You need to know that they're trying to have me removed as Jerome's lawyer."

"Can they do that?" asked Pearl anxiously.

"I was worried they might until Desiree showed up. Now I think we'll be okay."

Miss Jessup fixed a discerning gaze on Jack. "You talk to your daddy yet?"

"No, I haven't."

"Then you might want to. He took a chance comin' by my house again."

Jack stared at her, concern flicking over his features. "Did anything happen?"

"You go on and talk to him." She glanced at Pearl. "He tell you what *all* I said." Her gaze moved to DuBose. "And you can introduce Desiree to him, *and* your momma."

She and Jack had a little stare-down.

"Okay, I will."

"Tell your momma I said hello."

CHAPTER 27

WHEN JACK OPENED THE DOOR to his parents' house, Lucy appeared and gave her brother a crushing hug.

"Lucy, this is Desiree DuBose, a friend of mine."

Lucy next gave DuBose an embrace that almost knocked the woman off her feet.

"Lucy loves hugs," said Jack, grinning. "Getting and giving them."

A startled DuBose said breathlessly, "I can see that."

Lucy bellowed, "Momma, Daddy? It be Jack. And a *girl*!"

She turned and scuttled off. "Momma, Daddy? It be Jack. And a *girl*!"

DuBose looked at Jack with a questioning expression.

"My mother went to the dentist before she knew she was carrying Lucy. Laughing gas. Not good for a baby in the womb, apparently."

"I'm so sorry."

"Robert?" his mother called out.

Hilly Lee appeared a moment later and looked at him, smiling. "A girl?" When her gaze caught on DuBose she turned to her son with a stunned expression. "Robert?"

"Momma, this is Desiree DuBose. She's a lawyer. She's going to be helping me on the Jerome Washington case."

"Can't she take the whole thing on?" said Hilly hopefully.

"No. We're…partners on this."

"Francis?" Hilly called over her shoulder.

Frank Lee appeared a few moments later. "Jack? I was gonna call you about that…thing you asked me to do and—" He saw DuBose.

"This is Desiree DuBose. My new co-counsel on Jerome's case."

"Well, um…ain't that good," remarked Frank with an anxious glance at his wife.

"We just came from Pearl Washington's house. Miss Jessup was there. She told us about the man that came by to see Mr. Randolph and how he got angry."

"What man?" asked Hilly.

Jack looked at his mother. "Just something to do with the case."

"I—" His mother suddenly noted her son's injuries as he turned more into the light coming from the house. "Oh my God, what happened to you?" she exclaimed.

"It's nothing, Momma."

"When you end up dead, will it be nothing?" She shot DuBose an angry look.

Jack said, "I'll be fine. Now Daddy, I would like to find out what else Miss Jessup told you. She didn't seem to want to talk about it in front of Pearl."

"So *that's* where you went, Francis?" said Hilly.

"Yes, Hilly, that's where I went." He turned to his son and DuBose. "Why don't y'all come out to the garage? I'm working on that engine job." He shot DuBose a glance. "If you don't mind?"

"My father works on the delivery trucks for Marshall Field's in Chicago."

"I sure heard 'a them," said Frank appreciatively.

"I wanted to work on trucks, too, but my father wanted me to focus on my education."

Hilly grudgingly gave her an impressed look and said, "Smart man."

"Oh," said Jack. "Miss Jessup told me to tell you hello."

His mother gazed at him without speaking long enough for Jack to draw two breaths. "I'll be here with Lucy. Robert, you take care of yourself, honey. Y'all can just walk around the house to the garage, fastest way." She closed and locked the door.

Frank said uncomfortably, "Hilly's right. That'll save time—"

"—and trouble," his son finished for him.

As they walked to the garage DuBose said, "Why does she call you Robert?"

"It's a long story and not one worth telling."

In the garage Frank pulled up a wooden chair and wiped it off for DuBose to sit in before he commenced working on the engine.

DuBose watched him and said, "My father has forearms like you, Mr. Lee."

"Comes with the territory. But the aches and pains do, too."

"Miss Jessup?" said Jack in a prompting manner. "What else did she tell you?"

"Jerome has nightmares. About Vietnam. He wakes up fightin' and screamin'."

"But only when he's sleeping?" said Jack.

"Yeah, but..." Frank glanced nervously at DuBose.

"But the commonwealth could argue there's something wrong with Jerome's mind because of his war service," she said.

"You had nightmares, too, Daddy," said Jack.

Frank put down his wrench and pulled a cigarette and lighter from his shirt pocket. "You mind?" he asked DuBose.

"It's your garage, so you set the rules."

Frank glanced at the house. "You'd think so, right?" he said, his eyes lit with mild amusement. He took a puff on his smoke. "Yes, I had nightmares when I came back. To tell the truth, I still have them sometimes." He eyed DuBose. "It gets in you. Things you saw. And then it can't get outta you."

"I understand that your other son is a Green Beret?"

Frank shot Jack a look, who said, "Someone who knew us both told Desiree that."

"Why?" she said. "Is he okay? Is he in Vietnam?"

"He was," said Frank. "And now he's not. But he's okay. At least I think he is. Just got the one letter from him and that's been it."

"You never told me you got a letter, Daddy," Jack said. "You just said he called and told you what he was planning to do." He looked at DuBose. "My brother fought over there. They sent him home on leave. And then he wouldn't go back."

"He's a deserter," interjected Frank. "He's in Canada."

"It is a complex situation," said DuBose diplomatically.

"And not one we need to debate," added Jack.

"Did you tell her about your brother and the Randolphs' daughter, Christine?" Frank asked.

Jack said to her, "They used to date, way back in high school, so we all knew her. I ran into her at her parents' home when I was over there investigating things."

"Does she know you're representing Jerome Washington?" asked DuBose.

"I suspect she does now. Anything else, Daddy?"

"Just the fact that I'm not goin' back over to Miss Jessup's house anymore."

"Why?"

"Because I was told not to by someone who seemed like he meant it." He rubbed his stiff back. "And unlike you, my pain is where it *don't* show."

"Are you okay?" asked DuBose, looking concerned.

Frank wiped his hands on a rag. "I'm fine. Now I don't mind helpin' you out, Jack, but I ain't gettin' myself killed over it."

"Of course, Mr. Lee," said DuBose. "You needn't do anything else."

"Call me Frank. Even my daddy wouldn't go by Mr. Lee, and the man had airs about him."

"And I'm Desiree."

Frank said, "Can I ask you somethin', Desiree? A favor?"

"Certainly, Frank."

"Please don't get Jack killed. He's the only son I got left."

"Daddy! *You* wanted me to take this case on."

"I know that, son. And I know somethin' else now, too."

"What?"

"That I was damn wrong."

* * *

DuBose was staying at the George Wythe Hotel in the center of Carter City.

Jack stopped the Fiat in front. "Don't you have a suitcase?"

"I checked in already. I just walked here from the train station earlier."

"You take the train all the way from Chicago?"

"No, I was in North Carolina, so it wasn't that far."

"Trying another case?"

"No, I was visiting one of my sisters. She lives near Raleigh."

He looked at her finger. "No husband or kids?"

"I don't discuss personal issues with my law *co-counsel*," she replied tersely.

Jack glanced away. "Sorry. You want to meet up tomorrow at my office? I need to file a response to Battle's motion."

"I wouldn't bother filing any paper. We'll let the hearing do the job for us. Any idea which judge we'll be in front of?"

"Malcolm Bliley, most likely. He's the chief judge and with Battle being the prosecutor, I could see Bliley wanting to be in the loop on this from the word go."

"Tell me about him."

"He moved here from New Jersey and hung out his shingle before running for circuit judge. I've always found him fairer than most of the other judges we could get."

"I'll be at your office at eight in the morning. Is that okay?"

"I sleep right overhead. So I'll be there with the coffee hot."

"You like living over your office?"

"I liked it fine, until tonight. Now, I'm gonna watch you all the way into the hotel. Anything seems out of whack, you have my card with my phone number. Day or night."

"I can take care of myself, I assure you," she said sternly.

"I'm not worried about you in the least. It's everybody else that puts me on edge."

She seemed surprised and even touched by his concern. "All right. Good night."

He watched her until she was inside the front door of the well-lighted hotel. Then Jack Lee drove off to end what seemed like the longest day of his life.

CHAPTER 28

DUBOSE SAT ON THE BED in her plain room and surveyed the brittle and worn furnishings that looked like they had been here since the South had seceded from the Union. She had been in hundreds of such rooms in over a dozen of states ever since joining the Legal Defense Fund. They all looked and smelled alike. The only difference was in the last few years the hotels where she stayed also contained white people.

As she had told Jack Lee, this case had been made known to her, and DuBose had found it to be a golden opportunity. Her superiors at LDF had concurred, and she had taken the first available train from North Carolina to Freeman County, a name she found sardonic at best.

She undressed, put on her nightclothes, washed her face, and wrapped her hair in a silk cloth. She took out a photo from her wallet and gazed at the young couple captured there before putting it back. This was her ritual; she had several of them to sustain her, especially in foreign lands like this one.

Then she stood at the window and looked out over Carter City. She had traveled throughout the Deep South litigating cases to further the cause of freedom and equality for her race. She normally came into town with a contingent of other lawyers. She was not used to partnering with strange white men who had never lifted a finger to help the cause to which she had devoted her adult life. Jack Lee seemed sincere and willing, but she really didn't know him. She would have much preferred that he had withdrawn from the case. But Lee had not backed down, and she seemed saddled with him.

That's a bit harsh, Desiree. The man was beaten up and he could easily have turned tail and run for it. Give him some credit for that.

But Edmund Battle was a highly experienced trial lawyer and a tough opponent, and he had the full weight of the Commonwealth of Virginia behind him. If Lee faltered? If he couldn't handle the pressure of what was coming? Which was not simply a legal trial, she well knew. The publicity around this case would be immediate and unrelenting.

She moved away from the window, sat down at the small desk, took out a legal pad and pen, and began making notes. She had her standard strategic plans and checklists, but each one had to be revised to meet individual conditions on the ground.

I'm a battlefield officer without a uniform. No, that's wrong. My uniform is my Black skin.

In short order, she covered several pages with notes and thoughts. Then she laid down her pen, and her mind turned to something that the entire country was starting to focus on.

In November America would elect a new president. The men running for the country's highest office were conventional candidates, with one exception: George Wallace represented the American Independent Party, a far-right collection of people and policy platforms that were designed to carry America directly back to the past, where only whites enjoyed any rights and freedoms. DuBose could not believe that he would win, but his campaign was gaining momentum and his rallies were raucous affairs. Thousands of Americans filled the venues and expressed their undying loyalty for the man who they earnestly believed would lead them to their version of the promised land. This was not only the case in the South, but with working class folks in the North and Midwest.

DuBose had heard Wallace speak. He was a fiery orator who

could rile up a crowd far more effectively than the likes of Richard Nixon, Hubert Humphrey, or Eugene McCarthy, the other men in the running. Robert Kennedy also had had that effect over his supporters; DuBose had seen that firsthand. But he would not be president now. While the two official candidates would not be decided until August, according to people DuBose trusted, it seemed that Nixon would be the Republican candidate and Hubert Humphrey would represent the Democratic Party.

She was not terribly excited about either man, although Humphrey had vowed that, if elected, he would continue Lyndon B. Johnson's support of the Civil Rights movement. But she would prefer either of them over Wallace and his message of white supremacy and division.

DuBose and all the folks she respected were terrified that even if Wallace didn't prevail in the election, he would do well enough that the eventual winner would need to pacify Wallace and his followers by agreeing to some of their demands. And with the momentum for Civil Rights possibly stalled, the American people might slide back to old ways that would once more entrench Blacks in a second-class status.

However, Howard Pickett's being dispatched here by the Wallace campaign was the real reason DuBose had come to town. She and the man had had quite a few battles over the years, long before Wallace threw his hat into the presidential ring.

Pickett was arrogant, racist, and transactional, lacking empathy for anyone or anything that could not help him in some way. And the fact that he was here told DuBose that they sensed an opportunity in Virginia. Still smarting after the *Loving* case allowed Blacks and whites to finally marry, they would assuredly rejoice to see a Black man go to the electric chair for killing an elderly white couple, no doubt hoping it might compel enough Americans to turn against the effort to make Blacks fully equal with whites.

And it's my job to make sure that does not happen. So here we go again.

She turned out the lights and got into bed. Then she stared at the ceiling as she thought over tonight's events.

She had very much liked Pearl and Miss Jessup. Straightforward, good souls caught up in a legal nightmare. She assumed that the evidence against Jerome had been trumped up, as it often was with defendants of color, but she was not drawing any firm conclusions before viewing the facts. She knew that Battle would not have signed on to prosecute this case without good grounds to do so. Whether those grounds were factual or fabricated, she didn't know yet. But regardless of guilt or innocence, it was part of DuBose's task to make certain that whatever happened, it would not negatively impact her strategic mission of eventual racial equality.

She next turned to Jack Lee's family. His mother, despite what Jack had said about her grief at Dr. King's and Robert Kennedy's murders, seemed like a typical racist.

She clearly didn't want me in her house. And she was nearly apoplectic when she thought her precious son might be dating a Black woman. As if.

She had liked Frank Lee, who seemed down to earth and had the same occupation as her beloved father. But even he was clearly uncomfortable around her. And his plea at the end—for her to make sure his son did not die?

Well, Jack Lee was a grown man who could make his own decisions. DuBose had suffered the loss of many she cared for at the hands of racists. It was not her job to keep Jack Lee safe.

As she closed her eyes, she concluded that much of this case would probably unfold like many of the others she had handled.

But something told her that there would be differences, too.

Possibly profound ones.

With this troubling thought DuBose finally fell asleep, in another strange, uncomfortable bed, in another foreign, discomforting place.

CHAPTER 29

ALL RISE," SAID THE BAILIFF. "The Circuit Court for Freeman County, Virginia, is now in session. The Honorable Malcolm T. Bliley presiding. All those with business before the court draw near and you will be heard."

Jack stood, as did Edmund Battle and his two associates, and all the spirited public spectators in the pews. The front rows were occupied by—at least it seemed to Jack—the full force and credit of the local and statewide media. All these journalists had their notebooks and sharpened pencils, and full pens, and agile news reflexes ready to forge masterpieces in print.

A moment later the doors opened and in walked Howard Pickett. Every head in the place turned their attention to the millionaire man who firmly had George Wallace's ear. He surveyed the room like a reigning king looking over his court with mocking interest, before he took his seat in the back, so as to keep everything in front of him.

The door behind the broad bench opened, and out popped Malcolm Bliley like a rousted quail. He was short and rotund, with a pile of white hair topping his sixty-year-old head. He wore black-rimmed spectacles and had the air of a jurist in command of his courtroom.

Jack thought they would have to see about that.

"Be seated," said the bailiff.

"Mr. Attorney General," said Bliley. "Shall we get to your motion?"

Battle said, "It gives me no pleasure to do this, Your Honor, but, in good conscience, the facts will allow for no other action. It is clear that Mr. Lee has neither the experience nor the requisite legal ability to try this case. Heretofore, as was outlined in our documentation filed with the motion, the highest felony he has defended was armed robbery. Now, this is a murder case requiring extraordinary legal capacity. And this could indeed become a capital case if the death penalty is reinstated. Thus, we cannot allow the defendant to be represented by anything less than the best we can offer him."

"And who did you have in mind?" asked Bliley.

Battle pointed to the far end of the first row. "A man you know well. Mr. Douglas Rawlins of the firm McGuire, Russell and Williams. He's a graduate of the University of Virginia Law School, and has been assistant defense counsel on a number of murder cases and is highly recommended by the partners at his prestigious firm."

A now stone-sober Rawlins glanced over at Jack with a look of gripping fear.

Jack eyed him, shook his head, and got to his feet. "Judge Bliley, the commonwealth's motion has been rendered moot by the arrival of my new co-counsel."

On cue, the doors opened, and Desiree DuBose strode confidently up the aisle as all heads and notepads turned to her.

Jack watched Pickett's expression as his gaze lit on DuBose. It was not a look that Jack would ever want anyone to have when staring at him.

He said, "This is Desiree DuBose, Judge Bliley. Lead counsel in dozens of murder cases, and she has also won a case in front of the U.S. Supreme Court."

Bliley said, "I also read of her involvement in the *Loving* case which, as you know, commenced in Virginia." He eyed Battle. "And if memory serves, Mr. Battle, on that matter you were, at times, on the receiving end of this lady's legal skills."

Battle, who did not look remotely surprised at DuBose's appearance, said, "She is also not a member of the Virginia State Bar."

"The Virginia Supreme Court did not have an issue with that," said DuBose, coming to stand next to Jack. "I was waived in on a *pro hac vice* basis, as is normal."

"That was an *appellate* court appearance," countered Battle. "This is the *trial* component of what is shaping up to be a capital murder case. The lawyer defending the accused should be a full-fledged member of the bar where the killings occurred, not some *foreign* lawyer *flitting* in from out of state and who doesn't know our ways."

DuBose said, "So then you propose to put in Mr. Lee's place Mr. Douglas Rawlins, who we happened to meet the other night, and who described the man he would be representing as a 'colored errand-boy killer'?"

Bliley swung his gaze over to Rawlins. "Did you make such a statement, sir?"

"I was there, too, Judge, and he most assuredly did," said Jack.

Battle glanced at the mortified Rawlins, and the fury in the attorney general's expression was palpable.

Rawlins stood on trembling legs and said, "I don't really remember saying words exactly to that effect, Your Honor, but in my defense, I had been drinking maybe more than I should have that night."

"Well, that's surely a good attribute for counsel in a murder case, that he drinks too much," noted Jack.

Battle said in a booming, confident baritone, "This is easily resolved, Your Honor. There are numerous lawyers ready, willing, and able to step in." He gave Rawlins a dismissive glance. "And I imagine quite a few of them are teetotalers." He held up a letter. "And I have a document here signed by Mr. Washington whereby he acknowledges that Mr. Lee is inadequate to represent him and has requested that different counsel be appointed."

Jack exclaimed, "Do you mean to say that you visited my client without me being there? That is a most egregious breach of professional ethics."

"May we see the letter?" asked DuBose.

Battle made a show of handing the document to Jack and not her. They read down the typed letter and then looked at the signature.

"And you're claiming that Mr. Washington signed this?" said Jack.

"I was told that he did."

"A remarkable performance, since he uses an *X* as his signature." Jack opened his briefcase and took out the document that Jerome had signed appointing Jack as his lawyer. "Approach the bench, Judge?"

Bliley motioned them all forward.

Jack handed the document to Bliley. "Mr. Washington signed this in my presence at the jail. Put me under oath and I'll swear to it, and my client will do the same." He looked sternly at Battle. "And put him under oath and let him swear that *forgery* is my client's signature."

Bliley said, "Mr. Battle, you mentioned you were *told* the defendant signed this?"

"Yes. If there is any discrepancy, I'm sure it can be explained."

"I wish I was as sure as you," said Bliley doubtfully.

"That fact notwithstanding, I also need to object to Miss DuBose serving as co-counsel, which still leaves us with Mr. Lee being inadequate to try this case."

"On what grounds do you object?" asked a clearly puzzled Bliley. "She is more than competent to be defense counsel on this matter. And Mr. Lee can assuredly waive her in as local counsel, since I do not agree that a Virginia lawyer must represent a Virginia defendant at the trial level. I myself litigated such cases in New York after being waived in by local counsel, since I was admitted only in New Jersey at the time."

"I understand, Your Honor. However, the problem is actually due to her *race*."

"Excuse me?" exclaimed DuBose. "You can't be serious. A Black attorney *can* try cases in the Commonwealth of Virginia."

Keeping his gaze on Bliley, Virginia's highest-ranking lawyer said, "A Negro lawyer representing a Negro defendant accused of killing two prominent *white* people? There is a great deal of prejudice surrounding this case and I don't want to add to it."

"You're going to need to explain that, sir," demanded Bliley.

"While it pains me to say so, Your Honor, if we can't find a qualified white attorney to represent Mr. Washington, there is not a white juror in this entire area who will be able to objectively judge his guilt, or, in the tiniest of probabilities, his innocence. They will simply assume he is guilty because no white lawyer would take the case. And while we believe him to be guilty and the evidence for that is overwhelming, I have a reputation of being scrupulously fair in my dealings before the bar."

"Really, like Mr. Washington's signature that wasn't?" interjected Jack.

Battle ignored this and continued, "And the last thing that I would want is the race of Mr. Washington's counsel to be the deciding factor. One need only look around and see the state of this country today. There is a lot of anger on *both* sides. And we ignore that reality to the peril of Mr. Washington. And while Mr. Lee and Miss DuBose may be willing to risk a man's freedom on that, I am not. Ironically, I find myself playing defense counsel right now, standing my ground in support of the defendant's right to a fair trial. I would hope that opposing counsel understands my position, seeing as how I'm trying my best to do right by *their* client."

Well, that was slickly done, thought Jack. When he looked at DuBose, he could tell she was most likely thinking the same thing.

"All right, Mr. Battle, I see your point," noted Bliley.

DuBose said, "Your Honor, I have defended Black people in front of white juries all across the South. And I have also won more times than I have lost. Which directly cuts against the argument Mr. Battle is attempting to make here."

Jack added, "And I obviously *am* a white lawyer. And might I also add that the *white* public defender that represented Mr. Washington at his arraignment abruptly resigned shortly thereafter. And there were no other white lawyers apparently willing to defend Mr. Washington. So it strikes me as quite odd that Mr. Battle can apparently summon a legion of them at the drop of a hat. And besides that, Mr. Washington's family has already paid me monies to defend him. And surely a defendant should be able to choose his attorney."

Bliley said, "All right, Mr. Lee. Those are all valid points."

"Then let me make another one, Judge. If the standard is competency, then I would respectfully argue that competency also includes a *sincere* belief in a client's right to a fair trial, and a *sincere* desire to win the case. Contrast that with Mr. Battle being ready and willing to entrust the fate of a man to an attorney who already believed him to be guilty. Now, Mr. Battle may profess to a high standard before this court, but my daddy always taught me that words are cheap and actions are dear."

"Your Honor—" began Battle, but Bliley waved him off.

"Step back, all of you."

They returned to their respective counsel tables and Bliley said, "The commonwealth's motion to replace defense counsel is denied. It is clear to this court that defense counsel, on a collective basis, can provide competent legal representation, and that the defendant is not indigent and is entitled to the attorney of his choosing. Coupled with the fact that the commonwealth is unable to validate the document that the defendant allegedly signed," he added with a piercing glance at Battle. "Mr. Lee, do you desire to waive Miss DuBose into this court for purposes of this case?"

"I do, Judge."

"Have you filed the necessary paperwork to do so and paid the required fees?"

"We have, Judge."

"Then let's proceed with the formalities."

Jack said the requisite words, and DuBose added her accompanying piece.

Bliley declared, "Miss DuBose, you are duly admitted into the Circuit Court of Freeman County, Virginia, on a *pro hac vice* basis for the sole purpose of serving as co-counsel for the defense in the matter of *Commonwealth versus Jerome R. Washington*. Court is dismissed." He banged his gavel and scooted back into his chambers.

As Jack and DuBose were preparing to leave, Battle strolled over to them.

"Round one goes to you, Desiree."

"It goes to Mr. Lee and me," she replied.

Battle looked at Jack. "If you think you're leading the defense, think again. This young lady does not know how to play second fiddle to either man or beast."

"Do you have the cause and time of death for us yet?" interjected DuBose. "Or are you going to ambush us at trial? If so, we have a number of pretrial motions we can file, including a change of venue and a request for a preliminary hearing."

"That was waived."

"By incompetent counsel, rendering that decision null and void. I know the supporting case law by heart, Edmund," countered DuBose.

"We'll see about that."

"I saw your son last month. Brett is doing God's work with the Civil Rights Division at the Justice Department in Washington."

Battle glared at her. "You have a funny definition of *God's work*."

"I thought it was pretty straightforward. Right versus wrong?" noted DuBose.

Battle glanced away from her and looked over Jack's facial injuries. "No room for that in our legal system, Mr. Lee. I'm truly sorry it happened to you. But when you push them against the wall, some folks don't know any better than to strike back." He left with his legal posse.

The reporters flocked after him, pestering the man with questions.

A few moments later Howard Pickett came forward. "Miss DuBose, how nice to see you again."

She barely looked at him. "I wish I could say the same."

"You got the best of us a couple of times, but we returned the favor."

"Yes, by sending four innocent men to prison for life, and spending three years and hundreds of thousands of dollars of your money trying to keep little Black kids from getting the same education as white children."

Pickett laughed and turned to the reporters who had left the nonresponsive Battle and gathered around the pair, sensing blood. "A lawyer every second, twisting facts around to make it seem like she's doing good, when all she's really doing is destroying what America stands for."

"And what exactly does America stand for?" she asked. "Liberty and equality but only for some?"

"What *we* stand for are good family values, a strong defense, small government and the right to live the American Dream, and the true and natural supremacy of the white race in the greatest country on earth. And we can make it even greater if we can stop the damn federal courts from horning in where they don't belong."

"Well, good thing the Founding Fathers didn't agree with you on that," said DuBose. "Seeing as how they created the federal courts as an *equal* branch of government to do exactly what they're doing right now."

"And what is that, exactly?" said Pickett in a bland tone.

"Giving full force to the language of the founding documents we rely on to be a great and everlasting democracy, starting with 'all men are created equal.' I figure if we adhere to that one *literally*, but also include all women, good things will follow."

"Well, it'll be a long wait then."

"Oh, I'm a patient person," replied DuBose.

"It may not be up to you," retorted Pickett.

"Well, it certainly won't be up to *you*," she shot back.

Pickett grinned, spun on his heel, and walked out.

As Jack and DuBose exited, the flock of reporters turned on them, but Jack quickly led DuBose through the gauntlet, out onto the street, and down a narrow alley lined with dented garbage cans where eager blackbirds were trolling for their breakfast. The reporters finally gave up pursuit, and wheeled around to sprint to the nearest phone booth to report in. Jack and DuBose slowly walked back to his office.

"So I take it Pickett has a habit of showing up and getting in your way?"

"His idea of America is antithetical to everything this country *should* stand for. And yet millions of people believe the man makes perfect sense."

As they turned another corner, someone darted up to them. He was around fifty and unhealthily thin, not much more than flesh on bone. He was also breathing erratically, like his lungs were unwilling to perform in synchronicity.

"Jack Lee?"

"Yes."

"I saw you in court and wanted to talk to you," said the man, gasping for air.

"Look, if you're a reporter I—"

The man took a deep breath and said, "I'm Sam Randolph."

"Oh, I didn't recognize you. I'm truly sorry about your loss, sir."

"I've spoken with Mr. Battle. He seems to think the evidence is incontrovertible."

"Prosecutors always do. But that's why we have trials."

"I just want whoever did this to be punished."

"So do we," said Jack. "Only we don't believe it was Mr. Washington."

"Do you have any idea who it might be then?"

DuBose spoke up, "Mr. Randolph, with all due respect, we are in the middle of a murder trial. I'm sure you can understand that it would be against legal ethical standards and also against the interests of our client to discuss the case with you."

He wheeled on her. "I'm *not* going running to Battle with whatever you tell me. My parents have been murdered!"

"Which makes it critical that we adhere to the rules governing legal proceedings."

Randolph looked her over and his lips twisted. "You talk all high-and-mighty."

"I speak, I would hope, like a lawyer, which I happen to be."

He then glanced at Jack. "Is she the best you could do?"

Before Jack could say anything, Randolph turned and stalked off.

Jack said, "Do you think he *was* working for Battle?"

"I don't know. I assume he stands to inherit a lot of wealth. So maybe he's more worried about what we might find out during our investigation."

"Meaning *we* have to prove Jerome's *innocence* beyond any reasonable doubt?"

She gave him a patronizing look. "Welcome to my world, Jack."

CHAPTER 30

CURTIS GATES WAS AN OLD-SCHOOL trusts and estates lawyer with the dour look and dusty, estate-box-littered office that stamped the breed of attorney who presided over death, taxes, and property with a certain grisly relish. In his sixties with thinning white hair, blotchy skin, rounded shoulders, and a thickish belly, he eyed Jack and DuBose, as though he was bewildered as to why they were sitting across from him.

"The will is to be read next week, and then *only* to the bene-ficiaries."

He was interrupted by his secretary bringing in a pitcher of water and two glasses in response to Jack's and DuBose's requests. She poured out the drinks and exited, glancing at Gates with a dubious look as she nudged the door closed.

"I understand that, Mr. Gates," said Jack. "But we need to know *now* because we have a case to try, and this information is pertinent."

"What exactly are you implying?" said Gates, sliding his wire-rimmed specs onto his long, wrinkled brow.

"We just need to know where the estate is going. And if they left Jerome Washington—"

"Who?"

"He was a handyman who worked for them."

"I can tell you definitively that that name appears nowhere in the estate documents of Mr. and Mrs. Randolph. Wait, isn't he the man accused of killing them?"

"Yes," replied Jack.

"And you're his lawyers? *Both* of you?"

"Both of us," confirmed Jack. "And we need to know who gets what."

"Surely you are not suggesting that the beneficiaries had anything to do with their deaths? Wasn't that colored man found with the bodies?"

"We need to track down every possibility. His life is on the line."

"As well it should be, considering he ended two other lives," said Gates huffily.

"*Allegedly* did so," corrected DuBose.

Gates glared at DuBose as she sipped her water. "This is all highly irregular."

"Well, I would imagine so is two of your clients being murdered," pointed out DuBose. "We are duty bound to do our job, Mr. Gates. I hope you, also being a lawyer, can understand that."

Looking put out, Gates shuffled some papers, and said, "Christine and Sam split the money left by their parents equally."

"How much money are we talking?" said Jack.

"I will not give you a number until the will is officially read."

"And the house the Randolphs were living in? And the land?"

Gates hesitated. "That is dealt with separately."

"That's unusual, isn't it?" said DuBose.

"Who are you again?" Gates said abrasively.

"Co-counsel for the defense," replied DuBose. "Can you please tell us the testamentary provisions of the real estate?"

Gates cleared his throat and said, "The house and surrounding property goes to the *surviving* child, without exception."

"But there are currently *two* surviving children," pointed out Jack.

"I'm aware of that," growled Gates. "The property is to be held in trust until there is only *one* surviving child. The French had a

term for something like it. They called it a tontine. When one ben-
eficiary dies, the payouts to the survivors increase correspondingly.
It's a bit controversial because of the incentive to, well, you know."

"To *murder* the other beneficiaries?" suggested DuBose.

Gates cleared his throat noisily. "To put it bluntly, and crudely,
yes. And while this situation is not, strictly speaking, a tontine, in
a testamentary disposition of property owned outright by the tes-
tators, one can leave one's property to anyone they want and under
pretty much any stipulations. And this is what the Randolphs
wanted: that only *one* child should inherit the property."

"So you're saying they didn't care which of the two inherited?"
said Jack. "Christine or Sam?"

"I don't remember saying anything of the kind."

"Well then?" persisted Jack.

Gates said primly, "Well then, nothing. I assume you've heard of
attorney-client privilege?"

"Okay, and when was all this done?" asked Jack.

"Why does that matter?"

"If you could please answer the question?" said DuBose.

"No, I don't think I will," Gates declared petulantly.

"All right, just to be clear, if Christine predeceases Sam he gets
the house and property free and clear and Christine's children get
nothing?" said DuBose. "And vice versa?"

"Correct," Gates said grudgingly.

"Can you tell us how much the house and property are worth?"
inquired DuBose.

Gates perked up. "It was actually appraised about a year ago.
The valuation came back at nearly two million dollars. And I know
of at least three developers who would pay more than that and just
for the land. It's near the country club and is also adjacent to Faulkner's Woods. And that amount doesn't come close to its potential."

"What do you mean?" asked Jack.

"You knock down all those trees on the forested part of their
property, you could put up over fifty luxury estate homes and sell

them for over a quarter of a million or more *each*. My son, Walter, is a developer, so I know more about that business than most."

"Why would the Randolphs have done that?" asked Jack. "Making sure that only one child benefitted and having to wait until the other died?"

"Once again, that is privileged information and I have no intention of sharing it with you. Or...*her*," Gates said, glancing disgustedly at DuBose. "Now, if there's nothing else?"

He spoke into his phone and his secretary came in to take away the tray. She scrutinized the glasses after glancing at Gates, who inclined his head to the right. Neither of them noticed DuBose picking up on this unspoken exchange.

As they were leaving, DuBose poked her head into the small kitchen off the main reception area in time to see Gates's secretary dump one of the water glasses into the wastebasket. She was about to tell the woman that she had drunk from the other glass, just to let her know that DuBose knew what was going on. But her anger faded and she returned to Jack, who looked at her curiously.

"Anything wrong?" he asked.

"Nothing I haven't seen before," DuBose said wearily.

CHAPTER 31

WHEN THEY RETURNED TO JACK'S office, they found an envelope tacked to his door.

"Battle strikes again," he said after reading the document inside. "He's asking for the trial to commence in one week, and there's a hearing scheduled for that on Monday. He also says that based on the evidence they will make no formal plea offer. However, if Jerome confesses his guilt they will take the possibility of execution off the table, if the death penalty becomes active again. But he will be sentenced to life without the chance of parole. And he will have to provide an allocution in court." He looked up at DuBose. "We have to present this offer to Jerome."

"Which is why Battle made it."

It took DuBose showing her ID along with her Illinois bar card to three different guards, and Jack swearing on a stack of Bibles that she was his co-counsel, before they would allow DuBose in to see her own client.

Jerome gazed up curiously at DuBose while Jack introduced her.

She said, "I work for the Legal Defense Fund. Have you heard of them?"

"No ma'am."

"It used to be part of the NAACP. You've probably heard of it."

Jerome nodded. "But why they care 'bout the likes 'a me?"

DuBose sat in the chair opposite him. "Because it's our job to make sure you get the same rights as anyone else." She paused. "First thing, Mr. Washington, did you sign a letter asking that Mr. Lee be removed as your counsel?"

He shook his head. "Letter? Nobody brought me no letter in here."

DuBose glanced at Jack. "Okay. Now, the commonwealth has made an offer to you, Mr. Washington."

"Just call me Jerome."

"All right, Jerome. The offer says that if you plead guilty and stand up in court and say how and why you committed the murders, the state will waive any right it may have to ask for your execution, and you will spend the rest of your life in prison without the chance of ever being paroled."

"How I stand up and say stuff I ain't done?"

"I understand, but we were duty bound to present the offer to you. Do I take it that you do not want to accept that offer?"

Jack said, "Jerome, we mean to defend you with all we have. But they may very well bring back the death penalty."

"But even if we do lose at the trial level, I'm confident that we will win on appeal," said DuBose, drawing a surprised look from Jack.

"You may want to talk to your wife before you decide," Jack suggested.

"I ain't sayin' I killed them people, 'cause I didn't do it."

"Fine," said DuBose decisively. "We will communicate your decision."

Jack took a deep breath. "All right, Jerome. Now, do you remember anything about the man who came by to see the Randolphs a while back and where Mr. Randolph got so mad? Pearl and Miss Jessup told us about it. And do you recall the make and model of the car he drove?"

Jerome looked down at his shoes. "It be light gray with white trim. I remember that. It be a four-door…a Chrysler hardtop." He thought some more, scrunching up his features, and then he looked up. "Yeah, it be one of them New Yorkers. Nice car."

Jack wrote all of this down. "And the man? Can you describe him?"

"He a little shorter than you, and thicker. He got on a dark suit and tie and he was carryin' a black bag."

"A bag? What did it look like?" asked Jack.

"Uh, you know, like a doctor carries 'round."

DuBose and Jack exchanged a puzzled look.

"How old was he?" she asked.

"I reckon he maybe 'bout forty or so."

"And he was white?" asked DuBose.

"Oh, yeah. He gone in the house and all. And he come out the *front* door."

"Okay," DuBose said with a glance at Jack. "And Mr. Randolph said nothing other than nobody was going to make him leave his house?"

"That right. Ain't nobody makin' him get out his own house. He say that."

"And you never saw the man again after that?" asked Jack.

"No sir, not one time."

"Pearl said that the Randolphs invited you and your family over for lunch and a swim in the pool," said DuBose.

Jerome grinned. "Yeah. They take us 'round to the back and we ate out there o'course. But then Miss Anne say, 'Hey, kids, you wanna go swimmin'?' Now, Miss Anne tell me she gonna ask that, so Pearl had got 'em some swimsuits and she got one for herself, too. They changed in the garage. They ain't never been in no water 'cept the bathtub. But they had a real good time."

"And Christine Randolph showed up at some point?" said Jack.

"Yeah, Miss Christine and her husband and their kids walked in the backyard when we was fixin' to leave. They real nice. Asked how we liked the food and the pool and all. Just a real nice day. So I don't see how nobody think I could kill these folks who been so good to me and my family. Now I ain't got a job. And I'm in here." He shook his head in frustration.

Jack said quietly, "We understand that you have bad dreams from time to time?"

Jerome glanced sharply up at him for a moment before looking away. "I don't really have 'em no more."

"Did they make you angry or…?"

"I seen things, Mr. Lee, over in Vietnam, that I ain't never seen before. And I hope to God I don't never see again, so long as I live."

"I'm sure," said Jack, who was now thinking of his brother.

DuBose said, "We're only asking you this, Jerome, because the commonwealth may bring it up. Their argument might be that you had one of these…episodes, while you were at the Randolphs, and it caused you to attack them."

"I ain't never had none 'a that 'cept when I be sleepin'. I went in that house to get my money 'cause they didn't answer the door. And they didn't answer the door 'cause they be dead. That's all I got to say."

He bowed his head and looked at the floor.

DuBose eyed Jack. "Okay, well, I think that's all for now."

"We'll be back to see you soon," said Jack. "Anything you need?"

Jerome never took his gaze off the floor. "Just to get outta here."

"We're doing our best to make that happen," said DuBose.

Back in the car Jack said, "I wish we had let him talk to his wife before he made that decision on the offer."

"Jack, there was no way that man was going to agree to spend the rest of his life in prison." She looked at him. "Are you having second thoughts about trying this case?"

"No, but you told Jerome if we lost you were *confident* we'd prevail on appeal."

"I *am* confident."

"Did you win most of your appeals?"

"Every case is different, and I feel good about this one."

"We haven't even seen the commonwealth's case, Desiree. And we may not until trial. And I doubt that Battle would risk his reputation unless he was damn sure of winning it. And let me tell you, if they get that conviction they won't waste any time getting him in that chair if the death penalty gets reinstated."

"We will file appeals, Jack. That takes time."

"Not so much in Freeman County and the Commonwealth of Virginia. Before the moratorium on the death penalty came into effect, we used to execute more people faster than any other state, by a country mile."

"We better make sure we win at the trial level then," she said brusquely.

"And we're going to do all this in a *week*?"

"No, we will oppose Battle's ridiculous timeline."

"Look, as co-counsel, I thought I had the right to speak my mind."

She gazed at him coldly. "You do. But don't forget that I have a lot more experience than you. So I think we trust my professional instincts over yours."

Later, they walked to a restaurant near Jack's office and endured yet more stares and crude comments they could not fail to hear. They were finishing up when their attention was captured by a small TV that hung from a wall of the restaurant. It was a special news broadcast from Richmond.

The announcer, looking appropriately stern, said, "At a special session of the General Assembly in Richmond called by the governor, the moratorium on the death penalty was lifted and the bill was immediately signed by the governor. All murder cases satisfying the necessary elements that have been charged but not yet gone to trial can once more invoke the death penalty."

Jack looked at DuBose. "Well, that changes everything," he said.

DuBose said, "And it means when we win this case, Jack, it will bring even more attention to the cause."

"My only *cause* is getting Jerome off for murder," he said, frowning.

She glanced at him with an impassive expression. "I care about what happens to Jerome in ways you probably can't understand. But I also have to think of the bigger picture."

"What's bigger than a man's life?"

"You just don't get it, Jack, being white."

"I'm just trying to be a good lawyer for my client, Black or white."

"And you think I'm not?"

"I didn't say that."

DuBose leaned in closer, her expression a diamond-hard wall of determination. "I have been working my entire adult life to bring basic fairness and equality to my race, things you have never lived without for even one minute of your life. And I will do whatever I have to do, including taking on the Edmund Battles and Howard Picketts of this world, to make that happen, because, frankly, failure is not a damn option. Are we clear on that, Mr. *Co-counsel*?"

"Crystal clear," replied Jack.

CHAPTER 32

On Monday the bailiff ordered them to rise once more. The excitement in the packed courtroom was palpable; it had a carnival-like feel, as though they were all waiting for the bearded lady or a knife thrown within an inch of a frightened face.

Judge Bliley took his seat behind the bench and nodded at Battle.

Battle stood and said, "Your Honor, there is no reason on earth why this case couldn't be tried tomorrow, but to be fair we are giving the defense an additional full week in which to prepare. There is almost nothing in dispute and the facts are clear."

When Bliley looked at the defense table Jack rose and said, "We haven't even started our investigation, Judge. We also haven't gotten the autopsy report from the medical examiner. And we just found out that the death penalty was reinstated. So we don't even know if this is a capital murder case or not."

"Then let me allay any concerns you might have on *multiple* fronts," announced Battle. He nodded at his associates, who carried two large boxes over to Jack and DuBose's table and set them there.

Battle said, "In those boxes are all the exculpatory evidence required under *Brady*, Your Honor, little though there is. In addition, there is the commonwealth's complete theory of the case, its list of witnesses, the autopsy reports, and the facts and physical elements that we intend to introduce into evidence. We are not required to give the defense any of that, except for the *Brady* material, but are doing so voluntarily in the interests of justice and fair play. And we have duly amended our filed charges and are hereby asking that, if convicted, Mr. Washington be put to death. In addition, we have conducted a search of Mr. Washington's home and the results of that search are in with what we have just provided defense counsel."

DuBose said, "You searched our client's home without notifying us?"

"Just like you, Miss DuBose, we have the right and duty to conduct a thorough investigation of this matter and we have done so. And Mr. Lee is being more than a little disingenuous about having had no opportunity to undertake an investigation, since I personally allowed him to go through the entire crime scene and he took pictures and asked questions and we were thoroughly accommodating to him."

Bliley looked over at Jack. "Is that true?"

"I use an investigator to really dig into the case, since I'm no trained fact-finder. We're meeting with him shortly. And I don't know why the commonwealth feels like we need to rush this case."

Battle was clearly ready for this. "The Sixth Amendment to the U.S. Constitution and Section Eight of the Virginia Constitution require a speedy trial for the defendant. But unless the defense can point to any prejudice to their client I fail to see what leg they have to stand on. And we have presented our entire case to them. Indeed, I believe that once they review it, the next thing I'll hear from them is not about a trial, but a plea deal." He paused, gave Jack and DuBose a meaningful look, and added, "And the commonwealth is also amending its pleadings to include a murder charge against a second individual."

"And who is *that*?" demanded a stunned Jack.

"Mrs. Pearl Washington. I can assure you that our amended filing will make for interesting reading."

Bliley said, "I will take all this under advisement and apprise you of my decision by tomorrow." He looked ominously at Jack and

DuBose. "But I would advise the defense to waste no time in preparing its case."

He smacked his gavel and returned to his chambers.

Jack marched right over to Battle. "That is some cheap stunt to charge our client's wife and wait until we're in front of the judge to tell us."

Battle shrugged. "The ink is hardly dry on our filing."

"And where is Mrs. Washington?" asked DuBose, joining them.

"She was arrested this morning. And the indictment was handed down *before* her arrest, so you are not entitled to a preliminary hearing. She will be arraigned tomorrow, which will give you a chance to formally enter your appearance as her counsel, although, with what we have found out, she may want a separate lawyer. We will oppose any talk of bail. She's currently in the women's jail, which, I'm sure you know, is right next to the men's. Maybe she and her murderous husband can *holler* out the windows at each other."

"Are you claiming that she helped kill the Randolphs?"

"Yes, and we are seeking the death penalty against her as well, since she helped plan the killings and assisted in their execution."

"How can you imagine that Pearl Washington is involved?" exclaimed DuBose.

"I think your client, and his missus, might have some explaining to do. And piece of advice, next time, before taking on a case, do a little due diligence first."

With that stinging shot, Battle and his team left.

DuBose opened one of the boxes and stared down at the contents.

Jack looked over her shoulder and whispered, "I don't like the sound of that."

"Let's get these back and start going through them. And then we need to get ready for Pearl's arraignment."

"Well, first, we need to go by the Washingtons' house. We need to make sure everybody's okay."

DuBose glanced at him, a bit shamefacedly. "Yes. Of course."

"I'm going to call my investigator and have him meet us later today."

"I hope he's good."

"Donny Peppers is better than good."

Jack turned to look behind him when someone called his name.

Christine Hanover motioned to him from the front row.

Her hair was tied back in a single braid, which emphasized the delicate lines of crow's feet around her eyes. She had always been slender, but now she looked like she had lost weight just since he had seen her last.

He walked over and said, "Christine, I should have told you before that I was representing Jerome Washington. It was just mighty awkward at the time. In fact, I didn't even know that your parents were involved when I was first approached about taking on the case."

She nodded. "I understand that, I guess. It was still a shock to find out."

"How are your kids? I'm sure they took this hard," he said.

"Fortunately, they're all away at a summer camp. We called and told them about what happened. Leaving out the...details."

"Of course."

She glanced over at DuBose. "You have a new law partner?"

"Desiree DuBose. From Chicago. Oh, I saw your brother. He doesn't look too good."

"He has some health problems, but I don't know what they are. To tell you the truth, we don't really see one another anymore."

"Sorry to hear that. I'm sure your husband has been supportive of you."

"Gordon is always a rock," she said. "You ever hear from Jeff?"

"I just found out my daddy got a letter from him when he...when Jeff made his decision. But I don't know what it said."

"People are finding out this war is not all we were told it was. So I can understand why an honorable man like your brother would decide to do what he did."

She walked away as DuBose came over carrying one of the boxes.

"Who was she?"

"Christine Hanover, the Randolphs' daughter," said Jack.

"Do you think she knows about the tontine arrangement?"

"If she doesn't, she will soon."

CHAPTER 33

JACK AND DUBOSE PULLED INTO the front yard of the Washingtons' home. Miss Jessup answered their knock, with Darla Jean again wedged on her hip.

"We just heard," said Jack.

"Y'all come on in," Miss Jessup said curtly.

Inside, Jack saw another younger woman holding on to the hand of a little boy.

"This is Maggie, Pearl's ma, and my daughter. And this here is Elijah. Maggie, this is Jack Lee and Desiree DuBose, Jerome's lawyers."

Jack and DuBose greeted Maggie, who was petite with hair that fell to her shoulders. Her eyes were red-ringed, no doubt from crying, and her face puffy for the same reason.

Jack knelt and shook Elijah's hand. "You got yourself a strong grip, young man," he noted.

"You gonna be Pearl's lawyers, too?" asked Miss Jessup.

"Yes," said Jack, standing. "Her arraignment is tomorrow morning. We just wanted to make sure things were okay here."

Miss Jessup handed Darla Jean to Maggie and placed her hands over Elijah's ears. She said quietly, "Police come early this mornin'. Pulled Pearl outta bed. Good thing Maggie was sleepin' over, else the children woulda been left all alone."

"Surely the police wouldn't have done that," said Jack.

"The hell they wouldn't," snapped Maggie.

Miss Jessup said, "Maggie said Pearl was half-crazy when they took her away. The police were callin' her names so bad Maggie had to take the children out the room. Now, you two go on and see that poor woman right now, please."

On the drive over to the women's jail, DuBose read through the new filings. "Damn," she exclaimed.

"What?"

"You can hear when I ask Pearl about it. But it's not good."

At the jail they were led down a dark, bleak hall that smelled of equal parts bleach and urine. Behind a secure door, they were directed to a cell with a barred portal. Inside was Pearl, dressed in faded prison denim that was two sizes too large. It was so hot in here that Jack immediately felt a little nauseous. Knees drawn up to her chest, Pearl sat on the floor next to a filthy commode that bulged from the wall like a tumor.

"Pearl?" Jack said.

She looked up and then stood on trembling legs.

The jailer opened the door and locked it behind them.

"Are you all right?" said Jack, looking her over.

Tears slid down her cheeks. "I don't know what be happenin', Mr. Lee. They come and say I helped Jerome kill those people. The kids were bawlin'. My momma—"

She started hyperventilating. DuBose clutched her hand and said calmly, "Take some deep breaths, nice and slow. Now, sit on the bed. Take as long as you need and then just tell us what happened. We're here to help you. Deep, deep breaths. Take your time."

They stood in front of her bunk as Pearl composed herself.

After a minute or so, her breathing normalized. She said, "They come early in the mornin'. 'Bout knocked my door down. Pulled me out my bed, and I was in my undies. My kids were bawlin' and they put the handcuffs on me, and put me in the car. And all the time they jabberin' away about me helpin' to kill them people."

DuBose glanced at Jack. "They're saying that you went to the Randolphs' that day with clean clothes and shoes for Jerome. That you took the murder weapon from him, and his bloody clothes and shoes. They searched your property and found some money in the lean-to they assert you stole from the Randolphs."

"Ain't none 'a that true. And I don't know nothin' 'bout no money in the lean-to."

DuBose said, "The reason they brought you into this is because Jerome had no blood on his clothes or shoes, and no murder weapon or money was found on his person. Those are big gaps in the prosecution's case. To get around that they concocted this whole story about you and Jerome planning the murders together. That closes all the holes in their theory. And now that they found the money—or, more likely, planted it—that bolsters their argument."

DuBose perched next to Pearl. "But they're also saying that you weren't at your job the day that the Randolphs were killed. They must have checked on that before they laid out a plan to charge you, otherwise their scheme wouldn't have worked. Which means you *weren't* at work on that Friday?"

Pearl dabbed at her nose with her wrist and wouldn't look at either of them.

"Where do you work during the week?" asked Jack.

"Winston's. It only a mile from my house. It's where folks like me get our food."

"What do you do there?" asked DuBose.

"Unload the trucks. Stock the shelves. Hard work but it pays good."

"So you *weren't* there that day?" asked Jack.

"No," she said in a small voice. "I, uh, I had somethin' else I had to do."

"What was that?"

Her mouth twisted and she said defiantly, "My business."

"The commonwealth is making it *their* business, Pearl," pointed out DuBose. "If you tell us where you were, we can assert that as a defense."

"I ain't tellin' nobody where I was," Pearl said fiercely.

Jack and DuBose exchanged a worried glance.

DuBose said, "Okay, as I mentioned, the commonwealth also found fifty dollars in an envelope in your lean-to. You really have no idea where that came from?"

"No! All our money's in a coffee can on the top shelf of the pantry."

DuBose rose. "All right. Do you need anything?"

"Yeah, I need to get back to my kids," Pearl said tearfully.

Jack said, "We went to your house. Your mother and Miss Jessup are there."

"My grandma's there? What 'bout Ashby?"

"I don't know."

"She gonna lose her job. That old man don't care 'bout nothin' 'cept hisself."

DuBose said, "Do you want us to be your lawyers?"

"I guess so, yeah," she said distractedly.

"Then we need you to be truthful with us. Everything you tell us is confidential."

Pearl wavered for a moment, but then shook her head.

Jack said, "Your arraignment is tomorrow. We'll be back to prep you for it."

As they walked over to the men's jail DuBose said, "If she doesn't tell us where she was, we have no real way to defend her." She looked at the entrance to the men's jail. "Now, let's go see what Jerome has been withholding."

Jerome was sitting on his bed when they walked in.

They told him about Pearl being arrested and why.

A furious Jerome slammed his fist into the skinny mattress. "That be crazy. I didn't kill nobody and she didn't do none 'a them things. It all a pack 'a lies!"

"Only she wasn't at work the day the Randolphs were killed, Jerome," said Jack.

His anger instantly transformed to puzzlement. "Then where was she?"

"She wouldn't tell us. You don't know?" asked Jack.

"No, Mr. Lee. She never miss work. She miss work she ain't get paid."

DuBose urged, "We *have* to know, Jerome."

"Can I talk to her?"

Jack said, "We can arrange a phone call."

"You do that then."

"Now Jerome, the police searched your house and property," said Jack.

"Why they done that?"

DuBose said, "They found fifty dollars in an envelope in a hole in the wall of your lean-to. Do you know how that might have gotten there?"

Jack's gut clenched when he saw the expression on Jerome's face. It was not surprise, or confusion, but nervousness, perhaps guilt.

"Um…Miss Anne gimme that money."

"When and why?" asked Jack sharply.

"When we was at the house for lunch. Miss Anne, she pull me aside when they in the pool and she say I doin' a good job and I had a nice family. And—"

"And what?" asked DuBose.

"Pearl's birthday comin' up, and I wanted to get her somethin' nice."

"Did Mrs. Randolph know that?"

"Yeah, I told her. I think that one reason why she gimme the money. But I ain't ask for it. And fifty dollars is mor'n I make in a week. But she wanted me to take it, so's I did."

"Did you tell anyone else about this?" asked Jack.

"No sir, I wanted to surprise Pearl."

"Did anyone other than Mrs. Randolph know about the gift?"

"She maybe told Mr. Leslie."

"And now they're both dead," said DuBose, giving Jack an ominous look. She sat down next to Jerome. "See, the thing is, Jerome, the commonwealth will argue that you stole that money when you killed the Randolphs."

"But that be a lie!" he said angrily.

"With no one to show that it was a gift, it looks bad."

Jerome rubbed his face with his hand and shook his head wearily. "It don't matter. White man who brought you in here say they got the electric chair all fired up again. He say that where I be goin'."

"*Not* if we can do something about it," said DuBose. "And we can."

Jerome did not appear to be listening to her. "Look, how I get Pearl outta this? The kids got to have their momma. How do I do that?" He looked at them pleadingly. "How? Tell me."

Jack glanced at DuBose and said, "If you're really serious about this, we could talk to the prosecutor and see if he'll accept a guilty plea from you on the condition that the charges against Pearl are dropped, with prejudice, meaning they can never bring them again. Then she'll be free."

"Then you got to do that, Mr. Lee. You got to," Jerome said emphatically.

Jack again looked at DuBose, who was now gazing stonily at the concrete floor. He said, "We have Pearl's arraignment tomorrow. And then we can address it."

"Don't wait too long. Tear me up, Pearl bein' in a damn cage like this."

CHAPTER 34

JACK POURED OUT TWO MORE cups of coffee as DuBose sat at the worktable in his office. They had gone over all the documents provided by Battle, and DuBose had made a list of issues and follow-up items. But what was most troubling was what their clients had not told them.

Jack handed DuBose the fresh coffee and sat down across from her.

"When is your investigator going to be coming?" she asked.

Jack checked his watch. "Anytime now."

"He has his work cut out for him on this one."

Jack picked up her list and read down it. "The commonwealth's case is pretty straightforward," he said. "Jerome needed money. He had been inside the Randolphs' house before to use the bathroom."

DuBose nodded. "And on the day of the murder Pearl was not at work."

"And they found cash money hidden in Jerome's lean-to. Money that Jerome says he was given, but we have no way to prove that without putting him on the stand. Battle will then have the right to tear him apart on cross-examination, or else we're forced to instruct Jerome to plead the Fifth, and we could lose the whole case right there."

DuBose said, "They also have sworn testimony from Curtis Gates that the Randolphs were going to fire Jerome because they were afraid of him. No wonder he was so smug about Jerome being guilty," she added bitterly.

Jack picked up another piece of paper and read from it. "And the gardener, Tyler Dobbs, will say that Jerome had acted belligerently toward the Randolphs, which supports Gates's testimony and that Jerome told him he needed money. And they also talked to Gordon Hanover. He'll testify that Leslie Randolph thought Jerome had stolen from him and was going to fire him. And, lastly, Sam Randolph will testify that his father told him he was going to leave something to Jerome in his will. Which would be *another* motive." He dropped the paper and shook his head. "Does not look good, Desiree."

"This all seems woven *too* neatly," replied DuBose. "But yet it's also contradictory. Randolph was going to fire Jerome, but he was also going to leave him something in the will? Jerome was stealing, but Anne Randolph gave him a bonus?"

"I guess you've seen a lot of manufactured evidence," he said.

"Not that they needed to go that far. Most white juries have already convicted Black defendants before the trial even starts."

"And they have footprints from Jerome's shoes in that room. Not from the blood but from dirt he had on his shoes and that left an imprint."

"He doesn't deny he was there," pointed out DuBose.

"But the medical examiner's report says his footprints are the only ones other than the two deputies'," pointed out Jack.

"And he also said the murder weapon had a blade at least eighteen inches long. That was no kitchen steak knife. So whoever killed them came prepared to do just that."

"And where was Jerome going to hide that while riding his bike to work?" Jack said, shaking his head in frustration. "Except for Jerome being in the room, it's all speculation and circumstantial."

"They're also suggesting, as part of their grand plan, that Pearl called the police from a pay phone so they'd be sure to find Jerome there."

"If true, that was risky as hell," said Jack.

"But how would Jerome and Pearl know someone wouldn't

happen along *after* the maid and gardener left? In fact, someone did. The person in the blue convertible."

"If Jerome is to be believed about that," said Jack.

She shot him a harsh look. "You think he's lying?"

"You never had a client lie to you?"

"I could hardly blame them with the deck stacked against them."

"Whoever did it certainly knew the routine of the place. By one, the gardener was gone. By two, so was the maid. Jerome said he saw the convertible around four." Jack pulled out a document. "Okay, let's go through alibis. Cora Robinson and Tyler Dobbs both have solid ones for the time in question. Christine and Gordon Hanover were in Washington, DC, all day. They didn't get back here until very late that night."

"But Sam Randolph has no alibi." said DuBose. "So we'll need to talk to him."

Jack dropped the file and said, "But do we really have to do that? Jerome wants to sacrifice himself to save Pearl."

"What if Battle won't agree to waive the death penalty?'

"We won't know until we ask him."

"Jerome is not thinking clearly," she commented.

"You apparently thought he was thinking clearly when he *didn't* want to take the plea deal that Battle offered. So why not now?" When she didn't respond he added, "Hell, Desiree, if I were on a jury I might convict both of them on the evidence the common-wealth has compiled."

"So you believe they did it?"

"Doesn't matter what I believe. And I'm sorry if that doesn't dove-tail with your big-picture strategy. But if we can get Battle to do a deal, Pearl will get to go home to their kids, which is what Jerome wants."

"And he rots in prison for the rest of his life?"

"At the end of the day it's *his* decision."

She was about to respond when someone knocked at the door.

Jack rose and pulled his pistol from his desk. "Who is it?" he called out.

"Donny," the low voice answered.

CHAPTER 35

JACK OPENED THE DOOR AND there stood Donny Peppers, a bald, muscled man in his fifties, with a silvery mustache curved over his top lip. He had on black slacks and a white short-sleeved shirt that revealed thick, tattooed forearms. He lifted his sunglasses, revealing a pair of penetrating blue-gray eyes.

"Hey, Donny, come on in," said Jack.

Peppers noted the gun Jack held and said, "Heard you had trouble. Piece of advice, trade that peashooter in for something a little more robust, like this."

From his waistband clip holster Peppers pulled out a large revolver with custom wooden grips. "Single action Sturm and Ruger Super Blackhawk chambering the forty-four Remington Magnum cartridge. It's definitely a two-hander, but it'll drop a bear."

"Thanks for the recommendation," said Jack.

He introduced DuBose, who said, "We certainly can use your help."

"I heard some of it. Tell me the rest."

Jack and DuBose went through the entire case, and Peppers wrote down some things in a black notebook. He then leveled his gaze on DuBose. "What's your story?"

"Do I need one?" she said coolly.

"So you just dropped down from heaven to help Jack? What's in it for you?"

"Would justice for the accused work?"

"I don't know because I don't know you, at least not yet." He turned to Jack. "Word is there are important people *outside* the state who are watching this case."

"We've met one of them, Howard Pickett. One of George Wallace's cronies."

Peppers nodded. "Country's at a tipping point. And this Black-white stuff is right in the middle of it."

"Black-white *stuff*?" parroted DuBose in a scolding tone.

Peppers glanced her way. "I was just making an observation. And Bliley?"

"What about him?" asked Jack.

"Don't think he's going to be the judge on this."

Jack gaped. "What are you talking about?"

"They brought Battle in, so why can't they bring in another judge?"

Jack started to say something and then looked at DuBose. "No reason at all."

"Some people want to make a political statement by snuffing your clients." He looked at DuBose. "Which explains why you're here, even if you don't want to admit it."

"I have no trouble admitting my principles and beliefs, Mr. Peppers."

"Just make it Donny."

"So which side of the Black-white *stuff* do you come down on, *Donny*?"

Before he could answer, a tall, lanky Black woman in her early thirties and dressed in tight jeans and a red sleeveless blouse strode in. She wore big, chunky platform shoes that raised her impressive height another few inches.

"How much longer, Donny? I'm roastin' out there, babe."

Peppers frowned. "I told you to leave the engine running and the AC on, Shirl. I'm working here."

"Every time I do that the damn car overheats. And we're goin' out to dinner. I'll be a big ball of sweat. Again!"

"Okay, okay." Peppers turned to DuBose. "Shirl, I'd like you to meet Jack's co-counsel, Desiree DuBose. This is my wife, Shirley."

DuBose looked startled for a moment but then put out a hand. "I'm very pleased to meet you, Mrs. Peppers."

Shirley shook her hand. "Just make it Shirl." She paused and gave DuBose an appraising look. "I kind of dig your hairstyle, Desiree, but you could do a lot more with it. I have my own salon. Shirl's Curls." She slipped out a business card and handed it to DuBose. "If you're gonna be here awhile come and see me. I'll give you a new look. Guaranteed you'll love it."

DuBose looked down at the card. "Thank you. I might take you up on that."

"Now, as to what side I come down on?" began Peppers.

DuBose held up the card. "Don't give it another thought, Donny."

Peppers punched Jack lightly on the arm. "I'll start mowing through this."

"Thanks."

"Okay. Let's go, Shirl, I'm starving. And hustling business from my clients while I'm standing right here? It's embarrassing."

He grinned, chortled, and then belly-laughed before quickly walking out, leaving Shirl to stare after him, one hand on a thrust-out hip. She eyed DuBose with a sideways, long-suffering glance. "Girl, if I didn't love that man so much, one day, you know?"

DuBose smiled weakly. "I know."

Shirl left and Jack closed and locked the door. He turned to DuBose.

"You could have told me," she said.

"I wanted you to find out on your own that Freeman County is not exactly how you think it is."

"I already knew that, having met *you*."

"Donny fought in World War II *and* Korea. He also tried to

volunteer for Vietnam, but they said he was too old. He's the toughest man I've ever met in my life. And Shirl intimidates the hell out of him. He just tries to act cool with her to hide that."

"When did they get married?"

"A month after the *Loving* decision. But they've lived together for years."

"And how do people in Freeman County look upon their marriage?"

"They hate it. But everyone's too scared to tell them."

"So, a new judge?" said DuBose. "Any thoughts on who it might be?"

He eyed her resignedly. "Desiree, it doesn't really matter. Whoever it is will not be good for us. And that's another reason to cut a deal."

CHAPTER 36

ALL RISE," SAID THE BAILIFF. "The Circuit Court of Freeman County, Virginia, is now in session. The Honorable Josiah T. Ambrose presiding."

As the bailiff intoned on, they all stood. Through the chamber doorway strode a tall, slim man with a pencil-straight nose topped by gold-rimmed specs. His black robe was in conspicuous contrast to his white hair and trim beard.

The bailiff boomed, "Be seated."

DuBose whispered, "Do you know Ambrose?"

Jack shook his head. "Never heard of him."

He turned around to look at Howard Pickett. The man didn't appear to care one way or another about this development, which instantly made Jack suspicious.

He and DuBose had earlier made their formal appearance as Pearl's attorneys and had represented the woman at her arraignment, where bail had been denied.

Ambrose peered down at everyone with an oddly benevolent expression.

"Miss DuBose, may I welcome you back to the commonwealth? My friends on the Virginia Supreme Court sang your praises during the *Loving* appeal, though they ultimately ruled against you. But you and your esteemed colleagues of course prevailed in federal court."

"Thank you, Your Honor," she said, looking surprised.

Ambrose focused on Battle, who was sitting placidly with his hands on the table in front of him.

"Mr. Battle, one week preparation for a death penalty case? Really, sir?"

Both Jack and DuBose sat up straighter and looked on with heightened interest.

Battle stood. "Judge Ambrose, though we had no obligation to do so, we have provided our entire case to the defense. I also made a plea offer which would have precluded the need for a trial entirely, but they rejected it."

"You rejected a plea offer?" said Ambrose, eyeing DuBose and Jack, it seemed, with disappointment.

DuBose rose. "We did, Your Honor, because our client maintains his innocence." She did not mention the fact that Jerome now wanted to exchange his life in order to let his wife go free.

"Nonetheless, one week is more than sufficient time," said Battle.

Ambrose looked at DuBose. "Response?"

She said, "There is no reason to rush this case, Your Honor. Indeed, we just learned that the commonwealth has added another defendant. We need time to properly evaluate the evidence, do our investigation, and prepare an adequate defense."

"How much time?" queried Ambrose.

"One month."

Ambrose fingered his gavel and looked suitably troubled by the decision he was about to render.

"I would agree with you but for the fact that Mr. Battle has provided you with far more discovery than is required. I was a defense lawyer many moons ago, and I can't recall receiving anything near to what you did from Mr. Battle."

"But this is now a death penalty case," countered DuBose.

"That does not alter the fact that the commonwealth has been far more than accommodating with its pretrial discovery. Now, I would have preferred that a plea arrangement had been struck, but it was not. However, I agree with you that one week is not enough time." He considered for a few moments. "Trial will commence in two weeks. Jury selection will not exceed one day."

Ambrose smacked down his gavel. "Court is dismissed." He disappeared back into his chambers.

Jack looked at DuBose. "Well, it's better than a week but not by much."

Battle peered over at Jack and DuBose. "I assume by now you've had a chance to review the prosecution's case?"

"You covered a lot of ground in a short period of time," conceded DuBose.

"Well, it's an important case."

"Yes it is, but for whom?" said DuBose, glancing sharply at Pickett as he walked out of the courtroom.

Battle picked up his briefcase and left without responding.

A Black woman around Jack's age walked up to DuBose and him. "Miss DuBose?"

DuBose turned. "Yes?"

"I'm Cheryl Miller, with the local CBS affiliate." Miller eyed Jack and said, "Hey, Jack."

He closed up his briefcase and came over to join them. "Hey, Cheryl."

"You two know each other?" asked DuBose.

"Cheryl's dad works with my father at Old Dixie Transport."

Miller said, "I have a cameraman outside. It won't take long. Would you mind doing an interview?"

Jack began, "I'm sorry, Cheryl, I don't like to litigate cases in the—"

"I would be delighted," interrupted DuBose.

In an alleyway between the courthouse and another building they set up the shot.

Jack whispered to DuBose. "I don't think this is a good idea."

"I am not ceding the airwaves to the likes of *that* man," she said, indicating Howard Pickett, who was talking to a group of eager reporters at the next corner, while a cameraman filmed it. "And if used properly and judiciously, the press can be a valuable part of a sound defense."

"And it can also piss off the judge."

"I'm willing to risk it. And Ambrose seems fairer than I thought he would be."

"We're ready," said Miller.

On camera Miller introduced both Jack and DuBose, then asked DuBose some preliminary questions about her career and past cases. Then she turned to Jack. "And what is your opinion so far on how the case is proceeding, Mr. Lee?"

"It's moving along. We'll see how it goes," he said curtly.

DuBose stepped back into the shot. "I think the fact that we have the Virginia attorney general coming all the way here from Richmond to try the case speaks for itself. I'm afraid they are using this tragic event to advance a national political agenda."

Miller said, "Mr. Lee? Your thoughts on that?"

"Look, I just want folks to know that Jerome and Pearl Washington deserve the same presumption of innocence as any other defendant." He glanced at DuBose. "I'll leave the politics and rest of the country to my co-counsel."

DuBose's smile tightened at his words.

Miller said, "Miss DuBose, you have a sterling reputation as an advocate for racial justice in this country. What do you hope to accomplish with this case?"

DuBose glanced at Jack before saying, "To be clear, my focus is the successful legal defense of Jerome and Pearl Washington. No one should want to see an innocent husband and wife railroaded to a date with the electric chair, a punishment that was brought back in this case clearly to intimidate an entire race of people. After we prevail in this case the fight will go on, until Jim Crow is no more, and equal justice and opportunity actually applies to *all*, which is the real dream of this country."

They wrapped up the shot and Miller thanked them both.

"How do you really feel about the case, off the record?" she asked.

Jack said, "Well, there might not be a trial."

"What? Why?"

"Because a man loves his wife so much he's willing to go to prison for the rest of his life so she can go free to raise their children," said Jack somberly.

DuBose eyed Jack with a harsh look and hastily added, "That is strictly off the record. And it is by no means certain."

Miller said, "Absolutely. And I'm sorry if that's how it turns out."

"Can anybody join this party or is it some kind of private thing?"

They turned to see Howard Pickett striding purposefully up to them. He held out his hand to Miller. "Howard Pickett, ma'am, and you are?"

"Cheryl Miller, CBS."

"You folks have a grudge or something against the American people?"

"I'm afraid I don't understand," said Miller.

Pickett looked at the cameraman. "Can I get some equal time here?"

Miller hesitated, but then nodded at her cameraman, who readied his equipment.

"Okay, Mr. Pickett, you were saying?" said Miller.

"The American people are fighting a war against the commies in Vietnam, but to hear you folks and others tell it, we're the bad guys. But America is always the good guy, so we need to let our fine citizens know that our cause is just. The commies are godless. We are not. And we are fighting another war right here. For the soul of this nation."

"Thank you, Mr. Pickett," said Miller politely.

"Hold on there, I'm not finished, honey. The *soul* of this nation. George Wallace knows that. He hears the real people of this country, the moms and dads trying to keep a roof over their heads and bread on the table. Understands their concerns. Not the elites, not the wealthy."

"Wealthy like *you*, Mr. Pickett?" interjected DuBose, stepping into the shot.

"I use my money for the common man," said Pickett smoothly. "George Wallace understands that. We had great prosperity in the fifties and folks knew their place. Now, let me say up front and unequivocally, I got nothing against the Negroes, not a racist bone in my whole body. Colored man drives me around in fact, and I pay him fair and square. But the fact is, we are a country founded by white Anglo-Saxons. Now, so long as everyone knows where they stand, or can sit, or eat or sleep, things will be fine. I can't think of anything fairer than that."

Miller said, "Mr. Pickett, did you know that George Wallace used to advocate for equal treatment for Blacks?"

Pickett grinned at her. "Then he ran into John Patterson in the 1958 governor's race and got his ass handed to him 'cause Alabamans didn't want anything to do with being forced to associate with certain folks. That's not democracy, that's not freedom, that's what dictators do."

"So we all go back to Jim Crow then?" said DuBose. "That's your solution?"

"Worked fine for both whites and coloreds. Just ask 'em."

Miller motioned to her cameraman to cut the shot.

Pickett saw this and smiled. "Some people just don't like to hear the truth, do they? Could tell you were one of them just by *looking* at you, hon."

Miller thought for a moment and then said, "All right. While you're here I *do* have some questions to ask you." She motioned to her cameraman, who started to record once more.

"Fire away, little lady," said Pickett.

"Your coal mines have the worst safety record in the country with numerous fatalities, and your company has been fined more than fifty times for serious violations. In addition, pollution from one of your mines near Wheeling, West Virginia, tainted the area's entire water supply. And strikebreakers employed by you attacked and badly injured three miners, for which you have been sued and are also being investigated by the FBI. How would you respond to all that?"

Pickett slowly took out a toothpick from his pocket and rolled it around his mouth. "Your viewers will see right through what you're trying to do. Changing the subject to frivolous lawsuits against me and trying to hide the truth of my words from the American people. Well, good luck with that. My money is on average Americans knowing *exactly* what *I'm* trying to do, and how George is going to protect them from godlessness, and angry, dangerous folks that are as *different* from them as it's possible to be."

After he walked off, Miller said, "Just so you know, we will not run any of his lies. But I *will* show the piece on the coal mining." She smiled.

Miller and her cameraman departed, and Jack said to DuBose, "Let's go talk to Battle and see what deal he'll take, if any."

CHAPTER 37

BATTLE HAD SET UP HIS legal war room at the Carter City government building. They were ushered into his office, where he sat behind a large, cluttered desk. His jacket was off and his tie loosened. He was methodically packing a pipe with loose, pungent tobacco from a tin of it, and he looked up as they were escorted in.

"My, my, that didn't take long," he said with mirth in his eyes, as he struck a match and lit the pipe. "Have a seat."

They sat down across from him.

He puffed on the pipestem. "Well?"

"Our client would like to make a deal," began Jack.

"What sorta deal?"

"Jerome Washington will plead guilty in exchange for all charges against his wife being dropped with prejudice. And he will accept a life sentence."

"How kind of the man," replied Battle sarcastically.

"So?" said DuBose. "What do you say, Edmund?"

He eyed her with an amused expression. "You are royally upset, Desiree, because you so badly want to try this case."

"I believe my client to be innocent."

"And yet he's willing to say he did it?"

"To save his wife, and allow his children to have a mother to raise them."

Clenching his pipe in one corner of his mouth, Battle said, "Now, here's what I'm gonna do. I'm gonna try this case, and I'm gonna win this case. And I'm gonna get the death penalty for *both* of them. She's as guilty as he is, in my mind."

Jack said, "Jerome is willing to accept life in prison. Isn't that enough?"

Battle took his pipe out. "No, Mr. Lee, it's *not* enough. Two fine people who should still be alive are not. Because of your clients. And yet you ask me to spare his life? And let *her* go free to live her life? No, sir. Life for a life. In this case, two lives for two lives. So you can go back and tell your clients that the commonwealth has no interest in a plea from either of them now. And that the electric chair over in Richmond is where they will take their final breaths."

"They have young children," said Jack.

"You're not gonna persuade me trying sympathy, Mr. Lee. I'm plum out."

"You mean for defendants with a certain color skin?" said DuBose.

"As a judge and a prosecutor I've overseen many a *white* man on an appointment with Mr. Sparky," said Battle, referring to the electric chair. "And not everything in the whole damn world is based on *race*."

"It is for people like me," retorted DuBose.

"I'm real sorry to hear that. Whole years go by without me checking my skin. Now if I were you, I'd start preparing for trial." He motioned to the door.

Outside, Jack said, "Well, I guess we better let Jerome and Pearl know."

"A big, scary Black man and his evil, scheming wife kill two old white people in their home? Can you imagine how that will play out across this country?"

"And how does that added pressure make you feel?" asked Jack.

She glanced at him. "Nervous, but energized and optimistic. You?"

"Right now, honestly, I'm just feeling the nervous part."

CHAPTER 38

THEY MET WITH JEROME AND then Pearl, and told them both what had happened with Battle, and that the trial would commence in two weeks.

Jerome had broken down and sobbed into his hands, muttering the name of his wife over and over. They left him inconsolable.

For her part, Pearl was only upset that Jerome had even offered to enter a plea without talking to her first. "He didn't do it, so he shouldn't be punished. No, no, no."

"All right, but you really need to tell us where you were that day," said DuBose.

However, Pearl curled into a little ball of stiffened resistance and refused to answer.

Jack and DuBose headed out in his Fiat. Their next stop was the medical examiner's office to see the bodies.

Herman Till was tall and loose-jointed, with ruddy cheeks and curly gray hair, and wore a stained lab coat. He escorted them over to a wall with metal drawers.

"How's your momma?" Till asked Jack.

"Doing okay."

Till said to DuBose, "We go to the same church. She sings in the choir, has a fine voice." He eyed Jack curiously. "I know your daddy doesn't come anymore, but Hilly did with Lucy. Only they haven't been attending lately."

"Momma's going through some…things right now," replied Jack.

Till nodded. "Well, let's get to it."

He opened one door and slid out the tray. He picked up a clipboard lying on the chest of the sheeted deceased.

"Mr. Leslie Randolph. Very nice fella. He sponsored me into Willow Oaks." He lifted off the sheet to reveal the dead man. "Multiple slashes to the neck and chest. One hit the carotid artery right there," he added, pointing to a dark, jagged spot on the man's neck with his pen. "The slash is at a forty-five-degree angle and was struck with an upward motion. Almost completely severed it. Woulda bled out real fast. And the killer was almost certainly right-handed."

DuBose glanced at Jack, who recalled Jerome signing his *X* with that hand. He nodded.

"Time of death?" asked DuBose. "Your report said between three and five?"

"Yes. I'm confident with that range."

"And you noted the footprints," said Jack.

"That's right. Sheriff's deputies took the shoes the defendant was wearing and compared them to the marks found in the room. Perfect match."

"*Dirt* marks, but not blood marks with the shoes?" said Jack.

"Correct."

"How about Mrs. Randolph?" asked Jack.

"Her carotid was fully severed. It was strange, though."

"What was?" asked Jack quickly.

"She had a slew of old injuries. Bone fracture to her right scapula. Broken left wrist. Badly healed index finger on the same hand. And there were others."

"So not from her killer?" said DuBose.

"No, these were from years ago. Poor thing probably fell a lot."

"Can we see her body?" asked DuBose.

"Sure thing."

He opened another drawer, slid out the table, and lifted the sheet. The petite Anne Randolph looked supremely wilted in death as though only barely half of her remained.

Jack took out his Brownie camera. "You mind?"

"Fire away."

He took pictures of the mortal wounds on both bodies.

"You can see the cut right there on her neck. Same angle, only it came on a downward stroke," said Till.

"Looks like a deep bruise on her left cheek," said DuBose.

"It is. Probably during the struggle. Room was a real mess."

"I saw no injuries on Jerome, other than what the deputy did to him," Jack said.

"He's a big, strong young man and the Randolphs were old. They had no chance."

"So did Leslie Randolph have bruises or other injuries that would show he'd been in a struggle?" asked DuBose.

"No, nothing like that." Till slid the drawers closed.

"And Jerome Washington's footprints were the only ones there?" said Jack.

"Other than the deputies'. Let me show you." Till opened a file drawer and pulled out some photos. "That's your client. His shoes, his footprints."

Jack looked at a couple of the pictures and said, "And these are from where he was kneeling beside Mrs. Randolph as he lifted her into the chair?"

"I don't know about him lifting her, but they match his shoe soles."

"Lot of places where the blood spatter is all mashed together," said DuBose.

"Well, they were struggling, like I said," noted Till. "In fact, it smeared the Randolphs' footprints completely. Couldn't find a one of them in the blood."

"But how long could they really struggle?" asked DuBose pointedly. "Like you said, they were old, and Jerome is a big, strong man."

Till shrugged. "Don't know. I wasn't there. All I can do is look at the evidence."

"Do you have Jerome's clothes here?" asked DuBose.

"Yes, ma'am. Over in that closet."

They took a look at them.

Jack said, "There are no bloodstains on his pants or shirt. How is that possible if blood was flying all over the place?"

"He cut their carotids for sure. But if the blow caused them to face away from him, the blood spatter might've missed him."

"He said he tried to lift Mr. Randolph into his chair and *did* lift his wife. I'm assuming their clothes were covered in blood?"

"Oh yes, they sure were," replied Till.

"Then how did he not get blood on him?"

"Well, he *said* he put her in the chair."

"But she was *found* in the chair," said DuBose.

Till scratched his ear. "Well, after she was struck she could have just fallen into the chair, or she was attacked there in the first place. That might also account for the angle the weapon hit her from."

"Does the evidence show that was actually possible?" DuBose asked.

"Well, I don't think it shows it was *impossible*."

"But that doesn't explain her *handprint* being found on the floor, does it?" said DuBose. "That was also in your report."

Till looked uncertain. "No, ma'am, it sure doesn't."

"In your report you said a long-bladed instrument was the murder weapon," noted DuBose.

"Yes. Nearly cut poor Mrs. Randolph's head off. The mortician will have a job with that unless they're going to have a closed casket."

"How do you think it might have been wielded?" asked Jack.

Till squared his feet, lifted his right arm in the air, and took a downward swing with it, his hips rotating and the heel of his right foot lifting off the floor. "Sort of like a tennis player serving a ball.

Now that was Anne Randolph. With Leslie Randolph, the blow came from below his neck and hit him at an upward angle." He lowered his hand and lifted it. "Like that."

"And the blood patterns substantiate that?" said DuBose.

"Well, close enough. Anything else?"

"Can we see the shoes?" asked DuBose.

He opened another door and pulled out a pair of large, battered brogans that had no visible blood on them.

While DuBose held the shoes Jack snapped several pictures of them.

"Okay, we appreciate it, Mr. Till."

"You tell your momma to come on back to church. I miss her voice."

"I sure will." Under his breath Jack added, "There are a lot of things I miss about her."

CHAPTER 39

JACK DROVE DOWN A NARROW dirt and gravel street with run-down buildings on either side. Cora Robinson lived in a two-room apartment in one of them. Robinson was small boned and wiry with short, dark hair. Her wide eyes were brown and watery. She had Jack and DuBose sit on the couch while she took a seat in a chair across from them.

"I understand you have children?" said Jack.

"Yes, sir. Little boy and a girl."

"So that's why you always left at two from the Randolphs?" said DuBose.

"That's right. I go to the school to fetch 'em and we walk home together. Their last day of school was when the Randolphs were killed. Just awful."

"And your husband?" asked Jack.

She looked down. "Been four years now since he died."

"I'm sorry."

"Hard work with just one of me. After I get the children from school I do sewin'. I get paid for it. Place give me a Singer sewin' machine to do the work for them. My momma taught me. I do all sorts of dresses and coats and pants and what-not for their customers. After dinner and then when the children go to bed, I keep right on sewin'. But now I got to get another job cleanin' during the day. Sewin' alone don't pay the bills."

"Can you tell us about that day?" asked Jack.

She looked at him nervously. "I talked to the police."

"I know. But we're representing Jerome and Pearl Washington, and we need to hear it directly from you."

Her lips trembled. "I like Jerome. He a good man."

"You don't think he killed the Randolphs?" asked DuBose.

"I never thought Jerome would hurt a fly."

"Okay, just take us through the day and then we'll have some questions based on what you told the police."

Robinson cleared her throat. "I get to work 'bout nine 'less the bus is late. At the Randolphs I do the housework and help with the lunch and all."

"And did you see the Randolphs that day?"

"Oh sure, I seen 'em both."

"And they seemed normal?" asked Jack.

Her facial muscles tensed. "Y-yeah, nothin' off that I could see."

"And did you see Jerome that day?" he asked.

"No. Sometimes I do, but sometimes not. Depend on what he's doin' and all."

"When did you leave that day?"

"I cleaned up the lunch dishes, and give the kitchen a good wipe down till right 'round two. I got my purse and left."

"Did you say goodbye to the Randolphs?" asked Jack.

"No. After lunch they usually take a little nap at the back 'a the house."

"And do you lock the front door when you leave?"

"I don't go out the front door. I go out the back. Just close it behind me. I don't have no key."

"Did you see a blue convertible out front when you were leaving? Or did you see it driving by when you were walking to the bus stop?" asked Jack.

"No, I never seen nothin' like that."

"Did you see anyone else that day?"

"Mailman come round that mornin'."

"And he left a package on the porch, we heard?" said DuBose.

"Yeah, he did."

"Did you see the package?" asked Jack.

"Yes, sir. I took it inside and put it on the table in the front hall."

"Do you remember anything about it?" asked DuBose. "Who it came from? Who it was addressed to? Its size or shape?"

"I didn't look at the label or nothin'. It was about this size." With her hands she made a small, rectangular shape.

"Was it heavy?" asked Jack.

"No."

"Could you hear anything rattling around inside?"

"Nuh-uh. I think it might have paper inside. Felt like it."

"Was it still on the table when you were leaving?" asked DuBose.

"No. I figured the Randolphs got it after I put it there."

DuBose was writing all of this down while Jack asked, "Now, you told the police that Jerome had come into the house alone one time before that you know of?"

Robinson stared down at her hands. "I don't wanna get Jerome in no trouble. But he *was* in the house and he only supposed to come in if the Randolphs ask him to do some work in there. And Mr. Leslie, he always stay with Jerome when he do come in." She glanced at DuBose. "It just how he like to do things," she added quickly.

"Did you ask Jerome why he was in the house that time?" asked Jack.

"Yeah. He say he have to, you know, use the toilet." She looked down at her hands again, clearly embarrassed to be revealing this.

"Don't they have a bathroom for him to use?" asked Jack. "I mean, the man is there all day."

"No, they don't got no bathroom outside. Jerome, he just goes behind a tree if he has to pee. But that day he come in the back door and said he had to do the other one real bad. The Randolphs were out takin' a walk so I didn't see no harm in it. I showed him which bathroom to use, and I went in there after and gave it a real good scrubbin' down. Then I give Jerome a roll of toilet paper and tell him to keep it in the garage. That way he can go behind a tree for the other one and then take care 'a his business after."

Jack shook his head. In his mind was Miss Jessup being at Ashby's all day.

Surely to God he lets her...

"Did you tell the Randolphs?" asked DuBose.

"No. I never had no reason to tell 'em. I scrubbed it down real good. They never be able to tell he was in there."

"And how did you come to tell the police this?"

Robinson looked scared. "They ask me if I ever seen Jerome in the house before, without Mr. Leslie bein' with him. They say if I lie, I go to jail. I can't go to no jail. I told 'em he had to use the toilet."

"Okay, that's fine, Mrs. Robinson. Now, how were things between Jerome and the Randolphs?" asked DuBose.

"Oh, real good. They liked Jerome. A lot."

"You never heard any harsh words between them?" asked Jack.

"Harsh words? Why, no."

"Were you there when they had the Washingtons over for lunch and to swim?"

"No, but he told me about it. It was on the weekend and I don't work then. He say his children really liked it." She looked disappointed. "They never let me bring my children over there for lunch and swimmin', and I been workin' there longer'n Jerome."

"Did he tell you he saw Christine Hanover and her family as they were leaving?"

"Yeah, he did."

"Have you ever seen Christine, or Sam Randolph?" asked Jack.

"Miss Christine come pretty often. I haven't seen Mr. Sam in a long while. But he could come over when I'm not there."

Jack said, "Were you there when a man came by to talk to the Randolphs? Jerome said Mr. Randolph was very angry about it."

"Yep, I seen him. He was dressed in a nice suit and carryin' a black bag. I thought he a doctor or somethin'."

Jack asked, "Did you hear any of the conversation between them?"

"No, sir, but when the man left I hear Mr. Leslie say somethin' like 'I got me enemies all over the place. And I won't stand for it.' And Miss Anne? She was cryin'."

"Did you ask them what the trouble was?" said DuBose.

"Oh no, ma'am. I mean, I think they be mad to know I hear what I did. So I didn't say one word about it to them. But Mr. Leslie, he real mad."

"Did he get mad often?" asked DuBose curiously.

"Yeah, he had a temper all right. And…"

"And what?"

"I don't know if I want to say."

"Please, Mrs. Robinson, we really need to be told everything. We don't know what might help Jerome and his wife," said DuBose.

"Well, Mr. Leslie, when he gets riled sometimes at Miss Anne, he…he might hit her 'round some." She looked down and seemed frightened at having disclosed this.

DuBose and Jack exchanged glances. "You saw this?" she asked.

"They don't know I did, but I did, yeah."

"And what did Mrs. Randolph do?" asked DuBose.

"She calm him down. She real good at that. Then Miss Anne go on upstairs and fix herself up and Mr. Leslie go get himself a drink."

"Did he drink a lot?" asked DuBose.

"More'n he should," she said candidly.

"Well, I think that's all for now," said Jack, standing.

However, DuBose remained seated. "Mrs. Robinson, when Jack asked you if the Randolphs seemed normal that day, you seemed to hesitate for a moment. Is there something you were thinking about?"

Robinson fidgeted with her hands for a few moments. "It was durin' lunch that day. Mr. Leslie, he just seemed mad 'bout somethin'. Fumin', so to speak."

"Do you know what about?"

"No, but he had a real sour look on his face."

"And Mrs. Randolph?"

"She looked…worried."

"Well, thank you for telling us, Mrs. Robinson," said DuBose. "And were *you* allowed to use the bathroom at the Randolphs'?"

"Oh no, ma'am. But I'm only there for five hours. So's I just hold it. And there's some bushes behind the bus stop where I can do my business."

DuBose squeezed her hand. "Thank you for speaking with us."

"I hope…I hope Jerome will be okay and all. He never killed nobody."

"Now we just have to prove it," said DuBose.

CHAPTER 40

So THAT MIGHT EXPLAIN ANNE Randolph's old injuries that Herman Till told us about," said DuBose after they left Robinson's home. "They probably resulted from her husband beating her."

"So Leslie Randolph was not the nice guy everyone thought he was."

"So where to now?" she asked.

"Tyler Dobbs, the gardener."

As they were walking back to Jack's car a sheriff's patrol car slowed to a stop and two men got out and headed toward them. Jack whispered to DuBose, "The deputies who arrested and then beat up Jerome."

"What in the world are you doing in this part of the county?" said Jack as the pair approached. "You aren't following us now, are you?"

Gene Taliaferro eyed DuBose and then glanced at Jack. "I heard 'bout this gal, but I didn't believe it till I seen it with my own two eyes."

"Believe what, Deputy?" said DuBose pleasantly.

"I ain't talkin' to you, woman, am I?" barked Gene.

"Miss DuBose is in town to help me," said Jack.

"You mean to tell me you're *workin'* with this here n——?"

"I don't appreciate your offensive language, Deputy," said DuBose stiffly.

"And I don't *appreciate* you being in my county," Gene shot back.

Jack stepped in between them. "Okay, we'll be moving on."

LeRoy said, "They're gonna fry both of 'em now we got the electric chair all fired up again."

Gene got in Jack's face. "Hey, I wonder if we can get *you* fried at the same time?" He glanced disdainfully at DuBose. "Maybe they can strap both of you on. Chocolate and vanilla sundae on fire," he added gleefully.

DuBose edged up to Gene, who looked immensely pleased with himself. "Deputy, let me just tell you that I have been baited by white men far superior to you and they failed spectacularly. So someone with your decided lack of ingenuity and intelligence will have no chance whatsoever. But if you try to lay a hand on me, though I have given you no cause to do so, I will have you arrested. And then I will sue you for everything you have, everything your family has, and everything you or they might have in the future. And on top of that I will have a team of United States attorneys prosecute you for violations of the Civil Rights Act of 1964, which carry a lengthy sentence in a federal penitentiary. I hope I've made myself clear."

His patronizing grin vanishing, Gene took a step back.

LeRoy said, "Oh, we understand all right. And you understand this. You're in Freeman County now. The federal government don't count for shit here."

She turned to him and coolly said, "Two flags fly at every courthouse in this country, including Freeman County, and the one on top is always the Stars and Stripes."

Gene looked at LeRoy for a moment before turning to Jack. "Boys that came for you? They ain't done, I can tell you that."

"Well, I need to shoot the rest of that asshole's ear off, anyway. You can tell him that, since I'm sure you know him."

Gene and LeRoy got back into their cruiser and slowly pulled away.

DuBose said, "We need to really watch our backs now."

"I've been watching *both* our backs ever since you got to town."
He opened his briefcase to show her his gun inside.

* * *

Tyler Dobbs lived in a ramshackle cottage a few miles from Jack's
parents. In the backyard was a small greenhouse and stacks of gar-
dening supplies and tools. An old, rusted Dodge pickup was slant-
parked next to the house. Its bed was piled high with tools and bags
of seed and what smelled like manure. There was a trailer hitched to
it that held a lawnmower and other equipment.

They got out, and Jack ventured over to the greenhouse and
peeked inside.

"Hey, what the hell y'all doin' here?" barked a voice.

Jack looked over to see a cornstalk of a man with a cold gaze and
stubbly beard standing in the doorway of the cottage. He was holding a shotgun.

"Tyler Dobbs?" asked DuBose.

"Who wants to know?" he said.

Jack and DuBose walked over to Dobbs.

"Jack Lee and Desiree DuBose, attorneys for Jerome and Pearl
Washington."

"What's that got to do with me?"

"You're on the prosecution's witness list. You have provided testimony to them against our clients. Because of that you have to talk
to us."

"Who says?"

"The law."

"I don't see no law 'round here." He brandished the over-and-
under shotgun. "Just this gun."

"Well, let me put it to you this way. If you don't talk to us, we
can have your testimony stricken from the record and you may end
up getting our clients found innocent. I wonder what the police will
think of that?"

Dobbs said sourly, "What you wanna know, lawyer?"

DuBose took out her notebook. "You said that the Randolphs were going to get rid of Mr. Washington because he was belligerent?"

"You talkin' to me?" Dobbs snapped.

"Yes, I am. *Belligerent*? Can you give me an example?"

Dobbs came off the steps and said, "Who the hell are you? As a rule I don't allow coloreds on my property. They're always stealin' stuff."

Jack said, "I already told you who she is. She's an attorney for the Washingtons."

Dobbs looked like he might laugh. "A colored woman lawyer?"

DuBose said brightly, "They've actually been turning us out for a long time now."

"The hell you say?"

"Now, an example of *belligerent*?" she prompted.

"Well, that was the word the lawyer used, not me."

"What would be *your* word then?" asked DuBose.

"He was being, you know, uppity. Shooting off his mouth." He stopped and looked at DuBose. "They were scared 'a him."

"And when did this happen?" she asked.

"Lot 'a times."

"Then why did they keep him on?"

"They were scared 'a him, like I said. He's a big man. Could put the hurtin' on you. And he did, he killed 'em."

"Why would he do that?" asked Jack.

"'Cause he needed money. He told me so."

"When?"

"Few weeks ago. Said he needed money and was figurin' out how to get it."

At that moment they heard a dog barking. A few seconds later a large German shepherd hurtled from the open door and sprinted flat-out at them.

Jack jumped forward to block the dog, but Dobbs kicked the animal as it passed by him, sending the beast sprawling violently in the dirt. It lay there, whimpering and shaking one of its paws. Dobbs walked over and kicked the dog in the side, making it yelp.

"Damn dog. Now it's lame. Well, that's that." He pointed the shotgun at the animal's head.

DuBose rushed over to stand between him and the injured dog. She screamed, "Don't you dare shoot that dog!"

"The hell I can't. It's my damn dog."

DuBose knelt next to the panting and injured dog. She placed a calming hand on its heaving chest and said in a soothing voice, "It's okay, baby. We're going to take care of you." She looked at Dobbs. "What's her name?"

"She ain't got no name. Just a mutt I found wanderin' 'round. Damn useless. Shoulda got rid 'a her a long time ago."

DuBose noted the ribs showing and the filthy fur and skin of the animal. "She's obviously undernourished and has mange."

"So?"

DuBose looked at Jack. "Do you know a vet?"

"I do, yes."

"Can you carry her to the car, Jack?"

Dobbs barked, "You ain't takin' my dog. I'm gonna kill it."

"How much do you want for it?"

"What?"

"How much money do you want for the dog?" said DuBose.

Dobbs lowered the gun and scratched his chin. "Ten bucks."

DuBose pulled out a ten-dollar bill from her purse and handed it to him. "Now she's *my* dog."

Jack gingerly lifted the animal and put her in the back seat of the Fiat.

DuBose looked at Dobbs and asked, "You have any more animals?"

"Nope."

"Good. Keep it that way."

DuBose rode in the back with the dog and gently stroked her ears. Jack looked at her in the mirror. "I take it you like dogs?"

She eyed him with a sad smile. "Sunny. He was a chocolate Lab

I had growing up. He died in my arms when I was fifteen. I've never cried that hard in my life."

"I had one of those, too. What are you going to call her?"

DuBose looked the dog over and her features brightened. "Queenie. She has a noble look about her. Do you really think Dobbs would have shot her?"

"Hell yes. I thought he was going to shoot us, too."

They drove to a vet, who determined Queenie had no broken or fractured bones. They ran some blood tests, and the dog was given a bath. The vet gave DuBose some medications for the pain and said he would call when the test results came back, but he suspected Queenie had worms, among other things.

"Otherwise, it doesn't look like anything's much wrong with her that some good food and a lot of love won't fix," said the vet kindly.

They stopped at a store, and DuBose bought dog dishes, food, a leash, and a comfy blanket for Queenie to sleep on. She said, "I'll make arrangements for her."

"No need, Desiree. If you hadn't bought her off that bastard I was going to."

Jack carried Queenie inside his office. DuBose fed the dog and gave Queenie water and the first dose of her meds.

Queenie licked DuBose's hand appreciatively, a simple gesture that caused the woman's eyes to glisten. She sat on the floor next to Queenie, stroking her head, and the dog promptly fell asleep with her muzzle on DuBose's lap. Twenty minutes later DuBose slowly disengaged her, and Queenie rolled over and continued her slumber.

She said, "It's amazing what a simple act of kindness can inspire. Humans should try it more often."

"That 'unconditional love' thing is pretty damn powerful," noted Jack.

DuBose glanced at him with a troubled look. "And there always comes a time when it exacts a heavy price."

CHAPTER 41

DURING DINNER AT JACK'S PLACE, DuBose put her fork down. "Did you always know you wanted to be a lawyer?"

He smiled. "No. At first I wanted to be a mechanic like my daddy, then a pilot and then an astronaut. But growing up I had a neighbor named Ashby. He was a lawyer. Now, he was not the sort of lawyer I wanted to be, but he talked to me some about the profession. And I read all the Perry Mason books. I had just started law school when the TV show with Raymond Burr came on. It got me thinking."

"So you wanted to be Perry Mason then?" she said, looking amused.

"I wanted to be something, I guess," he said contemplatively. "At least more than what I was. But I believed I could help people who needed it. Criminal defense work is pretty much all I've ever done. Most of my clients aren't bad. They've just had bad things happen to them and then they made poor decisions because of that. My daddy always said don't judge anybody unless you've lived in their skin. And I don't. At least I try not to." He peered at her. "How about you? What were your dreams?"

DuBose sat back and looked off for a moment, gathering her thoughts. "I originally wanted to be a teacher. You know, exposing young minds to all the things they needed to know. And showing them how to be kind and tolerant. There's far too much hate and anger in folks."

"But you didn't end up teaching?"

"I had just finished my first year of college when a relative was killed in Louisiana by a local sheriff."

"What happened?"

"My cousin was trying to travel to the North for work, and the sheriff had been paid a bounty to stop any Black person trying to do that. They wanted to scare others from leaving because Black folks were needed to do the physical labor down there, or else the Southern economy would collapse. He waited at the bus station, said my cousin attacked him, and then shot him. In the back."

"Was he arrested?"

She looked at him funny. "This was the late 1940s in Louisiana, Jack. There was no earthly chance of a white lawman ever being charged for killing a Black person."

"And that made you want to be a lawyer?"

"That and the fact that when we went to the funeral, the man who shot him was at the church. And as we were walking out after the service, he tapped his gun and laughed."

"You must have wanted to kill the bastard."

"What I wanted to do was make sure his kind could never wear a badge or carry a gun. And I believed I could change this country one lawsuit at a time. And all these years later I feel both enormously hopeful and terribly depressed, often at the same time."

"If this isn't a fight worth having, I don't know what is, Desiree."

"How do you manage to live here if that's how you feel?' she said bluntly.

He picked at his food and then put down his fork. "This is my home, for better or worse. But if you want the truth, I've been wrestling with all these issues since I was little. Only I never did anything about it but think on things, get frustrated at how the country was divided up. I never looked for the chance to do something different, either. I guess I was just...I don't know."

"Since it didn't really affect you, Jack, you probably just went along leading your life. I'm not saying that was right, I'm just saying it was convenient. And why bring trouble on yourself if you didn't have to, especially when all you've been taught is that Blacks and whites should not mix?"

"Which makes me even more ashamed the way you just laid it out. Anyway, then Miss Jessup and Jerome came along, and I suddenly had this opportunity to do something…something risky, but important. But even with that, I had decided not to get involved when I got a phone call that said I was a—well it just called me a real bad name. And it was obvious that Jerome needed to be defended just like any other man because that's what he is, a man. But to be totally honest, I've had second thoughts, I've had doubts. I've been scared. I've never been involved in something like this. *You* go from one of these situations to another all the time. But this is my first. It makes a man think a lot about what he's done with his life, or what he *hasn't* done with it. And what he could do with it…if he had enough courage."

"You've *shown* courage," she said, eyeing the still-visible injuries on his face.

"Not like you. And you're doing it without my skin color, which at least gives me some protection." He paused and added, "Look, clearly I'm no Atticus Finch. I'm nobody's hero, or savior. Fact is, I can barely save myself most days."

"Despite what Harper Lee wrote in that book, I've never once met an Atticus Finch in the South. Quite the opposite." She gave him a look. "But maybe I will, as this case goes along."

He glanced up from his plate as her meaning broke over him and shook his head. "I'm not sure I have that sort of fortitude in me, Desiree."

"You never know until the opportunity arises."

"How do *you* keep doing what you're doing? With all the crap thrown at you?"

"After hundreds of years of slavery and then another century of

Jim Crow, which is slavery as well, just without the shackles showing, white people ask why Blacks can't get their act together. As
though white society is the victim and not the culprit. We live with
the fact that many white people in this country will do everything
in their power to break us. Every minute of every day, both by their
actions and their inactions. The sheer wrongness of that is what
keeps me going, Jack. And all that hell, all that misery, for *everybody*, is simply because of this."

She placed her hand next to his.

"But of course it's not just the color. It's everything that it represents. Whites may be ashamed of what was done to my race, but
instead of turning that into constructive action, it's like they have
decided that they will use that shame to make our lives as hard as
possible. Whether it's because they don't feel responsible since they
never owned slaves, or they just feel we are so different that we don't
belong here—even though the sweat and labor of *my* race helped
build this country—they seem determined to ensure that the lives of
Blacks will never be anything but nasty, brutish, and short, to borrow from Thomas Hobbes." She looked at Jack and added, "Maybe
in a millennium, if the human race is still around, they might look
back at this time and wonder how people could be so...cruel and
wrong." She shook her head. "But I doubt it."

"I hope you're mistaken about that, Desiree," he said somberly.

"I pray every night that I am."

CHAPTER 42

JACK DROPPED DUBOSE AT THE George Wythe Hotel and watched her walk all the way in before driving off.

DuBose headed across the lobby to the elevators, nodding and saying hello to the man at the front desk, who stared rigidly back at her without speaking. She ran into another fellow mopping the floors by the elevator. He was around sixty and Black, with a twisted spine that made him wince every time he thrust the mop out. He also had a large lump on one side of his face.

"Hello," said DuBose.

He looked up at her and smiled. "Evenin', ma'am."

"You look to be in some pain," she noted.

He shrugged. "Just got me the rheumatism and such, creak in the bones I call it."

"And the lump on your face?"

"Somethin' bit me, I reckon."

"Have you seen a doctor?" she asked.

"Naw, I be fine."

"I think you should see someone. It looks infected."

"Colored hospital a right long ways from here."

"The law now says they can't deny you care just because you're Black."

He looked surprised by this but said, "Well, doctors cost money."

She opened her purse and took out a twenty-dollar bill. "Here."

"I can't take that."

"Why not?"

"Well, I don't know you and I ain't done nothin' for it."

"Take it, go get the lump checked, and maybe they can look at your back, too."

"No, ma'am. I'm not gonna do that." He looked her over and said, "You dress mighty fine. You rich?"

"No, but I make a good salary."

"What is you?"

"A lawyer," replied DuBose.

He cracked a grin. "Go on now, missy. You say you a lawyer?"

"I am."

"What you doin' here?" he asked.

"Jerome and Pearl Washington? They're accused of killing the Randolphs. I'm defending them."

The grin slowly faded. "Then you best keep your money. You gone need it."

"What do you mean?" said a startled DuBose.

"*You* gone need a doctor after all is said and done."

He put the mop in his pail and rolled it off down the hall. DuBose slowly put the money back in her purse.

As DuBose waited for the elevator a man walked around the corner and stopped.

Judge Ambrose said, "I didn't know you were staying here, Miss DuBose."

"It's convenient."

"Yes, yes it is."

"Not to speak out of turn, but I was surprised that they removed Judge Bliley from the case and brought you in."

"Not as surprised as I was. I was retired when I got the call."

"So how did it happen?"

A moment later Howard Pickett joined them. "You two know each other?" he asked, looking surprised.

"No," said Ambrose. He glanced at Pickett with what DuBose took to be a mildly disgusted look. "But I understand you and Miss DuBose have a history."

"That's one way to refer to it," said DuBose curtly.

They all climbed into the car and Pickett said, "Which floor, Miss DuBose?"

She hesitated, not really wanting to answer. "Um, five."

He pushed the button for the fifth floor and then the third, while Ambrose selected the fourth.

Pickett said, "Not too long ago, this hotel would not have catered to Negroes. Sad they had to be forced to do so. I mean, it's against some folks' faith."

DuBose said, "What faith would that be? Ignorance or evil? Or both?"

Pickett said, "Come on, you know Blacks and whites are better off separated."

Before she could respond Ambrose spoke up. "I would strongly advise you to keep your mouth shut before you find yourself in trouble, sir."

Pickett slumped against the wall and kept quiet.

He got off on his floor. When they arrived at the fourth floor Ambrose nodded at DuBose as he stepped off.

DuBose shook her head, unable to make sense of what had just happened.

CHAPTER 43

DUBOSE UNDRESSED, WASHED HER FACE, wrapped her hair in the silk scarf, put on her nightgown, and sat on the bed. She opened the drawer of the nightstand and took out the Gideon Bible housed there. Instead of following the more traditional Southern Baptist religion, her mother had been a Catholic, and she had raised her children in that faith. However, unwilling to rely on the priests to interpret the Bible for her, DuBose had studied the scriptures. During her youth they had represented some of the most important lessons in her life, a touchstone that helped guide her through what the world had in store for folks like her. It was no coincidence, she believed, that Dr. King's undergraduate degree had been in divinity and his doctorate in theology; and he had been an ordained minister as well, preaching with his father at Ebenezer Baptist Church in Atlanta. Only deep faith could keep one going through times like these, she believed.

She had never known the Deep South as a child, other than driving there with her parents, or taking the train to attend marriages and funerals of relatives there. She would always remember that when the train got near the Mason-Dixon Line it would stop, and all the Black passengers would have to give up the seats they had paid for and move back to the decrepit "Jim Crow" car, as it was known. This was done so that whites could take the Black passengers' seats and travel the rest of the way without having to endure the sight of someone who looked like her. DuBose's family also had to pack picnic baskets because the availability of food largely ceased for Blacks on the Southern side of the country.

On the way north the process was reversed, and she and her family would retake their seats that they had paid for. Her parents didn't really explain any of this to her, but DuBose was smart enough to quickly figure it out on her own. And when they had traveled for the first time back to Louisiana to visit a relative in the late 1930s, her parents had made clear to her and her siblings the rules of the road, as they called them.

She was never to look at, talk to, or touch a white person. She was to move to the other side of the street when a white person was coming along. If the police stopped you, you made no sudden moves. And you never talked back. You never went in a white entrance. DuBose was also taught never to drink from a fountain marked for whites only. She had to use the toilet marked COLORED WOMEN, never the restroom with the sign that read WHITE LADIES. And she would always sit in the back of the bus with her gaze in her lap.

She also knew that if a white person made fun of her or called her a bad name, she had to keep on walking and bite her tongue. If they tried to pick a fight, she could not take the bait.

DuBose stopped making this mental list in her head and thought about the lives sacrificed to overturn almost every one of those "rules."

Restless, she once more slipped the picture of two people from her wallet to complete her nightly ritual. It was a photo of her and the man she had loved and hoped to marry.

A man who is now dead.

No one had been arrested. No one had been held accountable.

She had not told this story to anyone, because she could barely admit it to herself.

She traced the man's smile with her finger and then put the photo away. She rose and went to the window and opened it. The hotel did not have air-conditioning, and the light breeze coming in through the opening was welcome to her.

Her parents had liked Chicago well enough, but they had missed Louisiana's raw heat and humidity, and the absence of any real winter. And they missed the spicy Creole food. And the daily hugs and smiles from their families and friends. But those were really the only things they had missed about being Black while in the South.

But all the major Northern cities had their Black-concentrated areas: Harlem in New York. The South Side, where DuBose lived, in Chicago. There were slums and ghettos in Baltimore, Detroit, Philadelphia, St. Louis. This was accomplished by banks refusing to loan to Blacks in white areas; Realtors not showing Blacks any homes in white neighborhoods; and, of course, restrictive deed covenants that outright prohibited sales to Blacks.

Much like Native Americans forcefully sequestered onto reservations, Blacks had thus been relegated to areas where the housing—dilapidated though it was—and other associated costs were exorbitant, the jobs scarce and low-paying, the crime and drug use high, the loan sharks and pawnbrokers ubiquitous, the imperious police omnipresent, and the deep feeling of inferiority and isolation inspired and demanded by the white community rampant. How could anyone really be happy being *told* where they had to live? thought DuBose. And knowing that it was solely because Blacks were deemed not good enough to coexist with whites.

With all that, any hope by her race should have been nonexistent, DuBose realized. And yet folks got up every day and went about their lives as best they could. For DuBose, that was all she needed to show that Blacks were the equal of whites. Indeed, they had to work harder and more cleverly and cautiously for less than any white person she knew.

But then a politician or newspaper would tout that a few had made it out of these dire circumstances. If you just work harder, sacrifice more, tug those bootstraps with more vigor, you, too, can make it out, the message went. Even if it was only one in ten thousand.

Yet people's abilities and experiences were not monolithic and thus one method of success was not easily replicated for everyone. And touting the victory of one amid the "failure" of ten thousand was fine for the one, but it did nothing to aid the ten thousand, and it certainly should not be a reason to do nothing except encourage harder personal bootstrapping.

DuBose closed her eyes and mused:

If a heart surgery was only successful once every ten thousand operations, or a plane landing safely occurred only once every ten thousand times, what would people demand? Change the way it was done. Now.

From her satchel she slipped out an old copy of the *Green Book*, a publication that she and her family had used for many years and that told Blacks where they would be welcomed while traveling, allowing them to avoid danger. As a child she vividly recalled that her parents would always leave long before dawn when the family was driving to the South, to avoid traveling late at night. You didn't want to end up in a sundown town on the wrong side of the clock, when whites went looking for Blacks to arrest or kill.

This often meant that Blacks had to drive fifteen, twenty, or more hours without stopping if the distance was great enough, and nighttime driving could not be avoided. DuBose visualized the bucket of cold water and washcloths her mother would pack, and which she would apply to her husband's face and neck to keep him awake as they passed by places of rest unavailable to them. She knew of several families who had lost loved ones in car crashes because the driver had fallen asleep. That was another bite that Jim Crow took out of Black flesh.

She also was aware that white people often chastised or made outright fun of her race for "wasting" their money on large, fancy cars with powerful engines instead of buying homes. The reasons, at least to Black folks, were obvious.

Since Blacks weren't really allowed to purchase homes, nice cars were really the only way to show affluence and accomplishment.

And the automobiles they typically purchased were large because often whole families had to sleep in them. And the powerful engines were critical, to outrun whites intent on doing them harm, including the police.

Before they were old enough to really understand, DuBose and her siblings wanted to know why they couldn't stop at a motel or eat at a restaurant along the way like white people. Arguments ensued between them and their parents. DuBose more than once observed the look of deep shame on her father's face, though she now knew the shame had nothing to do with him or them.

The *Green Book* had ceased publication in 1967, after the passage of the Civil Rights Act. Still, DuBose carried the last edition with her because she never wanted to forget how far her race had come. Because if you did, you might end up back where you started. And while one Supreme Court had finally done the right thing in overturning the doctrine of separate but equal, a future Supreme Court could easily take it all away. Nothing was certain, or forever.

DuBose stiffened when she heard footsteps outside her door. She walked quietly over to it and put her eye to the peephole.

DuBose screamed and leapt back an instant before the fired bullet tore through the cylinder of glass, and lodged in the far wall.

She collapsed onto the floor because her legs had suddenly failed her. She frantically crawled away from the door and jerkily picked at the bits of wood and glass that had ended up on her hair, skin, and nightgown. She then wrapped her arms around her knees and sat there, trying to get her breath, her heart, and her nerves all under control.

When it was apparent no one was coming, she managed to rise and walk unsteadily over to the nightstand. She picked up the phone and called Jack.

"Hey, everything okay?" he said quickly.

"N-no, it's…it's actually not."

She told him. He was there in five minutes. He had called the police before he left. They met him there. Two patrolmen hurried up to the room with him and interviewed DuBose, and dug the bullet out of the wall. No one at the hotel had seen or heard anything, so they said.

"This has to stop," Jack told them. "It's only by the grace of God she's not dead."

One of the officers said, "Colored communities all up in arms what with their preacher gettin' himself killed. Riotin' and burnin' and such. Got white folks on edge. Make 'em do things they might not otherwise do."

"Dr. King didn't get himself killed," snapped DuBose. "Someone *murdered* him."

The same officer looked at her. "Well, I guess you're entitled to your opinion."

After they left Jack said, "Pack up, you're coming to stay with me."

"Jack, I can't. You know what people will—"

"I don't give a damn about that, Desiree," he interjected. "You almost died."

"All right, I'll stay with you *tonight*. Tomorrow we'll see how things are."

"You know as well as I do that they're not going to be any better tomorrow."

CHAPTER 44

THE NEXT MORNING, JACK, WHO had slept on the small couch in his office, rose to find DuBose already dressed and cooking breakfast in the kitchen.

Queenie was eating from her bowl. The dog glanced up and wagged her tail at Jack. He gave the dog a pat and sat at the kitchen bar in his robe and pajamas. DuBose poured him out a cup of coffee and then turned back to the stove.

"Eggs scrambled and bacon, and toast with butter and jam sound good?"

"Works for me, thanks. How'd you sleep?"

She gave him a playful smirk. "Much better with you and Queenie to protect me."

Jack sipped his coffee and watched her deftly preparing the meal. "You seem to know your way around a kitchen."

"My mother was a fine cook and she taught me."

"You said your father works at Marshall Field's. How about your mother?"

"Cancer took her two years ago."

"I'm sorry to hear that."

"I also have two brothers and three sisters."

"They all doing well?"

"Some are doing better than others. Just like every family, I suppose."

"Any of them follow you into the law?"

"No. My oldest brother is a doctor in San Diego. My youngest sister owns an art gallery in Harlem."

"That's impressive."

"He's a surgeon and a fine one. My sister exhibits established artists as well as up-and-comers. She's been very successful, and influential, in her field."

Jack watched her for a few moments before saying, "You okay after last night?"

She put his food on a plate and slid it in front of him, along with a paper napkin and utensils. "It wasn't the first time someone tried to kill me. And it won't be the last."

"But I suppose a person doesn't really get used to that. At least I hope you don't."

DuBose sat down on the stool next to him and cradled her coffee cup in her hands. She looked at Jack, clearly troubled.

"What?" he asked.

"Judge Ambrose and Howard Pickett are staying at the hotel. I was talking to Ambrose when Pickett showed up. We got into the elevator and Pickett asked me what floor I was staying on. I told him."

"And you think...?" began Jack.

"Anyone could have found out what floor I was on. But he didn't know what number my room was. Although he could have gotten that information. I was surprised because Ambrose was polite to me, and even stood up to Pickett when he started his racist stump speech."

Jack nearly dropped his fork. "Seriously?"

"Yes. He told me he was retired and then was called in to take this case. I asked him who had called him, but that's when Pickett showed up and I never got an answer."

"Well, Ambrose treated us pretty fairly on the trial date."

She put her cup down and studied him.

"What?" he said.

"Up till now it's just been the calm before the storm, Jack. Even with the attempt on my life. The real battle hasn't even started." She looked at him questioningly. "So are *you* good?"

"I'm good, Desiree," he replied immediately, meeting her eye.

"I hope so," she said. "I'm counting on you."

After Jack showered and dressed they headed over to Sam Randolph's home.

"I'd like to know how Battle was able to get that search warrant issued that found the money at Jerome's. He had to have a witness to tell him that it might be there."

"We should be able to confront that witness," said Jack.

"We'll move to get the search warrant and the affidavit and any other information they might have. Maybe we can have all of it excluded."

"Jerome doesn't deny he put the money in the lean-to."

"But I don't want the jury drawing negative inferences from that discovery. One frame does not make a whole picture. And the whole matters a lot more than the individual parts, because that conveys an entire story to the jury."

They turned down Cottage Street, which contained columns of small, aging homes, some better kept up than others. They pulled into Randolph's driveway, eased from the Fiat, and looked around. The lawn was dead, the flowerbeds sloppy and untended, the bushes overgrown, with clumps of dead leaves scattered among the green. The house itself was in disrepair; everything seemed to sag with time and lack of care. A one-car garage with peeling paint stood at the back of the property. Jack walked over and tried the banged-up overhead door, but it was locked.

They walked up the crumbling concrete sidewalk to the front door and Jack knocked. They heard footsteps and Randolph opened the door. He wore camel-colored slacks and a T-shirt. He held a newspaper and had on a pair of black specs with thickened lenses.

His body clearly looked withered, and his coloring appeared grayish in the light.

"What are *you* doing here?" he exclaimed.

"We need to ask you some questions," said Jack.

"Not now." He started to close the door, but Jack put a hand against it.

"You're on a witness list provided by the commonwealth. That gives us the right to question you and take your statement."

"I...I was actually going out somewhere. On business."

"Okay, we can follow you and then we can meet after you've finished your business. What kind of car do you drive, by the way?"

"Jesus Christ. All right, all right." Randolph stepped back and waved them in.

The interior held cheap furnishings, stacks of clutter, smells of fried foods, and an air of general neglect that corresponded with the exterior.

Jack noticed the pill bottles lying everywhere, along with some opened mail. Randolph hurried them into the next room, which was a small den furnished with a cracked leather couch and a wooden chair. The square of carpet underneath was badly faded, with loose threads sticking out.

"Let's make this as snappy as possible," he said irritably.

They all sat, and DuBose took out her notebook and pen. She made a show of looking around and then settled an expectant gaze on him.

Randolph fidgeted for a bit. "I've...some business prospects didn't pan out. And my divorce..."

DuBose said, "Those things can take their toll."

"What exactly do you want to know?"

Jack said, "We will take a sworn statement from you before the trial starts, but we need to get some information so we can prepare that. And it will be very, very soon because the trial will start shortly."

"Okay."

"So, what did you tell Mr. Battle?" asked DuBose.

"I told him that my father had mentioned to me that he was going to leave some money for Jerome Washington in his will."

DuBose said, "When did he tell you that?"

"About four months ago. I had gone by to see them one evening."

"Do you know the terms of your parents' will and the disposition of their estate?"

"No. Curtis Gates is supposed to tell us shortly."

"Mr. Randolph," said DuBose, "we were told by Mr. Gates that Jerome Washington is not mentioned in your parents' will."

Randolph looked surprised. "Then my father must have changed his mind. I thought it was absurd. He wasn't family. Why should my parents leave him anything?"

Jack said, "Did Jerome know your father was planning to leave him something?"

"I imagine so."

"Why?"

"Because my father liked to lord his wealth over people. And if he thought it would make this Jerome person work harder? So odds are very good that he *did* tell him."

"So you're saying that Jerome had a motive to kill your parents?"

"Yes. And I told Mr. Battle the very same thing."

CHAPTER 45

THOSE WERE PRESCRIPTION DRUG BOTTLES lying around," said Jack.

They were in the Fiat driving away from Sam Randolph's house.

"And there were bills marked 'Past Due' on his coffee table," noted DuBose.

"So the man is ill and clearly in need of money. Which gives *him* a motive."

"But the real wealth is apparently in the property. And it's held in trust until either Sam or Christine dies."

"Why would he do that to his children, Desiree?"

"Sounds like Leslie Randolph was upset about something."

"The man who visited with a doctor's bag?"

"Maybe," replied DuBose.

They next drove to the Randolphs' estate. The police were still there, and they were allowed inside. They were surprised to find Christine Hanover in the room where her parents had died, holding the picture of them that had been knocked to the floor.

Christine wore a pale blue day dress and black flats. A string of small pearls encircled her slender neck. Her light blond hair skimmed her shoulders.

"I'm sorry," said Jack. "The deputy outside didn't tell us anyone was here."

"It's all right. I just came to collect a few mementos."

"Christine, this is Desiree DuBose, my co-counsel."

"Nice to meet you, Miss DuBose."

"Likewise. My condolences on your loss. And please, make it Desiree."

"And I'm Christine." She held up the damaged photo. "I'll have to get this repaired. It's the only one of them we have before they were married."

"Nice to remember them by," said Jack.

"Yes, it is." She glanced at the bloodied carpet and then quickly looked away.

"While you're here, can we ask you some questions?" asked Jack.

"Okay. But I don't have much time."

"It won't take long. You and your husband were out of town when it happened?"

She paled and looked distraught. "Washington, D.C. Gordon is the president of Virginia Trust Bank and was testifying before Congress on some financial regulations, and was also attending some meetings. I just went along to do some shopping and see some of the sights. With the children at camp we had planned to stay the weekend. Then the news arrived about my parents. We got home around two that morning. My brother had already identified the bodies. I couldn't bring myself to go to the house. I sat home and bawled my eyes out. But I finally pulled myself together and we came here."

"And that's when I saw you and Gordon," noted Jack.

"That's right."

"Do you know the terms of your parents' will?"

"No. I assumed they would leave everything to Sam and me—my deceased siblings died young and had no children. I suppose the lawyer will tell us."

Jack nodded. "Curtis Gates. You know him?"

"Yes, he handles our estate matters, too. We recommended him to my parents."

"Do you know what a tontine is?" asked Jack.

"No, I've never even heard the word."

Jack explained about the terms of the will and how the house and property had been split off from the rest of the estate.

"That is quite odd," Christine commented.

"Is your brother having money and health problems?"

"His divorce was hard. And Sam has his...challenges. He's not working right now. And you're right, his health is not good."

"What's wrong with him?" asked DuBose.

"I don't know, really. But just looking at him it seems serious."

"So any money coming from the estate will be welcome to him?" said Jack.

"Look, the fact is my parents' cash ran out a while ago. Gordon and I have been supporting them for the last few years."

"We weren't aware of that," said Jack, giving DuBose a sharp glance.

"We have plenty of money. Gordon came from wealth and he's handsomely compensated at the bank. We live in Faulkner's Woods. It's only a short walk from here." She eyed Jack. "You know it?"

"Just by reputation. It's the nicest area in Freeman County."

"I would rather my parents' estate just went to Sam. He needs it. We don't."

"You care for your brother?" asked DuBose.

"He was going off to college when I was still an infant, so he and I had never been close. We *did* grow closer when we lost our brother and sister to illness. But the last few years have been...difficult for him."

DuBose said, "Did your father ever talk to you about a man visiting here who made him very angry? He has been described as carrying a bag like a doctor does. Your father was heard to say that he had enemies everywhere and no one was going to force him to leave his home. That might have prompted him to have Gates change their will, separate out the house and property and create the tontine-like arrangement."

"No, he never mentioned anything like that to me."

Jack glanced around and said, "Did your husband come here with you?"

"No, Gordon's at Willow Oaks playing golf with some clients of the bank."

"Do you think he would talk to us now?" asked Jack.

"I'm sure he would be happy to speak with you. He was going to have lunch there, too. You could probably catch him after that. He was the one who suggested helping my parents, by the way."

"That was good of him," said Jack.

"Well, if there's nothing else, I was planning on taking some things and going back home," said Christine. She added soberly, "I have the funerals to arrange."

"I didn't see a car outside. We can give you a lift."

"No, that's all right, Jack. It's just out my parents' rear gate here and a short walk, as I said, to Faulkner's Woods. I can actually use the fresh air."

Christine had turned to leave but then looked back. "If you ever hear from Jeff, tell him I said hello. And tell him I hope he's okay."

"I sure will," said Jack.

After she left DuBose said, "Why do I think she never got over your brother?"

"It's only fair, because I don't believe he ever really got over her."

CHAPTER 46

IN THE BOOKLINED STUDY, JACK found something in the trash can. It was an opened package that fit the description Cora Robinson had provided.

"This might be what was delivered on the morning of the murders. It's from Norfolk," he said, checking the return address. "I didn't search this room the first time I came to the house."

"Who's the sender?" asked DuBose.

He looked at the name. "Craig Baker, Attorney at Law," he said in surprise. "And the package was addressed to Anne Randolph. I wonder where the contents are."

"And I wonder why Battle's folks didn't find it."

Jack said, "I think the only thing they looked at in this house was the room where the murders happened, and they found Jerome."

"Presumably this is Leslie Randolph's study. Pipes in the rack. Hunting prints on the wall. So why would a package to her be in *his* trash can?"

"And we need to ask Craig Baker why Anne Randolph needed a lawyer." Jack glanced at the fireplace. "Hold on." He walked over there and moved the screen away from the opening. "Someone's built a fire here recently."

"In summer? Can you make out anything?"

He gingerly sifted through the ashes before plucking out a half-burned piece of paper.

"What does that look like to you?" said Jack, holding it up to her.

"It…it looks like a court pleading. But I can only make out a few words."

As Jack was holding it, the burned paper crumpled to bits and fell to the floor.

"Damn," they both exclaimed.

After completing their search inside, they walked past the large pool with its lovely blue water, and over to the garage where Jack admired the Randolphs' Buick, which sat in the first bay. The garage space was tidy and well organized.

"Jerome obviously took pride in his job," noted Jack.

He ducked his head inside the Buick and picked up the chauffeur's cap from the front seat.

"Jerome said he drove the Randolphs around sometimes. But were they vain enough to make him put on this hat? He didn't wear a chauffeur's uniform."

"I'm sure Jerome insisted on it," said DuBose.

He glanced at her, puzzled. "Jerome? Why?"

"If he drove them somewhere and they left the car to go shopping or to a restaurant, Jerome would be sitting in this fancy car all by himself. If the police didn't think he was the driver for some white people, they'd arrest him for stealing the Buick. With the chauffeur's cap on they'd probably leave him alone."

Jack dropped the cap back on the front seat and shook his head.

They drove to the sprawling Willow Oaks Country Club, housed in a grand building with enormous windows and sweeping views out to groomed lawns and flower beds, and an eighteen-hole golf course where educated, affluent men agonized over directing tiny white balls into small holes.

Jack angled his Fiat between a Mercedes-Benz sedan and a Porsche convertible.

"How much does it cost to join this place?" asked DuBose.

"I never asked. I'm just not country club material."

They inquired about Gordon Hanover and met up with him just as he was finishing a meal with a group of men also in golf attire. Upon learning what they wanted, he led them into an adjoining lounge that was outfitted with leather couches, small club chairs, and an array of small tables, with magazines fanned out on them.

A liveried Black attendant came forward. Hanover ordered an iced tea, and they joined him in that.

After the teas were delivered Hanover said, "Christine is devastated. The day we ran into you there? I tried to dissuade her from going into that room after you warned me. But she insisted. I thought she was going to faint."

"I'm sure," said Jack.

"Now, you say you're representing the man the police arrested?"

"Yes, Jerome Washington."

"Right. Jerome seemed like a good man. I thought Leslie and Anne liked him."

"That's what he says, too. And they had his family over for lunch and to swim recently," said DuBose.

"Yes. We actually saw them there. I forget his wife's name, but she and Jerome seemed tickled pink about the visit. And their kids were all smiles. Made me smile, too."

"They *were* all thrilled," said DuBose. "And her name is Pearl."

"That's right, Pearl."

"She's also been arrested," said DuBose.

Hanover sat up looking startled. "What? Why?"

"The commonwealth's theory is that they planned the murders together."

"That slip of a young woman I saw that day helped plan the murders of two people?" He shook his head and said forcefully, "No, I just don't see it. Not at all."

"We don't, either, but Mr. Battle seems confident."

He made a show of checking his watch and said, "Now, how can I help you?"

They asked him if he knew the terms of his in-laws' will and about the tontine.

"I didn't know until I spoke with Curtis Gates this morning and he gave me a heads-up. He handles our estate matters, too. I have no idea what Leslie was thinking with this tontine business. It's like something out of an Agatha Christie novel."

"We understand that you've been paying their expenses," noted DuBose.

He nodded. "Their problem was simple: They had outlived their money. So, we helped them. It just seemed like the decent thing to do."

They asked him about the man with perhaps a medical bag visiting the Randolphs.

He shook his head. "That's the first I've heard of it. Anne and Leslie had a regular doctor, Joseph Browder."

"Can you describe him?" asked DuBose.

"Around sixty-five, short, bald, and overweight."

"No, that doesn't match the man's description," said Jack.

"Are you close with Sam Randolph?" asked DuBose.

"No, as a matter of fact, I'm not. He was just never very friendly to me."

"He seems to be in ill health and in dire financial straits," commented Jack.

"Then he could come to me and I'd help him. I've actually tried reaching out to Sam, but he's rebuffed my every attempt."

"He told us that his father informed him he was going to leave Jerome some money in his will. Do you know anything about that?" asked DuBose.

"No."

"The files that Mr. Battle shared with us indicate that you have information about something your father-in-law told you?" said DuBose.

Hanover sighed. "I don't think you're going to like what I have to say."

"We know some of it, but would like to hear it from you," said DuBose.

"I was over at the house, about a week before their deaths."

"So *after* Jerome and his family came to eat and swim?" noted Jack.

"Yes. Leslie told me that he suspected Jerome might be stealing from them."

"Why, exactly?" asked DuBose.

"Some tools from the garage were missing, Leslie said. And he kept a box with petty cash in his study. Some of the money was gone as well."

She said, "And what was Mr. Randolph going to do about that?"

"Fire Jerome, I believe."

"Did he tell Jerome this?"

"That I don't know. But I can say that when Leslie got an idea in his head, he usually let you know it sooner rather than later."

Jack said, "This next question is delicate."

"Okay," said Hanover, looking apprehensive.

"It seems that Anne Randolph had some old injuries. And we were told that her husband might have had a drinking problem and might have...struck her sometimes?"

Hanover said slowly, "I *was* aware of the drinking. And the abuse."

"Did you try to intervene?"

"Several times. Christine was absolutely furious with her father. She called the police twice on him, in fact, although we did manage to hush that up. But then we got Leslie some counseling. We thought things were on a better, more even, keel. I wasn't aware of any recent...incidences."

"Okay, thank you for your frankness," said Jack.

Hanover said quietly, "My father was an alcoholic. Gave my mother fits. I remember their *encounters* as a child." He drained his glass of iced tea. "Which is why I never touch the damn stuff." He looked at his watch again. "I don't mean to be rude, but I have to change clothes and head to a meeting."

They all rose and shook hands.

"I wish you luck defending Jerome and Pearl," he said. "What little I've seen of them, I can't imagine how they could have done something like this."

"Seems like a nice, honest man," noted DuBose after Hanover left them.

"But what he just told us gives Jerome a prime motive for murder."

"And it looks like the Randolphs didn't tell anyone other than their lawyer about this tontine thing. Now we need to know why they set it up in the first place."

CHAPTER 47

As THEY WERE WALKING BACK to their car in the parking lot, a sleek red Ford Mustang stopped next to them.

It was Doug Rawlins, decked out in a garishly colored golf outfit that Jack had to fight hard to keep from laughing at.

"Jack, you have been busy," he called out.

"Well, I've got a murder trial to attend to. And I'm glad you *don't*."

"Not talking about that." He eyed DuBose and then tossed a rolled-up newspaper to Jack, who nimbly caught it.

"Leave it to you to mix business with pleasure." Rawlins laughed and drove off.

"What the hell is he talking about?" said Jack.

"Let me see that paper."

He handed it over. She searched the front page and held on a story, complete with pictures, at the bottom of the fold.

"Well, that explains it," DuBose said.

"What?"

She held it up. There was a picture of Jack and DuBose leaving the hotel with her luggage, and another photo of them carrying the luggage into Jack's place.

"Who took those pictures?" he asked.

"I suppose it was part of the plan. *If* I managed to survive the attempt on my life, which the story never mentions. So the gist is that we're basically shacking up."

"I wonder if Battle had something to do with this."

DuBose shook her head. "I think this more likely bears the fingerprints of Howard Pickett. Now, I would hope he had nothing to do with someone trying to kill me, but I've been surprised before on that score."

Jack dumped the paper in a trash can. "Let's prepare to be surprised then."

They returned to the office, where Jack looked up Craig Baker's number in Norfolk and placed a call to him. Baker was not in, so Jack left a message for the man to call him back and said it was urgent.

Later, after Jack walked Queenie, they both sat in Jack's office working. Around eleven DuBose put down her pen and said, "Talk to me about jury pools here."

Jack leaned back in his chair. "The last jury pool I selected from started with the usual twenty people, almost all of whom were white. I can tell you that that is roughly in line with all my other jury pools. My last ten jury trials were held before all-white juries, ninety-nine percent of them men."

"Are there not that many Blacks in Freeman County?"

"Oh, no, it's about forty percent Black. And here in Carter City, it's closer to eighty percent."

"Let me guess. People who look like me are either not picked to serve on juries or are somehow excluded from the pools to begin with?"

"Pretty much."

A bolt of lightning flashed outside. The following explosion of thunder was so loud it made them both jump. And then the skies opened and the rain fell so hard they could hear it viciously punishing the metal roof. Jack rushed over and opened the window, and the cool breeze immediately enveloped him. "Desiree, get over here and feel this breeze," he called out. "It is a-mazing."

DuBose smiled. "You sound like a little boy who's been given a new toy."

"Temperature must've dropped twenty-five degrees or more, thank you Lord."

She walked over and leaned out the window, right as a sudden burst of windswept rain splashed down on her, thoroughly soaking her blouse.

She ducked back inside and turned to him, laughing.

"I haven't run in the rain since I was a little girl. And when the police opened the hydrants in the summer in Chicago."

Jack smiled as he witnessed this unguarded side of DuBose. He had been dazzled, and intimidated, by her intellect and accomplishments. But now as he looked at her he thought, and not for the first time, that in addition to being a superb lawyer, she was also a lovely young woman.

She stared back at him, and seemed to be reading his mind. Her smile vanished and was replaced with pursed lips. "Well, that was stupid," she said, folding her arms over her soaked blouse.

"What was?" Jack said, confused.

"Ruining my silk blouse." She hurried over to the table and slipped on her jacket.

As a drenched Jack stood there watching her she said, "I'm going to bed. You too. Busy day tomorrow."

She hurried up the stairs, leaving him alone. Jack leaned back out the window, sucking in one lungful of cool air after the other. His head hung down with the weight of all the thoughts inside it.

* * *

DuBose dried off with a towel in the bathroom and put on her night-gown. She padded back into the bedroom, sat down on the bed, and glanced over her shoulder at the door to the downstairs. DuBose knew exactly what Jack had been thinking. He had given her that look, a critical tell that a woman could interpret as easily as a bird dog did the smell of quarry.

He cannot believe that I would become personally involved with a lawyer I'm working with, and a white one at that.

She sat up straighter. *Hold on, Desiree, don't think like that. You don't have to date the man, but not because he's white. That's how the other side wants the world to be. That's what you've been fighting against all this time.*

And you should be flattered that the "famous" Jack Lee finds you desirable.

She glanced in the small mirror hanging on the wall and DuBose's self-satisfied smile faded. She took the picture from her wallet and looked at the man there.

You know it has to be this way, in your heart. If only to show you still have one instead of a million pieces of shattered glass inside your chest.

CHAPTER 48

THIS TIME JACK WAS FULLY dressed and had the breakfast made and the coffee hot when DuBose came down the stairs.

"Good morning," he said with far too much enthusiasm. "Hope you slept well. I already walked and fed Queenie. What a gorgeous day. It can't be more than sixty degrees outside, not a cloud in the sky and no humidity." He paused and added sheepishly, "Guess I sound like a damn weatherman."

She looked at him quizzically. "Couldn't you sleep?"

He shot her a sidelong glance as he ladled fried eggs on her plate. "I slept fine. I...I just felt like getting up early, I guess."

They were eating, mostly in silence, their gazes averted from one another, when the phone rang. Jack answered it, listened, and then said, "Okay, we'll see you there."

He hung up and looked at DuBose. "That was Christine Hanover. She's invited us to her home for the reading of her parents' will."

* * *

The guard at the gate to Faulkner's Woods had their names on an approved visitor's list. He opened the wrought iron portal so the Fiat could pass through.

Jack asked, "Is this gate manned around the clock?"

The guard, a broad-shouldered, soldierly looking man in his thirties, nodded. "Yes, sir. Very secure here. Needs to be. Lot of money behind these gates."

Jack flashed his bar card. "We're investigating what happened to the Randolphs. We understand that Mr. and Mrs. Hanover got back here late that night from Washington?"

"They sure did."

"You sound positive," said DuBose.

"I was the one who opened the gate. Worked the graveyard shift that night."

"So you saw them?"

"Oh yeah. Big Rolls-Royce. Only one like that around. He was dressed in one of them monkey suits."

"A tuxedo?" said Jack.

"Yeah. And she had on a fancy dress with a pearl necklace. He looked like death and Mrs. Hanover was sobbing so hard the poor woman couldn't catch her breath."

"You happen to know the time?"

"I sure do. We don't keep a record of *owners* coming and going, but it was so late and seeing them at that hour was so surprising that I checked my watch. It was two in the morning. I remember thinking there were two of them in the car and it was two in the morning. How my mind organizes stuff."

"Thanks," said Jack and they drove on.

"Mercy," said DuBose as she looked at the brick and stone mansions they were passing, with their expansive lovely green lawns and professional landscaping touches, including stone fountains of varying states of grandeur. "You weren't kidding about this being the nicest area in town."

"Apparently, *nice* means you need a gate to keep everybody else out."

They pulled into the cobblestone driveway of a massive Tudor-style home draped with ivy and bracketed by towering crepe myrtles, fat hydrangea bushes, and lovely dogwood trees.

They parked next to a large Chrysler four-door. One of the three garage bays was open, revealing a red British Triumph convertible. After they got out Jack peeked inside the garage.

"Okay, no blue convertible lurking therein," he reported. "Just the silver Rolls-Royce and a burgundy Jaguar."

"The Hanovers were in Washington at the time," she reminded him.

"Someone else could have taken one of their cars while they were gone."

"That's true," she conceded.

They were admitted into the house by a Black uniformed maid who escorted them down a long, plush hall to a rounded maple door with brass fittings. She knocked, received an affirmative response, and ushered them into what turned out to be a booklined study.

Curtis Gates was seated behind an opulent walnut desk with a dark green leather inlay, while Sam Randolph and Christine and Gordon Hanover were arrayed in chairs in front of him. Next to Gates stood a tall, slim man in his late thirties and dressed in a navy blue jacket, light gray slacks, and a white dress shirt.

Gates introduced him as his son, Walter.

Jack shook his hand and said, "Your father mentioned you were in real estate?"

"That's right. I've done a fair amount of residential construction, including some of the homes in Faulkner's Woods, and a couple of small commercial projects. But I'm hoping to build up a more substantial portfolio."

"Good for you."

As they were about to sit down there came another knock at the door. Walter Gates opened it, revealing Edmund Battle.

Curtis Gates said, "Well, I think we're all here now. Let's get down to it."

They all settled into their seats as Gates cleared his throat. The estates lawyer then recited the provisions of the will that were already known to Jack and DuBose.

"This is absurd!" barked Sam Randolph. "Why would my parents have created this…this *tontine* device? It makes no sense at all."

Battle said, "Mr. Gates, how much cash is in the estate?"

Gates consulted a document and said, "About four thousand dollars."

"What?" exclaimed Sam. "Then how in the world did they continue to live there? How did they have money for a maid and to pay the man who ended up killing them?"

Gordon glanced at Christine, who nodded. He said, "We have been financially supporting Leslie and Anne for the last few years. Their money ran out, and we wanted them to be able to stay in their home and live out their lives in comfort."

"Good God!" cried out Sam Randolph. "Well, what you did was set them up to be murdered by a man looking for an inheritance."

"What do you mean by that?" said Christine, turning to look at her brother.

Battle answered, "He means that your father told Jerome Washington that he was to be included in the will. Then he changed his mind when Washington became belligerent." He glanced at Gordon. "And he also thought the man had been in his house and had stolen things from him. But Washington didn't know that your father had changed his mind. So he killed them in the hopes of inheriting money." He looked confidently at Jack and DuBose. "How do you think that will play out before a jury?"

"It'll sound somewhat plausible, until we have our turn," said DuBose.

He gave her a condescending expression and said, "Uh-huh, sure."

Sam said, "So Christine and I have to wait for one of us to die? That's outrageous."

"Your parents were of sound mind when they made the will," countered Gates.

"But what will happen to the property until one of us dies?" asked Randolph. "Who will pay for its upkeep, taxes and such? Will it just sit there and rot for years?"

"That was thought of and addressed," said Gates. "The estate will sell off five acres for development. That will raise more than enough money to keep the property up for a very long time. In addition, the will does provide that one or both of you can live in the house rent free for as long as you wish, until there is only one surviving child."

"I don't want to live there!" snapped Randolph. "I want the money. Now."

"I'm sorry," said Gates. "That is not how it will work."

Jack said, "Can you shed any more light on *why* they made such a will?"

"It's not my job to wonder about such things. It's my job to draft the documents that will implement my client's wishes," replied Gates testily.

DuBose said, "But are you saying that Leslie and Anne Randolph were independently aware of the legal structure known as the tontine? I find that very difficult to believe. I would venture to say that most *lawyers* in this country have never heard of it. I had to look it up myself after you told us about it previously."

Battle glanced sharply at her and said, "I have to admit, I had to do that, too, Mr. Gates, when you told me about it earlier."

They all looked at Gates who, for the first time, did not look so smug. "Well, in all candor, *I* suggested a tontine-style structure," he said.

"Why?" asked DuBose.

"Because Leslie told me that he wanted only *one* of his children to inherit the property. I told him that barring an outright testamentary disposition in favor of one child, which undoubtedly would have prompted a lawsuit from the other, a tontine-style arrangement was the most efficient mechanism to execute upon their wishes."

"So you're saying they didn't care which of us got the property so long as it was just *one* of us?" said Christine slowly.

"Oh, grow up, Christine," exclaimed her brother. "It was as good as left to *you*. I'm much older, not in good health, and I will almost certainly predecease you, and soon, as Dad obviously knew. And then you can walk away with millions."

She said, "I don't need *millions*, Sam."

"Of course you don't," he replied in a skeptical tone.

"Actually, she's right, we don't," said Gordon testily. "And if they had disinherited you, Sam, would you be surprised? You've done nothing the last several years except act abominably toward them. And toward Christine and me as well."

Randolph rose and stormed out, slamming the study door behind him.

Jack excused himself and followed the man.

At the front door, Jack watched as Randolph walked off at a rapid pace, turning the corner at the next street.

Jack hurried after him. He reached the corner to see that Randolph had slowed considerably and his breathing appeared to be labored. He started to cough violently. Next, he threw up in the grass. He took a few moments to recover, sucking in air in short bursts, before slowly walking off.

When Jack reached this spot, he noted the spatters of blood on the lawn.

At the next block, where Randolph had turned left, Jack paused and watched.

Randolph exited through the front gates and walked to the corner where there was a bus stop. Five minutes later he climbed onto a bus and it pulled away.

CHAPTER 49

LATER, AFTER THEY LEFT THE Hanovers' house, Jack told DuBose about following Randolph.

"He took a bus, so I don't think he even has a car. We'll have to confirm that, but something tells me he's not driving a blue convertible."

DuBose looked thoughtful. "But he clearly needs money, he even said so himself. So he had a motive to kill his parents to get what he thought would be a substantial inheritance. But he didn't know about his parents' lack of liquid assets, and the tontine. So if he *did* kill them, he's probably going to end up with nothing."

"Unless Christine dies first." Jack glanced at her. "Do you think he might…?"

"Desperate people do desperate things, Jack. But you said he threw up blood?"

"Yes. He's obviously seriously ill. Maybe he doesn't have much time left."

"Then why does he care about getting his parents' property?"

"Well, he has kids. He may want to leave it to them."

"Okay, it's time to meet with our clients."

They saw Jerome first. He was sitting on his bunk. The head bandage was gone and he looked and sounded better than he had the last time they had seen him. The first thing he asked about was Pearl.

"The last time we saw her she was doing okay," DuBose told him. "Now, Jerome, did Leslie Randolph ever mention to you that he was going to put you in his will?"

Jerome gaped. "What for? His wife already give me fifty dollars."

"Did you ever have angry words with Mr. Randolph?" asked DuBose.

His features scrunched up. "Angry words? With Mr. Leslie? You crazy?"

"Tyler Dobbs said as much. And the Randolphs' lawyer said the Randolphs were scared of you. That they were going to fire you. And there's another witness who will testify that Mr. Randolph thought you had been stealing from him."

Jerome shook his head. "I didn't steal nothin'. And if I do, why did he invite my family over for lunch? Why Miss Anne give me fifty dollars if they gonna fire me?"

"They might claim that Mr. Randolph thinking you were stealing from him happened *after* the lunch and pool visit," said Jack.

Jerome drew a deep breath and settled himself. "Look here, I ain't never stole nothin' from them, and I ain't never say nothin' angry to Mr. Leslie. Why I do that? He pay me good money that I need to help my family. With my bad leg and all, not too many jobs I can do. So I ain't gonna do nothin' to get me fired."

Jack said, "I arranged the call with Pearl. Did you talk to her?"

Jerome nodded, his expression turning even more despondent. "Only time she don't tell me the truth."

"She wouldn't say where she was that day?" asked DuBose.

"No, ma'am. Not one word."

They left him there and went to visit Pearl. She was standing next to the barred window and staring out.

"You seen Jerome?" she asked anxiously turning to them. "Is he okay?"

"We just came from there," said Jack. "He's fine. He said he talked to you?"

She sat down on her bunk. "Yeah, he did."

"And you didn't tell him where you were that day?" said DuBose.

She looked up at them pleadingly. "I...I can't."

"Were you...were you with another...man?" asked Jack quietly.

"I ain't never cheated on Jerome. Never, never, never," she said emphatically.

"Then I don't understand why you can't tell us," said Jack.

"I just can't," said Pearl miserably, not looking at them.

Jack glanced at DuBose and shook his head in frustration.

As they were heading down the hall to the prison exit Jack said, "She looks as bad as she did when I met her at my office the first time."

DuBose stopped walking. "What do you mean 'bad'?"

"She looked sick to her stomach and got all pale and shaky. I got her some water."

"Wait here," said a tense DuBose. She turned and hurried back down the hall.

Sitting next to Pearl, DuBose said, "Were you...were you pregnant?"

Pearl gasped and her eyes teared up. She put a hand to her mouth.

DuBose gripped her other hand. "I thought that might be it, when Jack said you weren't feeling well the first time you two met."

Pearl drew her hand away from her mouth and said in a trembling voice, "I was gonna have a baby." She placed a trembling hand on her stomach.

"'Was'? Did you miscarry?"

Pearl looked up at DuBose, her expression full of misery. She shook her head.

"Wait...Pearl, did you...did you have an abortion?"

The tears now streamed out of Pearl's eyes. She bent over and pressed her thin chest to her thighs, rocking back and forth, and sobbing.

DuBose wrapped her arms around the woman and held her tightly.

Pearl finally sat up and wiped her eyes with a tissue that DuBose handed her.

"But I don't understand, Pearl. Did you not want another child?"

"It…it wasn't…it wasn't Jerome's."

DuBose caught a breath. "But you said you had never cheated…"

"The man who owns Winston's where I work…he…he got me alone in the back room." She started to cry again. "He…he…"

"Okay, it's okay. I understand. You don't have to say any more."

The two sat there for a few moments, with Pearl clinging to DuBose.

As they drew apart DuBose said, "Where did you get…where was it done?"

"A place over behind the white hospital. A woman…she comes 'round every so often, so's I was told. She got a room. She did it there."

"And since abortion is illegal in Virginia, you didn't want to tell anyone?"

Pearl nodded. "And I didn't want Jerome to know 'cause he will kill that man."

"What time did you get there and what time did you leave?"

She wiped her eyes. "Got there 'round one or so. Didn't get out till after six. I was…bleeding some after…Felt real weak. She had me lie down and give me some medicine and all. Then she drove me home in her car. But I asked her to let me off 'bout half mile away. I got home in time to help my momma with supper. Then we found out 'bout Jerome, and my whole life just…*gone*."

DuBose said, "But that will show that you could not have been at the Randolphs' when they were killed. You see that, right?"

"Yes ma'am, I do."

"And since the commonwealth's theory hinges on you helping Jerome, that means it helps him, too."

"Yes, ma'am. I…I'm glad I told you."

"Did you talk to the police about the man doing what he did?"

"I went down there and told 'em, sure. But they asked me what was I wearin'? Was I flirtin'? When I told 'em it was a man I work for, they say, 'You tryin' to get him to pay you more money? You better watch out. That's a crime accusin' a man like that.' Then they told me to get on with myself before they put *me* in jail."

DuBose knew she should have been surprised by this, but she wasn't, not anymore. And this happened to *all* women, regardless of color.

"You said the owner did this. Is he white?"

"No, he colored. But he thinks he own all the women who work for him."

"Will the woman who…helped you, speak with us?"

"I don't know. Maybe."

"Can you give me her name and address?"

"She didn't tell me her name, but I know the place, o'course."

Pearl told her and DuBose wrote the address down.

"I know how hard that was for you, Pearl. But you did the right thing, okay?"

A teary Pearl nodded.

DuBose walked back to where Jack was waiting and told him everything she'd learned.

"Holy Lord," he said. "We need to nail the son of a bitch who raped her."

"First, we need to talk to this woman. If she can verify what Pearl told us, it blows up Battle's entire case."

CHAPTER 50

THERE IT IS," SAID JACK as they pulled up to a bland rowhouse two blocks behind the county hospital. "Doesn't look like much."

"Those places never do. That's the point."

He shot her a look. "You have experience with women getting abortions?"

"Not personally, but I know in some places you can get an abortion by a licensed physician. The doctor just says it's for *therapeutic* reasons, and the request to end the pregnancy gets approved by a review board. Or you travel to New York or one of the few states where it's legal. If you're not well-off or well-connected, you go to places like this, if there even is one nearby, and hope you don't die."

They knocked on the door. No one answered. They knocked again—no answer.

"She's gone."

They turned to see an elderly man smartly dressed in a suit and tie calling out to them from a house directly across the street, where he was sitting on the porch. A table with a water pitcher and a glass, and a small TV perched on it, was next to him. "Saw her leave the other day with her suitcase, and a box of stuff."

"Did you know her?" asked DuBose.

"No, not really, ma'am. She wasn't here long. Oh, about three weeks or so."

"Did you ever see anyone going or coming here?" asked Jack.

"Oh, yes. I sit out here on my porch every day and see lots of things. I've watched young ladies go in and out that place every single day. What do you think was going on there? Some sort of bingo parlor?" He glanced from side to side, looking intrigued. "Or maybe it's one of those houses of *sin*? Only I never saw any men go in, come to think."

"Do you have her name? Did you notice her car?" asked DuBose.

"First name was Janice, least that's what she said. Nice lady. Around forty. Redhead, like my dear, departed Emily. Car was a four-door Chevrolet Bel Air. Real pretty turquoise color."

"License plate?" asked Jack.

"Yellow numbers and letters and a blue background."

"Did you notice the state?"

"Oh yes, New York. Stood out, you see."

"Was she renting?"

"That's right. Woman who owns it lives right over there," he added, pointing across the street and two doors down. "Mrs. Burton. Angela Burton. Very nice woman. Makes the finest corn bread you'll ever put in your mouth."

"I'm sure," said DuBose. "Well, thank you."

The man nodded and sat back down in his chair.

Angela Burton *was* very nice, and did offer them corn bread, which they declined.

She readily answered their questions about her renter. "Janice Evans, said she was from Rye, New York. Rented the place for a month. Paid in advance. She had to leave early on account of her mother had taken ill."

"Was she here on business?" asked Jack.

"She didn't say. And I didn't ask."

"You have a phone number and address for her?"

"Yes, but I'm not sure I can give that out."

Jack held out his state bar card. "The thing is, she could be a very important witness in a murder case we're handling."

Burton's eyes swelled wide in alarm. "Murder? Oh my goodness. What sort of thing might she have witnessed in one of my rentals?"

"I'm afraid we can't disclose that. Client confidentiality," said DuBose.

She provided them the phone number and address in New York, and they left.

"What are the chances Evans agrees to come here and testify?" asked Jack.

"Slim and none. But it's better to know about her than not."

When they got back to the office, Jack called Craig Baker again. This time he was put through to the attorney.

Jack told him who he was and why he was calling. "So, we need to know what you sent Mrs. Randolph that day and why she needed your services."

"I can't possibly tell you any of that."

The line went dead.

Jack looked over at DuBose, who was seated at the worktable going over some files. "Mr. Baker is not going to be cooperative," he said.

"Well, that's why we have the right to subpoena," said DuBose as she added this to their to-do list. "And we can do the same for Janice Evans. If we can have her testify that Pearl was with her during the time the Randolphs were murdered, I think maybe even a white jury will be inclined to rule in our favor."

"I hope you're right."

"Oh, I did a phone interview last night while you were out walking Queenie."

"An interview? With who?"

"Huntley and Brinkley. They recorded it for their newscast last night."

"Chet Huntley and David Brinkley! How did that come about?"

"They heard I was here working on this case and wanted to interview me. I spoke to them last year during the *Loving* matter. And they told me George Wallace has commented on the Randolph case. Saying something like this is the line in the sand that white people cannot allow to be crossed."

"What'd you tell them about our case?"

Before she could answer, the phone rang.

Jack looked at it. "I wonder if Mr. Baker had a change of heart. I left my number the first time I called his office."

It was not Baker. Frank Lee sounded frantic.

"Jack, get yourself over to the hospital quick as you can, son."

"Daddy, what's wrong? It's not Momma, is it?"

"It's Lucy."

"Lucy!"

"Somebody hurt her, real bad."

CHAPTER 51

IT'S QUITE SERIOUS," SAID THE lean, gray-haired doctor. "She has a skull fracture. Hopefully, she'll pull through, but it will require a complicated, risky surgery. There are no guarantees, I'm afraid."

Frank, Jack, and DuBose looked through the round window into the room where an unconscious Lucy lay in the hospital bed, her head wound with bandages. Her mother sat stoically beside the bed, holding her only daughter's hand.

"What the hell happened?" Jack asked his agitated father, who was puffing furiously on a Camel.

"Your momma was hanging up the laundry outside. Lucy was with her. She went to get another basket of clothes when she heard Lucy screaming. She ran out and Lucy was lying in the grass, her head and face all bloody. Your mother saw a man jump the back fence and run off into the patch of woods there. If I ever get ahold of that son of a bitch…"

"But why in the world would anyone hurt Lucy?" asked Jack.

Frank eyed his son nervously.

Jack paled. "You…you think it was because of what *I'm* doing?"

Frank looked over at the local newspaper that was lying on a chair set against the wall. He grabbed it and held up the front page.

YOUNG NEGRO COUPLE ON TRIAL FOR MURDERING
TWO ELDERLY WHITE PEOPLE IN THEIR HOME

"Buddy of mine from the war called and said the same headline is running in his newspaper in North Carolina. His son's a reporter for the paper down there. He also said the Associated Press picked the story up. Says it's running in damn near every paper in the country. And you and Desiree are named as the lawyers."

The doctor glanced at DuBose. "I watched Huntley and Brinkley last night. They had this woman's picture up on the TV, and they had a phone interview with her where she was talking about fighting for equality for Blacks. They said it must be an important case to draw the NAACP's attention. Lots of folks around here probably watched that. Might've riled up someone."

Jack looked at DuBose. "So that's what you talked about with them?"

"Yes. We need that sort of media exposure when we're fighting back against the likes of Howard Pickett."

"Did you mention my family? Lucy?"

"No, I never talked about any of that. I never would."

"That's the truth," added the doctor. "I listened to the whole thing. They just talked about the case."

Jack turned and stalked off down the hall. DuBose hurried after him and caught up to him around the corner.

"Jack, I was just doing my job. I hope you can understand that."

He leaned against the wall and closed his eyes. "I don't blame you, Desiree. Lucy is lying in that hospital bed because of *me* and the choice *I* made."

He turned, slammed his fist against the wall, and screamed, "Goddammit!"

Tears clustered in her eyes, a shaky DuBose took a step back and said as calmly as she could manage, "I...I can get other lawyers on the case. You can withdraw and then maybe this will—"

"He's not withdrawing from anything," said the voice.

They turned to see Hilly Lee standing there.

"Momma?" said Jack. He wrapped his arms around her. At first she looked taken aback, but then Hilly Lee hugged her son fiercely.

"What do you mean he's not withdrawing?" said DuBose.

Hilly let her son go and said, "I didn't agree with your decision to represent that man, or work with *her*," she said, glancing at DuBose. "But what I know is whenever you let a bully make you turn and run, that bully will never go away. He will *own* you."

"But—" began Jack.

"I taught you and your brother that lesson when you were boys. And now I'm telling you, as a man, that you are not walking away from this. You go on and do your job. You and *her*," she added, drilling another stare at DuBose. "And you punch those people right in the damn face and you show them they don't control one thing about you, son. Not one goddamn thing."

Hilly turned and walked back to be with her daughter.

CHAPTER 52

JACK SAT BEHIND HIS DESK while DuBose stood on the other side watching him.

His hand trembling, he lifted the glass of whiskey to his mouth and finished it.

Another rain shower had just ended and a hot, dry summer had suddenly transformed into a wet, chilly one.

DuBose said, "I never expected your mother to react the way she did, Jack."

He set the glass down and glanced at her. "When I was twelve, Momma had me stand up to a bunch of bullies. As soon as I did, they never bothered us again. Now, I know this situation is not that simple. But...my mother's right. I walk away from this, it's like I'm saying they won. Hell, it's like I'm agreeing with them. And if people who want to do what's right run away, and the only ones left are like the man who hurt Lucy? Then what sort of world do we have?"

"I think people like Howard Pickett and George Wallace are counting on a vocal extreme minority dictating what this country will look like in the future."

He gazed up at her. "Have you lost anyone to this madness?"

DuBose now wouldn't meet his eye. "I have. Many people I work with have."

"They're operating on Lucy tomorrow."

"You need to be with her. I'll keep working on things."

He nodded and said, "You know how to shoot a gun, Desiree?"

She looked surprised by this question. "No, I don't."

He took out the Colt and a box of ammo. "Come on, it's time you learned."

*　*　*

They parked by an open field set next to some woods. There were no homes within a few miles in any direction. A column of old, battered tree stumps lined the field.

They got out and Jack picked up a bunch of shot-up tin cans that littered the grass.

"I think everybody who ever learned to shoot in Freeman County came out here at some point. You don't need a metal detector to find anything, just your hands."

He lined up four cans on four separate stumps and then marched DuBose back a short distance. He took out his revolver, then showed her how to load it and work the trigger and hammer. Jack aimed at one of the cans and shot it cleanly off its perch.

He handed her the gun and showed her how to grip it. He also tutored DuBose on correctly setting her feet and hips and squaring her shoulders. He then instructed her on how to use the gunsight on the end of the muzzle to aim.

Her first two shots hit nothing but dirt and the third struck a stump, blowing wood chips off. The fourth shot sent the can spinning off into the fading light.

She looked flushed, excited, and terrified all at the same time.

"It's not so easy to do that to a person," he said, his features grim.

"For some people it is. Like the person who shot at me through my door."

"I just hope you never have to use it, Desiree. Now, let's practice some more while there's still light."

An hour later they headed back. DuBose went to the bedroom

while Jack stripped down to his skivvies and lay on the couch with a blanket over him. Queenie came over and settled next to him on the floor with a contented sigh.

Jack reached down and gently rubbed the dog's head and muzzle. "How you doing, girl? You wish people were more like dogs? Most days I sure as hell do."

Queenie was asleep in under a minute. Jack listened to the dog's gentle breathing and then he rolled over on his back and stared at the ceiling.

Jack's thoughts rested solely on his sister. She loved everybody, wouldn't hurt anyone or anything, and someone had tried to kill her, apparently because he didn't like what Jack was doing. But there was a lot of depravity out there. People not listening to a damn thing that anyone who disagreed with them said. Making them out to be the enemies, simply for having a different opinion.

In the room directly above him was a young, determined woman who was spending her entire adult life fighting for the rights of people like her to just live free, and equal, with everyone else.

Jack thought about all of the people he knew here. They would use the courts and politicians who saw it their way to preserve the status quo and make sure it would endure well past their own lifetimes. And on and on it would go. Until...what?

He closed his eyes and put his arm over his face to make the room seem even darker than his thoughts.

CHAPTER 53

"I REALLY DON'T KNOW WHAT I can tell you, Miss DuBose," said Craig Baker.

DuBose had driven over in Jack's Fiat the following morning and was seated opposite Baker in his office in downtown Norfolk.

Craig Baker was a mild-looking man in his early fifties, paunchy with graying hair and a trim mustache, and wearing a finely tailored blue suit. DuBose was surprised that he had even agreed to meet with her. Yet his manner was decidedly cautious.

"Your client is dead, Mr. Baker. She was murdered. If you can provide any information that might show why someone else would want to kill the Randolphs?"

"The attorney-client privilege survives the death of a client."

"Yes, but I'm trying to prevent *my* clients from dying in the electric chair."

"For what it's worth, I *am* sympathetic to your position."

"Is there any way that you *can* help me then?"

"I just don't see how, I'm sorry."

"Can you at least tell me what sort of law you practice?"

When he hesitated she said, "Surely you tell people what you do for a living. That cannot be confidential. And maybe I'd like to hire you one day," she tacked on.

"You're not married, are you?"

She looked startled. "Uh, why no."

"Then I doubt you would have need of my services."

She looked puzzled, but as realization spread over her features, Baker smiled and nodded. "That's right. I'm a *divorce* lawyer. Does that help you?"

Later, DuBose drove back to Freeman County. She passed by broad tobacco fields, and also endless rows of tiny corn plants that would not be ready to harvest until September or so. She knew that tobacco plants ripened from the bottom to the top and that they took about two to three months to be ready for harvest. You could get multiple yields from one plant, and it was a good cash crop for both large and small farming operations.

DuBose also knew the whole country had profited off the cotton crop, from plantation owners in the south to factory owners in the north, as well as multiple countries that imported the commodity. Cotton production had made America an economic power, casting wealth across the land. The only ones who had not profited were the slaves who labored to plant it, pick it, and carry it to market. They had done all of that terribly hard work and helped build this country, for centuries. And in return they had received nothing except continued enslavement.

DuBose had spent years in the south litigating cases. Because of that she probably knew more about growing and harvesting tobacco *and* cotton than most people. And she had read extensively about what had happened once the Union prevailed in the war. And that had led directly to where they were right now.

After the Civil War, the federal government had given former slaves land to farm so they could become self-sustaining. This land was often part of plantations where they had once labored as slaves. Meanwhile, Black men were given the right to vote, and they registered in large numbers, electing to office many Black politicians. Schools opened to teach them to read and write, and the former slaves were on their way to building new lives in freedom, and becoming productive members of society. It had all looked promising as America seemed on the verge of turning the page on the ugliest part of its history and becoming far stronger and more robust in the process, as Black people were finally included in the American Dream.

However, under intense pressure from mostly Southern politicians, the federal government reneged on its promises to the former slaves, pulled troops from the South, and with the rise of the Ku Klux Klan quickly came voter suppression, riots, and murderous rampages, with whole Black sections of towns wiped out. Soon, there were no longer any Black elected officials, or Blacks who could vote without threat of being killed.

This had all happened with alarming swiftness, but then bad things very often did, while positive change took considerably longer.

Wealthy whites once more owned the land, and they made the laws. They fashioned arrangements with poor Blacks and whites to work the soil as sharecroppers all year without formal pay. Since these folks had no other means of supporting themselves or their families, they really had no choice. They were forced to purchase their seeds, food, and tools at inflated prices from the landowners and pay high rents for the shacks in which they lived—which was, ironically, often old slave housing. At the end of the year, after the crops had been harvested and sold, the owner would meet with the sharecroppers and go over the "books" of which the owner had sole control. And virtually every time the owner, who had already made his money, would tell the sharecropper that he owed the *owner* money. And this debt would be added to prior years, effectively making it impossible for the sharecropper to ever be free of this burden.

And when Black sharecroppers tried to leave and migrate north or west for gainful employment that actually paid them for their labors, the police would be waiting at the train or bus stations, where they would arrest them on some bogus charge. They would then be told that they would have to work for a decade or more in order to make good on the "wrongs" they had committed. It was just another form of slavery that continued to this day. And once more Black—and poor white—parents watched their children grow up in a country that really had no place for them, and that would do all it could to ensure no version of the "American Dream" would ever be possible, for them.

As DuBose passed a modest building set back off the road, she slowed and then stopped the car. She stared at the place for a few moments, trying to make up her mind. Finally, she pulled the Fiat into the parking lot.

CHAPTER 54

DUBOSE STARED UP AT THE church. Her mother had been a devout Catholic all her life. By contrast, DuBose's devotion had been haphazard over her adult years and then had totally faded.

She got out of the Fiat and stood in front of the house of worship, again wondering whether to go in. She turned back to the car twice but then finally reached an internal resolution and entered the Catholic church. She made the sign of the cross with a few drops of holy water taken from the marble font just inside the front doors. She walked slowly up the aisle, past the rows of pews, breathing in faded aromas of incense and the mustiness of the old building, until she reached the altar. She genuflected and stayed on her knees, her hands clasped, a remembered prayer forming on her lips that she wanted to say on behalf of Lucy Lee and her family.

"Excuse me?" said an agitated voice.

She turned to see an elderly priest in his black cassock and white collar striding purposefully toward her. Behind his thick specs was a pair of angry eyes.

"Excuse me, what are you doing here?" he demanded.

Flustered, DuBose quickly rose. "I...I just came in to pray, Father. The door was unlocked."

He waggled a finger in her face. "You are not a member here. I don't know you!" His expression was one of disgust as he looked her over. It was a countenance she was well used to and it made her face flame in anger.

As calmly as she could DuBose replied, "No, I'm not a member of your congregation. I was just driving by—"

"You must leave here right this minute."

"Father Matthew?"

They turned to see a young priest walking toward them.

"A visitor?" he asked.

Father Matthew rushed over to him. "Father Kelly, this...person is not a member of our flock." He glanced at DuBose with a disdainful look and added in a voice she could clearly hear, "And she's a Negro. You know how I feel about *them*."

"I believe I can handle this, Father. You can go to your meeting. Remember, the Parish Council? They're expecting you."

"Oh, right, yes." He clenched Kelly's arm and said in a cautionary tone, "Make sure she steals nothing. The chalices in the sacristy? Irreplaceable."

"All God's children, Father, the scriptures are very clear on that," admonished Kelly, inclining his head in DuBose's direction.

"Yes, yes, of course. But mind the chalices."

"Goodbye, Father, please convey my good wishes to the council."

The man hurried out, leaving Kelly and DuBose alone. The young priest walked over to her.

DuBose said, "Not to worry. I'll be leaving now."

"But have you finished what you came here for?"

"What, stealing the *chalices*?" DuBose shot back.

"My guess would be a replenishment of your spiritual faith, perhaps?"

"Excuse me?" she said, now looking puzzled instead of angry.

"I saw you from a window. I've noticed that sort of wavering before." He smiled graciously. "I'm Father Kelly. And you?"

"Desiree DuBose."

"Yes, I thought I recognized you. I read about you and Mr. Lee in the paper. I was horrified to hear what happened to his sister. I pray she survives."

"Yes, it *was* horrible, Father. But horrible things happen, every day. Even in *churches*," she added pointedly, looking in the direction of where Father Matthew had departed.

"Please, let's sit." When they did so, Kelly said, "So what brings you here today?"

"I'm not sure. Hence the wavering."

"You must have some idea."

"I...I just wonder what the point is. I mean, if a man of God can—"

"—can, by his actions, be in clear contravention with the teachings of the God to whom we both have committed our lives?"

She glanced sharply over at him. "It sounds like you've given this some thought."

"Every day. Sometimes every hour. Certainly when I pray, which I seem to be doing with ever greater frequency. Which isn't a bad thing for a priest," he added, smiling.

She shook her head. "I'm just tired of white people looking down on my race, destroying us bit by bit, while they simply go on with their lives, unaffected by it all, pretending the problem doesn't even exist." She looked at him. "All that time, money, and resources spent on keeping this country divided. If we had just honestly confronted our history, and spent far less than a tenth of that time, money, and resources on bringing us together, do you know what kind of country we would have right now?"

"I think I do actually, and it makes me want to weep at the wasted opportunity," he replied solemnly.

"Your race is going to have to *rethink* its opinions of my people at some point. The true obstacle is, while doing that, whites have to alter their opinions of *themselves*. And they clearly don't want to do that, because looking in the mirror that hard is no fun."

Kelly stroked his chin, looking thoughtful, and then said, "James Baldwin debated William F. Buckley at Cambridge Union in

England several years ago. I was fortunate to see a broadcast of it last year. I have never before or since heard such raw, powerful eloquence from a human being as I did from Baldwin. He spoke about many things that day. But, as a priest, one part particularly resonated with me. He said that, basically, whites may be even more emotionally and spiritually damaged by their racist beliefs and terrible actions than the Blacks are by those very same beliefs and actions." He noted the scar by her eye. "How awful it must be to think you have the right to harm another person...for no reason. I can only imagine that attacker's soul is...empty."

She said firmly, "I have a difficult time feeling sorry for any white person who seeks to subjugate my race."

"Oh, I hold no sympathy for their beliefs and actions, for they are repugnant. As a man of God, my sorrow is only for the damage to their soul." He paused again. "The news is full of the war being fought by this country." He added hastily, "I'm not speaking of Vietnam. The war I'm talking about is being fought right here, and it could end what has been a spirited if flawed experiment in self-governance. And as Winston Churchill once said so succinctly but brilliantly, democracy is the worst form of government there is, except for all the others."

"You sound more like an academic than a priest," noted DuBose.

He smiled. "I earned a degree in political science from Columbia University before receiving the calling and entering the priesthood." He glanced at her. "You know of the Golden Rule?"

"Of course."

"So simple and yet so *devilishly* clever. It's no secret that people are often self-serving. But society can still flourish because everyone basically wants the same things, and rising water lifts all boats."

"Not for people of my color. They didn't lift our boats, they carried us to slavery in theirs."

"Yes. Although, some argued against slavery from an economic point of view. It was felt that paid labor was more profitable, because it incentivized people to work harder, whereas forced labor did not."

"A whip and death threats can be great motivators," pointed out DuBose.

"Yes, they can," conceded Kelly.

She said, "And I'm not impressed with the morals of anyone who can only make an *economic* argument against slavery."

"I think those people felt it was the only tactic that would work with greedy slaveowners. Some philosophers favored an omnipotent monarchy free from all accountability. Slavery flourished in such a world. Whereas Jefferson and the other Founding Fathers chose the will of the people and the freedom to pursue life, liberty, and happiness as their ideal governing model."

"But they never managed to address the enslavement of my people, and now centuries later here we are."

"One would have thought a civil war would have laid to rest the indefensible, but somehow it didn't."

"On the contrary—the war was fought and won. The lack of political will to carry on the ideals that men and women gave their blood and lives for? *That* was the failure."

Kelly smiled. "Do I sense a fellow political science aficionado in my presence?"

"I thought the study of it *was* important."

"That and a good understanding of history, if only to not repeat the blunders of the past. But, back to the Golden Rule: 'Do unto others as you would have them do unto you.' It combines the knowledge that we are egocentric beasts, but that we must get along to prosper and live in peace. And really, is it such a burden to be nice and respectful to others?"

"Well, for more than a few, it certainly seems to be quite impossible. But the rule only works if we truly practice it for *everyone*," pointed out DuBose.

"Agreed. There can be no half measures, or the failure of society—of this country, in fact—will be inevitable."

"So what do you propose we do about it?" she said bluntly.

"I continue to do what I do, and you continue to do what you do, Miss DuBose."

"And the Father Matthews of the world?"

"He, and those like him, will not live forever."

Scowling, she said, "That doesn't work and you know it. Racism is a virus passed from the old to the young."

"So our job is not to merely wait for the source of the hate to die, but to touch the minds of those coming of age so that racism cannot take root."

"By preaching the Golden Rule?" said DuBose skeptically.

"By demonstrating that love and tolerance and empathy are far superior to their opposites, for all of us. Empathy brings out the very best in people. It makes them in God's image, the way he wants us to be. He was a humble servant who never sought material wealth; his fortune was in his faith. And in his love for others. *All* others."

"And the lack of empathy?" she said.

"Brings out the very worst in us. It just simply makes us angry, all the time, and looking for other people to hate for no good reason." He eyed the altar. "I believe you came here to pray. Would you mind if I joined you?"

"Father, you should know that I'm a fallen Catholic."

"There are no fallen Catholics, Miss DuBose. There are only imperfect human beings who work through the difficult challenges associated with living. Sometimes they fall, but then they rise again. As did the son of God. For our eternal salvation."

She said slowly, "Meeting you today has given me some hope, Father Kelly. What are the odds? I could have easily driven right past here and this encounter might never have happened."

"When one has faith, of any kind, the odds of good things happening become short rather than long. And even if we hadn't met today, I believe we would have achieved the same results elsewhere."

"Because of God's will?" she said, again in a skeptical tone.

"Because God endowed us with the best minds on earth. I would imagine he expected us to do *something* positive with them." He stood. "Shall we?"

They ventured to the altar together and knelt.

CHAPTER 55

WHEN SHE GOT BACK TO the office DuBose walked Queenie, and endured multiple stares and hushed comments from people, both Black and white. Apparently, her notoriety, or more likely
infamy, had made the local rounds.

DuBose then placed a long-distance phone call to Janice Evans
in New York. The woman didn't pick up, but she had an answering
service, and DuBose left a detailed message telling her it was criti-
cally important that they speak. She was not the least bit confident
that the woman would call her back. If she returned to testify, Evans
would likely be charged with assisting in an abortion, which in Virginia carried mandatory prison time. But without her testimony,
how could they corroborate Pearl's whereabouts on the day of the
murders?

She worked on finalizing the statements for all the witnesses to
sign, drafting pretrial motions, going through possible investigatory
leads, trial theories, initial outlines of their opening statement, and
thinking of possible surprises that she felt sure Edmund Battle would
employ. She also wanted to delve more into the search warrant Battle
had used to find the money in the lean-to. She knew Jerome hadn't
stolen it, but she would have to put him on the stand to get that into
evidence, and there was no way this jury would believe him. And
Battle would likely destroy him on cross-examination. It would be

like sacrificing your queen to gain a pawn. Jerome could of course plead the Fifth Amendment. And while a jury was not supposed to consider that as an admission of guilt in a criminal case, DuBose had never met a jury that had not done so.

That evening, when a knock came at the door, Queenie let out a low growl.

DuBose pulled the gun from her purse and walked over to the door, but kept to the right of it in case someone was going to try to kill her again by shooting through it.

"Yes?"

"It's Donny Peppers."

She exhaled a sigh of relief and opened the door.

Peppers eyed the gun. "Heard about you almost dying."

"Did you also hear about Lucy?"

He nodded. "Damn scum." He came in and greeted Queenie with a gentle voice and no sudden movements, and, with DuBose clearly at ease with the man, the dog lay back down.

Peppers looked DuBose up and down. "How you hanging after what happened?"

She laid the gun down on the desk and said, "I won't lie and say it didn't scare me. But I'm okay. And I have information to tell you."

"And I have things to tell you. You got any coffee?"

"Yes. I can make some," said DuBose.

"Nah, I got it. I know where Jack keeps everything. You want some?"

"Thanks. There's a chill in the air, although I'm not sure it's just the weather."

As Peppers was making the coffee he eyed her. "How are you and Jack doing?"

"He's devastated about his sister."

"I meant how are you and he doing?"

"The work is going fine. He's a good lawyer. We definitely have different styles, but I think we complement each other well."

He finished up and brought the coffees over and sat down across from her. "I guess I'm not making myself clear."

She stared deliberately at him. "I guess you're not."

"I told Shirl you had moved in here."

"Someone tried to kill me at the hotel. Jack insisted that I stay with him."

"Not disputing that. But Jack is a loner, always has been, at least after Jeff went away. Never married, hell, never had a serious girl-friend that I know about. So for Jack to invite you here, to stay with him—I'm not talking the race thing; I'm talking the man-woman thing—well, it's an indicator of how he feels."

"Our relationship is strictly professional."

"Shirl just thought there was something there, between you and Jack, I mean."

"Well, she's wrong. We certainly can't waste time on personal issues while we have our clients' lives at stake. And I have no feelings for him in that way."

"You sure he feels the same way?"

"That doesn't matter, since I just told you how *I* stand on it."

Peppers held his hands up in mock surrender. "Okay, okay, sorry. Now, do you want to tell me what you found out?"

She did so, filling him in on the tontine arrangement, Pearl's abortion on the day of the murders, and the fact that Anne Randolph was preparing to divorce her husband.

"But why would the lawyer have sent the package to the house? I mean, Leslie Randolph might have gotten his hands on it."

She said, "I think he *did* open it and read the contents."

"He must have been pretty pissed."

"Their maid said he looked ready to erupt at lunch."

"And Janice Evans? Any way to force her to come here and testify?"

"We can subpoena her but she'll fight it. So what do you have?"

Peppers opened his notebook. "Tyler Dobbs is a gambler—dogfights, street craps, blackjack, you name it. He was in debt to multiple folks for over three thousand bucks, which is more than what the guy makes in a year." He handed her some pages with notes on them.

"*Was* in debt?"

"It all got paid off *after* Dobbs talked to the cops."

"And you think someone paid him to say what he did about Jerome?"

"What I'm thinking, yeah."

She wrote down some notes. "What else?"

"Sam Randolph is flat broke. His crummy house is mortgaged to the hilt. He owes back taxes. He has no income. And…he's really sick."

DuBose looked up at him. "Cancer?"

"No, but it's something in his lungs." He looked at his notes. "He has an advanced case, and the treatments available here for that aren't exactly doing the job for him. He's looking to travel to Switzerland, where he can get experimental therapies."

"I would imagine that costs a lot of money."

"Doc friend of mine said about twenty thousand bucks."

"So he really needs his inheritance. What about the man who visited the Randolphs?"

"The guy's a shrink by the name of Anthony Richards. Apparently, Sam wanted him to find his parents incompetent so he could get a power of attorney and sell the property."

"Richards admitted that?"

Peppers nodded. "After a few drinks, he did. He was going to get paid on the back end if he got the parents committed."

"It backfired because I think it made his father change his will, almost ensuring Sam will get nothing. Now, what about the blue convertible?"

"Nothing yet. Sam sold his car about two years ago. It doesn't belong to Christine or her husband, either. I checked the records. I'll keep digging."

"Thanks, Donny, you've done great work."

"Oh, Shirl wanted me to remind you about the hairdo thing, if you're up for it."

DuBose fingered a few strands. "I actually might be due for something new," she said thoughtfully, as though she wasn't simply talking about her hair.

He handed her a card. "You ever feel unsafe or whatever, you call me, okay?"

She took the card and glanced up at him. "Thanks. And Donny?"

"Yeah?"

"I could not have been more wrong about you. I'm sorry."

"Book by its cover. We all do it. And I'm real glad you showed up, Desiree. Jack's a good lawyer, but he and I know you're at a whole other level on the legal spectrum." He left.

Ten minutes later the door banged open and a stricken Jack appeared there.

She stood and gazed at him fearfully. "Jack? What is it? What's happened?"

He put a steadying hand on the wall and looked at her, his eyes filled with tears. "Lucy died on the table."

CHAPTER 56

YOUR HONOR, HIS SISTER WAS brutally murdered, almost certainly by a man opposed to Mr. Lee's representation of Jerome and Pearl Washington. In light of that I believe that a continuance of the trial date for one month is appropriate." DuBose paused and stared up expectantly at Judge Ambrose.

He said, "I surely sympathize with Mr. Lee and his family. What a horrific event."

"Not to mention that someone tried to murder me in my hotel room," she added.

"Yes, I heard about that as well. I don't know what this country is coming to."

Ambrose glanced at Battle, who had risen to his feet. "Mr. Battle?" said the judge.

"It goes without saying that the commonwealth condemns these acts of violence, Your Honor. And I hope whoever did them is caught and punished." He hesitated and glanced at DuBose. "And... under these tragic circumstances, and in respect of the grieving Lee family, the commonwealth will agree to a one-month extension."

DuBose mouthed a thank-you to Battle, who nodded curtly.

Ambrose looked out at the sea of reporters, all of whom were eagerly awaiting his ruling.

The judge scratched his chin. "All of what you both said is perfectly reasonable."

"Thank you, Your Honor," said DuBose as Battle nodded.

"But let us consider that if we do postpone the trial date, are we not giving in to the person who performed this hellish deed? Clearly his intent was to disrupt these proceedings. And if we do postpone the trial, he'll believe he was successful. Then what will prevent him from trying to do something similar in the future?" He shook his head. "That is something that I, in good conscience, cannot allow. The trial will commence as scheduled."

After Ambrose returned to his chambers and the courtroom had emptied out, Battle drifted over to DuBose.

"It appears that Judge Ambrose has his own unique way of trying a case. But I suppose I understand his reasoning. And he certainly seems sympathetic to your case."

"Come on, Edmund. You know as well as I do that regardless of the defense we put on, the jury will find our clients guilty."

"Now hold on, Desiree, I still have to prove my case."

"You could sit in your chair over there the entire trial and not utter a single word and that jury will still send the Washingtons to the electric chair."

"You're getting a little paranoid, aren't you?" he said.

"I am living in reality. I suggest you join me there."

"Hell, you folks won the *Loving* litigation."

"And you know how that matter was decided in the state courts. It was a resounding win for racism. We only prevailed in *federal* court."

"You can appeal if you lose."

"There is no federal jurisdiction for this case. And you know full well how often murder convictions are successfully appealed in the South with Black defendants. It's basically zero."

He fidgeted with a button on his jacket. "I know that I declined your plea offer. And I want you to know that it was not my call."

"I appreciate your honesty that there is more going on here than a legal trial."

"How is Mr. Lee doing?"

"Devastated and guilt-ridden, as is his family. I'm sure your sympathy for him is genuine. I doubt you would have grieved if I had been killed," she added.

"Then you would be wrong, Desiree. Frankly, you're one of the finest lawyers I've ever faced. Professionally, I respect the hell out of you."

She took a step closer to him. "'Professionally'? But would you allow yourself to be a guest in my home? If I cooked a pot roast, would you eat it? Would you invite me to your home to meet your wife? Or simply take a walk with me? Or does the mere thought of that disgust you?"

Without meeting her eye he said, "My son Brett thinks I'm dead wrong about all of this. That's why he went to work with the Justice Department."

"I hope his disagreeing with you has not affected your relationship."

"Actually, it has." He looked at her now. "If you want the God's honest truth, Desiree, it's not really about what I think or believe or don't believe. If I were to do any of the things you just suggested. If I were to agree with my son...hell...I'd be...my family would be..."

"A wise woman once told me that if you let the bully win he never goes away. He *owns* you." She paused. "President Johnson said this wasn't a Negro problem or a Southern problem. He said this country's original sin was an *American* problem. The North was tired after the Civil War and let white people enslave mine again, just in a different way. Over a century of oppression, terror, and killings, all after we *won* the damn war. Talk about a Pyrrhic victory."

"I can understand how angry you must feel. Truly."

"Don't worry about *my* anger, Edmund. Concern yourself with this possibility: Maybe next time they tell you that the *religion* you practice isn't the right one, so change it. Or that free speech is only allowed if it comports with *their* views. Or that the right to vote is only for the rich. Will you never draw a line in the sand?"

She took a step back and drew an imaginary one with her shoe.

"Here is my line, Mr. Attorney General. They can come and kill me next time, and there'll be someone just as good or better to take my place. Because when right is on your side, it's amazing how many people find the courage of their convictions." She paused and added, "And you missed something *truly* special."

He looked thoroughly confused. "What are you talking about?"

"I make one *hell* of a pot roast."

She walked out of the courtroom.

CHAPTER 57

IT WAS THREE DAYS LATER and the church was far fuller than it would have been had Lucy Lee's death not been from an act of murder, and also a tragic part of a legal case that had captured the attention of the country. Frank and Jack Lee were two of the pallbearers.

DuBose slipped into the back pew right before the service commenced. She was startled when a man came to stand next to her.

Battle said, "I'm sure it means a lot to the Lee family that you're here, Desiree."

"It's...very nice of you to come as well, Edmund."

"I spoke with my son Brett last night. He sent his condolences. I've already communicated them and mine to the Lee family."

"I'm sure they appreciated it."

They turned their attention to the front as the funeral service commenced.

In a tremulous but emotionally riveting contralto, Hilly Lee sang "Amazing Grace" from the pulpit while Herman Till, the medical examiner and a deacon of this church, looked on, tears trickling down his face.

The rain held off just long enough for the gravesite service to be completed, and then it came tumbling down like heaven was crying.

Jack was the last to leave. He stood next to the coffin of his elder sister. Placing his hand on the wood he said, "Goodbye, Lucy girl. I will miss you for the rest of my days. You, more than anyone else I know, did not deserve this."

He put a hand to his face but failed to hold back the tears. "And I'm sorry...I'm so damn sorry, Lucy."

In a daze, Jack drifted back to his car, which was parked along the meandering, narrow lanes of Forest Lawn Cemetery, where towering oaks and beautiful canopies of pink and white crepe myrtles, and green flowing dogwoods sheltered both the dead and those who grieved for them.

DuBose walked up to him. "I'm so sorry, Jack."

He wiped his eyes and nodded. "I know. And it means a lot."

"I was thinking that I would move into the Oak Tree Motel. I saw it when I was driving back from Norfolk."

"Oh, you mean the *colored* motel?" said Jack, wiping his eyes again. "That's a long way away, and you don't have a car."

"That's my problem, not yours."

"Right now, they're totally interchangeable. Come on, we're going back to my parents' house. We're having a little get-together in Lucy's honor. You can ride with me."

"Jack, no. You need to be with your family and friends."

"Which is exactly why you're coming, Desiree." He stared at her. "I...*do* consider you a friend. I hope you feel the same."

She nodded curtly and said hesitantly, "Yes...of course."

About thirty people were packed into the Lees' small house. There were cold cuts and pastries and coffee and lemonade. The rain had picked up even more and the breeze was chilly.

DuBose poured herself a cup of coffee and hung back against the wall. She was well used to being the only Black person in a courtroom, but this was different. Every white face here held the anguish of an innocent life taken prematurely, and she felt herself constantly tearing up in the face of it.

Hilly Lee sat on the couch in the living room, holding a cup of black coffee, which matched the color of her dress, shoes, and spirits.

She stared down at the floor like she had no idea what planet she was on, or whose life she was actually occupying at the moment.

Jack had sat with his stricken mother and father, then risen to greet the visitors and helped serve food and drinks. After that he'd joined DuBose against the wall.

The Lees' neighbor, Ashby, had come by, dressed in an ill-fitting suit from his younger and leaner days. By the looks of him he was already three sheets to the wind before he walked in the door. But he conveyed his respectful condolences to the Lees, grabbed a pastry, glanced curiously at DuBose, nodded at Jack, and left.

DuBose said, "You'll be surprised to learn that Battle had agreed to our extension request, but Ambrose seemed to think that postponing it would mean the man who attacked Lucy would win somehow. So we're still on for trial."

"Battle was at the service, too. A second surprise."

DuBose sipped her coffee and glanced out the window at the falling rain. "After the hearing I saw another side of the man that I never expected to."

"People *can* change, Desiree."

"I…I know that," she said, but without much force behind it.

Little by little the people left until it was only the Lees and DuBose. She was helping to clean up when someone knocked at the door.

Jack answered it with DuBose next to him. "Miss Jessup? You're soaked."

Miss Jessup was dressed all in black, including a pillbox hat with a little veil. "Been waitin' outside till all the white folk left."

"You didn't have to do that," said Jack.

She gave him a look that made his face flush with embarrassment.

From a little cloth bag she took out a Mason jar and a small music box. "You give this here jar to your daddy. It's iced tea with a bigger splash of rye. I think he gone need it tonight."

"Thank you. And the music box?"

"Has Lucy's favorite song on there. 'Twinkle, Twinkle, Little Star.' Found it down at a little shop near my house."

"How did you know that was Lucy's favorite song?" asked a puzzled Jack.

"Because Miss Jessup helped take care of Lucy when she was a year old."

Jack turned to see his mother standing there like a pale monument in failing light.

She said, "Lenore, thank you for coming, and for the gifts. Please come in out of the rain."

A stunned Jack looked between the women. *Lenore?*

"You sure, Mrs. Lee? I can catch the bus right on down there."

"I am very sure. Robert can drive you home later, can't you, son?"

"Yes, ma'am," Jack said quickly.

He held the door open for Miss Jessup, and she joined Hilly and Frank on the couch. They listened to the music box song several times, shed many tears, and told a number of stories about Lucy as a little girl, long before Jack was even born, all while Jack and DuBose looked on in mesmerized silence.

Later, DuBose led Miss Jessup out to the Fiat while Jack grabbed his jacket.

"You never mentioned Miss Jessup taking care of Lucy," he said to his mother.

"Folks think she always worked for Ashby. Fact is, we recommended her to Ashby after…after I came home."

Jack looked puzzled. "You mean from the hospital after delivering her? But you said Miss Jessup took care of Lucy when she was a year old."

His father joined them. "Your momma was at *a* hospital, Jack. She had some *personal* problems after we found out what had happened to Lucy."

"The hospital was over in Petersburg," said Hilly, staring directly at her son.

"But the hospital in Petersburg—" began Jack.

"Yes, that's right. My problems were up here." She tapped her forehead. "Your daddy had a little child to take care of. And Miss Jessup had a good reputation."

"But—"

"Yes," said Hilly. "I know, son. You take Miss Jessup home now and then you go on and get ready for that trial."

His mother put her arms around her son and squeezed him with a strength that belied her lean frame but represented growing up in a daunting, unforgiving place, where the only person you could truly count on was yourself.

When she drew back her face glistened with tears. Hilly Lee picked up the music box, slowly walked down the hall to her bedroom, and closed the door.

CHAPTER 58

ON THE DRIVE OVER TO Tuxedo Boulevard, Miss Jessup told Jack and DuBose that she had visited Pearl. "She told me what she done, with the baby and all."

"You know the man who raped her?" asked Jack.

"I do now. And he'll be gettin' his, I can tell you that."

"Miss Jessup, you have to let the law—" began Jack.

"The *law*?" she parroted back to him. "Exactly what do I got to let the law do? No, let me say it 'nother way. What you think the law *gonna* do, Jack Lee? Pearl went to the police. She couldn't do that if he a white man 'cause *she* be the one endin' up in jail. But they won't even go after a colored man who raped a colored woman. Now if it were a white woman, the man would already be in jail or most likely dead. That why he went after Pearl in the first place. Some men bad all the way through, don't matter the skin color."

Jack eyed the woman in the rearview mirror. "Why didn't you ever tell me that you took care of my sister while my mother was... away?"

"'Cause she asked me never to speak of it, so I didn't. When she come back home she was not in a good way. But she told me to go and so's I went. But I got on with Ashby 'cause your daddy told him I did such a good job with Lucy."

"But my mother acted like she didn't even know you all these years."

"She *didn't* know me. People got to want to know somebody before that happens, and the will just wasn't there with your momma. Hell, on my side, too. See, I just don't get along with white folks for the most part. I'm too old and seen too much." She paused. "But your momma is a tough one to figure. I know 'bout her and your daddy helpin' out Black folks at his work. Sometimes when I look at her I see a white woman ain't got no time or will for folks like me. Other times...." She shook her head.

"What?" said Jack anxiously.

"Other times seems like I'm lookin' at somebody not that much different from me. Now, with what happened to poor Lucy, I think, well, maybe your momma's lookin' at the world a little different. Losin' somebody that way, it changes a person. Makes 'em see what really counts, and what doesn't."

DuBose said, "Have you lost...anyone, Miss Jessup?"

"White man got two of my boys. And my oldest girl, Wanda, she got real sick down in Alabama when she was young. Ain't no colored hospital where we lived. Tried to get her in the white hospital, but they wouldn't even let me bring her in the back door. She died right outside the buildin' where they had all them doctors and medicine that maybe coulda saved her."

Jack said softly, "I'm so sorry."

"Just the way it was. Still is, for the most part, all these years later."

"But not forever," interjected DuBose. "Things *are* changing."

Miss Jessup smiled sadly at her. "Girl, you for sure doin' God's work. But when I be dead, and even when you be dead, I don't see it bein' much different. Do you?"

Tears glistening in her eyes, DuBose said, "I *want* to believe that it will be different. I *have* to believe it will. If just to get myself out of bed every day, Miss Jessup."

The older woman nodded. "It's why I've gone to church all these years. Said lots of prayers, most not answered. Now, they say Jesus is white, but others say he come from part of the world where they ain't no white folks. So I say, what's that about? But I keep prayin'. He's my god, too, after all."

She looked up ahead and clutched her purse. "You drop me at the corner there, Jack Lee. Don't you come down the road. Daniel and his boys are out. It won't be good for you, and my chest's too heavy from cryin' to do much yellin'."

As she got out Jack rolled the window down and said, "I'm sorry I never asked about you and your family when I was a little boy. And I'm sorry so many years went by and I never spent any time with you." Tears trickled down his cheeks.

She patted them dry and said, "You take care 'a yourself and that gal over there. I can't do much no more, and you got your people to answer to. But that lady, well, maybe she got a shot. I'll go to church tomorrow, before Ashby, and pray for her. *And* you."

Jack watched her walk slowly to the home where she would most likely die. He hoped it would occur peacefully in her bed and many years from now.

CHAPTER 59

LATER THAT WEEK JACK AND DuBose finished their sworn witness statements, then went around and had them signed and notarized by all the people they had spoken with. Sam Randolph scrutinized his carefully before making one small handwritten correction and initialing it. Tyler Dobbs just signed his without reading it.

"How's the damn dog?" he asked DuBose in a surly tone.

"Doing just fine."

"Then I shoulda kicked it harder."

They worked until one in the morning. When their eyes would not stay open anymore, they turned off the lights. Queenie lay by the front door, while Jack went to the couch, and DuBose headed upstairs.

It was around two in the morning when Jack felt something touch him. Whoever it was nuzzled his arm, and then he felt warm breath on his face.

When Jack's eyes fully opened, Queenie backed up and started to whine and bark. And that's when Jack smelled it. He looked around. "Oh my Lord."

Flames were shooting across the front part of his office. Smoke was everywhere, and pouring up the stairs.

"Desiree!" he screamed.

Gagging and holding his arm over his face, he took the stairs two at a time; a barking Queenie bounded right behind him.

He pounded on the door. "Desiree!" He opened the door and saw her on the floor of the smoke-filled room gasping for air.

He raced over and picked her up as her eyes closed and she fell limp.

Jack carried her down the stairs. Flames had blocked the front door, so he slid open a rear window and clambered out with her. Queenie leapt neatly through the opening and followed.

Jack carried her well away from the building and set her down on a strip of grass. He breathed into her mouth, slapped her face, rolled her on her side, and pushed against her back to free up her lungs.

"Come on, Desiree. Please, come on now, breathe. Please!"

He kept driving air into her mouth and compressing her back. She suddenly gave a heaving breath, sat up, took another forceful swallow of air, then turned to the side and retched.

"You're okay, you're okay," he said softly as he helped her lie back. He turned to Queenie. "Watch her, girl!"

He passed back through the window and quickly filled boxes with their files, all the while coughing and gagging. Both their briefcases slung over his shoulders, he climbed back out through the window and put the items down. He made one more trip back inside to get whatever else he could before the place was fully engulfed in flames.

Jack could hear sirens now as, coughing and spitting up, he ran back to DuBose and Queenie. Only this time he found they were no longer alone.

"Son of a bitch," said Gene Taliaferro. "How'd you get outta there, man?" He was not in his deputy's uniform, but he had his service revolver pointed at Jack.

The man next to him was the same one whose ear Jack had shot half off. "Miss me?" he snarled. "Because I sure as hell missed you."

Gene looked at DuBose. "Get up, woman. Now! I ain't tellin' you a second time."

DuBose rose unsteadily to her feet.

Queenie was snarling and baring her teeth. Gene pointed his gun at the animal.

Jack stepped in front of the dog. "You're not going to do that, Gene. What you're going to do is get the hell out of here, right now. Before people show up and you get arrested."

Gene smirked. "What? You think the boys on the fire truck are gonna care? You simple, or what?"

"Simple like his sister," said his companion.

Jack slowly turned his gaze to him. "My *sister*?"

"Yeah, she screamed like a little baby when I hit her. Heard she died. You should thank me. Now you don't have to change her damn diaper no more."

With a roar of rage, Jack lunged at the man, striking him on the jaw so hard he knocked him down. But Gene struck Jack on the head with the butt of his revolver and Jack fell to the pavement, moaning.

Gene pointed his gun at Jack, but DuBose flung herself in the way.

"Help us," she screamed. "Help us, somebody."

"Ain't nobody gonna help you," said Gene, grabbing her by the hair and yanking her away. He aimed his gun at her and grinned. "Say goodbye to yourself."

A terrified DuBose closed her eyes and prepared herself to die.

She heard a cry of pain and a thud. When she opened her eyes, Gene lay stretched out on the pavement unconscious, his gun next to him.

The person who had put him there looked remarkably familiar to DuBose.

The man missing half his ear charged the intruder, and was rapidly and efficiently also beaten into unconsciousness. He dropped to the sidewalk and lay still next to the fallen Gene.

Jack and DuBose's savior stepped over the prostrate figures, as the fire trucks arrived and the firemen began battling the flames.

He held out his hand and helped DuBose to her feet. "You okay, ma'am?"

She nodded dumbly, amazed by the immense strength in the man's grip, as well as mesmerized by a pair of intense eyes she had seen before, on someone else.

"Good." He knelt down next to Jack. "Man, I haven't seen your butt go down like that since we played John Marshall High School in the state championship."

Jack rose up on his elbows, turned, and looked at the speaker, his jaw descending in shock.

"Long time no see, big brother," drawled Jefferson Lee.

CHAPTER 60

I GOT ME A LAWYER UP in Canada. He specializes in workin' out these types of situations. And I knew some things that the Army had done that, well, that they wouldn't want to see the light of day," Jeff Lee told Jack, his parents, and DuBose back at the Lees' home. "So we reached us a deal."

"So they can't arrest you now that you've come back?" said his mother anxiously.

"I got my general discharge papers. I'm good to go, Momma."

"How come you're back now, son?" asked Frank.

His youngest boy turned somber eyes on his father. "Heard about Lucy. When I got here, all the lights were out and nobody answered my knock. I remembered where Jack had his place, so I went over there."

"Good thing you did, or else we'd be dead," said Jack. "As it is, my apartment and office are gone. But they've arrested Gene Talia-ferro for arson and attempted murder. He was one of the deputies who arrested Jerome." He turned to his parents. "And the other man was the one who hurt Lucy. He admitted it right to our faces. He's going to prison, for life."

"Still too good for the bastard," snapped his father. "But what you gonna do now, Jack? You got the trial comin' up."

"You can stay here," said his mother immediately. "You and

Jefferson can have your old room. And Desiree can stay in Lucy's room."

"Mrs. Lee," said DuBose, "I can't possibly impose like that. Especially not at a time like this."

"You can and you will. And you can use the garage as your office. I'm sure Francis can fix it up for you."

Frank scratched his chin. "They got some old desks and chairs at work. They were just gonna throw 'em away. I can get it done tomorrow." He eyed the clock on the wall. "Well, I guess it already is tomorrow."

Jeff said, "And I'll stick around here in case anybody else tries somethin'. You still got your guns, Daddy?" When Frank nodded, he added, "We better make sure they're ready to go."

Jack said, "Now we just need to find some other clothes. The rest of ours got burned up. Lucky I had time to grab a pair of pants, my wallet, and your purse."

DuBose's face fell. "Oh. That's right." She looked down at the nightgown she was still wearing, though one of the firemen had given her a blanket to put around her.

Hilly said, "I've got some things you can use, Desiree; we're about the same size. Now, let's all get some sleep. Breakfast will be ready at nine. Which will be here before we know it."

Jack could tell that all this activity had given his mother a reprieve from her grief, allowing her to focus her energies on something other than her dead child.

Later, they sleepily met downstairs in the dining room, where they were greeted with fried eggs, bacon, ham, grits, biscuits, and hot coffee. Looking at his mother, Jack wasn't sure the woman had even been to sleep. But she swept around the kitchen and dining room full of vigor.

They ate their fill, and Frank went off with Jeff in his truck. Two hours later they came back with two desks, two chairs, a filing cabinet, and a chalkboard.

They unloaded it all and set it up in the garage.

"I can run a phone line out to the garage," said Frank. "And you can use the telephone we keep in the bedroom for out here."

"Thank you, that's very kind," said DuBose, who was wearing a pair of Hilly's jeans, and one of the woman's blouses.

Later that day, as they were organizing their files and setting their office up in the garage, they heard a car pull up into the driveway and someone honked a horn.

Jack watched as Donny and Shirley Peppers climbed out of a yellow Corvette.

Shirley said, "Where is that lady lawyer, Jack?"

"Desiree?" Jack called over his shoulder. "You're wanted out here."

DuBose came to the door and looked out at Shirley.

"Okay, Desiree, we heard what happened. Those damn assholes! Excuse my French. Now, we're goin' shoppin' for clothes and shoes and accessories, and then you're comin' with me to my salon and we are gonna work on a new hairstyle so you can knock 'em dead in court."

DuBose looked imploringly at Jack. "But we've got so much to get done."

"Well, neither one of us can do it without clothes," replied Jack. "You go with her, I'll go shopping at the Goodwill, we'll meet back here and burn the midnight oil."

"You're sure?"

Peppers glanced at his wife. "Well, I know that look, and Shirl is not going to take no for an answer."

Shirley and DuBose drove off, while Peppers walked over to Jack.

"Real sorry about Lucy. We were at the funeral but didn't want to bother you."

"Thanks, Donny."

"That's your piece-of-shit Fiat over there, right?"

"Yeah, why?"

"While Shirl is doing her magic with Desiree, we need to work on you. Let's go."

Jack returned later with two suits and four shirts and a new belt, along with some skivvies and a new pair of black shoes and a few pairs of dress socks. Peppers had insisted on paying for all of it.

"Until you get back on your feet, Jack, then I am billing your ass, *with* interest."

"Thanks, Donny, for everything. You need a ride home?" Jack asked.

"Nope. Shirl's old man is coming by to get me. We're about the same age, but we don't have a lot in common."

As soon as he said this, a dusty Dodge pickup truck pulled up with copper pipes and tool boxes and an old toilet in the rear bed. Driving was a massive, stern-looking Black man around Peppers's age with a bald head and rolled up sleeves revealing heavily muscled forearms. On the side of the truck was stenciled: BIG MIKE, THE PLUMBER.

Peppers said, "That's Big Mike."

"Yeah, I'd actually worked that one out for myself," replied Jack.

"He makes more money than I don't know what. I mean, who knew toilets were so damn lucrative? And he's really starting to come around on his opinion of me. Sort of going from outright revulsion to mild disgust."

"That's great. How long have you and Shirl been together now?"

"Seven years."

Jack's mouth fell open. "Oh, okay. Well, I guess keep doing what you're doing and Big Mike will be shaking your hand in no time."

Peppers climbed into the truck cab and they drove off, without Big Mike even once looking at his son-in-law.

Jack put his new things away, then went out to the garage to find that his father was hanging a sign on a wall.

"'DuBose and Lee'?" Jack said, reading off the names his father had burned into a piece of pine.

"Yeah," said Frank. "Think it has a real nice ring to it."

A handful of hours later the Corvette streaked into the driveway. Shirley got out, popped the trunk, and tugged out multiple shopping bags and a long garment holder.

The other car door opened and DuBose climbed out. Gone was the tight bun when her hair was up, and the demure locks when it was down. Her hair was shorter on the sides where it curved around her ears, with considerable volume on top. Though he knew little to nothing of women's hairstyles, the waves, dips, and intricate patterns DuBose's hair now possessed struck Jack as meaningfully artistic.

DuBose approached them, self-consciously swiping at her hair. She smiled in an embarrassed fashion. "Shopping with Shirl is...an experience."

Jack said, "You look...great, Desiree."

Shirley came up to them. "It was all there. It was like she was holdin' her breath all that time. And then finally she just let it blow." She handed the bags to Jack. "My work here is done. I've got to get home to feed my hungry man and my ornery father."

She kissed DuBose on the cheek and gave her a hug. "Good luck, girl. I know you are gonna kick some ass." In a far less strident voice that only DuBose could hear she added, "I walk and talk big, Desiree, because that's the only way some people will ever notice me. I married a good man and I built up a nice business after workin' my tail off for years. None of that would be possible without people like you. Not one damn bit of it. So...thank you."

DuBose saw tears sliding down the other woman's cheeks before she quickly climbed into the Corvette and kicked up gravel making her exit.

Jack pointed behind him at their garage office. "Ready to get to work at the law firm of DuBose and Lee?" he said nervously.

CHAPTER 61

LATER THAT NIGHT, JEFF WALKED through the dining room and found his father sitting at the table looking pensive.

"You okay, Pop?" asked Jeff.

"Take a seat, son, and let's talk for a spell."

Frank drew a paper from his pocket. "Your letter."

"You never wrote me back," said Jeff.

"Because when I read it I didn't agree with any of it. So I put it in my toolbox and mostly forgot about it. Until now."

"You wore the uniform, Pop. You did what you had to do. That was why I felt I needed to explain my actions."

"But it was a different time and a different war. We knew what we were fightin' for. And we were attacked."

"Did you arrive at that conclusion readin' my letter a *second* time?" asked Jeff.

"It helped me clarify things. *Clarify*. I never had no cause to ever use that word before now." He tapped the table with his knuckles. "So what I mean to do is apologize to you, Jeff. It's damn hard to fight in a war. But it's a lot harder to walk away from a fight that ain't the good fight, or the right one." Frank put out his hand. "Won't blame you if you don't want to shake your old man's hand, but I just wanted you to know how I felt."

Jeff clenched his father's hand. "You still got a strong grip for an old man."

Frank smiled.

"I'm real sorry about Lucy, Pop. I know Momma's takin' it bad."

"Your momma has dealt with a lot in her life, son. But this truly might be the hardest."

"Well, that's why she has you. You got her back, right?"

"Right, son. I do."

And the way he said it, it seemed that Frank Lee actually believed his answer.

* * *

Jack stood in front of the chalkboard. He had diagrammed out the commonwealth's case, and he and DuBose were looking over it to see the gaps.

DuBose said, "Okay, they have the victims, the opportunity, and the motive, but they don't have a murder weapon."

"We can hit them on motive by showing that Sam Randolph also had plenty of incentive to kill his parents and then lie about what he told Battle."

"But Gordon Hanover will testify that Leslie Randolph thought Jerome was stealing and had been in the house without permission, and that he was planning on firing Jerome. And *he* has no motive to lie," noted Jack.

"But there's no proof Randolph told Jerome that he was going to fire him. And Anne Randolph *was* planning to divorce her husband. She might have told Sam and *he* decided to kill them."

"So we make Sam and his situation our reasonable-doubt strategy?" said DuBose.

"Only we can't place him at the crime scene."

"We don't have to prove that he did it, only that he *could* have. Because he doesn't have an alibi."

Jack said, "I hope Donny can somehow tie the blue convertible to Sam."

"But in order to get that evidence in, we have to put Jerome on the stand. He's the one who saw the car. Now, is Sam the only one with a motive?" she mused.

"Well, Christine and her husband were in Washington, DC. And they were financially supporting her parents. They clearly don't need the money. So there's no motive, means, or opportunity for her or Gordon."

"And we're sure they *are* in good financial shape?"

"I had Donny run a check. The Hanovers are worth at least three million dollars with little debt."

"I guess that answers that." She paused. "You and your brother look an awful lot alike. Same eyes."

"But the war changed him," Jack said earnestly. "Before that, he was pretty basic. Beer, football, girls, and guns but…it just changed him."

"War often does to that people."

He looked at her. "You're in a war, too."

"And now so are you," she replied, a bit sadly, Jack thought.

He looked back at the chalkboard. "The Randolphs liked Jerome and his family. They paid him a cash bonus, according to Jerome. They invited them over for lunch and the pool, or rather Anne Randolph did. Apparently, she was more enlightened than her husband on such things. And who would have been upset that the Randolphs were divorcing?"

"Sam? A divorce might mess up his inheritance. Or so he thought."

"What if he hired someone to kill his parents before they divorced?"

"But we can't show he even knew of the divorce," she replied.

"Right."

DuBose said decisively, "I'll take Janice Evans, and you have a go at the divorce lawyer, and let's hope for at least one miracle between us."

CHAPTER 62

THEY DROVE TO COURT ON the first day of the trial. When they turned the last corner Jack exclaimed, "Damn!"

"What exactly did you expect?" said an unfazed DuBose.

There was a large crowd outside the courthouse. Some held signs with images of a Black man in a noose. Another large placard proclaimed, THE KILLER COLOREDS MUST FRY. Other signs used even more graphic language and images. Confederate battle flags were waving everywhere. A few streets over, Jack's old home and office were now still-smoldering ruins.

DuBose glanced to where Howard Pickett stood next to his chauffeur-driven car as he was being interviewed by the local NBC station. News trucks were parked out front, cameramen were filming journalists reporting on the case, and other media members were interviewing folks in the crowd.

Jack did a quick U-turn and parked on a side street.

"We'll go in through another entrance near the rear," he said.

* * *

Twenty minutes later the bailiff announced, "All rise."

The packed courtroom followed this directive, and Judge Ambrose marched in and took his high seat.

The angry chants from the mob outside could be heard inside, further fueling an already emotional atmosphere.

Jack had watched Jerome come into the courtroom, dressed in his church suit and tie, and take his seat with him and DuBose. It occurred to Jack that he had never seen Jerome walk or even stand before. He was a truly large man. But his left leg had a pronounced limp.

Pearl had been brought in from another doorway. She looked nervous and fearful in the simple blue dress her mother had brought her to wear. But when she saw her husband she appeared to relax a bit.

Jack maneuvered the chairs so that the couple could sit side by side and converse in low voices.

DuBose explained, "This is jury selection today. We can challenge potential jurors and the commonwealth can, too. Our goal is *not* to end up with people who have formed an opinion about this case, and not in a good way for you and Pearl, you understand?"

Jerome said, "Yeah, but damned if I can see how you gonna do it."

Jack said, "Now, we have unlimited challenges for cause, but we only get four preemptory challenges, meaning we can disqualify a juror for any reason."

DuBose said, "And we may end up using them all."

Battle and his two lieutenants looked ready to go to war. Ambrose peered over the courtroom with an excited if benevolent air.

Jack's parents and brother were in one of the middle rows and had smiled encouragingly at Jack. Miss Jessup was seated to the left of Hilly Lee. Their presence made his small stomach butterflies turn into ones the size of condors. He noted Sally Reeves, the clerk of the court, was seated near the front, with what looked to be some of her older children. She looked at Jack and then whispered something to the teenage towheaded boy next to her. He laughed. Then he turned his gaze to Jack, and a mask of loathing descended over his youthful features.

Jack turned to look at DuBose, who seemed both relaxed and expectant. But then she'd litigated high-profile cases all over the country. She'd argued and won a case before the highest court in the land. She was used to this level of scrutiny.

You are so far out of your depth, Jack Lee. Is this a dream? Or, more accurately, your worst nightmare? No, what happened to Lucy was your worst nightmare. But this is an uncomfortably close second.

He felt a surge of panic coming on. Then strong fingers closed around his under the table, and he turned to see DuBose's reassuring gaze on him. She smiled and whispered, "You can do this. You *deserve* to be here, Jack."

He smiled back and his nerves did ease some. The condors had now reduced to mere hawks in his belly.

Ambrose said, "Bailiff, bring in the juror pool."

The bailiff nodded at the deputy standing next to the rear doors. He opened them and motioned to someone out there. A moment later a column of twenty people walked down the center aisle and over to the juror box.

"That be the folks gone be on the jury?" exclaimed Jerome. "They all white men."

DuBose rose and said, "Judge, this juror pool is prima facie unconstitutional. It requires a jury of the defendants' peers. There is not one Black person or a female."

Ambrose nodded. "I sympathize with you, Miss DuBose. I truly do. But it's the same all across the state. I will keep an eye on things. And you have your challenges to fall back on." He eyed the attorney general. "No funny business today, Mr. Battle."

"Excuse me, Your Honor?" said a stricken Battle.

Ambrose eyed him cagily. "We all know why you're here, sir. And why the death penalty was reinstated. And I was made aware of your actions with a certain dubious letter regarding representation of the defendant?"

Battle began to protest but the judge cut him off. "Let's get to it."

Ambrose intoned to the juror pool, "Now, the process of jury selection is called voir dire, which is old French meaning, 'to speak the truth,' which we expect all of you to do. Jury pool member number one, please take the witness stand."

A man in a brown pin-striped suit came forward and was sworn in. He gave his name as Nathan Talmadge. The judge asked the usual questions, whether sitting on the jury would cause undue hardship, or whether the juror was related to the defendants by blood or marriage.

To this last query Talmadge uttered a firm, "*No, sir.*"

Talmadge went on to swear that he had no preconceived opinions about the case and had no financial interest in the outcome.

"Mr. Battle?" said the judge.

"No questions, Your Honor."

"Defense counsel?" said Ambrose.

Jack and DuBose had decided to handle the voir dire together, with each taking half, unless there was a compelling reason for one of them to interview a particular juror.

DuBose rose and approached Talmadge. She had read about his background in the materials provided to both counsel. But she had faced so many white men in so many trials that she had developed a sixth sense about what they truly felt behind their soft, evasive words. It usually wasn't difficult.

In this case, the closer she drew, the farther Talmadge leaned back in his chair.

"Mr. Talmadge, nice to meet you."

"Uh-huh," he said, frowning.

She glanced down at the paper she held. "You sell cars for a living?"

"Yep, Talmadge Chrysler-Dodge," he replied curtly.

"Does your business do well?"

He shifted in his seat as DuBose drew even closer. "Keeps food on the table."

"You meet a lot of people in your business, I would imagine."

"Sure do."

"You have any Black customers?"

He noticeably flinched. "What?"

"I said do you have Black customers? Do you sell to Blacks?"

"I sell to anybody has the money." He glanced at the crowd in the courtroom and smiled in a cocksure manner. "Green's the only *color* I care about."

That drew laughter from around the courtroom.

"So you have and do sell to Black customers?"

His grin faded. "Well, I...I'd have to check my records."

"You can't remember a single Black person you sold a car to? I mean, if it was that rare, I think you would remember."

"Well, I don't. Coloreds want a vehicle, I'll sell it to 'em."

"But you can't remember having done so?"

"Not offhand, no. Those folks, well, they usually have trouble gettin' a loan. Bad credit and so on."

"'*Those* folks'?" she said, moving still closer.

Ambrose interjected, "Miss DuBose, I know the point you're trying to get across, but we have a lot of jurors to get through, so please move on."

"Judge, the law gives me the right to question a prospective juror about bias or prejudice that would impair his ability to objectively hear the case."

"The man has already said he would sell cars to Black folks. I empathize with what you're trying to do, but you can't beat a dead horse."

DuBose composed herself and said to Talmadge. "Did you know the Randolphs?"

"No. Like I already told the judge."

"Had you heard of them?"

"Yeah. They were a well-known family hereabouts. Never sold 'em a car."

"But you can be impartial in this case?"

"Yes."

"You're aware, no doubt, of the murders of Robert Kennedy and Dr. Martin Luther King Jr.?"

Ambrose said, "We're not getting into any of that, Miss DuBose. No politics in my courtroom. And I'll hold the other side to the same standard," he added, pointing his gavel at Battle and shooting Howard Pickett a stern look.

"Do you have any Black friends or business colleagues, Mr. Talmadge?"

"Colleagues!" he barked before catching himself. "Um, got a boy does the cleanin' up, and another ni—another *man* does the detailing on the used cars I sell."

She turned to the bench. "Judge, I'd like to strike this potential juror for cause."

"What cause?" said Ambrose, looking surprised.

"That he caught himself right before he called a Black person a n——."

He looked at Talmadge with a grim expression. "Is that what you were going to say, sir? And I'll remind you that you're under oath."

"No, Judge. I was gonna say...*nice* man. I got me another *nice* man."

Ambrose gazed at him skeptically for a long moment. "All right. Miss DuBose, if you want to strike him you'll have to use one of your preemptory challenges."

"Then I'll have to seek to strike him on that basis, Judge."

Ambrose said sternly to the man, "You are excused from this jury pool, sir."

A scowling Talmadge got off the stand and left the courtroom.

DuBose walked back to her chair as Ambrose called up the next potential juror.

Jack looked over at Jerome and Pearl. He was staring down at his hands, and Pearl had her gaze fixed resolutely on her husband. She reached out and took his big hand in hers, until a deputy rushed over and removed it.

In the audience, Hilly Lee had her gaze directly on Judge Ambrose.

Jack rose to question the next potential juror after Ambrose had finished with his standard line of questioning and Battle, again, had no questions.

"You're a mechanic, Mr. Runnel," he said.

Runnel nodded. "How'd you know?"

"Well, it says so right here on this paper. But I would have known anyway. It's your hands. My daddy pulls wrenches for a living and he has the same set of thick, strong fingers you got."

"Work over at Associated Truckin'. Been there twenty-four years."

"Hard work?"

He grinned. "Yeah, but I don't mind it. Keeps me outta trouble, or so my wife tells me."

"Associated Trucking? Now, I read about them in the papers recently. They were just unionized, correct?"

"Yes sir, about damn time, too."

Ripples of laughter swirled around the room and Runnel looked embarrassed.

"And unless I'm mistaken they also were the first large trucking company in the country to do away with separate bathrooms for Blacks and whites."

"About damn time for that, too," said Runnel.

"We accept this juror, Your Honor."

Jack started to walk back to his chair.

"Mr. Battle?" Ambrose said, as the lawyer started to rise.

DuBose exclaimed, "Judge, the commonwealth has already had the opportunity to question this juror."

Ambrose said, "Come on now, Miss DuBose, we haven't even started the trial yet. Let's try to get along and let this play out fair and square. I am doing all I can to accommodate your every request."

Caught off guard by this, DuBose turned and looked at the reporters scribbling furiously in their notebooks; several shot DuBose unfriendly looks.

Battle said, "Thank you. Commonwealth moves to strike this juror for cause."

"On what basis?" asked a clearly surprised Ambrose.

"He's in the same occupation as defense counsel's father, and there might be a natural bias because of that. He might even know the man."

"Wait, do you know the defense counsel's father?" asked Ambrose.

"I...I might've met him at a union event. Don't know for sure."

"You should have acknowledged that when I questioned you, sir."

Runnel now looked unnerved. "I'm sorry, Judge."

Ambrose looked sternly at DuBose and Jack. "In the future, any possible connections between potential jurors and parties, attorneys, and their families to this case *must* be disclosed," he said in an admonishing tone. "Motion to strike for cause granted."

Hours later, after many disputes and sidebar conferences with the judge, and the proceedings twice being interrupted by protestors invading the courtroom before being forced back out by a contingent of law enforcement, the jury was finally seated. Jack and DuBose had asked for cause strikes on nine potential jurors. Ambrose had rejected seven of their challenges, but he had disallowed several of Battle's challenges as well.

Court was adjourned for the day.

At the counsel table Jerome shook his head. "We ain't got no chance now."

"Listen here, Jerome, we got Miss Desiree and Mr. Jack," said his wife firmly. "You let 'em do their job. I believe in 'em and you should, too."

They were then escorted away by a pair of deputies.

Jack looked at DuBose. "Well, we have a jury. Just not one of our clients' peers."

She said, "We only have one way through this. We have to prove they *didn't* do it. Because that's what it's going to take with this damn jury."

CHAPTER 63

JACK DROPPED OFF DUBOSE AT his parents' house and then immediately left for Norfolk to speak to Craig Baker, the divorce lawyer for Anne Randolph.

Meanwhile, DuBose again called Janice Evans in New York, and this time she answered.

DuBose explained who she was and what she wanted. "With your testimony we can show that Pearl could not have been at the Randolphs' when they say she was."

"I understand that, Miss DuBose. But if I come back to Virginia and testify, can you guarantee that I won't be arrested and charged with a crime?"

"No, I'm afraid I cannot."

"Then I can't possibly do as you ask. I'm terribly sorry about the Washingtons, but women need my services and I can't perform them if I'm in prison."

"But would you at least be willing to provide an affidavit?"

"No, I'm sorry. I can't be involved in this."

"Then I'm afraid I'm going to have to subpoena you. I have no other choice."

"You do what you have to do and I'll do the same." Evans hung up.

DuBose sat back and sighed. "Damn."

"Trouble?"

She looked up to see Jeff Lee standing in the side doorway of the garage.

"A witness we really, really needed is not going to cooperate."

"Can you force her to come in?"

"Maybe, but it will take time, time we don't have," replied DuBose.

"I guess you can't prove what you need some other way?"

"I suppose I need a miracle."

"Well, here's prayin' for one," said Jeff.

"I guess you did that a lot in Vietnam. Did you ever find one?"

"I'm standin' here, aren't I?"

* * *

Jack sat across from Craig Baker in Norfolk. The divorce lawyer stared stoically back.

Jack said, "Okay, let's look at this logically. The rule in question covers privileged communications between counsel and client."

"Correct," agreed Baker.

"And what you sent to Mrs. Randolph was such a communication?"

"Yes."

"I saw a scrap of it. They looked like pleadings."

"They were draft pleadings that were to be filed in court once finalized."

"But why on earth did you send them to the Randolphs' house?"

Baker now looked confused. "No, no, they went to a P.O. box that Anne maintained for our correspondence, not her home."

"Well, someone at your office got that wrong. And we found the empty package in Mr. Randolph's study. So I think he read and then burned the pages."

"My God," muttered a clearly distraught Baker. "I can't believe this."

Jack thought of something. "I understand that you specialize in divorce?"

"Yes. I told your colleague that already."

"Okay. Revealing that specialty in court would not break the attorney-client privilege, since I assume you hold yourself out publicly as a divorce lawyer."

Baker nodded slowly. "Y-yes, that is correct."

"Now, the *fact* that you were Mrs. Randolph's lawyer involves no disclosure of attorney-client privilege, does it? I mean, you were going to file a lawsuit for divorce in court where it would be a matter of public record. So you could say that you were Mrs. Randolph's lawyer without disclosing communications between the two of you. Right?"

"Yes, that's right."

"Would you be prepared to do so under oath?"

Baker sat up straighter and smiled as what Jack was proposing dawned on him. "I liked Anne Randolph very much. So I would actually be delighted to do so."

CHAPTER 64

LATER, DUBOSE AND JACK MET up in the garage to prepare for their opening statement.

"So Baker will testify?" she said after Jack told her about his meeting.

"Yes. And Janice Evans?"

"Working on it. We won't need her until the prosecution rests."

It was eight o'clock when they both realized that they had not eaten since breakfast.

"You want to go out somewhere?" asked Jack.

"What, to get spit or worse in my food?"

At that moment the door opened and Hilly came in carrying a tray, with Frank and Jeff right behind her doing the same.

"Dinner is served, y'all," Hilly said.

"You shouldn't have gone to this trouble," said DuBose, as Hilly and the others set their trays down on a sheet of thick plywood laid over two sawhorses Jack and DuBose had been using to organize their legal files.

Hilly laid out paper napkins and utensils. "It's nothing fancy, but it's filling."

"It smells wonderful," said DuBose, lifting the lid off one pot revealing beef stew.

As they started filling their plates, Hilly said, "That judge has it in for you."

DuBose glanced up to see Hilly staring at her. "He's actually been reasonably fair. I thought it would be much worse."

Hilly took a newspaper off the tray and handed it to DuBose. "Evening edition."

DuBose looked at the headline.

JUDGE BENDING OVER BACKWARDS TO AID DEFENSE

She glanced at Hilly, who said, "You get more flies with honey than vinegar."

DuBose gazed at Hilly in understanding and said, "Okay, he wants to look good for the media. And Ambrose is probably going out of his way to appear to be on our side so we'll have no way to argue that this whole trial has been fixed from the very start."

Hilly said, "You see, I know when white folks are trying to pretend they're not racist because I've done it myself." She looked down. "But…I wasn't always that way."

"Momma?" said Jack. "What are you talking about?"

Hilly smoothed down the front of her apron and clasped her hands in front of her. She eyed the concrete floor like there was something fascinating there. She looked nervous and unsure of herself, which clearly shocked the other Lees, who knew her to always be a confident, decisive person.

"I can't believe I'm about to say this but with what happened to Lucy…" She drew a deep, calming breath. "I was the youngest of ten. Most of my siblings were long gone by the time I came along. My momma was in her forties when she had me. I was…unexpected. On the day I was born I also died, or so my momma told me years later. My daddy was a practical man, if not a nice one, so he built a little coffin for me that very day. I was laid out in my white burial clothes, and I would have been put into the ground behind the barn if the doctor who delivered me had not pressed a mirror against my mouth and got a little fog of life on it. That man saved me from being buried alive." She glanced up at DuBose. "That doctor was a Black man named Isaac Taylor."

Jeff said, "How did a Black doctor come to deliver you, Momma?"

"We were farmers, and the farm right next to ours was owned by the Taylor family. Isaac was from my daddy's generation, only Black doctor I ever heard of. After medical school he came back home to serve the community and farm the land. When Momma went into a bad labor with me, one of my brothers went to fetch him. Where I'm from everybody just helped everybody." She looked at DuBose. "Back then I just saw good and bad, that was all. Well, Isaac had a son about the time I was born. He was named Joshua. We were best friends growing up, couldn't keep us apart. Roamed all over those mountains together. Now, my parents had their troubles from time to time and left me alone up there. When they did, the Taylors watched over me as best they could."

"You never told me that, Hilly," said her husband.

She looked at him, her features tight and anxious. "And I also never told you that I was...sweet on Joshua, either."

Frank and his sons exchanged startled glances, while DuBose kept her gaze fixed on the woman.

Hilly continued. "He grew up to be one handsome man—and even better, a kind one. And he could play the fiddle so good it was like his soul was coming out his skin as music. Many an evening his bow and fingers would dance on those strings, and I would sing along. 'Old Black Joe,' 'O Ride On, Jesus,' ''Tis Me, O Lord.' Still remember the words after all these years. It was...a nice time during hardship." She looked around. "And then I moved here and then suddenly I started seeing color, because everybody around me was seeing it, too. And I just went along, like sheep being herded, because I was weak."

"I don't know anybody who would describe you as weak, Hilly," said Frank.

"But I was," she said sharply. She looked dead at DuBose. "I *was*. On the mountain the Blacks were always poor. And most of the white folks were, too. The Taylors were the best friends I ever had. And I would like to think I was the best friend they ever had."

She looked at Jack and her son gazed back at her. "You found that picture of me and Joshua when you were a little boy. Well, now you know, son."

Jack nodded and then glanced away from his mother's vulnerable gaze.

"Do you know what happened to Joshua?" asked DuBose quietly.

Hilly nodded dumbly, her mouth trembling. "He went away to college. And the man never came back. And then I became...what I am..."

She turned and walked out, leaving them all staring at one another.

CHAPTER 65

WHEN GIVEN THE GO-AHEAD BY Judge Ambrose, Edmund Battle rose, buttoned the jacket of his three-piece light gray suit fronted by a yellow tie, made a sharp left turn around the counsel table, and approached the jury box containing twelve men who stared earnestly back at him.

He eyed every one of them, lingering a few seconds on each face, smiling, like he'd known them all his life. Back at the counsel table his two associates were readying documents and jotting down notes and being fine little foot soldiers for their leader.

Battle began, "Gentlemen of the jury, I am Edmund Battle and I represent the interests of the Commonwealth of Virginia. We are here today to prosecute Jerome R. Washington and Pearl H. Washington for capital murder. It is the most egregious felony in this state, and any other state, as it should be. And we will ask you to return a verdict of guilty of murder in the first degree. And then we will ask you to impose a sentence of death on both defendants. We do not undertake this action lightly, I can assure you."

He spread his hands wide. "And let me tell you why we are asking you to do this, because it's not an easy thing to take the life of another, nor should it be. But that is exactly what both defendants are charged with. Taking the lives of Leslie and Anne Randolph, while they were in their home, an elderly couple enjoying their time together, when those lives were brutally ended by the defendants."

He stepped back and put his hands in his pockets and glanced down at his polished dress shoes, as the jury's attention remained riveted on him.

He looked up and said, "The evidence will show that on the fourteenth day of June of this year, Jerome and Pearl Washington entered the home of the Randolphs between three and five p.m. They found them in a room at the back of the house where Jerome Washington knew they would be because he worked for them and knew their routine. Using a sharp, long-bladed knife wielded with considerable force, he repeatedly stabbed and sliced both victims until they were dead. After doing so, the defendants stole money from the Randolphs. And then his wife"—Battle pointed at Pearl— "in accordance with a plan they had concocted *together*, took his bloody clothes, shoes, the murder weapon, and the money, provided clean clothes and shoes for her husband, and then left. It is the commonwealth's belief that she made a phone call to the police telling them of the murders. We have traced a call from a pay phone that was very near the Randolphs' home to the police dispatcher at the relevant time in question."

Here Battle paused once more and looked around the courtroom. Christine Hanover and her husband were staring resolutely back at him.

Battle continued. "While she did that, Mr. Washington stayed with the bodies until the police came, to make it seem like he was innocent and had no weapon or money on his person, nor was he wearing bloody clothes. Now, the defense will no doubt argue that no sane killer would wait around for the police to come and arrest him. But the fact is, Mr. Washington worked for the Randolphs and was known to have been there that day. In fact, at the time of their murders, he was the *only* person other than the Randolphs who was there. Were he to have fled the scene, the man would have been hunted down and arrested immediately." As he said this Battle pointed directly at Jerome and Pearl. "The Washingtons knew this. Thus, their plan was slickly designed to cast off suspicion. Luckily for us, and the interests of justice, they made mistakes or overlooked things along the way."

He held up one finger. "Our evidence will show, first, that cash money they stole was found hidden at their home, by police executing a lawful search warrant. Second, you will learn that Mrs. Washington was absent from her work that day, indeed the first time she ever was, without explanation. Well, the reason was because she had to help prepare for the crime, and then travel to and from the Randolphs' home to aid her husband in the execution of said crime. Third, the medical examiner will testify that the killer was right-handed, as is Mr. Washington. Fourth, only Mr. Washington's footprints were found at the crime scene. Fifth, we have witnesses who will testify that Mr. Randolph had decided to fire Mr. Washington, because they had grown afraid of him, and for his belligerence and also due to the fact that Mr. Randolph believed Mr. Washington had stolen things from him. And you can all see that Mr. Washington is a large, powerfully built young man. He would intimidate most people, especially an elderly couple like the Randolphs. Sixth, we have testimony that Mr. Washington believed Mr. Randolph had also left him something in his will. Therefore, he had the strongest possible motive for killing the couple, as that would hasten his inheritance. Seventh, we have testimony that Mr. Washington had been in the Randolphs' home without their knowledge or permission and was no doubt casing the place for this future crime. Eighth, we have testimony that after coming back from Vietnam, Mr. Washington was prone to violent outbursts. And finally, we have testimony that the Washingtons desperately needed money, and the Randolphs represented their best possible chance to gain that money both by robbery and also, they believed, by inheritance. An inheritance that would come to them sooner rather than later, by his and his wife's criminal actions."

Battle turned once more to the gallery. "The Randolph family

members are in this courtroom today and they obviously want justice. As do I. As we all should."

Christine, looking miserable, rubbed at her watery eyes with her
gloved hand, while her husband put his arm around her.

Battle placed his hands back in his pocket and gazed at the jury.

"What we have here is a calculated double murder committed
for that age-old motive: greed. The Randolphs had something the
Washingtons wanted: money. Under these facts, the only possible
verdict is guilty. And for these premeditated and gruesome crimes,
the only acceptable punishment is death. I am confident that the evidence and your own common sense will lead you to that same conclusion. Thank you."

He walked back to his table as Ambrose looked at Jack and
DuBose.

"Defense? Your turn."

CHAPTER 66

JACK ROSE AND LET HIS jacket remain unbuttoned. He and DuBose had talked at length about who should deliver the opening statement. And she had finally won out, insisting that *he* do it.

She had argued, *You're the hometown boy. And you connect with people. So go out there and* connect.

And he had practiced his remarks over and over again in front of her, with DuBose praising some, critiquing some, and suggesting some. And he had learned a hell of a lot from the woman in doing so. DuBose was far more strategic in her approach than he was. While he often winged it in court, she thought about how every point and argument moved into the next one, and the one after that. And then how the whole case came together after you built it deliberate block by deliberate block.

He approached the jurors and took a shallow breath.

He glanced over and saw his family anxiously watching. Then his gaze alighted on DuBose and held there for a moment before moving over to Jerome and Pearl.

Right now their lives were in his hands, and that was a big responsibility for any mortal. Maybe too big.

No, Jack, you got this. You can do this because you have to do this.

He turned to the jurors. "My name is Jack Lee. I was born and raised right here in Freeman County. Never really been anywhere else except over to Virginia Beach to get a sunburn once a year. I know this place, and its people real well. Certainly better than Mr. Battle, who they recruited all the way from Richmond to come and prosecute this case. The commonwealth clearly has a lot of firepower focused on this. And it is an important case, but then again there are lots of important cases. So you might wonder, why are they so bound and determined to win *this* one?"

He indicated the packed courtroom. "We got reporters, and TV and radio folks from all over the country right here. We got a crowd of people outside that you can hear yelling out their opinions on this matter." He pointed at Howard Pickett in the back row. "And there we got the millionaire mouthpiece for a presidential candidate who I'm sure you've seen on the TV or heard on the radio, trying to score political points talking about this case. It's like this has become some sort of national flashpoint for all that's going on in this country. And there is a lot going on, some good, but, to be honest, more bad. So far, nineteen sixty-eight has been...*memorable*."

He turned and pointed at Jerome and Pearl. "But for Jerome Washington and his wife, Pearl, this case is as *personal* as it gets. What the commonwealth wants you to find is that they are guilty of murder, and then it wants you to condemn them to death by electrocution. Doesn't get any more personal than that."

He turned back to the jury and drew closer. "The evidence will show that Jerome Washington faithfully labored for the Randolphs, giving them his best effort in return for forty dollars a week. This was his first job after coming back from the war, where he was severely wounded fighting on behalf of his country, on behalf of all of us. He rode his bike fifteen miles each way to the Randolphs', leaving his house early in the morning and returning long past suppertime each night.

"Now, the commonwealth wants you to believe that Jerome rode his bike to work that day. Worked hard all day. And then sometime that afternoon, he and his wife snuck into the house, brutally killed the Randolphs, and stole fifty dollars from them. Then his wife took the murder weapon and his bloody clothes and shoes and the money, and gave him a new set of clothes and a new pair of shoes, and then left. Just to be clear, the commonwealth cannot produce a single witness or a lick of evidence to show her doing any of this, or her calling the police from that pay phone. And they have yet to find the murder weapon or the bloody clothes and shoes.

"You will also hear evidence that the Randolphs might have told Jerome that they would leave him something in their will. They say that is the motive, and yet he steals fifty dollars? And Pearl, after helping to develop this very careful plan, hides the cash in a place where the police easily find it?"

Jack looked over at Christine Hanover and saw her listening intently to what he was saying. Her husband was now gazing at the floor.

He turned back and let the palms of his hands rest on the top rail of the jury box.

"Now, ask yourself, would any person contemplate committing *any* crime in that clumsy way, much less the murders of two people?"

He paused, then took his hands off the rail and lifted his gaze to the dozen men who would decide the Washingtons' fate. "Now, let's deal with the elephant in the room. Jerome and Pearl Washington are Black. The victims were white. This country has a history when it comes to the two races, and it's not a good one. We all know it, none can deny it, and that history is still being written, day in and day out, often with bloodshed."

He spread his hands and pointed at the floor. "But in here, in a court of law, in the United States of America, is this one absolute truth that each of you most hold on to as the holy grail of your duty as a juror during this trial. And here it is: Every person, regardless of race, creed, or color, is presumed to be innocent of any crime of which they have been charged. And that presumption of innocence is only overcome—" Jack paused here and pointed a finger at the jury "—is only overcome by the commonwealth proving a person's guilt *beyond* a reasonable doubt. *Beyond a reasonable doubt.* Four words that seem pretty clear. But quite frankly, having practiced law for a number of years, I can tell you, firsthand, that those four words are anything but clear in the hearts and minds of most people."

Jack ran his eye around the courtroom, landing on his family and Miss Jessup, then the Hanovers, Howard Pickett, Curtis Gates, and then to the Washingtons sitting side by side. And finally, to DuBose, who gave him an encouraging smile.

He drew close again to the jury. "But here's what those words mean to me. And here's what I think they should mean to you. If the case against the Washingtons, as proven by the commonwealth, leaves no reasonable doubt in your mind that they murdered the Randolphs, then a verdict of guilty is required. But if you do have doubt, even just a sliver in your mind, then you must acquit them. That is the standard. To send a person to their death, I think all of us will agree, we need to be pretty damn sure we're getting it right. There are no second chances. There is no bringing the dead back to life."

He leaned down and looked, in turn, at each juror. "And the evidence will demonstrate that not only has the commonwealth failed to show guilt beyond a reasonable doubt, but it proves that the Washingtons, in fact, are innocent of this crime. But we do not need to show that in order for the defendants to walk out that door over there and return to their three small children. The burden of proof forever remains on the commonwealth. Us showing y'all that they are innocent is just gravy on the mashed potatoes."

Jack stepped back and contemplated the jurors for a few moments. "I used to go duck hunting with my daddy. When I was a kid I would ask him how I would know if it was a duck I was shooting at, the durn things being so high up in the sky and flying so fast. And do you know what my daddy told me? He said, 'Son, if it looks like a duck, and flies like a duck, and quacks like a duck, then it's a damn duck.' And as you see the evidence presented, and you listen to the testimony of the witnesses, and use the common sense that

God gave us all, I am confident that you will conclude that someone did indeed murder the Randolphs. And you will also find, I am
certain, that the commonwealth has failed to prove that the Washingtons were the ones who did it, *beyond a reasonable doubt*. Which
is what the laws of the United States of America and the Commonwealth of Virginia require. No more, but surely...no less."

He straightened, buttoned his jacket, nodded his head, and said,
"Thank you."

CHAPTER 67

DEPUTY RAYMOND LEROY WAS CALLED as the common-wealth's first witness.

LeRoy testified to being dispatched to the Randolph residence and arriving a few minutes past six o'clock. He then described what had happened when they found Jerome Washington there, including his partner's physical tussle with the man. After Battle was done with his questioning, Jack rose and walked toward the deputy.

Jack asked, "Was the defendant in custody at the time when he allegedly attacked your partner? Was he restrained?"

"Well, yes. He was handcuffed and on his knees."

"So neither you nor your partner were in any danger from him?"

"Well, not really."

"Did your partner say anything to provoke the defendant?"

"Not that I recall. But Gene was naturally upset with what the man had done."

"*Allegedly* done. But I understand that right before the defendant lashed out, your partner had said he was going to go visit Mr. Washington's wife and do something to her? Maybe have himself a good time?"

LeRoy looked uncomfortable. "I don't remember that."

Jack was handed a paper by DuBose and glanced over it. "You want to try that again? You are under oath, and perjury is a crime."

LeRoy glanced nervously at the paper and said, "Well, Gene might have gotten a little carried away and said some things he shouldn't have about the man's wife."

"And then your partner beat the living daylights out of the defendant with his billy club even though he was handcuffed and presented no threat?" said Jack.

"I don't know about that, either."

Jack went over to DuBose, who handed him another document.

"I have his medical records right here with the injuries suffered during his arrest. The list is a long one. I can read them out. Or do you want to take another swing at my question?"

LeRoy fussed with his tie and said, "Okay, Gene beat him up pretty good, yeah."

"And why is Deputy Taliaferro not here today to speak for himself?"

LeRoy glared at him. "You damn well know why."

"Oh, that's right—he's in jail after trying to murder me and Miss DuBose."

Battle got to his feet. "Objection. We have Deputy LeRoy here to testify. Deputy Taliaferro's testimony would just be superfluous."

"Sustained," said Ambrose.

Jack looked at LeRoy, who was now smirking. "When you entered the room where the bodies were, what did you see?"

"Two dead people!"

"And what was the defendant doing?"

"Well...it looked like he was settin' Mrs. Randolph in the chair. Probably to do somethin' weird to her."

"Move to strike the last statement—nonresponsive, argumentative, speculative, and probably five other bad things that this court should not tolerate," barked Jack.

Ambrose told the jury to disregard the remark and added, "And please stick to the facts, Deputy. Personal commentary like that is *not* helpful."

DuBose turned to see Hilly staring pointedly at Ambrose. Then she noted the reporters probably writing their next headlines.

"So it looked like he was lifting her into the chair, yes or no?" said Jack.

"Yes," said LeRoy, now looking confused.

"Thank you, I have nothing further to ask this man."

Next, Herman Till, the medical examiner, was called to the stand and sworn in by the bailiff.

"Move to show the jury the crime scene and autopsy photos that have already been stipulated into evidence," said Battle.

"Objection," said DuBose. "That would be prejudicial to the defendants and far outweighs the probative value of the photos. Mr. Till can testify to everything having to do with the crime scene and autopsy reports."

Ambrose said, "It's well-established law in Virginia to allow a jury to see this material, and I'm a stickler for observing precedent. Your objection is thus overruled." He turned to Battle. "Be efficient about it, sir."

Battle had his associates hand the photos out to the jury. Jack and DuBose watched as expressions of revulsion appeared on all of them. More than half glanced at the Washingtons with obvious anger.

Battle led Till through his forensic findings before sitting back down.

When DuBose rose she could feel the eyes of every juror on her as she strode purposefully to the witness box. She turned quickly to look at the jurors and found, by her swift tally, at least nine who held looks of outright hostility toward her.

"Your Honor, can we have the photos removed from the jury? That is not something anyone should have to look at for long."

"Certainly." Ambrose nodded at the bailiff to collect the photos.

DuBose said, "Now, Mr. Till, you said that only Jerome Washington's footprints were visible in the room?"

"Correct. Well, other than those of the deputies who arrested him."

"But what about the Randolphs'? They were obviously in the room, too."

"Well, it seems that during the course of the struggle, their footprints were smeared around so much as to be unidentifiable."

"So during the struggle *their* footprints were erased, but not Mr. Washington's. Does that seem odd to you?"

Battle rose. "Objection, calls for speculation by the witness."

"Sustained," said Ambrose. "You can disregard that question, Mr. Till."

An undeterred DuBose said, "How many murder cases have you handled, sir?"

Till said, "Well, before I came here I worked over in Norfolk. Bigger city, had more homicides. Best I can figure, more than three hundred."

"In any of those cases which involved considerable blood loss, have you ever seen where the alleged killer's footprints were visible, but the victims' were not?"

Ambrose seemed ready to say something but he held his gavel, looking uncertain. Then he glanced at the gallery and saw a row of journalists staring at him, their pens poised over pads. Ambrose slowly set his gavel down and looked on attentively.

In the audience, Hilly Lee and Miss Jessup exchanged whispered comments.

"Well, I can't say that I have, ma'am," replied Till.

"So you would classify *that* as unusual?"

Ambrose eyed Battle, who had not risen. He rapped his gavel. "Calls for speculation. Move on."

DuBose looked at him for a long moment as if to say, *I thought the lawyers were supposed to object, not the judge.*

"You said that the murders occurred between three and five p.m.?" she asked.

Till nodded. "Yes."

"Mr. Randolph was found on the floor and Mrs. Randolph in a chair?"

"Correct."

"Was Mrs. Randolph killed in the chair?" asked DuBose.

"I don't believe so, no."

"Then how did she end up in the chair?"

"She might have fallen into it after she was struck down."

DuBose went back to the counsel table and picked up a photo. "Defense Exhibit Four previously stipulated into evidence. Can you identify what's in this photo?"

Till examined the photo. "They're palm prints and fingerprints that were found in the blood by the chair. We matched the prints and blood type to Mrs. Randolph."

"Why would her prints be in the blood on the *floor*?" DuBose asked.

"Because she had fallen there, I suppose."

"But she was found in the chair. Can you explain that?"

"No, I cannot," replied Till.

"Could she have lifted herself from the floor into the chair afterward?"

"With the injuries she had sustained it would have been impossible."

"Now, you heard Deputy LeRoy's testimony that the defendant was found on his knees with his arms around Mrs. Randolph and her mostly in the chair. Would that explain it? That he was putting her there?"

Battle rose to his feet. "Objection. Defense counsel is not allowed to testify!"

She wheeled around. "I am in no way testifying, merely attempting to have Mr. Till explain a piece of previous testimony in conjunction with the forensic evidence, of which he is the expert of record for the commonwealth."

Ambrose said, "Objection sustained." He eyed DuBose severely. "Now, come on, Miss DuBose, an attorney of your experience surely knows better than that."

Unruffled by this nonsensical ruling, DuBose pulled out some photos from a file that Jack handed her and showed them to Till.

"These have been previously entered into evidence by Mr. Battle, Commonwealth's Exhibits Ten and Eleven. Can you describe them for the jury?"

"These are the pictures my people took of the clothes and shoes Mr. Washington was wearing when he was arrested."

"All right. Is there blood on his clothes?"

"No."

"Is there blood on the tops of the shoes?"

Till put his glasses on and looked at the pictures more closely. "Uh, no, none."

"Is there blood on the soles of the shoes?"

He looked again at the photos. "Well, just a little on this one right there."

"Just a little on that one right there," repeated DuBose, looking at the jury. "Now, you testified that the attack on the Randolphs was furious and violent, and that they lost a lot of blood. How much blood?"

"Between them, nearly fourteen pints."

"How many pints of blood does a human body have on average?"

"Ten."

"So fourteen of their combined twenty pints of blood was on the carpet and on their clothes and the furniture? Everywhere literally?"

"Yes."

"Is fresh blood sticky? I mean if you step in it, will it adhere to shoes and clothing?"

Ambrose interjected, "Mr. Till, does that not call for speculation on your part?"

A puzzled Till looked at the judge. "Not at all. I can say for a fact that fresh blood sticks to pretty much everything. When it gets on your clothes, it's damn hard to get out, as my missus will tell you because she has to launder mine."

The courtroom tittered at this.

DuBose waited for the noise to quiet down because she wanted to make absolute certain the jury heard every bit of what was to come next. "Mr. Till, you went to the crime scene, and walked where the blood was?"

"Yes, ma'am. No way around it. Had to get to the bodies."

"And were your shoes covered in blood?"

"No. I mean I wasn't there obviously when they were being murdered. You know, when the wounds were spewing blood and it was fresh."

"But if you had been?"

"Well, both the victims' carotid arteries were cut, so blood would have been flying out of both bodies like water from little fire hoses."

Jack looked back at Christine in time to see her shudder and cover her eyes.

"So would you expect some blood to end up on your clothes and shoes if you had been there when the murders occurred?" asked DuBose.

Battle rose and objected to this line of questioning.

DuBose turned to the judge before he could rule. "Surely a medical examiner with as much experience as Mr. Till is qualified to give an opinion about blood residue on clothes and shoes and blood patterns in a crime scene. For why else is he here?"

"I am giving you a lot of leeway, Miss DuBose, but there are limits. Objection sustained. Move on," said Ambrose.

DuBose said, "All right, Mr. Till, let's get to some facts you apparently *can* testify about. Did your wife have to clean the soles of your shoes when you got home that night?"

"What? Uh, no. There wasn't any blood on them. I mean just a tiny bit."

"A tiny bit? Like the amount on the bottom of *one* of Mr. Washington's shoes?"

"Yes, that's right."

"And in your opinion, why was that the case, I mean with *your* shoes?"

"Well, it's fairly obvious. I got there when the blood had dried and hardened. When blood does that it loses its viscosity, meaning its stickiness."

"What time did you get there?"

"Around ten past seven."

"So you had very little blood on your shoes despite the enormous amounts on the carpet because the blood had dried and lost its *viscosity*?"

"That's right."

"And what would be the reason why Mr. Washington's shoes would have almost no blood on the soles?"

Ambrose made to raise his gavel but DuBose saw this and added, "In your professional opinion, of course?"

"Well, same reason as for me. The blood was…" Till looked puzzled now.

"Mr. Till?" she prompted.

"Um, well, it could be because the blood was already dry when… he entered the room, and had lost its viscosity."

"And in your opinion, how long would it take for blood to dry to that extent?"

"On a warm day like that on a porous surface such as that wool rug, the blood will begin to dry in about a minute. But it will retain its viscosity for up to half an hour."

"So let's get this as clear as possible for the jury. In your professional opinion, if Mr. Washington killed the Randolphs, would you expect to find blood on his clothes and the tops and soles of his shoes?"

"Now, isn't that speculation?" asked Ambrose.

"I asked for his *professional* opinion, Judge."

"I'm sorry. That's still speculation and I cannot allow it." He eyed the audience. "Same as I would rule if the commonwealth had tried something like that." He turned to the jury. "You are instructed to disregard that last question by defense counsel."

"All right," said DuBose. "Mr. Till, the dirty footprints you found of Mr. Washington's, the ones you've already testified to?"

"Yes?"

"Did they show him to be standing in the victim's blood?"

"Absolutely."

"If the blood was fresh with full viscosity would it have stuck to the soles of Mr. Washington's shoes?"

"Absolutely."

"Was that level of blood found on Mr. Washington's shoes?"

"No. Not even close."

"Thank you. No further questions."

"Mr. Battle, redirect?" asked Ambrose.

Battle rose. "Mr. Till, if Mr. Washington changed his clothes and shoes after he killed the Randolphs, would that account for the lack of blood on those items?"

DuBose, who had not yet reached her table, whirled around and exclaimed, "Objection, calls for an opinion about facts that have not been introduced into evidence and for which the commonwealth has offered no proof whatsoever."

"Mr. Till can certainly answer that," said Ambrose amiably. "It's a perfectly appropriate question."

"Mr. Till?" prompted Battle.

"Yes, it would account for it," replied Till.

DuBose looked at the jurors to find all of them of them smiling and nodding.

Battle said, "Thank you, no further questions."

CHAPTER 68

AFTER A STRING OF OTHER witnesses took the stand, Cora
Robinson, the Randolphs' maid, was called by Battle. She testified
as to Jerome's coming into the house one afternoon without the
Randolphs' knowledge.

When she tried to explain why he had, Battle cut her off. "Nothing further."

Jack walked up to her and immediately asked Robinson the reason Jerome had come into the house on that particular day.

"He had to use the bathroom real bad. After he was done I
cleaned the bathroom up real good."

"Thank you. No further questions."

Battle rose looking pleased and eager. "Did you tell the Randolphs that the defendant had been in their house without their
knowledge?"

Robinson looked fearfully around.

Battle said, "I remind the witness that she is under oath and that
perjury is a serious crime."

"No, I didn't tell them."

"Why not? It was their house and this man was not supposed to
be in there."

"I...well, I didn't want him to get into trouble."

"So, you were covering up for one of your own? Not informing the people who were paying your salary of an unlawful trespass into their home?" Battle tacked on a disappointed expression.

Looking both anxious and frustrated, Robinson answered, "I just didn't want him to get into trouble for havin' to use the durn bathroom. I mean, we all got to go."

DuBose glanced over at the jurors who were, to a man, staring at Robinson like *she* had just committed a terrible crime.

A deputy sheriff was called to the stand. He had been one of the officers who had found the money in the lean-to. Since Jack and DuBose knew that Jerome had secreted the money in there they could not argue that it might have been planted, but they could still attack its connection to the case.

After Battle released the witness DuBose rose and approached him like a predator coming through the high grass for its next meal.

"Fifty dollars cash found in a hole in the wall of the defendants' lean-to?"

"That's right," said the deputy confidently.

"Do you know who put it there?"

"I assume that—"

"No, the question was, do *you* know who put it there? For certain?"

The deputy seemed to shrink under her intimidating gaze. "Uh, no ma'am, I don't."

"Can you show that this money was taken from the Randolphs' home? Did it have anything on it proving where it came from?"

"Uh, no."

"In fact, for all you know, Mr. Washington could have earned that money from his job and placed the funds there, isn't that right?"

"I…" The man looked at Ambrose, but the judge would not meet his eye.

"Isn't that right?" said DuBose in a louder voice.

"Yes, that's right."

"And isn't it possible that the Randolphs could have given that money to the defendant for a job well done?"

Battle rose and said, "Objection, speculation."

"I am only asking him if it's possible." She shot Ambrose a determined look. "Plainly goes to reasonable doubt, the bedrock principle of all criminal law."

Ambrose gave her a look of grudging respect. "Answer the question, Deputy."

"Yes, it's possible that they could have done that."

"So despite your having found the money in the lean-to, you have no evidence, no proof whatsoever, that the defendants stole that money from the Randolphs, do you?"

"No ma'am, I don't," said the man, now thoroughly defeated.

"Thank you for your honesty, Deputy," she said brightly. "It's refreshing."

Curtis Gates was next called by Battle and asked whether the Randolphs were planning to fire Jerome because he had been belligerent to them.

"Yes, Leslie Randolph told me that." Gates glanced at the Washingtons. "They were scared of him. And from where I'm sitting they had good reason to be."

DuBose leapt to her feet. "Judge, I move to strike that last sentence. He answered a question that was not asked, and not only is it highly prejudicial it is personally repugnant."

DuBose and Gates did a stare-down that she won when he looked away.

Ambrose turned to the jury. "You are to disregard the witness's statement that he believes the defendant to be a frightening person."

DuBose gazed stonily at the judge as he turned back around to look at her. "Anything else, Miss DuBose?"

After Battle was done, Jack questioned Gates about the tontine provisions of the will and had the lawyer explain it fully to the jury along with the wealth of the Randolphs being almost wholly in their house and land.

After he had done so, Battle rose and said, "Relevancy?"

Ambrose looked at Jack. "Well?"

"The relevancy will become clear when the defense puts on its case. Mr. Gates's testimony on these points is critical to lay the foundation for this line of inquiry."

"I hope it is, Mr. Lee," said the judge. "Otherwise you are wasting our time, sir."

Miss Jessup was called next and talked about Jerome's nightmares, which Battle's people had unearthed during their investigation. Battle twisted her words around so much that even on his gentle cross-examination, Jack could do little to straighten it out.

As she got off the witness stand she turned and smiled sweetly at Ambrose. "Afternoon, Judge," she said in a friendly tone.

He quickly looked away from her without replying.

After more testimony, court was adjourned for the day. Jack and DuBose had a hurried conversation with their clients as the jury filed out. DuBose kept a close eye on them until they left.

Jerome said, "How we be doin', you think?"

"It always looks bad when the prosecution is putting on its case," said Jack. "But we'll get our turn."

"You think you want us to testify?" asked Pearl anxiously.

Jack glanced at DuBose. "We haven't decided yet. If you do take the stand, Battle can question you, and he's good at twisting things around. You saw that for yourself."

"Yeah, we did," said Pearl. "But I don't got no bag big enough to carry all the stuff they say I did. It just ridiculous."

The deputies came for them. When Jerome rose from the table, his left knee buckled and he had to grab the table to right himself.

Jack took a hold of his other arm to steady the man.

"Damn leg," said Jerome, breathing hard. "I forget sometimes not to put all my weight on it."

"Jack said that happened in Vietnam?" noted DuBose.

"Yeah. Ain't never gonna be right again." He looked around the courtroom. "Nothin' ever gonna be right again, I guess."

Jack watched Jerome limp awkwardly off. Then he and DuBose gathered up their things and left the courtroom.

CHAPTER 69

ONCE THEY REACHED THE HALL Jack said, "Come on, we can avoid all the reporters if we go out a side door."

"Who said I wanted to avoid the press?" DuBose countered.

She marched out the front doors and into the sea of journalists.

Battle had just stepped away from the podium that was lined with microphones. He glanced at DuBose. "Have at it," he said before walking off.

DuBose stepped up to the podium, while Jack hovered behind.

One reporter called out, "How do you think the first day went?"

She said, "It always looks dire when the prosecution is putting on its case. But there are two sides to every story, and we will get our chance to tell ours."

"How do you feel about the jury?" asked another, a thin woman with glasses.

"I would feel a lot better if it had some people on there who looked like my clients. But that wasn't my call. It was the judge's. I will let others *judge* that while we try to win this case."

Some of the reporters laughed while protestors across the street yelled and jeered.

Jack touched her arm. "Desiree, let's go."

Another reporter said, "Seems like Ambrose is doing all he can to help you."

"And who are you with?" asked DuBose.

"The *Review of the News*."

"Ah, yes, the John Birch Society. Well, all I can say is you and I have a difference of opinion on what helping someone looks like."

"Desiree," hissed Jack. "Enough."

Another reporter, a large man with a soft dark hat and hanging jowls, said, "Why do you think colored people keep killing white people in this country?"

DuBose appraised him coolly. "Do you know what I pray for, sir?" She didn't wait for him to reply. "I pray for the day when this country moves forward *together*, as one mighty nation, and one *united* people. It wasn't that long ago that Senator Joe McCarthy sought to tear this country apart, pitting one American against another with his slanderous accusations and pieces of paper with nothing on them. Divided is when we are at our weakest, our most vulnerable. We are called the United States of America for a reason, because when we are truly united, there is nothing on earth that can defeat us, including whatever bogeyman someone puts up to turn one American against another. Dr. King may no longer be with us, but he loved the *possibility* of this country. And his spirit and his message of hope, his cry for equality, will forever be part of us."

Jack noted that a number of people in the crowd were actually nodding their heads in agreement with her words. He looked at DuBose with a fresh level of respect.

DuBose also seemed to sense some support in their ranks. She had taken a step back but now moved up to the podium once more and glanced at the journalists arrayed around her obviously eager for more, and the crowd of everyday people just beyond them.

She said, "A great nation can never realize its full potential until *all* its citizens are allowed to realize theirs. And the rest of the world is not waiting for us to get our house in order. They are moving forward in ways that are best for them, not for us. By battling each other we're literally fighting with one arm tied behind our back, and for no good reason at all." She gazed around the crowd and then spied Pickett standing near his Lincoln watching and listening. And DuBose allowed herself the barest of smiles.

She continued, "It would be like taking pretty much every cent of wealth created in this country by all of you, and giving it to a handful of folks at the very top. Who thinks that's a good idea?"

One man called out, "They already got too damn much as it is."

There were cheers throughout the crowd that clearly showed they were in agreement with DuBose and the man on *that* point.

And then another voice spoke up. "So you mean socialism, communism, Miss DuBose? You're a socialist?"

She looked at Howard Pickett as he finished speaking. By his slick smile she knew the man thought he had trapped her.

DuBose said, "On the contrary, it's socialism when the government divides up the wealth and everyone gets the same share no matter what. However, what we have in this country, I believe, is outright theft."

Pickett's smile faded.

She continued, looking out at the crowd, "As a lawyer I can tell you theft is the illegal taking of something that does not belong to you. So when all of you work hard all day long and the lion's share of the wealth you create goes to someone else? How would you define that?"

Pickett immediately said, "As the American way. The individual pulls himself up by his own bootstraps. Like I did."

With the triumphant look that DuBose gave him, Pickett was suddenly aware that he had made an ill-advised move on the chessboard.

She said, "Really, Mr. Pickett? You got into Princeton through your family connections, not on merit. And bootstraps? After you graduated, your uncle, a millionaire many times over, *gave* you your first coal mine, which you subsequently drove into bankruptcy through a series of grossly incompetent business decisions. As you did your second coal mine. Then you received a government loan to bail you out, which you subsequently defaulted on, leaving the

American taxpayer to foot the bill. But then luck shone upon you, because some valuable mineral rights became available through a government program, and you were awarded those rights. Not in an auction, as it was supposed to be conducted, but by an administrator with the Department of the Interior. You then hired that man as your vice president at ten times his government pay. Last year your income exceeded the combined salaries of every coal miner you employ. I don't call that bootstrapping, sir. I call that...*bullshit*."

Pickett looked up at her with more loathing than Jack had ever beheld on another person's features. The coal magnate then turned and walked away as people in the crowd started to clap and hoot in appreciation of her verbal assassination of the man.

She stepped away from the podium and looked at Jack. He said, "You sounded like a politician, not a lawyer."

"I actually have to be *both*," she shot back. "Because while we have the law on our side now, they have the actual politicians on theirs."

"I didn't mean that as a bad thing, Desiree. I think you might have gotten through to some of the folks in the crowd."

"One can only hope."

"How'd you know so much about Pickett?"

"Many years of digging into his career. You see, I often know more about my enemies than I do my friends. I find it far more useful."

They left the area and turned the corner heading toward Jack's car. Halfway down a side street something hit Jack in the head.

He looked down and saw that he was covered in the remains of a burst tomato.

He looked up and saw several of the protestors jeering and pointing at him and DuBose.

One of them was Sally Reeves. And the person who had launched the tomato was her towheaded son, who was cranking up to hurl another one.

A smirking Reeves called out, "Just be glad it's not a bullet, Jack."

After dodging a second tomato, they hurried along, turned down another street, and stopped as the man loomed up in front of them.

Raymond LeRoy barked, "What the hell you think you doin' in that courtroom?"

"My job," Jack shot back.

"It's your *job* to ask stupid questions and make good people upset?"

"It's my job to see that my clients have a strong defense."

LeRoy drew closer, his right hand edging close to his holstered weapon.

"Gene's in jail 'cause 'a you."

"Gene's in jail because he tried to kill us. And his asshole buddy *did* kill my sister."

"Well, I don't know nothin' about that," LeRoy said dismissively.

"*I* do. And I hope they both rot in hell."

LeRoy shot a glance at DuBose. "They say you gettin' in bed with this colored gal. Have you lost your goddamn mind?"

"Okay, we need to get on," said Jack.

He and DuBose started to walk away.

LeRoy hooked Jack's arm. "You ain't gonna win, you know that?"

Jack removed the man's hand. "We'll see. Trial has a long way to go."

"Not talkin' 'bout the damn trial. I'm talkin' 'bout her kind and our kind."

"I'm not part of your kind."

"The next generation is gonna do the right thing," spat LeRoy.

"I dearly hope so," said DuBose.

"I ain't talkin' to you!" snapped LeRoy. His hand now gripped his revolver.

"You pull that gun, I'll lay you right out on the pavement," said Jack. "And then I'll sue your ass off."

"Daddy!"

They all turned to see a boy around sixteen running up to them. He was taller than his father and leaner, but they shared the same facial features.

"Daddy," said the boy. "Come on, Momma's waitin' in the car." He gripped his father's arm, all the while glancing anxiously at Jack and DuBose. "Come on, Daddy, Momma said we got to go."

"All right, all right, Kenny," said LeRoy. He pointed a finger at Jack. "This ain't the end of it. No sir."

"Daddy, come on. You ain't doin' no good here talkin' to *those* people."

As they walked off, Kenny LeRoy glanced back apprehensively at them.

"The next generation," said Jack. "Let's hope to God they do the right thing.'"

"But *our* generation has to do its share, too," countered DuBose.

On the drive back to the Lees' house, Jack said, "You did a first-rate job on Herman Till's cross."

"And Battle blew it all right out of the water with one question that Till should never have been allowed to answer, but Ambrose let him, the son of a bitch."

"So now Pearl was carrying a big knife, Jerome's bloody clothes, fifty dollars cash, and his size fourteen shoes that are about as big as she is?"

"If the jury *wants* to believe it, logic doesn't have to play a part," pointed out DuBose. "And from what I've seen there is very little logic on that jury."

"But unless you want to give up right now, we have to keep going," noted Jack.

"Oh, we're going to keep fighting, all right."

"Until justice runs down like water and righteousness like a mighty river?"

She looked at him appreciatively. "Now you're talking like a civil rights lawyer, Jack Lee."

CHAPTER 70

LATE THAT NIGHT DUBOSE WENT to Lucy's old room to go to bed. Queenie was already asleep on her blanket.

DuBose undressed down to her slip, and wrapped her hair. Then she idly wandered around the room, looking at the possessions the dead woman had cherished so much that she had displayed them. Some stuffed animals from her never-ending childhood. A picture book full of toads. A frilly pink dress. A Mickey Mouse figurine.

She picked up an empty glass bottle of Coca-Cola that had a large, floppy artificial sunflower inside it. On the wall was a photograph of the Lees. Jack and his brother were tall, angular teenagers. They stood on either side of their older sister, arms protectively around her. On either side of them were Hilly and Frank Lee. They looked happy, thought DuBose. With no idea what the future held for them—the loss and accompanying heartache.

Just like every family. Just like my family.

She carried the Coca-Cola bottle over to the bed and sat down with it in her lap.

How much longer are you going to do this, Desiree? Because there will always be another train to catch, or plane to hop on, another city to go to, another case to try, more justice to secure. Are your shoulders wide enough? Can you sacrifice just a little bit more of your time

*on earth for a cause that will probably never be fully realized while
you're still breathing?*

She put a hand through her new hairdo under the wrap and liked
how it felt; her fingers seemed to tingle with the freshness of the style.
But then a depression seized her, as it sometimes did. She set the Coke
bottle on the nightstand, slipped off the bed, stood in front of a mirror
hanging on the wall, and took a good, long look at herself.

In less than a handful of years she would be forty. Then, before
she could blink, fifty. Then, in another heartbeat, sixty.

If I haven't been killed.

Then what comes after that, Desiree?

Distressingly, she found she had no answer.

DuBose had just slipped under the covers when there was a
knock on the door.

"Yes?"

"It's Hilly. May I come in?"

DuBose sat up. "Of course."

The door opened, revealing Hilly wearing a long pale blue robe
that accentuated her lean frame. She sat in a chair by the bed, and
looked around. "Lot of memories in this room."

"I'm sure."

Hilly picked up the bottle with the sunflower, her face easing
into a sad smile. "This was Lucy's first Coca-Cola. And Jack won
the sunflower for her at the county fair."

"A nice piece of family history."

After a few moments of silence Hilly said, "That judge is playing
one slick game."

"I guess they saw that the likes of Bull Connor using firehoses
and attack dogs on men, women, and children was not a winning
strategy to capture the support of the public. So they sent a wolf in a
judge's robe."

"You'll have to outsmart him at some point, Desiree."

"I just have to find the right moment."

"If I can help you with that, I will."

"Thank you, Hilly," DuBose said slowly, unsure where all of this was going.

A lengthy silence was broken when Hilly spoke. "Joshua Taylor?"

"I…I'm sure that was so difficult," observed DuBose.

"I wanted to marry him," Hilly bluntly said.

DuBose looked startled, which drew a resigned look from Hilly.

"I've never told anyone that. Not even Francis. But I wanted you to know."

"O-okay," said DuBose uncomfortably.

Hilly seemed to read her mind. "I'm not telling you this to relieve some guilty secret, Desiree. I wouldn't do that to you. And, frankly, I have no reason to feel guilty for how I felt. But what I want you to understand…is me. Why I am how I am. Without knowing that, I don't see any way forward for *us*, do you?" she added.

"No, I guess not," said DuBose, still clearly uncomfortable.

Hilly took a small photograph from the pocket of her robe and passed it across to DuBose. "That's Joshua. And me."

DuBose looked at a decades-younger Hilly in a long dress with her auburn hair done up and a brilliant smile on her face. Next to her was a tall, handsome Black man. His arm was around Hilly's waist, and his smile matched hers in its luminous intensity.

"You make a truly lovely couple," noted DuBose, handing it back.

Hilly looked down at the photo and smiled. "I made that dress from the sacks the cow feed came in. First time I ever wore hose. And those shoes sure hurt something fierce. I was so used to going barefoot. But that was one of the happiest days of my life."

"Where were you two going?"

"My high school dance was that night. We couldn't go together, of course."

"So what'd you do?'

"We had our own little party down by the McClure River. Obviously way back then it was illegal pretty much everywhere for a Black and a white to marry. Not that I cared a whit for what the law said. I knew where my heart was."

"Did you talk to Joshua about it?"

"Yes. Before he went away to college. I didn't want him to go. Begged him not to. Or at least to take me with him. But that was crazy talk. I mean, how could he show up at a Black college with a white woman in tow? I waited a year for him. When I didn't hear anything, I left the mountain and moved to Richmond, stayed with one of my sisters for a while, before moving here and meeting Francis and getting married."

"I take it you really loved Joshua?" said DuBose quietly. "Because loving a Black man would have involved a lot of...sacrifice."

"If you want the God's honest truth, Desiree, it was something more than love, at least the way I looked at it."

"I don't understand."

Hilly set the Coke bottle down. "It was like I couldn't exist without him. It was as though I couldn't *breathe* without him. I had no purpose without him by my side, but with him next to me, I could accomplish anything in my life. *Anything*. And I had dreams back then, Desiree. As big as the Appalachians. The things I wanted to do with my life. With Joshua. That's why it hurt so bad when he went away. I didn't tell all of you the exact truth earlier. After I left home I wrote his mother every week for news. She only sometimes wrote me back."

"Why is that, do you think?" asked DuBose.

"How much hatred and abuse and anger do you think Blacks and whites have endured for simply loving each other?"

"Far too much. And none of it was right."

"And what mother would want that pain, that danger, for her child if there was an easier path to take?"

"So you think his mother didn't want you and Joshua to be together?"

"I *know* she didn't, because she told me so right to my face. I would ruin her beautiful son's life. I would take him away from his world, his kind. And worst of all, I would be condemning him to death."

"And how did that make you feel, Hilly?" asked DuBose in a cautious tone.

Hilly's features clouded over. "It angered me. It...it made me think there was no way through, no way at all. And before then, Desiree, I always figured out a way to keep moving ahead. No matter what life threw at me, and it was a lot, I figured out a way to keep going. People calling me a stupid hick all those years because of where I came from and the way I talked? The fact that I didn't have a good education? The fact that my momma and daddy would just leave me up there by myself like I didn't matter? Like I wasn't worth anything? It all just made me fight harder. Made me more determined to prove them wrong." She paused and drew a shallow, nervous breath. "But with this damnable thing I couldn't punch through it. It swallowed me whole. It turned me into a person without a lick 'a hope about anything. And that's as low as a body can get."

DuBose felt her chest grow heavy. "And so you...?"

Hilly's features tightened and she nodded. "And so I just accepted it. The way everybody told me how my life was to be led, that's what I did. I was weak, like I said before. It's always easier to follow, isn't it? See, that way you don't have to face the hard problems. You don't even have to think for yourself. You just do what others want you to do, become the person they tell you that you already are." A solitary tear slid down her cheek.

"But wouldn't you know deep down it was all a lie?"

Hilly dabbed at her eyes and then resettled herself. "I had my issues with how Lucy turned out, as you now know. The guilt was beyond any pain I had ever felt. What I'd done to that poor, innocent child. But it wasn't physical pain. It was all in my mind, my heart. And even after I came back from that hospital over in Petersburg, I believed that I could not...survive, without some help. So I went to the preacher who used to be at our church here. I talked to him about Lucy. And I told him about me and Joshua, because I just had to tell somebody about it. The things I was feeling, what was in my soul. Regrets I had. Everything so mixed up in my head."

"What did he say? Was he helpful?"

Hilly lifted her gaze to DuBose, and the woman's expression of crushing hurt was all-encompassing.

"He said that God had made Lucy the way she was as punishment for me being in love with a colored man, though he did not use that term."

DuBose caught a quick, erratic breath, and her thoughts went back to her encounter with Father Matthew. "Then he was no man of God."

Hilly touched her eye where a tear clung to it, letting it leach into her finger. "But I believed his words for the longest time. And then I thought: How can that be? God created the heavens and the earth and every single thing on it. God doesn't say one creation is better than another. For God there is no color. There is only love. So these folks can't have it both ways."

"I'm so sorry, Hilly."

"The law case that allowed Blacks and whites to finally marry?"

"What about it?"

She smiled, bittersweet and deep. "The white man's name was *Loving*. I always thought that was one of God's finest ironies."

She rose and gazed around the room of her dead daughter before looking back at DuBose. "You and my son *both* give me hope. And that's a powerful thing when it looks like the whole world is spinning right out of control, when we should all know better if we just opened our damn eyes."

After she left, DuBose stayed sitting up in the bed.

When you're fighting for the rights of the millions, Desiree, never forget that the millions are made up of single people, like Jerome and Pearl. And...Hilly Lee.

CHAPTER 71

THE NEXT DAY, AFTER CALLING a series of witnesses as part of the prosecution's case, Edmund Battle brought Albert Custer to the stand. He was a Black man, slender in physique, wearing a three-piece cream-colored suit and a colorful bow tie. He was sworn in and faced the crowd with an assured, superior manner. Several of the jurors looked at him with contempt.

Battle said, "You are the owner of Winston's Food Market?"

"I am."

"Do you employ the defendant Pearl Washington?"

Custer looked at Pearl, who had her head bowed, clearly unwilling to meet his eye. He smiled and licked his lips.

"Yes I *do*," he said.

"In what position?" asked Battle.

"Gal does what I tell her to do," he said casually. "Monday to Friday. After that, guess she does what her husband tells her to."

Now Pearl glanced up and gave Custer a look of singular disgust.

"Is she a good worker?" Battle asked.

"Yeah, she's a good gal, knows her place."

"Can you tell us if she was at work on June fourteenth of this year?"

"No, she was not," answered Custer.

"Did you know she was going to be absent from work on that day?"

"No, I didn't. I was pretty upset. I had things for her to do that day, for *me*."

He grinned and Jerome glanced at Pearl in a quizzical manner.

"So, all day she was not at work?" queried Battle.

"That's right," answered Custer.

"And when she came in on Monday, did you ask where she had been?"

"I sure did."

"And her answer?" asked Battle.

"She didn't have one," replied Custer.

DuBose said something to Pearl and she whispered back. DuBose pressed her point, but Pearl glanced fearfully at Jerome and shook her head.

Battle said, "Thank you, nothing further."

DuBose rose and approached Custer. "You're in the store all day?" she asked.

"I am."

"Never take a lunch, or a break, or leave the premises?"

"I go in the back room sometimes." He smirked at Pearl. "If there's a reason for me to be there."

"Did you ever have a reason to go in—"

DuBose halted and looked back at Pearl, who was staring at her with pleading eyes. She then glanced at the smug Custer and said, "Nothing further, Your Honor."

Custer chuckled, but as his gaze roamed over the courtroom it fixed on Miss Jessup, who was staring at him with an intensity that struck the self-satisfied look cleanly off the man's face. Then, when he glanced on either side of Miss Jessup, he saw Daniel on the left and his friend Louis Sherman on the right. They were also staring rigidly at him.

Custer started to breathe fast.

Ambrose said, "You are excused."

"I...I..."

"You're excused!" snapped Ambrose.

Custer got up and hurried out of the courtroom.

Miss Jessup nodded curtly at Daniel and Louis Sherman.

They rose and followed Custer out.

DuBose, who had been watching all this, eyed Miss Jessup. The woman didn't look at her. She stared straight ahead with both hands clenching the handle of her pocketbook.

DuBose turned back when she heard Jerome say to Pearl, "Where *was* you that day? You *got* to tell me, Pearl. Ain't no secrets between us."

DuBose leaned over and said, "She was getting some medical treatment, Jerome."

"What?" he exclaimed.

"It was for a *woman's* issue," said DuBose.

Jerome now looked at Pearl with concern and said, "You okay, baby?"

She smiled weakly and nodded. "I am now."

* * *

The gardener, Tyler Dobbs, was wearing jeans that were stained, and his corduroy jacket was threadbare. He hadn't shaved, and when Battle approached him to begin his questioning, his nose wrinkled at the sour smell wafting off the man.

He led Dobbs through a series of questions that were answered for the most part with one-word responses. But his message to the jury was clear: Jerome Washington had acted belligerently toward the Randolphs, *and* he needed money.

When Battle was done Jack picked up a piece of paper from the table that had certain items listed on it that Donny Peppers had previously given to DuBose.

He approached Dobbs and smiled. "So you say the defendant acted belligerently towards the Randolphs?"

"Yes he did."

"And he told you that he needed money?"

"Yep."

"For what purpose?"

"He didn't *confide* in me. Not like we were buddies or nothin'." Dobbs winked knowingly at the jurors and several of them smiled back.

"Mr. Dobbs, are you a gambler?"

"Objection," said Battle. "Relevancy?"

"I will make the relevancy real clear in just a few moments," said Jack.

Ambrose frowned down at him from the bench. "Well, please do so quickly."

"Are you a gambler, Mr. Dobbs?" said Jack, glancing at the paper in his hand.

"What do you mean by gamblin'?" snarled Dobbs.

Jack looked at the paper. "Dog fights, poker, street craps, and blackjack."

"Ain't gamblin' illegal in Virginia?"

"That's not what I asked. And just remember, you are under oath, and also know that I am prepared to call a half-dozen witnesses depending on your answer."

Dobbs sat up straighter and crossed his arms over his chest. "Yeah, I done all that." He glanced at the bailiff at the back of the courtroom. "But I don't do it no more."

"Since when?"

"Since you just told everybody."

"What is your yearly income?"

Battle once more said, "Relevancy?"

"If the witness would answer a little faster, we'd be done by now," retorted Jack.

Both men looked at Ambrose, who slowly nodded. "Answer the question."

"Depends on the year," said Dobbs.

"Last year, then."

Dobbs shifted in his seat. "Oh, 'bout two thousand dollars."

"How about this year? You doing better or worse?"

"Little worse. Probably won't end up makin' fifteen hundred this year."

"You come from money? You inherit a bunch?"

Dobbs laughed. "I wish."

Jack didn't crack a smile. He just stood there awaiting an answer.

Dobbs stopped laughing and said, "No, I ain't come from no money."

"How much do you have in the bank right now?"

"I don't use a bank. I keep it on me."

"Okay, how much?"

Dobbs pulled out his wallet and counted out the money. "Forty dollars, satisfied?"

"Have you taken out a loan from anyone recently? Anyone given you a gift? Anything like that?"

"No! What the hell is all this about?"

"Okay. Isn't it true that you owed three thousand one hundred and fifty dollars in gambling debts?"

Dobbs looked wildly around the courtroom. "What?"

"Over three thousand dollars in gambling debts, you owed that to a number of individuals, correct?"

Dobbs clenched the top rail of the witness box. "I—"

"Correct?"

Dobbs swallowed heavily and nodded. "Yeah, that's right."

"You must be a really, really bad gambler."

Battle rose to his feet. "Your Honor, can counsel tell us where this is going?"

"I am right now," said Jack. "And isn't it true, Mr. Dobbs, that those gambling debts have been satisfied in full? *Shortly* after you told the police and Mr. Battle that the defendant was belligerent toward the Randolphs and that he needed money?"

DuBose glanced at the jurors, to see several of them stiffen and look more attentive. Ambrose also looked concerned by this revelation.

Dobbs said, "I...see, the thing is..."

"A simple yes or no will do," said Jack.

"Well, yeah," admitted Dobbs.

"Yes, your gambling debts were paid off?"

"Yeah."

"*How* were they paid off?" asked Jack.

"I...see...I won me some money in a craps game."

"You won over *three thousand dollars* in street craps in Freeman County?"

Dobbs glanced at the jury to find them staring at him in complete disbelief. "Yes...I mean, no. I mean..."

"Who gave you the money to pay off the debts?"

Dobbs slumped back, a resigned expression on his face. "Nobody give it to me."

"Mr. Dobbs," began Jack.

"I'm tellin' the truth. Nobody give it to me. But they paid off my debts."

"Who did and why?"

"I don't know who. I found out when some folks come by. I thought they...I thought they were there to collect and might hurt me. But they said the money had come in and I was free and clear."

"And someone did that out of the goodness of their heart?"

Dobbs leaned forward. "Yeah, I guess so."

"No, Mr. Dobbs, someone paid those debts off so you would provide false testimony about Mr. Washington, isn't that true?"

"No, sir, that ain't true at all."

Jack was handed another piece of paper by DuBose. He said, "I will give you one more chance to tell the truth, Mr. Dobbs, and then I will refer you for prosecution to the commonwealth for the charge of perjury, which carries a stiff prison sentence."

"Shit." Dobbs stood. "I'm gettin' the hell outta here."

But the burly bailiff came forward to intercept him.

"Sit down, sir," ordered Ambrose. "And no profane language in my courtroom!"

Dobbs slumped down in the witness chair and started to chew on a fingernail.

Jack said, "Answer the question. Who told you to lie?"

"Okay, you're right. I got a note. It told me what to say and that if I did, my debts would be taken care of."

"And you seriously expect us to believe that you don't know who it is?" said Jack.

"I swear to God."

"Where's the note?"

"I burned it."

Jack glanced at the paper. "One more chance."

Dobbs was desperate now. "Listen, Mr. Lawyer, I'd love to tell you, but I don't know who done it. I swear."

"And the people who were paid off?"

"They told me the money just showed up with a note sayin' it was to pay off what I owed. That's all they know, too. It's why they come by, to see if I knew about it."

He had half risen in his anxiety and then sat back down. "Am I in trouble?"

"Oh yes, a lot," said Jack. He glanced at the judge expectantly.

Ambrose said, "Bailiff, take this man into custody and hold him for perjury charges."

"What!" exclaimed Dobbs.

Ambrose peered down at him with a withering expression. "You lie in my courtroom, sir, you pay the price."

A protesting Tyler Dobbs was removed from the courtroom by the bailiff and an armed deputy.

Jack handed the paper he had used to intimidate Tyler into telling the truth back to DuBose. On it were simply doodles she had made earlier. He said to the judge, "Move to strike all of the last witness's testimony on the grounds that it was all lies in return for cash."

Ambrose looked at a deflated Battle, who said, "No objection."

The judge turned to the jury. "You are hereby instructed to

disregard the testimony of the last witness as it dealt with all matters related to the defendants."

"Thank you, Your Honor," said Jack.

"Mr. Battle, call your next witness. And let's hope he's not a liar, too," Ambrose snapped.

CHAPTER 72

BATTLE CALLED SAM RANDOLPH, WHO walked up to the stand and provided his testimony under the prosecutor's careful direction.

"Now, you're of the mind that your father definitely told Mr. Washington about wanting to leave money to him?" Battle asked.

Before he could answer DuBose was on her feet. "That's speculation on his part, Your Honor. The witness cannot answer that question unless he has direct knowledge that Mr. Leslie Randolph did in fact tell the defendant about his intent to leave him money."

Battle said, "Your Honor, I am relying on the legal principle of *res gestae*. We have heard previous testimony from other witnesses that Mr. Randolph was a blunt, forceful person who meant what he said. Under *res gestae*, if he told his son that he intended to leave money to the defendant, the jury can draw an inference that he indeed went through with that and duly informed the defendant."

"I renew my objection," said DuBose. "The commonwealth has not laid an adequate foundation to raise the extremely narrow principle of *res gestae*. Otherwise, it's simply a back door for hearsay to be admitted as factual evidence and should not be allowed."

Jack looked confused. It was clear he had no idea what the term even meant.

Ambrose said, "Your objection is duly noted, but I think

Mr. Battle *has* laid an adequate foundation. You may answer the question, sir."

"When my father got a thought in his head he acted on it," said Sam. "The defendant knew he might get something, count on it."

When Battle was finished, Sam Randolph perched nervously in his chair on the witness stand as Jack approached.

"Hello, Mr. Randolph. Now, you just testified that your father told you that he was planning to leave something to the defendant in his will. And you also just testified that it is your firm belief that he did indeed tell Mr. Washington of that intent."

"That's right."

"But turns out he didn't leave Mr. Washington anything."

"Then he changed his mind or was killed before he could amend his will."

"In your sworn statement you expressed surprise that he would have thought about leaving the defendant anything at all, correct?"

"Yes. I mean, he wasn't family. He'd only worked for my parents about a year."

"Now, do you have any direct knowledge that your father actually told Jerome Washington that he was going to leave something of value to him in his will?"

Battle rose. "We already established that under the principle of *res gestae*."

Jack said, "Well, I was never any good with Latin, so I just thought I'd try old-fashioned English."

The courtroom erupted into laughter, with DuBose, Pearl, and Jerome joining in. Even Battle managed a grudging chuckle. DuBose turned to see Hilly smiling proudly at her son's quick wit.

Ambrose said, "Go ahead and answer, Mr. Randolph. In *English*."

"No. I have no direct knowledge of that."

"Thank you. Now, you are in desperate need of money, are you not?"

Battle stood. "Objection. Relevancy?"

DuBose rose and said, "Your Honor, this is the common-wealth's witness, meaning we can treat him as a hostile one. And we have every right, in trying to show reasonable doubt, that other people had motive to kill the Randolphs. I can cite you ten Virginia Supreme Court opinions that back me up on that point. And your denying our right to do so will *guarantee* a swift appeal, which we will seek immediately depending upon your ruling."

DuBose stared at Ambrose, and the judge stared right back at her.

Come on, thought DuBose, who had been intentionally provocative with her words to the judge. *Show yourself. You know you want to, Jim Crow.*

However, before Ambrose could respond, Battle said, "I withdraw my objection."

"Get on with it, Mr. Lee," barked Ambrose, who then shot DuBose another withering look. "But you watch how you address this court, you—" He seemed to catch himself, glanced at the reporters, and added, "I have treated you with respect this whole time, and all I ask is for you to do the same, Miss DuBose." He tacked on a forced smile.

"Of course, Judge. Just trying to be an effective advocate for my client."

Jack continued. "You were in need of money, correct?"

Randolph replied, "I…I could use money, yes."

"And did you expect an inheritance from your parents' estate upon their deaths?"

"Of course I did."

"But under the terms of their will, you didn't get it, did you?"

"No."

"But you didn't know that before they were killed, correct?"

"Are you implying that—" sputtered Randolph.

"Just answer the question," interrupted Jack.

Randolph eyed the judge, who said dully, "Answer the question, sir."

"No, I was not aware of the contents of their will until *after* they died."

"And where were you when your parents were killed?"

"I was at home."

"Alone?" asked Jack.

"Yes."

"So no one can corroborate your whereabouts at that time?"

"No!" snapped Randolph.

"So you could have been at your parents' home that day?"

"I wasn't."

"Are you ill, Mr. Randolph?" Jack asked.

"That is none of your business!"

Jack said, "Ordinarily it wouldn't be, but under the circumstances, I'm afraid it is." Before Ambrose could say anything, Jack said, "Goes to motive, state of mind, and an alternate theory of who committed the murders, Your Honor, all to demonstrate reasonable doubt."

Ambrose sat back, looking irritated. "Go on and answer the question, sir."

"Yes, I am sick," said Randolph.

"And you're seeking treatment outside of the country?"

Randolph shot him an angry look. "How the hell did you—"

"Just answer the question, please," Jack prompted.

"Yes. Switzerland."

"Well, I hope you're successful, Mr. Randolph."

"Sure you do," Randolph said snidely. "But I did not kill my parents."

"Move to strike the witness's last statement," Jack said automatically.

Ambrose turned to the jury and said offhandedly, "You are to ignore the witness's last statement as though it had not been said."

Jack knew this was really impossible, but he garnered immense satisfaction in forcing Ambrose to have to say it. "Now, you had a psychiatrist visit your parents," he said to Randolph. "Can you tell us why?"

Randolph nearly came out of his seat. He looked over Jack's shoulder.

When Jack turned around he saw Christine once more staring intently at her brother. Jack turned back to him. "Mr. Randolph?"

"I-it's true that I retained a doctor to examine my...parents. There's nothing illegal about that," he added quickly.

"For what purpose did you want them examined?"

Randolph kneaded his fists into his thighs.

"I thought they were both losing their minds."

"Why would you think that?"

"Just little things."

"But you didn't see that much of them, did you?"

"I saw enough," countered Randolph.

"Isn't it a fact that you wanted to have them declared incompetent so that you could get your hands on your inheritance sooner rather than later?"

"Objection, leading question," barked Battle.

"Once again, as my colleague already pointed out, he's the commonwealth's witness, thus I am entitled to treat him as a hostile one."

"Answer the question," Ambrose ordered reluctantly.

"My only purpose was what was in the best interests of my parents."

"Is it true that your father told your doctor to get out and that no one was going to make him leave his home?"

"I have no idea what you're talking about."

"And that this stunt made your parents change their will so that you're almost guaranteed not to get a penny from the estate?"

"Go to hell," barked Randolph.

"I hope neither one of us gets to see that place."

"Objection, Your Honor," said Battle. "Argumentative, even for a hostile witness."

"Sustained," said Ambrose brusquely.

Jack held Randolph's gaze. "You must have hated your parents very much."

"Objection," roared Battle.

"Withdraw the statement. Did you ever ask your parents for the money for your treatment?"

"Objection, relevancy?" said Battle.

"Goes to motive and state of mind, Judge," retorted Jack firmly.

"Answer the question," said Ambrose, with a quick glance at the journalists in the courtroom.

"Yes, I asked my father."

"And what was his answer?"

Randolph didn't reply right away. When he did, Jack couldn't help feeling sorry for the man.

"My father said that even if he had the money he wouldn't give it to me. He...he said I wasn't worth it." Randolph bent his face into his hands.

Jack stared sympathetically at the stricken man for a few moments. "Well, I'm very sorry about that. I really am. Nothing further." He walked back to the counsel table.

Randolph got off the witness stand, walked down the aisle, ignored his sister's outstretched hand, shoved open the double doors, and kept right on going.

CHAPTER 73

BATTLE NEXT CALLED CHRISTINE HANOVER and ques-
tioned the woman about her and her husband's trip to Washington,
DC, and Hanover's relationship with her parents. And also about
her shock at learning of their deaths. She continually looked at her
husband as she testified.

DuBose rose when Battle turned the witness over to the defense.
She approached Christine. "I'm very sorry for your loss, Mrs.
Hanover."

"Thank you."

"Were you aware that the defendants and their children attended
a pool party and luncheon at your parents' house a couple of weeks
before their deaths?"

"Yes, my husband and I were arriving with our family as the
Washingtons were getting ready to leave."

"Can you describe that event, please?"

"They were all happy and having a wonderful time. The kids
were still wet from the pool, and they had little brown lunch bags
my mother had filled up with leftovers for them to take home."

"Did you speak to your parents about why they had invited
them over?"

"Yes. My mother said that Jerome had been working hard, and
had fixed so many things, and was extremely pleasant in his manner.

My parents had learned about his family, and she thought it would be fun to have them over. And my father agreed."

"As sort of a reward for a job well done?"

"Yes."

DuBose glanced at the jury, who seemed to be listening to this exchange intently.

"So you saw no animosity or fear or anything else negative between your parents and Jerome and his family that day?"

"That's right. It was all very pleasant."

"And that made you happy?" asked DuBose.

"Yes. They're people, too. I don't care what color their skin is."

DuBose closed her eyes for a moment and then glanced at the jury.

Never ask an open-ended question like that, Desiree. That allows a witness to tack on an opinion. The jury will now discount every-thing she just said.

"Anything else to ask the witness, Miss DuBose?" Ambrose said politely.

When she glanced at his smug features she could just tell he was thinking the very same thing.

"Thank you, Mrs. Hanover. Nothing further."

Battle next called Gordon Hanover to the stand. "Mr. Hanover, have you and your wife been financially supporting her parents?"

"That's right. We knew what their expenses were, and they were promptly paid."

"So if your father-in-law wanted to fire someone, like the defendant, it would not have been over money?"

DuBose said, "Objection, calls for speculation."

"Sustained," said Ambrose, which almost made DuBose fall out of her chair. But then she understood.

He knows the jury has made up its mind. He can afford to appear magnanimous. And look good for the media.

"Did your father-in-law have occasion to speak to you about Jerome Washington?" asked Battle.

Hanover looked down and nodded. "He did."

"Can you tell us the substance of that conversation?"

Hanover glanced up and found his wife in the gallery. His gaze locked on her as he said, "Leslie, I mean Mr. Randolph, told me that he suspected that Mr. Washington had been in his house without permission."

"Anything else?" prompted Battle.

"I'm not sure that I recall, really."

Battle tensed. "I can show you your *sworn* statement if that will refresh your memory, sir."

"No, no, that's all right," Hanover replied, looking nervous. "He said...he said that he thought Mr. Washington had stolen some tools or some such from the garage and some money from a cashbox in the study, and was going to fire him because of it."

"I ain't steal nuthin'," called out Jerome from the counsel table.

"Silence," barked Ambrose. "Another outburst like that and I will have you removed from this courtroom."

Jack put a restraining hand on Jerome as Ambrose scowled down at him.

Battle turned back to Hanover and said, "So your father-in-law was going to fire the defendant for stealing?"

"Um...apparently."

"You were there the day that the defendant and his family were at your in-laws'?"

"Yes," answered Hanover.

"Now, did your conversation with Mr. Randolph happen before or after the Washington family was at the Randolphs?"

"It was...after."

"And on that day everything seemed fine to you, too, as your wife testified?"

"Yes."

"But apparently your father-in-law's opinion changed since, after that time, he told you he was going to fire the defendant, isn't that right?" noted Battle.

"Calls for speculation," said DuBose.

"Sustained," said Ambrose.

Battle continued. "Do you believe that your father-in-law told the defendant that he was going to fire him or might have already done so?"

"Objection," said DuBose. "Speculation!"

Battle said, "Once more I am relying on *res gestae*."

"And once more I am pointing out that you have woefully failed to lay the proper foundation to invoke it," she retorted.

Ambrose said, "Miss DuBose, you know I've already ruled on that. Please respect this court's decision. Objection denied. Answer the question."

"Yes, I do believe he told Mr. Washington that he would be terminated."

Battle went back to his table, where his associate handed him a piece of paper. "Your Honor, after Mr. Hanover identifies this document, I would like to move it into evidence as Commonwealth's Exhibit Number Thirty-One." He passed it to Ambrose.

Jack got to his feet. "Objection. We have not seen this exhibit, nor was it listed on the schedule."

Battle turned to him. "Under Virginia law we do not have to show you every scrap of evidence we collect, Mr. Lee. Indeed, we provided to you far more than the law says we have to, so you have no standing or reason to object." He motioned to his associate, who handed a copy to Jack.

The judge looked at the piece of paper and said, "Commonwealth's Exhibit Thirty-One will be accepted into evidence once it is authenticated by the witness."

Jack ran his gaze down the paper while DuBose, sitting next to him, did the same.

Battle handed the paper to Gordon Hanover. "Do you recognize this, sir?"

Hanover looked at the paper. "I do."

"Can you tell the jury, please?"

"It's a bill for a water delivery at my in-laws' home."

"You had this bill paid?"

"Yes."

"What sort of water was it?"

"It's a bill for *pool* water. My...in-laws had their pool emptied and then refilled with fresh water."

Battle was handed another piece of paper from his associate, who also passed a copy to Jack.

Battle handed it to Ambrose and said, "Motion to move Commonwealth's Exhibit Thirty-Two into evidence, Your Honor, once authenticated by the witness."

Ambrose looked at the paper and said, "Commonwealth Exhibit Thirty-Two to be moved into evidence once validated by the witness." He handed it to Hanover.

After looking at the document Jack glanced curiously at DuBose. Her dour expression showed she now knew exactly what the attorney general was doing.

Battle said, "Can you identify that document for the jury?"

"It's another bill for pool water that I had paid."

"What is the date on that, sir?"

"May twenty-fourth of this year."

"And what is the date of the first document I handed you, Exhibit Thirty-One?"

"Um...June eighth."

Battle assumed a confused expression. "So let me get this straight. On May twenty-fourth they filled the pool with fresh, clean water, I suppose, for the start of the summer season, correct?"

"Yes, that was around the time when they usually did so."

"And yet on June eighth they had water that was only two weeks old replaced? That wasn't cheap, I imagine."

"No, but it was what they wanted."

"Did you ever ask them why they did that?"

"No, I didn't."

"Was it normal for them to replace the water *twice*?"

"No."

"And when exactly did you see the defendant and his family at the Randolphs'?"

Hanover fidgeted.

"Mr. Hanover, do I need to refresh your recollection?"

"They...we saw them there on June first."

"So *one week* after the defendants and their family used the Randolphs' pool, the Randolphs had the pool completely emptied and refilled with *clean* water, is that correct?"

Hanover looked out over the courtroom and found his wife once more. His expression was forlorn, thought DuBose, who was watching him carefully.

"Mr. Hanover?" prompted Battle.

"Uh, yes, yes, that's right," he said curtly, his mouth curving in displeasure.

"And you have no idea why they would have changed the water after this *Negro* family swam in their pool?"

DuBose, her face burning with indignation, rose to her feet. "Objection, counsel is leading the witness."

Before Ambrose could rule Battle said, "Withdraw the question. Thank you, Mr. Hanover. Nothing further."

"Defense?" said Ambrose. "Any questions for this witness?"

DuBose said, "Mr. Hanover, do you have any direct knowledge that your father-in-law told the defendant that he was going to be fired, or had, indeed, fired him?"

"None whatsoever," Hanover said firmly, staring at the jury.

DuBose looked at the jury as well and found that at least half of them did not even appear to be listening.

"Nothing further," said DuBose, and Hanover was excused by Ambrose.

Battle rose and said, "Commonwealth rests, Your Honor."

DuBose immediately said, "Motion to strike the commonwealth's case."

"On what grounds?" asked Ambrose.

"That the commonwealth has utterly failed to prove guilt beyond a reasonable doubt. And it has, in particular, failed to provide any proof whatsoever that Pearl Washington was even at the scene of the crime while it was being committed, or did anything that the commonwealth alleges that she did. They have offered only one witness, who merely testified she was not at work that day. And without that, the evidence presented by the commonwealth vindicates our clients because Jerome Washington could not have committed those murders while having no blood on his clothing or shoes. The county's own medical examiner was clear on that point. Further, the commonwealth has utterly failed to provide the murder weapon, or come up with any reason, bolstered by evidence, as to why it was not found on the defendant's person. And, lastly, they have no proof that the money found in the lean-to was taken from the Randolphs' home."

Ambrose took off his glasses and cleaned them on his sleeve before putting them back on. "I know you're only trying to do right by your clients, but the fact is the commonwealth has put on more than sufficient evidence to take this case to the jury, and you know it, too." He glanced at the audience before continuing. "But you have the opportunity to rebut that case starting tomorrow. Your reputation has preceded you, Miss DuBose. I'm sure we all expect a powerful defense to the commonwealth's long lists of proofs." He rapped his gavel. "Court is dismissed and will reconvene at ten tomorrow morning."

CHAPTER 74

JEFF!" SAID CHRISTINE OUTSIDE THE courthouse. "I heard you were in town."

Jeff Lee smiled warmly. "Good to see you, Chrissy."

"Haven't been called that in years. In fact, you're the only one who ever did."

His smile faded. "I'm sorry. I'll just make it Christine."

"No, I always liked Chrissy. Christine seems so formal, and that's just not me."

"Sure not the gal that I knew," said Jeff, grinning once more.

"So if you're back, does that mean everything is okay?"

"I'm no longer in the Army and I can lead my life however I want to."

She touched his arm. "I'm so glad. And I'm happy you came back to Freeman."

"Well, it is my home. And my family is here."

"And I'm so sorry about Lucy. She was just the sweetest thing under the sun."

Jeff's grin vanished once more and didn't return. "Yes...yes she sure was."

A horn sounded, and they looked over to see Gordon driving up in his elegant silver Rolls-Royce.

"Wow, that is some car," said Jeff.

"Gordon likes nice things."

"Heard you got kids. I'm really happy for you."

"Thanks. Maybe we could talk some time, over coffee?"

He glanced at Gordon, who was staring at them from the car. "Anytime. Just let me know. I'm staying at my folks' house."

"I will."

She walked over to the Rolls. Before she climbed in, a man ran across the street and started screaming at her.

"Rich bitch!" he yelled. "You love you a n——? You better watch yourself."

He pushed her up against the Rolls.

Before Gordon could intercede, Jeff Lee had rushed over, picked up the man, and thrown him across the pavement. When two other men, fists raised, came at Jeff, he knocked them both down. So swift had the beating been that both men lay on the street, seemingly unsure of how they had gotten there.

Another man came at Jeff with a knife. A few moments later, Jeff had the knife and was holding it against the man's pulsing neck.

"Anybody else have a problem they want to 'discuss' with me?" asked Jeff, as he shoved the man to the ground. He tossed the knife into a prickly holly bush. "Anybody?"

No one took up the challenge.

Jeff turned to Christine and helped her into the Rolls. "You okay?"

"Yes," she said breathlessly. "Thank you."

"Yes, thank you," said Gordon Hanover from the driver's seat. "This mob is getting out of control."

"You best get on out of here," warned Jeff.

"Will you be okay?" asked Christine. "You can ride with us."

Jeff surveyed the crowd. "I'll be fine. I think *they* have to worry about *me*."

She smiled and touched his hand, and Gordon swiftly drove off.

"What are you doing?"

Jeff turned to see his brother standing there. Jack had obviously come out of the courthouse too late to see the altercation.

"What do you mean?"

Jack stared after the Rolls. "You know what I mean."

"We were friends, Jack."

"You know and I know you were a lot more than friends. And she's married, little brother. So tread carefully."

Jack walked away, leaving Jeff to stare pensively after the Rolls.

* * *

Jack and DuBose were sitting in the garage working that night when Jack said, "I heard you on the radio earlier. When did you do that interview?"

"From a pay phone near the courthouse before we came back here. What'd you think?"

"You know how I feel about litigating in the press."

"I want to *win* this case, Jack, not lose and then file endless and pointless appeals while Jerome and Pearl rot in prison."

"That's my *point*. We have to put all our energies into the trial. You said your piece out on the courthouse steps and it was damn powerful. But let that be enough."

"I'm also a realist, using different tactics than other lawyers because I have to."

"You've lost me."

"With that jury we have almost no chance unless we deliver the real killer right to the police—and that is not something I can count on, can you?"

"Then what exactly are you doing?"

"I am taking every opportunity to blast to the heavens how blatantly unfair this all is. At some point, it should get through even the thickest of heads."

"There are a lot of white people you will never convince that the races are equal."

"I don't need to convince everyone. We just have to reach critical mass. At some point the tide will turn. We made the laws change, now we just have to bring the majority of *your* race along."

"So, should we tell Jerome and Pearl that they're just *pawns* in a bigger game?"

She looked at him darkly. "They know more than you ever will the powers stacked against them. Do you really think they expect to be found innocent by *that* jury?"

"Well, we haven't put our case on yet."

"Our clients are Black, not white. And if we can't get into evidence where Pearl was that day, the jury will infer that she was there helping Jerome."

"Then we have to figure out a way to get it in," said Jack.

"I've subpoenaed Janice Evans, but she's fighting it, and the clock will run out."

"Okay. In the meantime, how about some dinner? I'm starving."

"I really don't want to be stared at, not tonight."

"That won't be a problem. Trust me."

He hurried inside the house and came back out with a picnic basket.

She blanched. "Please don't tell me your mother made that."

"No. Miss Jessup dropped it off earlier. It's part of our legal fee."

"Okay, but where are we going?"

"You'll see," he said.

CHAPTER 75

JACK DROVE THEM TO THE abandoned Penny Bridge. He grabbed the picnic basket and led her out onto the span, stopping about halfway across. He laid out a blanket from the basket, then he and DuBose set out roasted chicken, green beans, mashed potatoes, soft rolls, and a pitcher of iced tea, and plates, glasses, and utensils.

They sat on the blanket, and when DuBose bit into the chicken she moaned.

"Oh my God, that is so good it should be illegal."

Jack took a bite. "I suspect it might have something to do with bacon fat, Crisco, prayer, or a combination thereof."

They ate and enjoyed the breeze that was constant along the river below.

"When did they close this bridge?" she asked.

"When I was little." He pointed to the east. "That is unofficially the Black side of the county. Used to be a lot of white people who lived there, but it changed after the *Brown* decision."

"White flight to the suburbs," noted DuBose. "So their children wouldn't have to sit in class with Black kids."

"But it's not just segregated by race. Rich whites live in the northwest part and folks like my family in the southwest."

"Wealth and race are truly insidious dividers," noted DuBose.

"We'd ride our bikes over to the Penny and lie down and do

some star gazing, pick out the Big and Little Dippers, Ursa Minor, Polaris, Orion. See if we could spot a shooting star; it's supposed to bring good luck. We'd swap dreams and baseball cards and chew our bubble gum and then spit it into the McHenry River. Stupid stuff that boys do."

"You and your brother were close I take it?"

"We were each other's best friends growing up. Played ball together, did everything together, really. Momma and Daddy had to focus on Lucy, of course. But that was okay, we understood. We got more freedom and we always had each other's backs." He looked at her. "What about you? You said one brother's a surgeon and you have a sister in North Carolina. And you said a younger sister owns an art gallery in Harlem."

"Yes, Judith. I see her whenever I'm in New York. We're closest in age."

"So were you best friends growing up?"

DuBose tensed as she picked at a piece of chicken. "No. No, we weren't. My mother played favorites, you see, and I was her chosen one, even over Nathaniel, my doctor brother. When I graduated from Yale Law School, my mother clapped louder and longer than anyone else. She told me that now I had the tools to accomplish great things. To right the world, for our people."

Jack took a swallow of iced tea and said, "No pressure there, of course."

"Judith was only a year younger, so there was going to be some natural rivalry. But she's truly extraordinary, in every way. Hoping for my mother's praise, and love, but never really getting it. My mother wanted me to take care of her funeral, take care of our father, handle the estate. I'm not sure she and Judith even spoke much."

"That must've been tough for everyone."

She looked squarely at him. "I saw it while it was happening, Jack, but I did nothing about it. I actually reveled in my mother's praise. In being the chosen one."

"We all want our parents' love."

"Anyway, after my mother died, Judith and I sat down and had a come-to-Jesus sort of talk. It ended with us reaching common ground and becoming...closer."

Noting her depressed look, he lifted the picnic basket top and pulled out a bottle. "I can't swear my daddy didn't bring this wine back after the war, but I thought we'd give it a go."

He pulled out two glasses, opened the wine, poured generous portions into the glasses, and handed one to DuBose. They moved over to the side of the bridge, took off their shoes, and let their feet dangle over the edge.

"So you really don't think we can win this case?" he asked.

"There are lots of ways to win, Jack." Her tone was distant and troubled.

"The only win for *me* is if Jerome and Pearl are found not guilty."

DuBose looked to the sky. "Maybe *we* can spot a shooting star, bring us some luck." She drank her wine and gazed at the heavens.

And Jack watched her, a woman seemingly with the weight of an entire race on her shoulders, with growing anxiety.

CHAPTER 76

THE NEXT DAY JACK ROSE in the courtroom and called Craig Baker to the witness stand to commence the defense's part of the case.

"Mr. Baker, can you state your occupation for the jury?" asked Jack.

"I'm an attorney in Norfolk with the firm of Day and O'Connor."

"And did you have occasion to send a package to Mrs. Anne Randolph?"

"I did. Although it was supposed to go to a P.O. box she had provided me. But my secretary mistakenly sent it to the Randolphs' home."

Jack picked up the empty package from his counsel table and showed it to Baker. "Did you send the communication in this?"

"Yes, I did."

Jack showed the package to Ambrose. "Move to admit this into evidence as Defense Exhibit Five, Your Honor."

Battle got to his feet. "For what purpose?"

"My line of questioning will make that clear," said Jack.

Ambrose chewed on a nail while he considered this, shooting glances at the crowd of journalists in the courtroom. "I'll take you at your word, Mr. Lee. Motion to admit evidence granted. Proceed."

"Can you tell us the contents of the communication you sent to Mrs. Randolph?"

"I'm afraid that would run afoul of the attorney-client privilege."

"Oh, so Mrs. Randolph *was* a client of yours?" said Jack.

"Yes, she was."

"And her husband as well?" asked Jack.

"No, he was *not* my client."

"Without telling us exactly what was in the communication can you tell us, generally, the nature of it?"

"They were draft pleadings."

"Pleadings? So Mrs. Randolph was taking someone to court?"

"Correct."

"Can you tell us who?"

"That may once more run afoul of the privilege."

Jack turned to see Christine Hanover listening intently to all of this. He next glanced at the jury to see that they were doing the same.

"Okay, Mr. Baker. Can you at least tell us what sort of law that you practice? Are you a general practitioner? Do you handle lots of different things?"

"No, I confine my practice to one specialty only."

Jack shot Battle a sidelong glance. "And what is that specialty?"

"I'm a *divorce* lawyer."

A gasp went up throughout the courtroom. Jack turned to see Christine Hanover. She looked relieved. Or, more accurately, resigned. She glanced around the courtroom, and her gaze found and held on Jeff Lee, who mouthed the words, *I'm so sorry.*

Jack said, "So, to be clear, Mrs. Randolph was divorcing Mr. Randolph?"

Baker looked at the jury as he said, "That can be inferred from what I said, and that inference would be correct, yes."

"Your Honor, this was not disclosed to us previously," Battle complained.

"Why, Mr. Battle," said Jack. "We don't have to show you every 'scrap of evidence' that we've uncovered, do we, sir?"

Bursts of laughter sparked around the courtroom.

"Everyone just quiet down," growled Ambrose as he banged his gavel.

"Can you tell us on what grounds she was doing so?" asked Jack.

"I'm afraid I cannot."

"But it was serious enough for her to engage you to commence a divorce action?"

"Obviously," replied Baker.

"And serious enough for you to keep the fact of her filing for divorce secret from her husband, hence the P.O. box?"

"Yes. Divorce can be a...delicate matter that elicits...strong emotions."

"Thank you, no further questions."

Jack walked back to his table.

Ambrose peered down at Battle. "Commonwealth? Anything for this witness?"

"Uh, no, Your Honor," said Battle, obviously still processing this development.

"Then I recall Herman Till to the stand," said Jack promptly.

The medical examiner sat back down in the witness box.

"Mr. Till, you examined the bodies of the Randolphs thoroughly, did you not?"

"I did."

"Now, in addition to the wounds they received from the attack, did you observe any other injuries on Mrs. Randolph's body that had been there previous to her murder?"

"I did," replied Till.

"And at our request you went back over them again, did you not?"

"Yes."

"Can you describe these injuries?" asked Jack.

Till looked at the jurors. "She had multiple bone fractures that had healed over time. On both her arms, left leg, cheekbone, and shoulder blade. There were also what appeared to be knife gashes on her arms and legs that had healed. And one of her fingers had been broken a while ago and then healed badly. It was all twisted."

"It's been stipulated that Jerome Washington worked for the Randolphs for only one year. Did all these other injuries predate his time there?"

"Without question," answered Till.

"What is your professional opinion on how she sustained these injuries?"

"Well, at first I thought perhaps she fell a lot, but after taking another look at everything at your request, I'd say she was beaten and rather badly on multiple occasions."

A gasp went up around the courtroom.

"And did she have a more recent injury of that nature, aside from the wounds to which she succumbed?"

"She had a bruise on her cheek that had most certainly been inflicted on the day she died."

"Thank you, Mr. Till, nothing further."

Battle rose. "Mr. Till, could that bruise have been caused by the struggle with her attacker?"

"Yes, I suppose so."

A confused-looking Battle had no further questions for Till, who was excused.

DuBose now took over and recalled Christine Hanover to the stand. "You had occasion to call the police about your father's physical abuse of your mother, did you not?"

With a tissue pressed against her nose she said, "Yes. On two occasions. I could have called them a dozen times more, I suppose. And maybe I should have."

"So there was a history of a violent, troubled marriage?"

"Yes. They were not affectionate toward one another. I think it was their children that kept them together all those years."

"And your mother's injuries?" she said quietly.

"I...knew that my father could be a violent man. Before he was married he fought in World War I in the Army, and my mother told me that he brought back...bad memories from that time. And...and that sometimes he could fly into rages. I was the youngest child. But my brother, Sam, he told me of some things that, well, frankly, shocked me. And while I knew that my father was abusive toward her, I didn't know the extent of my mother's injuries that Mr. Till just talked about."

She began to weep into her hanky.

"Did you ever speak to your father about it?" asked DuBose.

"Many times. And then when they ran out of money and came to us, I told him we wouldn't help him financially unless he sought professional counseling."

"And did he?"

"Yes, he did. And I thought...I thought things were better."

"But the divorce action apparently shows that things were not, in fact, better?"

"Yes, that's right."

"Did you know your mother was seeking a divorce?"

She hesitated. "No."

"So you said your brother knew about the abuse?" asked DuBose.

"Yes. I didn't know that Sam had tried to get a psychiatrist involved. But if I had known my mother was still being physically abused, I would have tried to put a stop to it. Even if it required having my father institutionalized."

Battle rose and said, "As tragic and sad as all of this is, Your Honor, what possible relevance does it have to this case?"

Before Ambrose could make a ruling, DuBose looked directly at the jury and said, "With a troubled marriage like that, you could have people who knew the Randolphs, and who were taking sides in such a bitter relationship. Or who did not want a divorce to take place for some reason. Could that have led to violence against the

Randolphs by one of these parties? And if you have others with reasonable motivation and opportunity to commit the crime, then that equates to the basis for reasonable doubt in the minds of the jury." She now looked directly at Battle. "I can't think of anything *more relevant*."

Ambrose said grudgingly to her, "Go on ahead."

DuBose turned back to Christine. "You testified that as far as you could see your parents had a good time with the defendants' family when they went there for lunch and to swim in the pool?"

"That's right. They all were happy. Even my father."

"And yet it seems that your father had the pool water replaced after the Washingtons were in it."

"Yes," she replied, looking disconsolate.

"Can you explain that?"

"My father was a...complicated man, Miss DuBose. I could see him having the Washingtons over, and letting them swim, and eating lunch *outside*. But I could also see him wanting to replace the water before any of *his* family used the pool again. It was just the way he saw the world, I suppose."

"Do you believe your father liked or respected Black people?"

"I think my father knew there would always be Black people in his life...to *serve* him, I mean. And to ones who worked for him, he could be generous and...he perhaps enjoyed showing off his wealth, his *superior* position over them. I don't mean that he would do it necessarily in a mean or cruel way. I just mean that he saw it as something to be expected of him. As...as a *benevolent* white person."

"You mean being kind to...those *beneath* him?"

"Yes, I guess that does describe it pretty accurately from his point of view," she said sadly.

"Thank you for your candor. I know this can't have been easy."

Christine wearily shook her head. "None of this has been easy, for anyone."

CHAPTER 77

LATER THAT DAY BATTLE RECEIVED a message in the court-room and immediately asked for and received a recess.

Ambrose ordered the trial to recommence on Monday.

On their way out of the courthouse Jack told DuBose, "I bet Battle is licking his wounds right now. We put a real dent in his case."

"A dent but not a crack. And Battle could come back with something unexpected after the weekend. The people behind all this may sense vulnerability in the commonwealth's case and want to do something about it. That's probably the message Battle got. And why he asked for the recess. And, frankly, that has me worried, Jack."

They drove to the men's prison to meet with Jerome.

"It real good what you did talkin' to Miss Christine 'bout her daddy and the pool water," said Jerome.

"It was all outrageous is what it was, Jerome," said DuBose sharply.

He shrugged. "Naw, it just be how Mr. Leslie was. We got cleaned up real good before we went there, but he didn't know that."

"You could never scrub hard enough to turn your skin white, which would have been the only thing that would have worked for that man," commented DuBose.

Jerome glanced away as Jack said, "We've got some more

witnesses to put on, and we have to be prepared for whatever else Battle throws at us, Jerome, but we feel pretty good about things."

"So maybe I be outta here soon?" he said hopefully.

"We'll have to see," said Jack cautiously.

"But even if we lose we already have strong grounds for appeal," added DuBose.

"How long that take?"

"It's hard to say," she replied.

"So maybe a week, somethin' like that?"

Jack eyed DuBose, who said, "Let's just take it one step at a time."

Later, as they walked out, Jack said, "I feel like we're misleading him, Desiree."

"He knows we could win or we could lose. And if the latter, we appeal."

"But he seems to think an appeal will happen in a snap."

"And if we come to it we'll explain all about that in greater detail. But telling him that it could take months or years *now*? What good will that do? For either of them?"

* * *

They walked over to the women's prison and were escorted to Pearl's cell. The young woman rose from her bunk and gave DuBose a hug. "Thank you, thank you, thank you for what you done yesterday, not tellin' everybody 'bout what happened."

"I would never do that, Pearl, not unless you gave your permission."

"You think all them white men goin' to see the truth for what it is?"

"If they use their brains, they will," said Jack.

"Well, from where I'm sittin', that be askin' a whole, whole lot," said Pearl.

DuBose said, "We're going by your house. Can we bring your kids anything?"

Pearl slid her hand under her thin mattress and pulled out a slip of paper. She handed it to DuBose. "This here is a letter I wrote for 'em."

Jack looked curious because he obviously didn't think Pearl could write.

DuBose looked at it and said, "Oh, it's pictures."

"Yeah, that how...that how I like to write to 'em." She glanced anxiously at Jack, who was studying the paper.

He said, "Pearl, you are one fine artist. When did you draw these?"

"Momma brought me the paper, and the guard here say it okay if I have a pencil. And I ain't got nothin' else to do 'cept worry 'bout everythin'."

* * *

That evening they drove out to the Washingtons' home. Miss Jessup was also there helping Pearl's mother, Maggie.

"I've seen you in court; I'm surprised Ashby gave you time off," said Jack.

"Me and Mr. Ashby have made us a deal," said Miss Jessup. "Leastways I told him where I needed to be. I made him enough food to last him a while and the house is all clean. And he's got his liquor."

"How about Albert Custer, Pearl's boss?" said Jack.

"That man ain't never gonna trouble no woman again."

"They didn't kill him, did they?" exclaimed Jack anxiously.

She said primly, "No, but he probably wishes they had."

"Wait a minute. You don't mean—"

Miss Jessup cut him off. "I mean he ain't gonna be troublin' *no* woman *no* more."

DuBose showed Pearl's letter to the two older children,

six-year-old Elijah, who was tall like his father, and four-year-old Kayla, who was petite like her mother. Darla Jean perched quietly in her playpen, watching all of them.

"Your momma is quite an artist," Jack told the children.

"How are Momma and Daddy?" asked Elijah solemnly.

DuBose said, "They're doing okay. They miss all of you so much."

"When they comin' home?" asked Kayla in a small voice.

"I hope soon," said DuBose.

"Come on, children, time to eat," said Maggie, and she led them into the kitchen after picking up Darla Jean.

Miss Jessup said, "Now you can tell me how you really feel."

"It's Virginia, and our clients are Black," said DuBose candidly.

"So not good then?" said Miss Jessup.

"We have to hope for the best and prepare for the worst," said DuBose.

"Honey, I been doin' that my whole life, and the worst is pretty much all I ever got."

CHAPTER 78

JACK PARKED IN FRONT OF his parents' house, and he and
DuBose got out. When Jack heard someone calling his name, he
turned to see the old man waving at him from the large, rambling
house several up from his parents.

After telling DuBose that he would meet her in the garage, Jack
strode off and met up with the man in the latter's front yard. "Hey,
Mr. Ashby, how you doing?"

Ronald Ashby would have been around Jack's height, but his
spine was bent painfully forward and his spindly legs were clearly
failing. He was thinly built, except for his pot belly, and his hair was
nearly all gone, the exposed scalp burnt by the sun. He wore a faded
blue shirt, wrinkled beige slacks, and comfortable-looking slippers
with no socks. He had a cane in hand and had it pressed firm against
the earth to hold himself up.

"Doin', Jack Lee. Doin'," he drawled.

"I just saw Miss Jessup over at her granddaughter's house. She
said—"

"She said what!" broke in an agitated Ashby. "What was she
sayin' to you?"

"That you gave her the time off to help with her family and
watch the trial. But she made sure you had food and the house was
clean."

Ashby looked at him suspiciously, but then nodded. "You want to come on in? I...I wanted to ask you about the trial, son."

"Okay, but I can't stay long."

"Nobody stays long anymore," said Ashby, with one of the saddest faces Jack had ever seen. "My children never come to see me. Did you know that?"

Jack simply shrugged.

"Come on then."

He led Jack into his immaculate house, which smelled of Pine Sol and Pledge. Fresh flowers were in vases on various tables. Ashby led him into what was clearly the study. Jack noted the worm-eaten floorboards, shelves filled with old law books and framed photographs. There was a lawyer's partner's desk with a tall leather-backed swivel chair, a small couch and two upholstered chairs, and a full bar, which Ashby headed straight to.

"You thirsty?" he asked Jack.

"Um, what do you have?"

"I got everythin', son. Just name your poison."

"A finger of scotch neat."

"I'll join you in that. Been tryin' to cut down on the bourbon. Better for my health." He cackled at his little joke.

He brought the drinks over. Jack held Ashby's until the man carefully made it down to the couch and then he handed the drink to him. He sat in a chair opposite Ashby.

"Wish my place looked like this. Well, before it burned down."

"This is all Miss Jessup's work. Up to me, I'd be lyin' under a heap 'a old newspapers deader'n a runover squirrel."

Jack nodded appreciatively. "She's a right fine housekeeper."

Ashby looked into his glass. "Don't know how I would have made it without her, not after Alice...did what she did."

"Yes sir," said Jack, who was now regretting his decision to join the man.

"You know 'bout Alice?"

"Well, I heard, like everybody else."

"You sure Miss Jessup didn't tell you anythin' more?"

Jack took a sip of his scotch. "Anything more what?"

"Oh, never mind. Now, tell me how the trial is goin'." He squinted at Jack. "You gonna get them colored folks off, you think?"

"You know as well as I do that predicting a jury is a fool's mission."

Ashby sat back, looking disappointed. But then he nodded and said, "Hear tell they brought in Eddie Battle all the way from Richmond."

"And Josiah Ambrose to be the presiding judge. Don't know much about him. You know anything? He's around your age."

"I know he was in the KKK as a young man."

Jack sat up so fast he nearly upended his drink. "How do you know that?"

"I know 'cause I was right there with him. Josiah and I grew up with each other in the Piedmont, over near Danville. Had too much time on our hands and nothin' excitin' to do. Remember we went to the pictures and saw *Birth of a Nation*. The Klan was damn heroic in that flick. Don't know how much was true, but it got our blood goin', so we joined up."

"Yeah," said Jack, trying hard to keep the disgust out of his voice. "So how'd he become a judge with that in his background?"

Ashby chuckled. "Hell, back then, pretty much every white man I knew was either in the Klan for real, or in spirit. You use that as a disqualifier, son, you wouldn't have many judges or lawyers left. Or police. But they gonna win in the end," he added.

Jack looked confused. "Who is?"

"Coloreds, o'course." Ashby laughed so hard he nearly spilled his three fingers of scotch. "Won't that be somethin'. Rile up a bunch 'a folks, yes sir."

Jack studied the old man. "And how do you feel about that, Mr. Ashby? Will *you* be riled up?"

Ashby gummed his drink and got some of it down his shirt.

"You know your end is comin' fast when you can't even sip good scotch without dribblin' it down your shirt like a goddamn infant."

"Yes, sir."

Ashby let his cane go and used both hands to get the drink properly to his mouth. He smacked his lips and said, "Now, that is mighty fine." He looked over at Jack. "I find myself actually quite inspired by the idea that old Jim Crow is about to breathe his last."

"You mind me asking why?"

Ashby grinned. "You think only coon hunters live in Freeman County, Jack Lee?"

"Not by a long shot, since I'm here. But I imagine your parents raised you to think a certain way when it comes to that issue. And you said you were in the Klan."

"My momma and daddy raised me to believe that white people were up here"—he lifted his shaky arm as high as he could—"and n—s, though I do not use that term anymore, were down here." He got his quivering hand as close to the floor as he could.

"Well, what changed you then?"

"Miss Jessup did, that's what."

"How?"

"You know her, right?"

"Yes, I do. She's a remarkable woman."

"And remarkable women do remarkable things. Particularly when it comes to men." He gave Jack a penetrating stare. "You sure Miss Jessup didn't tell you nothin'?"

"Nothing other than what I already told you."

Ashby nodded, then set his drink down and wiped his mouth. "What the hell. I'm old and feel like shit, and how much time do I have left really?" He looked at Jack. "You ever wonder why my wife killed herself?"

"I guess so, yeah."

"She thought that way back when, me and Miss Jessup were, well, you know."

Jack narrowed his eyes. "I'm not sure I do know." He took a sip of his drink.

"She thought me and Miss Jessup were...gettin' it on, like the teenagers say."

Jack nearly spit out his scotch. "What!"

"Exactly, son. Exactly. Absurd, on its face."

"So why did she suspect?"

"Oh, little things she saw here and there, looks and words exchanged, which she transformed into paranoid fantasies of debauchery on my part."

"So it wasn't true then?"

Ashby looked at his scotch, as though he wanted another sip but wondered if he could manage the lift. "Well, I can't say I didn't *want* it to be true."

This statement knocked the wind out of Jack. "I don't understand."

"Alice was...difficult. Well, maybe *I* was difficult and Alice didn't know what the hell to do with me. Yeah, that's far more likely the case."

"And where does Miss Jessup come into all that?"

"She was here. Takin' care of the kiddies. Doing everythin', really, while Alice played the role of my society wife. A sometimes prosperous lawyer who was flush with cash till he wasn't. And for my part, I wanted a go at Miss Jessup because she was as different from Alice as could be. And back then, she was a mighty fine-lookin' woman."

Jack put his drink down. "I don't think I need to hear anymore."

"But she wouldn't have me," said Ashby, seemingly not hearing Jack's response. "Flat-out turned me down. Schooled me, really."

Jack's interest was piqued once more. "How do you mean?"

"She told me that I was married to a good woman and that was where my affections and loyalties should lie. She didn't use those words, you understand, those are mine, but that was the gist of it. She wasn't married then. Her husband had died young from somethin' or other. But she did say that the two races were not capable of bein' mixed. This was a long time ago, you understand. Before you were even born." He pointed a shaky finger at Jack. "That's right. Before she come here she worked for your folks takin' care 'a your sister. God damn the sons of bitches that killed poor, sweet Lucy. Then your daddy told me to hire her. We had all our kids by then, and sure needed the help, because Alice had her headaches and I don't think motherin' came natural to the woman."

"And Miss Jessup continued to work for you after...?"

"She needed the job and I was payin' her twice what she could make anywhere else. It was a decision she made for her family and I respected that. And I never did anythin' to her, never brought it up again. Like she told me to, I turned my affections to Alice and tried my best to make it work." Here Ashby stopped, grabbed the drink in both hands, and finished it. "And then the woman ups and kills herself in the garage in the goddamn Plymouth." He dropped the glass to the floor. "I just don't get it, do you?"

"No sir, I can't say that I do. But you can marry her now if you want to, and if she's agreeable."

Ashby glanced at him sharply. "What the hell you talkin' 'bout, boy?"

"You can marry Miss Jessup if you both want that. Law now says you can."

"I know what the law says, but why the hell would I do that?"

"Well, if you wanted to get it on with her, I thought you might love her. She comes here every day. If you got married she could live here while she's taking care of you. And it would save her a long trip both ways."

"Marry her and live here, with *me*? Are you out your mind, Jack Lee? Do you know what people would say?"

"You just told me you're old with not much time left. Why do you give a damn what people think?"

"I...I just do. And love her? Look, son. I said she was different.

Exotic, so to speak. This house here, do you know it stands on the exact spot where the plantation owner's home used to be?"

"No, I didn't know that."

"Bet he slept with his slave women."

"And I'm also sure those poor women had no choice in the matter."

Ashby settled back and assumed a pedantic tone. "It was sort of economics, you see. More babies, more slaves. Like printin' money or some such, because the law back then was if you're born into slavery, you're a slave for life."

"They were *people*, Mr. Ashby, not property."

"Well, technically, back then, they were both, son," Ashby said offhandedly.

His temper barely under control, Jack rose. "I have to be going now."

Ashby said in a distracted tone, "Thank God I still got Miss Jessup. Nobody else comes to visit me. Not even my own damn kids."

"Well, don't always think Miss Jessup will be here for you."

"What the hell do you mean?" Ashby said, looking startled.

"She might just get sick of being around you. Like everybody else."

Jack left Ashby and headed to his parents' house. He thought back to the time when he was a child and he'd overheard Mrs. Ashby and Miss Jessup arguing. It must have been about her suspicions regarding her husband and Miss Jessup.

Oil and water do not mix.

Inside the garage DuBose was working away at her desk. Jack pulled up a chair across from her.

She held up a copy of a national news magazine. On the cover were the Washingtons in their shackles, and next to them a photo of the very white and very elderly Randolphs.

"What does it say?" he asked.

"Not that it matters much after that cover photo. But nothing good about us or our clients. Howard Pickett and George Wallace are both quoted and they cherry-picked some of my statements to make it seem like I want to overthrow the government and put all white people in prison. Oh, and listen to this."

She opened the magazine and read off a page. "'The one constant source of legal integrity has been the thoroughly professional manner of Judge Josiah Ambrose, who has shown himself to be not only fair but compassionate. He has exhibited great tolerance and restraint in the face of some of Desiree DuBose's outlandish tactics in her bag of legal tricks. However, appropriate ethics authorities should show no such leeway to the woman, and relieve her of her ability to practice law for good. But certainly, if the Washingtons are convicted they will have no cause to claim any racial animus on the part of the esteemed judge.'"

"Well, that esteemed judge was in the KKK when he was a young man."

Eyes widening, DuBose put down the magazine. "How do you know that?"

"Ashby, the man I just met with, told me. He and Ambrose grew up together and joined the Klan after seeing *Birth of a Nation*."

DuBose looked reinvigorated. "A judge presiding over a racially charged case used to be a Klansman?"

"I imagine there were a lot of men back then who wore the white hoods."

"How many become judges?"

"Okay, I grant you that is troubling. But it was a long time ago."

"Doesn't matter. We can still use it."

"How?" asked Jack, looking confused.

"Not only is that a powerful foundation for a successful appeal, it's plausible grounds for me to go directly to federal court under the Civil Rights Act. Not to mention every TV network and newspaper in the country will want to run with the story. I can see the headline now: 'Handpicked Judge for a Murder Trial Involving Blacks Was a Klansman.' Then we use that fact, once it's confirmed, to demand a mistrial, a new judge, *and* a jury of the Washingtons' peers."

"But they'll just get another racist judge who wasn't in the Klan and you're never going to get a jury of their peers, at least not in Virginia."

DuBose did not seem to be listening. "Do you think Donny can confirm Ambrose was in the Klan? I can start writing the press release."

"I think Donny can do anything, but I'm not sure that's the path we should take."

She looked at him blankly. "Why not?"

"Desiree, I actually feel good about our case. I think we can win it on the merits."

"And if we lose? They go to the electric chair." She sat back and scowled at him. "You know, you keep berating me for thinking too big-picture, but here I am trying to win *this* case, and you're still complaining. What is it you want from me?"

"Can I ask you a question?"

"What?" she said icily.

"Did you become a lawyer to defend people's rights, or to pen press releases and talk into microphones?"

"I do whatever I have to do to get the job done. I've told you this many times before—yes, I focus on individual cases, but I have to always remember it's bigger than that. I wish I didn't have to be concerned with all of that, but I don't have that luxury!"

"I'm sure your mother meant well when she told you to make the world equal and just for Black folks, but no one person can be the savior of an entire race."

She shook her head. "You will never understand me or what I'm trying to do."

"Well, let me tell you what I *do* understand."

She looked at him crossly. "What?"

"That you're one hell of a trial lawyer, Desiree DuBose. So why don't we focus on *that*?"

They stared at each other.

"Okay, Jack, we'll play it your way. For now."

CHAPTER 79

ALL RISE," BEGAN THE BAILIFF as he called the court into session on Monday morning.

Ambrose appeared behind the bench and looked over at DuBose and Jack. "Call your next witness."

Surprisingly, Battle got to his feet. "Your Honor, if I may interrupt. The commonwealth has just come into possession of a new piece of evidence, and a new, vital witness to be heard. We therefore request a special motion to have the evidence introduced and the witness testify before the defense recommences its case."

DuBose rose. "Objection. The prosecution already rested."

"It is *vital* to the commonwealth's case," insisted Battle. "And in the interests of justice, it must be heard and seen by the jury."

"Motion granted," said Ambrose. He eyed the jury. "Our job is to find the truth and nothing can get in the way of that." He smiled benignly as he glanced at the row of reporters writing this down.

DuBose looked at him and concluded the man must have read the magazine article about his being an esteemed and fair-minded judge.

Battle nodded at his associate, who opened a case that was on the floor and pulled out what appeared to be a long-bladed knife wrapped in plastic.

"Wait, are you saying that's the murder weapon?" exclaimed DuBose.

"Yes," conceded Battle.

DuBose said, "Your Honor, this is truly outrageous."

"Let's just keep the drama to a minimum and hear what the man has to say," admonished Ambrose. "Go on ahead, Mr. Battle."

"I recall Herman Till to the stand," said Battle.

Till took his seat, and Battle approached with the knife still sheathed in plastic.

"Can you identify this, sir?"

"Yes, over the weekend it was provided to me by the Sheriff's Department and I examined it."

"And where was it found?"

"I was told in a rotted stump on the defendants' property."

DuBose leapt to her feet once more. "Objection! This witness does not have firsthand, direct knowledge of any of this. He was *given* it? He was *told* it was found on the defendants' property? I fail to see even one evidentiary *fact* in there."

"Your Honor," said Battle, "while perhaps a little out of the ordinary, Mr. Till is the commonwealth's medical examiner. He has testified that in his official capacity, he was given this potential piece of evidence—which was found pursuant to a lawfully issued search warrant—to examine and to maintain the chain of evidentiary custody. I can have the deputy who actually found it testify to that, but in the interests of time, I took a bit of a shortcut. But if the defense insists?"

"We do," said DuBose immediately.

"Overruled," said Ambrose. "We are not going to waste time over that. The word of the attorney general suffices for this court."

DuBose, however, was clearly not ready to concede. "Motion to strike the admission of this item into evidence."

Battle barked, "On what grounds?"

DuBose said, "The failure to identify the person named in the affidavit from which the search warrant was issued. That person would need to have personal observations of the area purportedly covered by the search warrant, as well as any information from any sources believed to be reliable. None of that has been provided. Without that, neither the defense nor the jury can reasonably evaluate the veracity of this *supposed* evidence."

Battle said, "Your Honor, the search warrant was validly issued by a magistrate of this court on a showing of probable cause. And a search warrant can be issued for the fruits of the crime and the tools, of which this knife is undoubtedly one. And, furthermore, *Hester v. U.S.* holds that open fields or woods do not even require a search warrant, while *McClannan v. Chaplain* states that any place remote from the defendant's dwelling and not in his presence also does not require a search warrant."

DuBose countered, "That is *not* the issue. Mr. Battle *got* a search warrant, so *Hester* and *McClannan* are irrelevant to this discussion. Thus, the defense should have the ability to cross-examine the person who told the police of the object and its location. Your Honor, they are holding this out to be the alleged murder weapon and that it was found on the defendants' property. Thus, it constitutes evidence so critical to our clients' ability to receive a fair trial that it must be held up to the strongest possible scrutiny. Otherwise, any fairness to our clients is irreversibly destroyed. It would be like having an eyewitness to a crime on the stand and not allowing defense counsel to cross-examine that person."

Battle snapped, "Counsel is attempting to impugn the integrity of the evidence."

DuBose retorted in a deeply strident voice, "I'm trying to *evaluate* the *integrity* of this *purported* evidence, but the prosecution doesn't seem interested in allowing us to do that. So, is it admissible on its face, or do we get an opportunity to question the person who told the police where the object was located, so we can determine if that person is reliable and has no conflict that might taint his or her motive in leading the police to the proffered evidence? I can't think of a better example of a defendant's rights under the Sixth Amendment to confront one's accusers than that! And my clients deserve *nothing* less. No one, regardless of who they are or what color their skin is, deserves less in any court of law in this whole damn country!"

Battle apparently had nothing left in his legal repertoire to respond to DuBose's pinpoint barrage. He just stared pleadingly up at the judge.

Ambrose seemed totally unsure of what to do. He looked around the room and Jack followed his gaze until it came to rest on…Howard Pickett. The coal millionaire didn't say anything, didn't move a muscle. He just stared right back at the judge.

Jack turned to see the reporters writing down every word DuBose had uttered.

A thoroughly out-of-his-depth Ambrose rubbed his mouth and said, in a halting voice, "I'm…I'm going to…deny your motion, Miss DuBose, and allow Mr. Till to testify without putting on the stand the person named in the affidavit."

DuBose stared at him and he looked back at her for a moment that seemed to stretch to eternity, before Ambrose flinched and dropped his gaze.

She said, "I renew my objection and I will take it up posthaste with the Virginia Supreme Court, and we will get this piece of *alleged* evidence thrown into the garbage, where it belongs."

Ambrose cast her a nasty look and snarled, "I'm sure you'll try!"

A seething DuBose sat back down to find Jack beaming at her. "What?" she snapped in a sharp tone, scowling at him.

"Now *that* was Desiree DuBose, the legendary trial lawyer fighting for her clients to the fullest. And I have to tell you, it was pretty damn awesome to behold."

DuBose's cheeks flushed and she smiled self-consciously at his praise.

A clearly rattled Battle turned back to the witness. "All right, Mr. Till. Did you examine this object?"

"I did."

"And your findings?"

"I'm no expert, but it looks to be a pretty old Army-issued

bayonet or weapon of some kind. It has blood on it. The blood matched both the Randolphs' types, though I can't tell for certain that it is *their* blood, since there is no medical test to determine that. However, the blade does correspond with the wounds I found on the couple."

"And it's a matter of public record that Jerome Washington served in the Army," Battle said to the jury.

DuBose got to her feet. "Mr. Till said it was pretty old, but the record also shows that Mr. Washington just got out of the Army a little over a year ago. So how old is old?"

Battle turned to her. "I'm not necessarily saying this thing was issued to him while he served, but since he was in the military he probably would have access to God knows how many weapons and such, including ones like this."

"You have no proof it *was* issued to him," retorted DuBose. "Or that he had access to weapons like this one. And I thought trials were all about *proof.*"

Ambrose smacked his gavel. "Your position is duly noted, Miss DuBose. But I'm going to let Mr. Battle continue with his examination of this witness."

Battle said, "Thank you, Your Honor." He turned back to Till. "Any fingerprints on it?"

"No, sir, it was wiped clean."

"Deliberately?"

"Objection, speculation," instantly barked DuBose.

"Sustained." Ambrose eyed her severely. "I'll give you that one."

"I have no further questions," said Battle.

"Defense?" said Ambrose.

Jack and DuBose held a hurried conference. "May we see the weapon first? Or is that asking too much?" DuBose said coldly.

Battle handed it over.

"Defense requests a two-day recess," said DuBose.

"What for?" asked Ambrose, appearing shocked by this.

She said slowly and carefully, trying to keep her temper in check,

"We have just been handed what the commonwealth is alleging is the *murder weapon*, Judge, and that they also allege was found on the defendants' property. We'd like some time to investigate this further *outside* of court so that we can prepare for our next steps *in* court."

Ambrose seemed to have lost patience with appearing fair-minded. "I'll give you ten minutes. Make good use of it." He rose from the bench and disappeared into his chambers.

DuBose scowled at Battle. "I didn't expect this kind of dirty-handed trick from you, Edmund."

He looked uncomfortable. "It really just came to our attention, Desiree."

"The hell it did!" She looked away in disgust.

Jack was checking out the weapon, turning it over and over. He asked Jerome if he'd ever seen it before.

Jerome shook his head. "No sir, never."

Jack felt someone tap him on the shoulder. It was his brother, leaning over the railing separating the gallery from the front of the courtroom.

"Let me see that thing," said Jeff.

Jack handed it over and Jeff examined it thoroughly. Then he smiled, pointed to a barely visible marking on the blade, and whispered to Jack, who stiffened when he saw what his brother was indicating. The two brothers conversed in low voices for a couple of minutes. Then Jack took the weapon and spoke, at length, into DuBose's ear. She nodded in agreement.

When Ambrose returned, DuBose rose. "Your Honor, in light of the seriousness of this piece of 'evidence,' the defense would like to call an expert witness to validate it."

"Mr. Till?" said Ambrose.

"No. Mr. Till has already acknowledged that he is no expert on this subject. I call Mr. Jefferson Lee."

"Who?" barked Battle.

"Mr. Jefferson Lee, a decorated war veteran with the United States Army."

"I don't see how that makes him an expert on knives," protested Battle.

"Let me put him on the stand and show you then. You always have the right to cross-examine him, Mr. Battle. And you dumped this on us, and the judge will not grant a recess, so we have no time to find another expert. Thus, I don't see how you have any grounds to object."

Battle exclaimed, "Wait a minute. Lee?" He looked at Jack. "Are you related?"

"He's my younger brother."

"Your Honor," exclaimed Battle. "We can't allow defense counsel's *brother* to testify. That is outrageous."

DuBose pounced. "What *is* outrageous, Mr. Battle, is your ambushing us with this purported murder weapon without even allowing us to question the person who led you to it. And if the judge isn't convinced he's an expert, he won't be able to testify."

"And if he is no expert, I'm putting a stop to this real quick," said Ambrose.

"Defense calls Jefferson Lee to the stand," said DuBose immediately.

Jeff Lee rose, walked ramrod straight to the witness stand, and was sworn in. DuBose approached with the weapon in her hands.

"Mr. Lee, did you serve in the United States Army?"

"I did."

"For how long?"

"Nearly fourteen years."

Battle flinched and looked over at Jack.

"What rank did you achieve?" DuBose asked Jeff.

"I was an enlisted man. I came out as a sergeant major."

"Did you serve in Vietnam?" asked DuBose.

"Yes, ma'am, two years total in-country."

"Were you a Green Beret?"

"Yes. Still consider myself one."

Even Ambrose looked impressed by this.

"Were you wounded?"

"Twice. Knife to the leg. Bullet to the arm."

"So two Purple Hearts?" said DuBose.

"Yes."

"Any other medals?"

"Silver Star, two Bronze Stars, among others."

"So you were quite brave?"

"I did my job."

"You're a hero," noted DuBose.

"No ma'am," Jeff said firmly. "The heroes are the men who didn't make it back home. I was just one lucky SOB."

DuBose glanced at the jury. The men were all nodding in agreement. "Were you issued weapons like this one in the Army?" she asked Jeff.

"I was."

"For what purpose?"

"Well, for example, Vietnam's a jungle, ma'am. And you have to cut your way through it with a machete. I've also used bayonets and combat knives. And in hand-to-hand fighting I killed many of the enemy with them. Before they could kill me," he added.

The jurors were all staring and listening, captivated.

DuBose looked at Ambrose expectantly. "Will you accept this witness as an expert on equipment with which he is intimately familiar? A wounded Green Beret with Silver and Bronze Stars who served his country bravely for nearly fourteen years, and defended it with his own blood?"

Ambrose looked at Battle, who glanced nervously away. Then he stared at the jury who, to a man, were gazing in awe at Jeff Lee. "Mr. Lee is accepted as an expert witness for purposes of the examination of the evidence in question," he said. "And thank you for your service, young man."

DuBose handed Jeff Lee the weapon, and when their gazes met, they exchanged a brief smile. "Is this knife the same type that was issued to you while you were in Vietnam?"

"No ma'am, it's not. Looks nothing like the bayonets we use today, or even the ones used in World War II."

Battle rose. "I would like the record to reflect that I already pointed out this weapon is old but that the defendant may have had access to it while serving in the Army. Maybe he stole it from an armory or a museum or some such."

"Duly noted," said Ambrose.

DuBose looked at Jeff Lee. "What do you say to that, Mr. Lee?"

"That Mr. Washington would never have been able to obtain this weapon while serving in the United States Army."

"Why not?"

"Because this is not a U.S. Army weapon at all." He pointed to the letter etched on the blade. "Look right there."

"*C*?" read off DuBose.

"The letters *S* and *A* have worn off. *CSA*. Stands for 'Confederate States of America.' This is a socket bayonet used during the Civil War by Johnny Reb."

All around the courtroom people started talking in hushed voices.

DuBose glanced first at Ambrose and then at Battle. "And have you ever seen this particular item before, Mr. Lee?"

Battle and Ambrose exchanged startled looks.

"Yes I have."

"Where?"

"It belonged to Leslie Randolph. I used to date his daughter and visited their home many times. He showed it to me and told me his ancestor fought with it when he served with General James Longstreet in the Civil War. It was handed down in the family."

This revelation threw the courtroom into a complete uproar, and Ambrose had to slam his gavel down several times before order was restored.

Ambrose barked, "Lawyers, my chambers! Now!"

CHAPTER 80

AMBROSE STRIPPED OFF HIS ROBE once he was in his office. Underneath he wore a white dress shirt, no tie, and dark slacks. Jack noted the sandals on the man's bare feet.

The agitated judge paced up and down behind his desk for a few moments before whirling around on the trio of lawyers.

"What in the goddamn hell is going on here?" snapped Ambrose.

"I'd like to know that as well," said DuBose. She turned to Battle. "What were the events that led to this Confederate bayonet being found?"

Battle said, "The police received an anonymous tip that the murder weapon was hidden in a tree stump on the defendants' property. They went there and found it."

"An anonymous tip," said Jack incredulously. "Convenient. How did you get a search warrant issued on the basis of *that*?"

Battle had no response.

"It obviously doesn't belong to our client," said DuBose.

"Doesn't mean he didn't use it. It has blood on it," said Battle. "He could have seen it at the Randolphs' home. And it was found on his property."

DuBose said, "And what are the odds the anonymous caller *placed* it there? Just like an anonymous caller knew about the murders and called the police in time to seemingly catch Jerome

Washington red-handed. And then we still don't know who paid off Tyler Dobbs to lie on the stand."

"You have no proof of an anonymous caller phoning the police about the murders, not a scintilla," snapped Battle.

"And you have no proof it *didn't* happen that way," retorted DuBose. "Which, *prima facie*, absolutely leads to reasonable doubt because the burden of proof is on *you*, not us, as you damn well know!"

Someone knocked on the door.

"Come," shouted Ambrose.

It was the bailiff with a note. He handed it to the judge.

"This is extraordinary," said Ambrose after he'd read it.

"What is it, Judge?" asked Battle anxiously.

He looked up. "The maid, the little Negro gal who testified earlier? While you all were looking at that bayonet with Mr. Lee's brother she got a gander at it, too. Said she's seen it many times sitting in the umbrella stand by the front door of the Randolphs'."

"She'll need to testify to that," said Battle quickly. "And that shows that the defendant had access to it and could have used the weapon to kill the Randolphs. He'd been in the house before, had probably seen it then, like I just suggested, and it was right there when he came through the door on the day of the murders."

"And it also could have been planted in the stump by the real killer," said Jack.

Ambrose donned his robe and said emphatically, "And that's a fact for the jury to consider. Okay, let's head back in."

"Good," said Battle. "Because I have another witness to call."

"Who?" demanded DuBose. "And what will this witness say?"

"You'll find out in a few minutes."

CHAPTER 81

BATTLE RECALLED CORA ROBINSON TO the stand. She recounted seeing the bayonet in the umbrella stand by the front door in the house on the day of the murders. She also confirmed that was where Leslie Randolph kept it.

"So anyone going into the house would be able to see it?" asked Battle.

"Oh, yes sir," she said brightly.

"Including the defendant when he went into the house that time?"

Her features crumpled. "Um...I don't know 'bout that."

Battle said in a scolding tone, "Mrs. Robinson, could the defendant have seen the bayonet if he came into the house? Yes or no?"

"Yes," she said, thoroughly frightened now.

"So he could have used it to kill the Randolphs, could he not?"

DuBose said, "Objection. Speculation."

"No, I'm going to allow that," said Ambrose, glancing at the row of journalists.

"Mrs. Robinson?" prompted Battle. "Answer the question."

"Yes, I guess he could."

"Thank you. Nothing further."

"Defense?" said the judge.

Jack walked up to Robinson. "Did the defendant ever indicate to you that he had seen the bayonet?"

"No sir," she said.

"Never touched it that you know of? Never asked questions about it?"

"No sir, never."

"You said it was in the umbrella stand by the *front* door?"

"Yes."

"When he came in the house by himself that time, did Jerome use the front door?"

"Oh, no, sir. He ain't never come in the front door. He always come in the back."

"Nothing further."

Battle stood. "Redirect, Your Honor. Now, Mrs. Robinson, were you with him every second while he was in the house?"

"No."

"So he could have been in the front foyer and seen the bayonet then, correct?"

"I guess so," replied Robinson.

"Nothing further."

"Witness is excused," said Ambrose.

"The commonwealth now calls Linda Drucker," said Battle.

The doors opened and a petite, mousy woman appeared in the courtroom. She was dressed in an ankle-length skirt and flat shoes. Spectacles perched on her nose. Her hair was dark and short with irregularly clipped bangs.

She walked nervously up to the witness stand and was duly sworn in.

Battle approached and said, "Miss Drucker, where are you currently employed?"

"I'm a bookkeeper, but I'm between jobs right now."

"On June fourteenth of this year did you have occasion to ride a bus?"

"I did."

"Which bus?"

"The bus that picks up on Tyler Street."

"And why were you on the bus that day?"

"I had done some shopping in the west end and I took the bus to meet a friend of mine at her house."

"About what time were you on the bus?"

"I got on at around five thirty."

"Did you have occasion to see someone get on the bus that day?"

"Yes," replied Drucker.

"Is that person in the courtroom?"

"Yes."

"Could you point the person out?" asked Battle.

"That's her," said Drucker, indicating Pearl.

Pearl shook her head violently. "No, no, no," she said to herself. "That ain't true."

Battle said, "Let the record reflect that the witness identified Pearl Washington."

"You are lyin'. My granddaughter ain't never been on that bus."

Everyone turned to see Miss Jessup standing and pointing at Drucker.

"Sit down, woman!" barked Ambrose. "And keep quiet."

Pearl looked at her grandmother standing there like a wall of granite.

"She ain't never seen my Pearl on that bus," declared Miss Jessup.

"How dare you call me a liar!" called out Drucker.

"'Cause you sure are one," said Miss Jessup calmly.

Ambrose roared, "Sit down, woman. I will not tell you again."

Miss Jessup did not sit down. "You can't let people come in here and lie. You a judge, act like it. Tell her to stop lyin'."

Ambrose snapped, "You will not speak to me that way you... fat..." He looked at the bailiff. "Remove her. Now! Drag her out if you have to. But remove her from *my* courtroom."

The bailiff looked at the elderly Miss Jessup standing there defiantly, and then he saw Daniel and three other Black men sitting directly behind her. They were staring right at him, and their intent was clear. The bailiff glanced nervously at Ambrose.

"Uh, Judge...?"

"Get that *person* out of here!" barked Ambrose.

Now Hilly rose to her feet. "You throw her out, you throw me out, too." She locked arms with Miss Jessup. "Both or none," added Hilly, staring down Ambrose.

The judge looked flummoxed facing a white woman in solidarity with a Black.

Pearl then got to her feet and pointed at Drucker. "My granny is tellin' the truth. You are lyin', lyin', lyin'. You ain't got no right to do that. Shame on you."

Drucker screamed, "*You're* a filthy liar who doesn't know her place."

Ambrose's face flushed crimson as he stood behind the bench and shouted at Pearl, "Sit down or you will be removed. Bailiff, I told you to remove that old fool of a woman—"

Pearl glared at Ambrose. "My granny ain't no old fool." She looked at the bailiff. "And don't you dare touch her! She got every right to be here, same as you." She pointed at the judge. "And you, too!"

Hilly barked, "You go through me to get to her! That's *our* right."

Ambrose was seething with indignation now. "I am the *judge*! *I* tell *you* what rights you have and don't have. Bailiff, do your duty and remove *all three* of them! Call in armed deputies. But do it now!"

Pearl screwed up her courage and said, "You ain't nothin' but an old white man who thinks he knows everythin'. But you don't know nothin' 'bout me or my granny. So *you* just sit down and *you* shut up."

Eyes near to popping from their sockets, an apoplectic Ambrose screamed, "Why you filthy little n——!"

The courtroom instantly became still and silent. Ambrose stood there frozen for a moment before looking around in a daze, as though he only now realized he was in front of people other than Pearl.

The reporters were scribbling furiously.

Hilly and Miss Jessup shared a satisfied look before retaking their seats.

Pearl fell back in her chair, looking astonished. Under her breath she said, "I can't believe I just done that."

In the absolute silence of the courtroom, Ambrose plopped down in his chair and fiddled with his gavel, looking disoriented. He glanced up and saw all the reporters writing away. He finally said, in a desultory voice, "I, uh, I apologize for that little outburst. Don't know what came over me. Now you go on ahead, Mr. Battle."

A shaken Battle cleared his throat and asked the witness gingerly, "Now, do you recall about what time that was, Miss Drucker?"

Drucker, also obviously upset by all that had just transpired, said, "Um, I do. We were, um, yes, we stopped at the First Virginia Bank building on Strawberry Street around that time and the clock on the bank said six fifteen. She got on at that stop. Right in front of the bank."

"Let the record show that that First Virginia Bank branch is only one-quarter mile from the Randolphs' home," said Battle. "And the pay phone used to call the police was nearby. Anybody else get on other than her?"

"No, just her."

"And did you notice anything unusual about her?"

"Well, she looked nervous. And she was carrying a large duffel bag. When she sat down she was almost right across from me."

"Did you see anything else?"

"She opened the duffel and I saw a big old shoe in it. Looked like a man's shoe. You know, a workingman, not a businessman."

"Did you notice anything on the shoe?"

"Yes, it had what looked to be blood on it."

The folks in the courtroom started murmuring.

"And did she get off the bus before you?" asked Battle.

"Oh no. My stop was Cavalier Street, just two stops after she got on."

Battle said, "Let the record reflect that the defendant would need to get on two more buses to go to her home in the far east end." He turned to Drucker. "Thank you for your testimony. Nothing further, Judge."

"Defense?" said Ambrose in a hushed tone.

Jack rose and walked over to Drucker. "How did you come to be here today?"

"I don't understand."

"Did someone tell you to come or did you call somebody or what?"

She pushed her glasses up the bridge of her nose. "Oh, I see. I was following the trial in the papers and on the TV. And when I saw a picture of that gal over there"—she paused and gave Pearl a withering look—"I knew I recognized her. So I called up the police and told them what I had seen. They asked me to come in and give a statement and then I met Mr. Battle over there and told him."

"I see. What stores did you shop in?"

"Excuse me?"

"You said you shopped that day in the west end. What stores?"

"I went into the Belk department store to look for a dress." She tucked her hair behind her ear and looked down at her drab clothes. "I wanted to get something...a little more fun."

"Anyone see you, talk to you? Did you try on any dresses?"

"Your Honor," complained Battle. "Where is this going?"

"I have every right to probe this witness's recollection and the truthfulness of her testimony," pointed out Jack. "She remembers times and faces and duffel bags and bloody shoes and bus stops real well. You'd think she'd remember where she shopped that day. Otherwise, it seems fishy."

Drucker said stiffly, "I went to Belk. I didn't find anything I liked. I got on the bus and saw her."

"You remember the bus driver?"

"I do actually. He was a white man in his fifties. I think his name was Barry, but I can't be sure. I glanced at his name tag when I got on."

"This friend you were meeting? What's her name?"

"Bella Andrews. You can talk to her. She'll verify it."

"So, you're saying a woman resembling the defendant—"

Drucker interrupted, eyeing Pearl. "No, not resembling. It *was* her. I'm sure."

"Okay, she was carrying things from a murder scene and she opened it up on a bus for all to see, including bloody shoe?"

"No, there weren't many people on the bus. I was the only one close to her and who could see anything. And I already said she was nervous. I'd have been nervous, too, if I'd just helped kill some people."

"Motion to strike that last part, Judge. Argumentative and non-responsive," said Jack automatically.

A still-distracted Ambrose murmured, "Disregard the witness's last statement."

"And with one glance you can say it was a man's large work shoe?" said Jack.

"My father was a bricklayer. He had shoes like that. Big ones."

"And you said it appeared to be blood, so you're not sure?"

"I'm pretty sure it was blood."

"Did you speak to the defendant?"

"No. I didn't know her."

"Did she see you?" asked Jack.

"I don't think so. She was keeping her eyes down."

"But you somehow got a good look at her? Enough to positively identify her?"

"I got a good look at her while she was walking down the aisle to her seat. Look, I didn't have to come down here and testify. I'm just trying to be a good citizen."

"And the court appreciates that," said Ambrose, pepping up. "Anything else?"

Jack said, "Not at the moment, but I reserve the right to recall this witness due to the way in which she was dropped in our laps at the last minute."

DuBose rose. "Considering the recent developments of today, defense requests that court be adjourned until tomorrow morning."

Battle looked at her and said, "No objection."

"Court is adjourned until ten tomorrow," said a relieved-looking Ambrose.

CHAPTER 82

BACK AT THEIR GARAGE OFFICE, Jack said, "Well, thanks to Miss Jessup, my mother, and Pearl, at least Ambrose has been revealed as the racist he clearly is."

"Yes, he has," agreed DuBose, who did not look cheered up by this small victory at all.

"I don't think we have any option now but to put Pearl on the stand to refute Drucker's testimony."

"That is really risky," cautioned DuBose. "We will need to instruct Pearl to plead the Fifth Amendment in response to some of Battle's questions. And *this* jury will interpret that as proof positive of her guilt if they're not already there."

"But if we leave Drucker's testimony out there unchallenged, we are as good as dead. And now that Ambrose let the bayonet in and Battle got Cora Robinson to testify that Jerome could have seen and used it?"

"And you think that jury will believe a Black woman over a white one?"

Jack shot her a glance. "They might."

"Are you willing to risk our clients' lives on 'they might'?"

A dejected Jack stared down at the grimy concrete floor. "I guess not."

"But you are right in your analysis—it really is over unless we can counter that testimony. And Drucker looks respectable and her story is plausible enough for the jury to believe her. But we know she's lying because we know Pearl was not on that bus."

Jack jerked up. "Donny found out why Tyler Dobbs was lying."

DuBose shot him a hopeful glance. "So maybe he can find the same about Drucker?"

Jack called Peppers and explained the situation. "As soon as you can, Donny."

He put the receiver down. "He's on it. But if he can't find anything, what then?"

DuBose abruptly stood, looking excited. "Can I borrow your car?"

"Sure, but where are you going?"

"To run down a hunch."

"You want company?"

"You better stay here in case Donny calls back."

"Okay." He tossed her the keys and DuBose rushed out.

* * *

Two hours later, a car pulled up in the Lees' driveway. Jack thought it was DuBose but it turned out to be Donny Peppers in the Corvette.

"You are in luck, Jack," said Peppers as he got out of the vehicle.

"I could use some luck right now."

He handed Jack a sheaf of papers. "Linda Drucker. That will make interesting reading."

"Thanks."

"Wait, there's still more."

"Okay," said Jack expectantly. "You have been a busy man."

"I finally found the blue convertible. It's the only one actually registered in Freeman." Peppers pulled out a copy of the registration and a photo of the car. "You can show it to Jerome, see if he can ID it."

"Thanks," said Jack, his enthusiasm dimming.

"What?" said Peppers.

"To get it into evidence, I have to put him on the stand. And if I do that, Battle will rip him apart."

"I see your dilemma, but it might be worth it."

Jack looked at the car registration. "Walter Gates? Curtis Gates's son?"

"Yep."

"We met him at the reading of the will. What the hell was he doing at the Randolphs' house that day?"

*　*　*

When DuBose returned she was looking immensely pleased. She told Jack where she had gone, whom she had met with, and what she had found out.

"Damn, Desiree, how did you think of that angle?"

"Desperation, it's a great motivator."

He then informed her about what Donny Peppers had unearthed.

"So Curtis Gates's son was over at the Randolphs' that day?" she said.

"And we need to find out why. Give me the car keys."

She handed them to him. "Where are you going?"

"*We're* going to Curtis Gates's house."

As they were heading to the Fiat, they saw Jeff climbing out of a Jaguar. Driving it was Christine Hanover. After she pulled away Jack walked up to his brother.

"Jeff, come on, what are you doing out with Christine?"

"We just went for coffee. To catch up. And she wanted to talk."

"Well, I hope that's all."

"What's that supposed to mean?" retorted Jeff.

"I just don't want you to get hurt."

"By havin' a cup of coffee with an old friend?"

"You know exactly what I'm talking about," said Jack, growing angry.

"I'm a big boy, Jack. I can live my own life."

"Do I have to kick your ass to make you see straight like when we were kids?"

Jeff looked him over. "No disrespect, big brother, but you couldn't kick my ass now with two other guys helpin' you."

"Is that right?" barked Jack, his fists balled.

"Yeah, that's for damn sure right," his brother barked right back.

DuBose got in between them and said, "Act your age, and park your male egos. Nobody is kicking anybody's ass unless it's me knocking you two idiots on yours."

Jack unclenched his hands and stepped back. "Like you said, it's your life, Jeff. I guess you can go ahead and screw it up if you want." He stalked off to the Fiat.

Jeff glared at DuBose. "What the hell is his problem?"

"He just got you back and he's terrified he'll lose you again."

Jeff walked into the house and slammed the door.

DuBose took a deep breath.

Boys.

CHAPTER 83

THE DRIVE TO CURTIS GATES'S home took about twenty-five minutes. He lived in an area that was upscale, but not in the price range of the Hanovers'.

"How'd you know where his house was?" asked DuBose as they drew to a stop several homes down from the substantial two-story painted-white brick house. Parked in the front circular drive was a blue convertible.

"The son lives with his father; the address was on the copy of the car registration Donny gave me."

"He lives with his father? I thought he was a successful real estate developer."

"And that's him," said Jack, as Walter Gates came out of the front door of the house, got into the convertible, and drove off.

They followed.

"Where do you think he's going?" asked DuBose.

"Maybe to have a clandestine meeting with Pickett and Ambrose."

"That's not funny, Jack," she said sternly.

"Hell, Desiree, after today, I'm thinking anything is possible."

They drove for another twenty minutes before the convertible slowed.

"Faulkner's Woods," noted Jack.

As Walter Gates approached the gate, the guard there waved to him and opened the portal without checking to see if the man was on a list, as had been the case with DuBose and Jack when they had come for the will reading.

DuBose commented, "Looks like they know him here, which is interesting."

"Wait here," said Jack after he'd parked on a side street. He opened the car door.

"I'll come with you."

"No, you won't."

"Why not?" she demanded.

"Can you scale a six-foot-high fence in heels and a dress?"

"Well, don't let anyone see you. Your being arrested for trespass will not help our case."

Jack hurried to his left and slipped between two trees that stood next to the fence and well out of sight of the guard. He grabbed the top rail, pulled himself up, and nimbly dropped to the other side onto a soft bed of pine needles.

He quickly walked to the main street, hung a left, and soon found himself on Compson Lane, where the Hanovers lived. He got to their house just about the time the same maid he'd seen on the earlier visit was opening the door for Walter Gates.

Jack didn't see any sign of Christine, or the Jaguar, but it might be in the garage. He looked around carefully, and then inched up to the garage, the doors of which had windows set at eye level. He saw the Rolls in one bay and the Triumph he had seen earlier in another, but he saw no sign of the Jaguar. So what were Gordon Hanover and Walter Gates meeting about while Christine was absent? There was nothing more he could do without giving himself away, so he left, clambered back over the wall, and returned to DuBose.

"Well?" she asked as he opened the car door.

He told her where Gates had ended up.

"What do we do with this information?" she said. "Call Walter

Gates to the stand and ask him what he was doing at the Randolphs' the day of the murders?"

Jack shook his head. "All we have is Donny's report that it's the only blue convertible registered in Freeman County. But Jerome didn't get the license plate. So we don't even know if it's the right car. And maybe someone drove a blue convertible in from *outside* the county. So Gates says it isn't his car and we have nothing to hit him back with, unless we put Jerome on the stand, and even that won't be conclusive. And then Battle gets to tear Jerome apart on cross. It could blow up in our faces."

"I guess you're right," said DuBose. Next, she smiled.

"What?" he said, noting this.

"You're thinking a lot more strategically now than you were a couple weeks ago."

"Well, look at my teacher."

CHAPTER 84

THE FOLLOWING DAY JACK RECALLED Linda Drucker to the stand.

"Nice to see you again, Mr. Lee," she said with a warm smile.

"I doubt that will last," he replied.

Her smile vanished as Jack held up a piece of paper. "This is a public notice from the county water department. On June fourteenth, the only Belk department store in Freeman County was closed. Water main break." He handed the paper to Battle before turning back to Drucker. "So how did you go into a store that was closed?"

"I...I must have misremembered. It must have been another store. Yes, that's right."

"And you seemed so sure yesterday." He pointed to a woman in the second row. "You see your friend Bella Andrews right there? You suggested we reach out to her? Well, my investigator took her statement, after he showed her the water department notice and told her about your previous testimony. She is now prepared to swear that you told her to lie for you if we contacted her, and that she hasn't seen you in person for over a month."

"Oh, for God's sake," bellowed an infuriated Ambrose. "Is that true, woman?"

Drucker started to sob. "Please, I didn't want to do it, but they made me."

"Who made you?" demanded Jack.

"I don't know."

"Just like Tyler Dobbs?" said Jack, wheeling around and pointing at Battle. He turned back to her. "*How* did they make you? The
truth now!"

Drucker sobbed, "I...I embezzled some money from the place
where I used to work. These people found out and said if I didn't
testify, they'd have me arrested."

"You never saw Pearl Washington that day, did you?"

"No. I...I was on a bus, but...she wasn't."

"So who told you about the details? The bag, the work shoes?"

"It was in a note I got."

"And you have no name to give us? It just appeared out of
nowhere?"

"Yes, that's right."

Jack stared at her in disgust and then said, "Motion to strike
every bit of this witness's earlier testimony from the record."

"Motion granted," spat Ambrose. He turned to the jury. "There
is now no evidence presented by the commonwealth that Pearl Washington was ever on that bus carrying the things this *witness* said she
was carrying. You are not to consider her testimony from yesterday
in any of your deliberations. It is as though it never happened." He
pointed his gavel at Battle. "I will expect her to be charged with perjury and obstruction of justice. You think you can do that without
screwing it up, Mr. Battle?"

The bailiff swept forward and led away a distraught Drucker.

DuBose glanced around in time to see Howard Pickett get up
and hurry out.

Ambrose continued to stare at Battle. "If this keeps up, sir, I'll
hold you in contempt and *you'll* spend some time behind bars, too."

Edmund Battle looked like he wanted to vanish into the floor of
the courtroom.

DuBose rose and said, "Defense calls Peter Clancy."

"Who?" said a clearly overwhelmed Battle. "He's not on the list."

"Well, as you so cavalierly told us once, we just became aware of him," shot back DuBose.

Clancy, the elderly man DuBose and Jack had met while looking at the rowhouse where Pearl had had her abortion performed, rose and walked slowly to the witness stand.

That was where DuBose had gone off in Jack's car. It had occurred to her that Clancy might have seen Pearl go into the row-house, since it appeared that with his TV and water pitcher out on the porch with him, Clancy might spend a great deal of time out there. And she had turned out to be right.

After he was sworn in, Clancy took his seat in the witness box and adjusted the glasses he wore. DuBose approached him.

"You are Peter Clancy?"

"I am."

"And your address?"

"One fifteen Fauntleroy Avenue. Over behind the county hospital. It's a lovely neighborhood."

"Were you there on June fourteenth of this year?"

"Oh yes."

"Are you sure?'

"I'm always there. I never leave my street, you see, at least for the last ten years or so, except on the Sabbath. And today, of course."

She glanced at the jurors, who were listening attentively to the man. "What was your profession?"

"I was a traveling salesman. That's why I don't go anywhere any-more. For decades all I did was go from city to city. Sounds glamor-ous, but it gets old fast."

"Does your home have a front porch?"

"Oh yes. That's where I sit before I take a walk up and down my street at seven thirty in the evening after my dinner. Exercise is good for the digestion."

"Now, on June fourteenth, did you have occasion to see anyone who is now in this courtroom?"

"Oh yes."

"Who?"

"That young lady there." He pointed at Pearl.

"Let the record show that the witness has identified Pearl Washington," said DuBose. "And where did you see her?"

"She was going into the rowhouse across the street from mine."

"Do you know who lived in that house?"

"A woman named Janice from New York was renting it from a lady named Angela Burton, who makes the very finest corn bread you'll ever put in your mouth."

The crowd collectively chuckled over this endearing comment.

"And you're sure it was June fourteenth?"

"Oh yes, on account of the movers were at Mrs. Abigail Ward's house that day. She had gotten on in years and was going to live with her son in Ashland."

"And can you tell us when you saw the defendant go into that house on the fourteenth?"

"At one p.m. sharp."

"How can you be so sure?"

"The hospital clock bonged the hour just as I saw her."

"And you're certain it was her?"

"Yes. I actually said hello to her and she said hello back, very nice, and polite, although she didn't look too good. Seemed like she was having tummy trouble."

"And did you see her leave?"

"Oh yes."

"Do you know the time?"

"It was four minutes past six. She got in a car with Janice and they drove off together."

"Again, how can you be so sure of the time?" asked DuBose.

"In the summer I keep my little TV out on the porch. Run the cord through the window. Run my fan cord through there, too. Walter Cronkite had been on four minutes when I saw them leave. I'm a stickler for time and punctuality. As a traveling salesman, you had to be. Never missed a train or a bus or an appointment in over forty years."

"But how do you know she didn't leave before then?"

"She couldn't have. I was out on the porch the whole time."

"You never went inside from one to six?"

"Whatever for?"

"To eat, to use the facilities?"

"I have a large breakfast and an apple for my lunch. And I have a very regular constitution," he added primly. "So after breakfast, and my apple at twelve fifty, I sit on my porch and watch the world go by. And then I watch Walter Cronkite for thirty inspiring minutes. And then I prepare and have my dinner, and then I take my walk at seven thirty."

"Might she have earlier gone out a back door and then returned the same way?"

"There are no back doors in those places. Other rowhouses on the rear side are connected to them. One has to come out the front."

"So from around one o'clock to four minutes past six o'clock, Pearl Washington was in that house on June fourteenth?"

"Yes, she was."

DuBose turned to the jury. "You have heard sworn testimony that the Randolphs were killed between three and five p.m. You have also heard testimony that the police arrived at the house at a few minutes past six, while Pearl Washington was at least fifteen miles away during all of that time, and would have had no opportunity to do any of the things the commonwealth alleges she did." She looked back at Clancy. "Thank you, no further questions."

Battle stood but stayed behind the counsel table. "I see you wear glasses, sir."

"I do."

"Did you have them on that day?"

"Oh yes," replied Clancy.

"So your eyesight is not that good?"

"It's excellent with my glasses on. That's why I always wear them."

"How far would you say it is from your front porch to the house across the way?"

"Oh, I would say no more than fifty feet or so. It's a narrow street."

Battle marched off some distance toward the back of the courtroom.

"About here?"

"Yes sir. About that."

Battle held up three fingers. "How many fingers am I holding up?"

"Three. And I'm afraid you also have a spot of grease on your left lapel, sir."

Battle wiped at the spot while some of the spectators chuckled. "No further questions," he said in a dispirited voice.

CHAPTER 85

JACK NEXT CALLED HERMAN TILL back to the stand. "Mr. Till, we've heard how big and strong Mr. Washington is, correct?"

"Yes."

"But looks can be deceiving, right?"

"I don't follow."

Jack picked up the autopsy report from his table and brought it back to Till. "Now, you described for the jury the attack on the Randolphs when Mr. Battle was questioning you. You said it was like someone was swinging a tennis racket? You described it the same way for me and my co-counsel when we met with you."

"Yes, that's right."

Jack picked up the murder weapon, still wrapped in plastic, and handed it to Till. "Could you step out here and demonstrate for the jury *exactly* what you mean?"

Till took the bayonet and stepped out of the witness box. He squared his shoulders, and said, "The blows were delivered by a right-handed person, like I am. And, I believe, like this."

He rotated his hips, pivoted his left foot, putting most of his weight on that leg and then swung the bayonet up and then forward and down with his right hand, bringing it across his chest. Jack noted that Till raised his right heel as he did so.

"Just like that, then, you're sure?"

"Pretty darn sure, yes. Though with Mr. Randolph it was an upstroke. The depths of the wounds demonstrate they were administered with considerable force and velocity. No matter how big you are, you'd have to get your body into it. And no one will stand rigid when wielding a weapon like that."

"Okay, you can step back into the witness box. Hang on to that thing for now. Your Honor, I request permission to have Mr. Washington assist me in a little experiment right here in the middle of the courtroom. Only take a minute."

"Be quick about it," groused Ambrose.

Jack rolled up the autopsy report and held it out to Jerome. "Now, Jerome, you just saw what Mr. Till did. I want you to stand up and copy his movements exactly, with this paper serving as your weapon."

Jerome said gamely, "Okay, Mr. Lee, I give it a try."

"Come on out here in the center of the room so the jury can see you."

Jack watched the jury closely as Jerome used the table to lever himself up and then limped heavily out to where he was standing in front of them. Jack could see that several of the jurors looked surprised at the big man's limited mobility and weak leg.

"Okay, Jerome, go ahead. Swing it just like Mr. Till did," instructed Jack.

Jerome raised the paper, took a breath, and tried to move his legs. But the instant he put all his weight on his bad leg, he fell heavily to the floor.

He cried out in pain and grabbed at the limb.

Till and Jack rushed to help him up, as did the bailiff. The three of them managed to get the big man back on his feet.

"Sorry," said a shamefaced Jerome as he hopped over to the table and used it to support himself. "I ain't able to put all my weight like that on my left leg. Stupid to try."

Till looked stunned. "You got that injury in the war?"

"Yes sir."

A puzzled Till glanced over at Battle, who caught the man's look and frowned.

Jack thanked Jerome and helped him back to his seat.

Till returned to the witness stand, and Jack said, "Okay, after seeing all that, is it your professional opinion that the defendant could have wielded the murder weapon in such a way as you described to kill the Randolphs?"

"Well, I don't see how," said Till. "You'd have to move your feet like I showed you or something close to it. You'd have to put your full weight into it to inflict the sorts of injuries that were on the bodies."

"Now, in your report, you said the blows on Mrs. Randolph were delivered above to below, like this, correct?" Jack lifted his arm and then brought it downward.

"Yes."

"But on Mr. Randolph, you said the blows were delivered down to up, like this." He made the corresponding upward motion.

"That's right."

"Why the difference?"

"Well, the downward strokes make sense if the killer were taller than the victim."

"How tall was Mrs. Randolph?"

"Five four."

"And Mr. Randolph?"

"Six feet exactly."

Jack looked at the jury. "I had Mr. Washington measured this morning at the jail. He is six feet five and one-half inches. So, if Mr. Washington were the murderer, wouldn't all of the killing strokes be downward? He's far taller than *both* of the victims."

"I have to confess, Mr. Lee, that I'm confused."

"Don't be too hard on yourself, Mr. Till. I think everyone in this courtroom is confused. Including the jury. Nothing further, Judge."

"Witness is excused," said Ambrose after Battle declined to ask any questions.

DuBose rose and said, "Motion to strike the commonwealth's case, Your Honor."

"On what basis?"

"That they have completely failed to carry the burden of proof of guilt beyond a reasonable doubt required to send this case to the jury."

"Denied."

"Well, that was a shock," DuBose remarked under her breath.

Jack said, "The defense rests."

CHAPTER 86

AFTER COURT WAS ADJOURNED FOR the day, Battle dismissed his associates and walked over to DuBose and Jack.

"Y'all got a minute?" he said.

"Okay," said DuBose, looking at him like she suspected a trap.

"Let's find an empty room."

Dodging the journalists rushing at them, they hustled out of the courtroom and down the hall. At the bottom of a set of stairs Battle instructed a deputy to keep the reporters at bay. They walked up to the second floor, where Battle found an unlocked room. They slipped inside, and he bolted the door after them.

There was one table and two chairs.

"I don't feel like sitting," Battle said. "Go on ahead."

They sat and watched him pace for a bit before he stopped and faced them.

"I don't mind telling y'all that this damn case is embarrassing as hell."

DuBose said, "And do you find it suspicious that lying witnesses keep crawling out from under rocks to testify?"

"Or evidence keeps showing up that was clearly planted?" added Jack.

"But despite that, the fact is, I have enough to convict Jerome Washington."

Jack said, "I don't see how. Mr. Till pretty much said it was impossible that Jerome could have wielded that bayonet to match the evidence. And your whole case is based on the fact that Pearl took him clean clothes and shoes and got rid of the bloody ones, and the murder weapon. Otherwise, none of the physical evidence makes any sense. And you have no proof she did any of that because your witness was blackmailed to lie about it. And *our* witness proves she was nowhere near the Randolphs' at the time of the murders."

DuBose added, "I think the least you can do is dismiss the charges against Pearl Washington, Edmund."

"The thing is, if I do that, Desiree, I will be taken off this case, and another prosecutor will be appointed."

"By the higher-ups?" said DuBose. "The same ones that brought us *Josiah Ambrose*?"

"And compared to my replacement, you'll think I'm a drugged-out hippie."

"What do you want, Edmund?" said DuBose. "Why did you want to meet?"

"Jerome Washington pleads to involuntary manslaughter. The maximum sentence for that is ten years. I'll recommend he serve five. And charges against his wife are dropped, with prejudice. She'll be free to return to her family immediately."

"But not her husband," retorted DuBose.

"I can't work miracles, Desiree. This is my best and final offer. Otherwise, we'll do our closing arguments and it goes to the jury, and you roll the dice."

"But you said if you dropped those charges against Pearl, they would replace you," said Jack.

"Not if I get a plea deal on Jerome. He has to spend some time in prison. That is nonnegotiable."

"So this is all about saving face?" said DuBose. "Something for George Wallace to trumpet on his way to the White House?"

"What it is, is an offer worth considering," replied Battle.

DuBose said, "And if we take our chances with the jury?"

He gave her an incredulous look. "You want to risk putting your clients' fate in *that* jury's hands?"

DuBose tapped her shoe against the floor. "We need to discuss this with the Washingtons."

"Don't take too long. Once it goes to the jury, no more deals." He nodded at them both and left.

DuBose leaned back in her chair, looking weary. "In any fair system, we would have gotten a directed verdict. And even if we didn't, there is no impartial jury that would ever return a guilty verdict on these ridiculous facts. But we don't have an impartial jury, so I *am* scared to death to let twelve white men who have looked at me with disgust this entire time decide our clients' fates."

"And Battle knows that. It's the only leverage he has to make Jerome and Pearl take the plea deal."

"We still have our closing argument to make," she pointed out.

Jack looked at her fixedly. "In *To Kill a Mockingbird*, Atticus Finch gave one of the finest closing arguments I've ever heard. And the jury still found his client guilty."

"And then the police shot him." DuBose rose. "Let's go talk to our clients."

Howard Pickett was waiting for them outside. His big Lincoln purred at the corner, its engine kicking fumes into the warm, humid Virginia air.

"You left the courtroom mighty fast today," said Jack.

Pickett said, "I'm an important businessman. This is just one of a dozen things I got going on. That's the thing when you're so damn *rich*. Lots of responsibilities."

DuBose looked him up and down. "Is part of your *business* recruiting Ambrose to oversee this trial?"

"Nothing to do with me."

"I've noticed that George Wallace has tempered some of his racist talk lately."

"It's all about winning. You know that. Same thing you're trying to do in there."

"What do you want?" said Jack. "Because we're pretty busy, too."

"Take the offer."

"And how do you even know about *that*?" demanded DuBose.

"Just take it. Otherwise, things will not turn out well. For any of you. And that's not a threat. It's a given."

CHAPTER 87

PEARL AND JEROME HAD ALREADY been taken back to their jail cells. But Jack and DuBose received permission to speak with them at the courthouse later that day.

DuBose went through the offer with them slowly and clearly.

Pearl shook her head and said, "No, he ain't gonna do that. Lock him up like an animal for years for somethin' he didn't do? No! Ain't gonna do it."

"Look, Pearl, honey," said Jerome. "It won't be that long. Man say five years."

"*Maybe* five years. You don't know that for sure. And what if that judge say you got to go to prison longer?" She looked at DuBose. "Can he do that?"

"He can."

"See?" said Pearl. "That man will *screw* you, Jerome. He hate colored people."

"But you get to go home, to the kids, baby. That be what counts. They need you."

"They need *both* of us."

"You think that jury gonna let us both off?" countered a frustrated Jerome. "Hell, we'll both end up in the chair. Then where will the kids be, huh?"

Pearl wiped away tears and hung her head while Jerome lifted a

shackled hand and placed it gently on her back. He looked up at Jack
and DuBose.

"Tell that man we take the deal."

"Okay, Jerome," said DuBose resignedly. "We'll tell him." She
looked at her watch and then glanced at Pearl. "Nothing can be done
now. But first thing in the morning. And Pearl will be able to go
home right after. And then we'll see to your officially pleading to
manslaughter. Battle will make his sentencing recommendation and
we will do all we can to make sure that Judge Ambrose goes along
with it."

They left the Washingtons, drove to Jack's parents' home, and
went into the garage. Queenie greeted them with tail wags and yips.
They petted her, and then sat, depressed, at their desks..

DuBose gazed around at their little war room. "I have to say,
this is the first time I prepared for a case in a place where people normally park their cars."

"I'm glad I could provide a new experience for you." He paused
and studied her. "I know that look. What are you thinking?"

"I confirmed that Ambrose was in the Ku Klux Klan."

"How?"

"Colleagues at the NAACP. They know all the slimy holes to
look in."

"And?"

"And I'm wondering whether I should leak it to the press and
then go into court and ask for a mistrial."

"If you do that, no telling how long Pearl will be sitting in jail
until the next trial."

She rubbed her eyes. "I know. Which is why I haven't done it
before now." She stood and paced. "God, I'd like to know who is
giving Battle his marching orders."

"It's got to be Pickett, don't you think? He knew about the plea
offer. He probably insisted on it after Drucker was shown to be a
liar. He wants to save face and help Wallace's chances for the White
House, like you said."

She sat back down. "I guess the racists win this round."

"So what's next for you?" he asked quietly.

"Back to Chicago to catch up on laundry and paying bills. And then there's a case in Georgia that I'm needed on. And then one in Texas after that."

"And on and on goes the carousel?"

"My work is *not* a game, Jack," she said curtly.

"Never said it was. It's the most important work a lawyer can be doing. But—"

"But what?"

"But you *are* entitled to a personal life, Desiree."

She snapped, "I don't have a husband at home taking care of everything while I'm working. I don't have someone to have the babies I'm too busy to carry, and then raise them. Okay? This *is* my life. All of it. I have room for nothing else!"

Jack held up his hands. "All right."

DuBose looked down for a moment, as though she were making an important decision. She leveled her gaze on him. "I *was* engaged to be married. His name was Paul."

"What happened?"

"He—"

Before she could finish the garage's side door opened and Jeff walked in.

"Where have you been?" asked Jack.

"Over at the Hanovers'."

"Why?" demanded his brother.

"I went to see Christine, but she wasn't there."

"So you just left then?"

"Well, I did talk to Patsy for a while. I gave her a ride home after she finished up for the day. Daddy let me borrow his truck."

"Who's Patsy?" asked Jack.

"Their maid. She's been with Christine since Christine was a kid. She brought Patsy with her when she married Gordon. They're real close."

"Right. We saw her when we went over there for the will reading," noted Jack.

"How is Patsy doing?" asked DuBose.

"Not good. She's totally devoted to Christine, and Christine is not doin' well."

"She's been through hell, all right," noted Jack.

"Patsy said Christine was cryin' her eyes out the day her parents were killed."

"Wait a minute. The *day* her parents were killed?" said Jack.

Jeff said, "What?"

"Christine and Gordon were in DC and didn't get home until very late. Didn't you hear Christine's testimony?"

Now Jeff looked confused. "I guess I wasn't really focused on that. Patsy told me that Christine told her to go home early that day."

Jack said, "What the hell are you talking about, Jeff? Christine and Gordon were *both* in Washington when her parents were killed."

"Not accordin' to what Patsy just told me. She said Christine went out in the afternoon, and then came back later. Patsy said she looked like death itself. Told Patsy to go home and not to talk about anythin' to anyone."

DuBose said quickly, "Can you go with us to Patsy's home? Right now?"

CHAPTER 88

PATSY LIVED IN A SMALL house on a narrow gravel road with four other similar homes. The Black woman was in her fifties, and her long graying hair was tied back into a bushy ponytail. She was surprised to see the Lees and DuBose at her door, but quickly invited them in. She had taken off her uniform and was in blue jeans and a white shirt.

They sat in her front room.

Jack said, "We understand that Mrs. Hanover was very upset when she got back from her parents' home the day they were killed?"

"Oh, yeah. Sobbin' and everythin'. I ask her what was wrong and she say somethin' bad had happened to her momma and daddy. I was real upset, too. I used to work for them when Christine was just a little thing."

"What was she doing at her parents' that day?"

"Miss Christine say her momma called and was upset 'bout somethin'. So she went over there to see what was the matter."

"Did she drive?" asked DuBose.

"No, it just a short walk over there."

"But wouldn't she have to go out the main gate?" asked DuBose.

"Oh, no. They got a locked gate back 'a the home. She go out that way, then through a little path in the woods and right to her momma and daddy's through *their* back gate. I done it lots of times. Only takes five minutes."

"That's right," said Jack. "She told us about the back gate at her parents' house. What time did she go over there and what time did she get back?"

"Oh, she leave the house 'bout quarter past three or thereabouts."

DuBose glanced sharply at Jack. "And what time did she get back?"

"She got back close to five."

"Did she walk back?"

"Well, I thought she would. But then I see her gettin' out a car over by the garage. I see it through the kitchen window when I was cleanin' up."

"Was it a blue convertible?" asked Jack.

Patsy smiled. "How you know that?"

DuBose said, "Was she wearing the same clothes that she had on when she left?"

"Well, I guess so."

"You *guess* so?"

"I couldn't really tell. She had on a long coat. I guess she got it from her momma and daddy's house. I wondered why she had it on 'cause it was real hot that day."

"And when she came in? What did she say?" asked DuBose.

"She say somethin' bad happened. She told me to go on home right then."

"And she told you not to talk to anyone?" said DuBose.

"That's right. Then come to find out they dead." She shook her head. "So sad. They was real good people."

"Have you been following the trial?" asked Jack.

"No. I mean it make Miss Christine sad, so I just closed my eyes and ears to all that. And she told me not to bother with it, so I didn't. I ain't talk to nobody 'bout it. That be Miss Christine's business, nobody else's. 'Course, I did talk to Mr. Lee here 'cause he and Miss Christine were such good friends."

DuBose looked at her keenly. "You're very fond of Mrs. Hanover, aren't you?"

"Oh, yeah. I took care 'a her when she was a little girl. Now I helpin' to raise Miss Christine's children. They real sweet, just like their momma."

Jack looked at his brother, who was gazing at Patsy in astonishment. Then he said, "Patsy, we don't want to distress Mrs. Hanover, so can you not tell her that we came over and that you talked to us about all this?"

"Oh, yeah, I can do that. I don't like talkin' 'bout it anyways. So sad."

Outside Jeff said, "Does this mean that…" But he couldn't finish his thought.

Jack looked at DuBose. "The evidence is starting to make a lot more sense."

She said, "And I could kick myself for making assumptions about certain people just because of who they are."

"So what are you going do with what we just found out?" asked Jeff.

DuBose eyed Jack. "Probably one of the hardest things we're ever going to have to do. And we *have* to do it."

"I know we do," said Jack.

CHAPTER 89

JACK AND DUBOSE SPENT THE next morning making phone calls and verifying some information. They also called Donny Peppers, explained the situation, and he did some additional legwork for them. Jack phoned Battle's office, and, without specifically telling him what was going on, said that they had one more witness to call before they made their closing arguments.

Battle said, "Okay, but after today my plea offer goes away, Mr. Lee. And it won't be coming back."

"I don't think we'll be needing it, Mr. Battle, to tell you the truth."

"Who's the witness?"

"The person has already been on the stand."

"Then what else is there to ask?"

"A lot, actually. You'll see and hear it all."

They had arranged for the court to return to session at three o'clock.

The place was once more full, with everyone expecting the closing arguments to be made by the respective counsel before the judge sent the case to the jury for deliberations, and, eventually, a verdict.

Thus, all were surprised when DuBose rose and said, "Your Honor, we need to recall one more witness."

"You rested your case," retorted Ambrose.

"We have just become aware of some extraordinary evidence that this court and the jury need to hear."

"This is highly irregular," said an irritated Ambrose. "Mr. Battle, what do you have to say about this?"

Battle stood, shot DuBose a glance, and said, "Well, considering we did the same thing to them, and in the interests of justice, we should hear from their witness. So, no objection."

DuBose then turned to survey the courtroom. Her gaze moved from person to person until it came to rest on one.

"Defense calls Mrs. Christine Hanover."

Gordon Hanover was sitting next to his wife, and they both visibly reacted when DuBose called out her name.

Gordon exclaimed, "What is this about? My wife has already testified."

DuBose said, "Please, Mrs. Hanover, this will not take long."

Christine slowly stood, glanced at her husband with a sad expression, and then walked down the aisle and stepped into the witness box. She was reminded by the bailiff that she was still under oath.

DuBose approached her, while Jack sat next to Jerome and Pearl, who both looked on curiously.

She said, "Mrs. Hanover, I'll try to make this as quick as possible, but I can't promise it will be painless."

Christine was shooting nervous glances at her husband. "A-all right. But I...I don't understand."

"You testified previously that you were with your husband in Washington, DC, the day your parents were murdered, correct?"

"Yes."

"And that you received word there about their deaths, and that you and your husband arrived home very late that night?"

"That is correct."

"But that is *not* correct, is it?"

Christine turned as pale as the jacket she was wearing. "I...I don't..."

"We spoke with the hotel where your husband was staying in Washington. He checked in alone. We also spoke with people in Congress. You were never seen with him. We have affidavits from three people that we will be entering into evidence that will corroborate this. We have also talked to your maid, who confirmed that you were home that day."

Christine looked up at her as though she could barely hear a thing DuBose was saying. "W-what? Patsy?"

"Who is as loyal to you as anyone can possibly be. We all just accepted your account that you were with your husband because he *was* in Washington. But in a capital murder case no assumptions should be made." She glanced at Battle. "We all should have taken steps to confirm your whereabouts, but we didn't. Until now."

Christine simply looked at her blankly, and remained silent.

DuBose continued, "Now, were you at your home in Faulkner's Woods when you received a phone call from your mother on the afternoon of June fourteenth?"

"My mother?"

"Yes. Was she upset about something? And you walked over to their house, which would only take about five minutes? Did you go out through your rear gate, pass along a path in the woods where no one would see you, then enter their property through your parents' rear gate?"

"I—"

"Can you tell us what happened when you went inside the house?"

No one in the courtroom was making a sound. Battle was staring open-mouthed at Christine, and he didn't even object to what amounted to DuBose stating all these questions as facts without being under oath. The jurors were all leaning forward, seemingly not wanting to miss a syllable of what was being said here.

Christine stared out at the gallery of people, who were all looking back at her, wholly dumbstruck.

She found her husband and fixed her gaze on him. She looked

like a swimmer who knew she was caught in a riptide and was probably going to drown.

"I...you say I went over there? But I was in—"

"No, you were not in Washington, DC. Did you return from your parents' house around five o'clock in a blue convertible owned by Walter Gates?"

"W-Walter Gates?" said a trembling Christine.

"Yes. A witness, whom we will call if necessary, said that you were wearing a long coat that you did not have on when you left your home. Did you get the coat from your parents' house? Was that to cover all the blood?"

"B-blood?" Christine swayed in her seat.

Gordon leapt to his feet. "Stop. Stop this right now. Christine, don't say another word. My wife wants a lawyer. She is entitled to a lawyer. Right now."

"Please, sir, sit back down," said a thoroughly confused Ambrose.

DuBose turned to Hanover. "She's actually *not* entitled to a lawyer, because she has not been arrested and charged with any crime. Yet."

"Then she'll plead the Fifth. Christine, honey, just take the Fifth Amendment." Hanover glared at Ambrose. "Judge, this is a mockery. She is not saying another word. This is a disgusting trick...I have never. I..." When Ambrose said nothing, Hanover seemed to lose all energy and fell back into his seat, breathing heavily, the sweat glistening on his forehead.

DuBose turned back to Christine. "Your husband is right, Mrs. Hanover. You are entitled to plead the Fifth Amendment right against self-incrimination if you believe that what you might say in answer to my questions could implicate you in a crime." She looked at Jerome and Pearl. "Mr. Battle offered a plea deal to the defendants. A maximum of ten years in prison on a manslaughter charge for Mr. Washington, and in return Mrs. Washington gets to go free. Mr. Washington wishes to accept that offer, though he did not kill the

Randolphs, in order for his wife to be able to return to their three young children. I just thought you might want to know that because it could possibly influence whether you want to tell us the truth, or plead the Fifth."

Christine looked at the Washingtons, and tears spilled down her cheeks as she shook her head.

DuBose handed her a tissue, which Christine used to wipe her eyes. "Mrs. Hanover, are you going to plead the Fifth Amendment right against self-incrimination?"

Christine's gaze once more flitted around the courtroom until it came to rest on Jeff Lee. Seeing him seemed to calm and steady her. She tucked the tissue away in her jacket cuff, wiped her eyes clear, and shook her head. Composing herself she said, "No, I'm not."

"Christine!" called out her husband, but she put her hand up.

"It's all right, Gordon. It's…time the truth finally came out." She looked at the Washingtons and said, "I'm so, so very sorry for everything you've gone through." She turned back to DuBose and began.

CHAPTER 90

CHRISTINE SAID, "I WASN'T TRUTHFUL before. I knew that my mother was planning to divorce my father. She couldn't take the abuse anymore. I actually encouraged my mother to do so. I didn't want…anything bad to happen." A sob escaped her throat.

"And she phoned you on the afternoon of June fourteenth?" said DuBose.

"Yes. My father had found out what my mother was planning. She was afraid because he was so very angry. He had struck her already that day. She asked me to come over. So I did."

"And there was no one there, other than Jerome?"

"I knew the maid left at two. I didn't know Jerome's hours, or where he was. I wasn't even thinking about that. I just hurried over to try and defuse the situation. I had planned on having my mother come back to my house with me for the time being."

"Then what happened when you got there?"

Now Christine showed visible signs of distress. "I walked into that room…and…my…my mother…was…" She let out another sob.

"She was dead?" said DuBose, her own voice now cracking, as the other woman's misery seemed to bleed into her.

Christine rested her head on the rail of the box and slowly nodded. "Yes."

"And your father?"

She lifted her head, her face littered with tears. "He...that damn old bayonet. He had...Blood was everywhere." She let out a low moan. "My mother was...on the floor. Her...head and neck were..."

"Yes, we know. You don't have talk about that," DuBose said quietly.

Christine abruptly sat straight up and let out a long, violent gasp. "My father was out of his mind."

"He had killed her?"

"Yes."

"And he struck the picture of them that was on the table, didn't he? Cutting their faces in the photo?"

She nodded. "It was taken when they were courting. I guess he...he..."

"Yes, I understand."

Christine clutched the sides of the witness box. "He looked at me and then he started screaming. That my mother had told him that I knew about the divorce, that I wanted her to get one. That I had betrayed him...that...he was going to do to me what he had done to her. He rushed at me with..." She closed her eyes and the tears seeped out. "I picked up a book and hit his hand with it. The bayonet fell to the floor. I...I managed to grab it. We struggled. He was stronger than I was, but after I saw what he had done to my poor mother, I knew I was fighting for my life." Her features screwed up as she moaned, "And I hated him for what he had done to her. And I just wanted to hurt him. To make him feel—"

"Christine!" bellowed her husband. "Please, don't say another word, honey."

Jack turned around to see Jeff rush over to the man, sit next to him, put his arm around his shoulders, and speak in a low voice until Hanover sat limply in the chair, leaning into Jeff.

DuBose said, "You picked up the bayonet? You were struggling with him?"

"I finally broke free from my father and I struck him with it. But he kept coming at me. And I struck him again. And again. Until…he fell down. Until he…couldn't hurt…anybody else…"

"Had he hurt…*you*, before?"

Christine looked up at DuBose and her features once more calmed. When she next spoke her voice had regained some rigidity though her gaze and voice were distant. "Yes. And Sam. And my other brother and sister before they died. My father could be so kind. And then he could be so very…cruel."

"That explains why the wounds on your mother were on a downward motion. Your father was much taller than she was. But you're shorter than your father, and your blows were coming from another angle."

"I was just striking at him blindly. To make him…stop."

"So now they were both dead. And then what happened?"

"I couldn't believe what…what I had done. I was numb, paralyzed. Then I realized how bad this would all look. I didn't know what to do. So I made a call. I couldn't reach Gordon because he was out of town."

DuBose turned and scanned the crowd until she saw Curtis Gates near the back. The man looked like he had been turned to stone. "So you called Curtis Gates?"

"Yes. He was our lawyer, our friend. I thought he could help. I told him what had happened. He…he sent his son, Walter, right over."

"And what did Walter do?"

"He brought me a coat to cover the blood on my clothes. Then he smeared the blood on the rug to cover my footprints. I had held the bayonet, so he took that, and he wiped down the phone I had used. Then he drove me home."

"How did you get past the gate without the guard seeing you? And why would they let Gates in without you?"

"He had put the top up on the car, and I hid in the floorboard with a blanket over me. Walter has a pass to get into the gate because his company does work there."

"Didn't the police come by your house to try to notify you of what had happened?"

"That's why I sent Patsy home. They *did* come by, but I didn't answer the door, or the phone. I had stayed inside all day so none of my neighbors saw me. I *was* planning to go to DC with Gordon, but I was feeling unwell and decided at the last minute to stay home. Later that evening, pretending to be his secretary, I reached Gordon at his hotel in Washington. I told him what had happened. He drove straight home."

"But the guard at the gate to your neighborhood said he saw Gordon *and* you arrive around two in the morning."

"I got dressed up, snuck out of the neighborhood, met Gordon at a prearranged spot, and we drove home together so the guard would see us both coming in at that time."

"And then Jerome was arrested for the crimes."

Christine slumped forward and moaned. "I...I couldn't believe it. I didn't even know he was there. I never, ever expected him to go into the house like that."

"But you didn't come forward then?"

She shook her head. "Curtis told me that I would go to prison. "

"It sounds to me like it was self-defense, Mrs. Hanover."

"Curtis said people would think that I had killed them both."

"Who called the police on Jerome?"

"Later, Curtis told me that Walter had gone back to see if we had missed anything and he saw Jerome going into the house. He went to a pay phone and called the police."

"To implicate Jerome?"

"Yes."

"But then evidence began appearing that further framed both the Washingtons. Witnesses like Tyler Dobbs and Linda Drucker? The discovery of the money in the lean-to, the bayonet in the tree stump?"

Christine shook her head, her expression one of misery. "My mother had told me about the bonus she paid Jerome. I told the

Gateses about it. I guess they had an idea that if the money was found at their property that it would make things look bad for the Washingtons. I don't know how they found out where Jerome had put the money. And of course my mother wouldn't be around to say that it had been a gift."

"Do you know if they anonymously called the police about the money *and* the bayonet?"

"They told me they did. And they said they paid or threatened those people to say those things."

"Objection, hearsay," said Battle feebly.

Ambrose gave him a fierce look. "I'm going to allow her testimony, Mr. Battle. You just keep quiet."

DuBose turned to look at Gates. "Mr. Gates also testified that your father was going to fire Mr. Washington."

"That was a lie." Christine stared directly at Gates. "Curtis said that he would take care of everything so long as when I inherited my parents' estate, when my brother died, we would sell it to him and his son at a very *favorable* price."

"Did he know of your brother's illness?"

"Yes. He was Sam's estate lawyer, too. I believe he knew that my brother didn't have long to live. Before all this happened, when my father decided to change his will, I think Curtis came up with this tontine idea so that the property would, realistically, only come to me. He and Gordon were friends, so maybe he thought Gordon would sell it to him and his son because Walter had grand plans to turn it into a luxury neighborhood and make a fortune. Then, with my parents' deaths, the Gateses saw a way to get the property for a fraction of its true value, and a lot sooner because now they just needed my brother to die."

Battle started to rise, no doubt to object to all of Christine's speculations, but Ambrose, seeing this, pointed his gavel at the man and barked, "Don't. This fine woman has been through hell and back and she's entitled to have her say. Sit down!"

Battle meekly retook his seat.

While Christine had been talking, Gates had slowly risen and was attempting to leave the courtroom. However, Jack spotted him and called out, "Hey!"

Ambrose saw this and called out to the bailiff, "Place Mr. Gates under arrest and take him away. And have deputies find his damn son and take him into custody, too."

The bailiff did so, and Ambrose looked back at Christine. "Go on," he said.

"Gordon and I hoped that the jury would acquit the Washingtons, but then when things seemed to turn against Mr. Battle, the Gateses made up all that evidence. I told them not to, but they wouldn't listen."

DuBose said, "Your husband testified, too, that your father was going to fire Mr. Washington because he had stolen from him. But that was not true, was it?"

"He didn't want to lie, but Curtis threatened me with exposure if he didn't. Gordon was just protecting me."

"But why did Mr. Gates want the Washingtons to be convicted of these crimes? Why did it matter to him?"

"He said if they were acquitted the police might keep looking for the killer, and could find out the truth." She closed her eyes for a moment. "It just got so out of control. I...I just couldn't believe it. It was horrible enough what happened with my parents. It was like a nightmare I couldn't wake up from. I'm just so sorry."

"No further questions," said DuBose.

Ambrose eyed Battle, who shook his head. The judge said, "You're excused, Mrs. Hanover. But now I'm afraid that both you and your husband will be taken into custody. It truly saddens me to do this, considering all you have suffered." He gestured at two deputies, who came forward with their handcuffs out.

After she was arrested, Christine turned to the Washingtons. "I'm so sorry. I...never meant for any of this to happen to you."

Pearl looked down while Jerome dumbly nodded.

Christine and her husband were led out of the courtroom.

DuBose looked at Ambrose. "Defense moves to have all charges against the Washingtons dropped and that this case be dismissed *with* prejudice."

Before Ambrose could even look at Battle, the latter said, "No objection."

Ambrose fiddled with his gavel. "Well, Mr. Washington *did* assault the deputy who arrested him."

"You mean the same deputy who tried to murder me and Miss DuBose?"

Ambrose gave Jack an angry glance and said in a curt tone, "All charges against Jerome and Pearl Washington are withdrawn and this case is dismissed with prejudice. You are both free to go."

"Perhaps an apology from the commonwealth, Your Honor?" said DuBose.

Ambrose shot her a stern look. "They can go home to their little colored kiddies. Isn't that enough?"

He turned to the jury. "On behalf of the commonwealth, I thank you for your service. The jury is dismissed. Court is dismissed." He slammed his gavel down and disappeared into his chambers.

On that, the courtroom erupted.

CHAPTER 91

JEROME AND PEARL WERE CRYING and hugging one another.

Battle shook both DuBose's and Jack's hands. "I hope to hell I never have to face you two in court again," he said.

DuBose said, "Who knows, Edmund, next time we might be on the same side, if your thinking continues to evolve."

Battle next extended his apologies to the Washingtons for all that they had endured, and left with his associates scurrying along behind.

Jack said to DuBose, "Same side? That man and you? Really?"

"Do you know the best thing to make of your enemy?"

"What? A friend?"

"No, an ally," she replied.

Jack and DuBose joined the Washingtons in their celebration.

"Thank you, thank you, thank you," said Pearl, hugging them both.

DuBose smiled warmly and said, "It's always a good day when justice prevails."

Jerome shook his head and said, "I feel real bad for Miss Christine."

Pearl shivered. "Can't imagine walkin' in that room and seein' your daddy done killed your momma. Then he come after her. What you think gonna happen to Miss Christine and her husband?"

"I think with who they are and the lawyers they can afford, they'll be just fine," opined DuBose dryly.

Jack said, "I hope they throw the book at the Gateses, though."

"You and me both," said DuBose.

Jack looked around and saw his parents, and smiled and waved. However, his brother, who was standing near the back of the room, appeared a shadow of himself.

Outside, they faced a crush of media. DuBose stepped to the podium and, with a glance at Jack, said, "I wish we lived in a world that was just and equal for all, and that lawyers could concentrate on being simply lawyers and not spokespersons for a cause. But today we saw justice done. It was tragic and heartbreaking and should remind us that we're all human, and we can all rise high or fall low, but we should all be judged by the same standard. That is the only way we can move forward as a country, as a people."

As she stepped away from the podium, Jack said, "Do you mind if I say something?"

DuBose was clearly surprised by this but said quickly, "Of course, Jack. You don't need my permission."

He stepped to the podium and looked out at the crowd staring back at him, many with hostile expressions.

Jack pointed at DuBose. "Desiree DuBose is a far better lawyer than I ever have hopes of being. And yet she's closed off to parts of the world where I'm freely welcome. Why? First, because she's not white. And second, because she's a woman. What's fair or right about that? Nothing, that's what."

He stared out over the sea of people and noted many women, both black and white, glancing at the men next to them. When they looked back up at Jack, there was grim agreement in their expressions with what he had said.

Then he continued, "Now, I see many an upset person out there among y'all. The result of the trial was maybe not to your liking." Jack pointed at Jerome and Pearl Washington. "It was conclusively proven that they had nothing to do with the deaths of the Randolphs.

So they will not be going to the electric chair, but rather home to their young children. If it had been your family members, wouldn't you be happy? So ask yourself, why is it different for them?"

He glanced over at a man holding a Confederate battle flag. "I've heard a lot about us needing to break up this country into two parts. We can't agree on a damn thing, so why not just walk away from each other?" He stopped and again surveyed the crowd, going from one face to the next. "We've been through wars and sickness and depressions. We've been through so much *together*, and we all actually agree on a lot of fundamental principles. Yet I never hear anyone talk about that. Just about what we *don't* agree on. What divides us, not what unites us." He paused and composed himself because he could feel his heart racing and his voice rising, and he didn't want that, not now.

He looked at Sally Reeves in the crowd, her son next to her. She was looking angrily at Jack, but her boy's expression was more muted; he actually appeared to be listening.

Jack said, "But the thing is, we're the United States of America through thick and thin. Not 'the United States of America, except when the going gets tough.' And to accept anything less than that from ourselves is to disrespect every single American who came before us."

He leaned into the microphones. "I'm not naïve enough to think that I'll change a single mind today, or tomorrow or the next day. The most eloquent orators in the world couldn't do that, and I'm certainly not at that level. But y'all just need to start listening to each other, talk things out. It takes a lot of work to be angry all the time. And what good ever comes out of it? What good comes out of hating folks for no reason? Now, kindness and respect go a long, long way. We learned that in school and at church, and those lessons should last a lifetime and maybe we need to get back to them. And then maybe when enough of us have done that, we might have a decent shot of being united for a long time to come. Now I don't know about you, but I think what we have here is worth fighting for. At least that's my hope and my prayer. And maybe it should be yours, too."

He stopped, stepped back from the podium, and looked at DuBose. She did not look happy, he thought. "What's wrong, Desiree? Did you not like what I said?"

"I liked it very much. It was thoughtful and powerful, Jack."

"So why do you look so sad then?"

"I…"

"Desiree?"

She glanced out at the crowd and then looked back at him. "I…I fear for you now, Jack."

He gently took her arm. "It'll be okay, Desiree. Let's go."

They pushed through the crowd with Jerome and Pearl in tow.

"I can give you a ride home," Jack offered to the couple.

"Can't wait to hug my babies," said an excited Pearl.

They turned toward where Jack's car was parked.

"Hey, Mr. Washington? Jerome?"

They turned to see a teenage boy running up behind them.

"Yeah?" said Jerome.

The teen raised his gun and fired.

Jerome clutched his chest as the bullet hit him. The boy fired again, and this bullet struck Jerome in the neck, ricocheted off his spine, and exited his body.

Pearl screamed.

Jack felt something strike him with tremendous force. He looked down to see blood streaming from his torso. He slowly looked at DuBose, who watched in horror as Jerome fell dead to the pavement. Then she cried out as Jack collapsed a foot from Jerome.

The crowd rushed in every direction to get away, knocking each other down and trampling over one another. Confederate and American flags hit the ground as terrified people scattered.

Deputies raced forward, guns drawn.

A sobbing Pearl was cradling Jerome's head in her lap, as other people rushed over to them to see if they could help.

DuBose gripped Jack. "Someone call an ambulance. Hurry!"

Hilly Lee ran to them, pulled a large handkerchief from her bag, wadded it up, and placed it against the wound to stop the bleeding. "Hold on, Jack. Hold on, son." She held his hand and kept eye contact. "Look at me, Jack. Stay with us. Help is coming. Stay with me, son."

Frank Lee knelt down next to his son. "Come on, Jacky, breathe, son. Breathe."

Jack looked up at them. Despite the copious blood loss and his body commencing to shut down, he still seemed able to see his parents and DuBose, but could say nothing. He managed to move his head to the right to see the shooter still standing there with his gun pointed outward. And then Jack Lee's eyes closed.

The deputies had their weapons leveled at the shooter, but didn't fire.

"Put the gun down, son," one of them said. "Before you get hurt."

The teenager did not put the gun down. "That n—— deserved what he got."

"Put the gun down," bellowed the deputy, looking nervously at his colleagues.

"And so does she!"

When the teen aimed his gun at Pearl, who was holding her dead husband, and started to pull the trigger, a hand grabbed a deputy's gun and shot the teenager. He fell to the pavement, his blood spilling all over him from a gaping wound in his chest.

"Kenny!" screamed a voice.

Deputy Raymond LeRoy raced through the crowd, shoving people out of the way until he reached his dead boy. He stared down, helpless, and then dropped to his knees and clutched his son's body in his arms. "Kenny," sobbed the lawman. "No, boy, no."

Jeff Lee handed the gun back to the deputy, who scowled at him.

"Why in the hell did you shoot him?" asked the man.

"Because he was going to shoot *her*," Jeff barked. He pointed at Pearl Washington, who was now sprawled on top of her lifeless husband, crying her heart out. "Why the hell didn't *you* shoot him?"

The furious lawman just shook his head.

DuBose looked frantically around as she heard the ambulance coming. That was when she saw Howard Pickett standing on the corner. With a smile, he made a gun with his right hand, pointed it directly at DuBose, and pulled the trigger. Then he turned and walked off, leaving behind the dead and the dying, and those who mourned them.

CHAPTER 92

NEARLY THREE MONTHS TO THE day after being shot, Jack Lee drove his Fiat slowly down the street to his parents' house and parked out front.

The air was cooler and the sky held not a single cloud. Leaves were changing color and had started falling from trees. Jack liked this time of year. Things seemed to slow down and a person could get their bearings and think clearer.

He had been in the hospital for six weeks. Things had been touch and go for a while, as he had lost a lot of blood and the internal damage had been considerable. And then infections had set in, nearly killing him twice. After multiple operations he was sent for a lengthy stay in another facility, where he slowly regained his strength and relearned how to move his limbs.

His parents had been with him every day in the hospital. And for the first month of his rehabilitation they'd helped him to do his exercises hour after hour, until he had had to literally chase them out of the place.

He eased out of the car and stared back up at Ashby's house. The man had died a month before, he had learned. Too much alcohol and not enough to live for, Jack reckoned. The house had been put up for sale, and he had heard a young couple with small children had a contract to buy it.

He had been unable to attend Jerome's funeral, although his parents and brother had been there. It was a beautiful service, his mother had told him, with a large crowd in attendance.

"A lot of white folks were there, too," she had added. "They didn't know the family, but came to pay their respects."

They also had told him that Miss Jessup had left her home on Tuxedo Boulevard and moved in with the widowed Pearl to help with the children.

He walked in the front door, half expecting to be hugged by Lucy and to hear her call out, "Momma, Daddy, it be Jack." But there was no Lucy. Not anymore.

His brother came around the corner and gazed stoically at him. Jeff would be leaving in a few weeks. On his last visit to see Jack, Jeff had told him he was moving to England. He had gotten a job there with a large security firm to train its field personnel. He wasn't sure if he was ever coming back.

He glanced at Jack's surgically repaired shoulder. "How is it?"

Jack slowly moved his arm in a small circle. "I won't be throwing any more touchdown passes, but I can wield a pen and carry my briefcase." He added, "And I'm alive."

"That was always the best test for me."

"Christine?" asked Jack. He had not been paying attention to anything other than his long recovery and was anxious to know what had happened during that time.

"They didn't charge her. Gordon, either. But Curtis and Walter Gates are both going to prison."

"Nothing less than they deserved."

"And Gordon and Christine bought Pearl a real nice house, and they're paying her so she doesn't have to work. And they have a tutor teaching her to read and write so she can get a good job one day. That was nice of them, wasn't it?"

"Hell, Jeff, it was the absolute least they could do, considering what they did to that family."

Jeff glanced down. "I guess you're right." He paused. "Nobody ever figured out why that boy shot Jerome."

Jack gave his brother an incredulous look. "Really? Seems pretty damn obvious to me."

"I never killed a kid before."

"That 'kid' was going to murder another person if you hadn't stopped him."

Jeff rubbed his jaw and glanced away. "Christine and Gordon gave Sam the money to get the treatment in Switzerland. He's been over there for the last month. Sounds like he might get a few more years of living out of it."

"Good. And Momma and Daddy?"

"Out in the garage."

The desks, file cabinets, and chalkboard were long gone. His father was working on another engine for another neighbor, for cash. They had bought the dishwasher with the proceeds of the other motor rebuild. Hilly was handing him the tools he needed. The recliner and TV were gone. His father was not smoking and it seemed that his breathing had eased some.

The sign, though, was still up on the wall.

Jack glanced at it: DUBOSE AND LEE.

His mother carefully embraced him, and his father shook his son's hand, but did so gently.

"I talked to your doctor and he said you're almost eighty percent," Hilly said.

"I guess." He looked at the engine. "You should open up your own shop. With Daddy's mechanical know-how and your energy and attention to detail, Momma, you two could make a real go of it."

"What I told her," said Frank as he went back to fiddling with the carburetor.

Hilly looked steadfastly at her oldest son. "You still planning on heading out?"

Jack had already communicated this intention to them. "I am. It feels right."

His mother wrapped her sweater around herself more tightly and said, "Well, for what it's worth, I think so, too."

"It's actually worth a lot, Momma."

"Think you'll ever come back, son?" asked his father.

"I never say never, at least not anymore."

Hilly said, "With the way the world is right now, what's the point?"

CHAPTER 93

JACK HAD NEVER BEEN ON a plane before, and he found it equal parts terrifying and exhilarating. When it landed, he picked up his suitcase, hoisted his briefcase, and grabbed a taxi outside the bustling airport.

He hadn't written, or called. He just wanted to show up. He thought it might be best. But it also could be a disaster. He had come amply prepared for both, he hoped.

The taxi ride was long and carried him to a section of the city where children played stickball in the street and vendors sold their wares from little carts. The air was colder than in Virginia and the breeze brisk. He had seen the body of water they had flown over that looked as big as the whole of the Chesapeake Bay. But the passenger seated next to Jack had told him it was merely a lake.

"Lake Michigan," she had said.

"Calling that thing a lake doesn't do it justice," Jack had replied.

He paid the taxi driver and got out at his destination. He took a moment to adjust his tie and shirt cuffs. He picked up his bag and briefcase and took a deep breath. The building had no elevator, so he trudged up the four floors. His body ached some and probably always would, the surgeon had told him.

"Grazed your subclavian artery and tore up some bone and muscle. If that artery had been severed, you wouldn't be here. You're a very lucky young man."

"I feel lucky," Jack had said. "And also very unlucky."

"And if that bullet hadn't passed through the other man first...?" The doctor shook his head and looked grim.

I owe Jerome my life. I wish I could thank him.

He arrived on the fourth floor and walked to Apartment D. He set his bags down and rapped on the door, taking another moment to adjust his tie and cuffs. He saw the peephole and wondered if the woman could bring herself to ever look through one again.

When he heard two discrete sets of footsteps coming, his breath quickened along with his pulse.

The speech he had prepared simply drifted from his mind. He was flying by the seat of his pants, just like always.

When the door opened, she looked back at him.

Desiree DuBose looked thinner and her features were drawn. But her eyes brightened at the sight of him, and her mouth eased to a wide smile. Next to her was Queenie. The other pair of footsteps he had heard were actually the dog's claws on the hardwood floors. She barked in greeting and sniffed Jack's hand, perhaps to make sure it was really him. Then she licked his fingers as if to say, *It's good to see you again, friend.*

"Jack? What in the world are you doing here?"

As he stroked Queenie's ears he said, "You talked about Chicago so much I thought I'd have to see it for myself."

"You look all healed."

"Pretty much."

She ushered him in and he set his bags down. "Nice place," he said.

"I like it."

"How about Queenie?"

"She loves running up the stairs, and the cooler weather suits her."

"Been traveling much? I know you said you had those cases to work on."

"Yes, I just got back last week from another one in Mississippi. I have a neighbor who takes care of Queenie while I'm gone. Older woman who just loves animals, and Queenie loves her. Almost makes me jealous."

They sat in the front room, he in a chair, she on the couch, and Queenie on the floor between them, sighing contentedly with her gaze darting back and forth.

"I heard that Judge Ambrose pretty much disappeared," said Jack. "After an exposé by my friend Cheryl Miller came out about his Klan past. Did you have anything to do with that?"

A smile playing over her lips, DuBose said, "I plead the Fifth." Then her expression turned serious. "I didn't leave town until they told me you were out of danger, Jack."

He nodded and then looked down. "I know."

"And I wrote and called your mother. She kept me up to date."

He glanced up at her. "But you didn't call or write *me*."

Now she looked down for a moment. "No, no, I didn't."

They gazed awkwardly at each other.

She said briskly, "So, you came for a visit? You can stay here if you want. I have a spare room. You put me up once. It's only fair I reciprocate." She tacked on a smile.

"Actually, I'm moving here. Going to start looking for a place. If you have any recommendations? But keep it on the cheap side. I'm not a rich man."

She stared at him, obviously trying to process this. "You're moving to Chicago?"

"Hell, I needed to see something other than Freeman County for once in my life."

"What will you do?"

He opened his briefcase and held the sign up for her to see.

"DuBose and Lee?" she said, her eyes widening.

"Still has a nice ring to it, don't you think?"

"You want us to practice law together?" she said incredulously.

"I thought we could do some good."

DuBose eyed him and said, "Donny told me that Shirl thought we were a couple."

Jack sat back. "I didn't know that."

"I told Donny that was not true. We were just professional colleagues."

"That's right."

"It's the way I feel. Is it the same for you, Jack?"

"I care for you, Desiree. I'm not ashamed of that. We're friends."

"That's fine, but it can't ever be more than that."

"You can predict the future now?"

"I understand myself, Jack."

"So you'll be the same person you are forty years from now as you are right this minute?"

"That's not what I said," countered DuBose.

"I believe it's exactly what you said."

They sat in silence for a few moments until Jack spoke up. "You never told me what happened to Paul, the man you were going to marry."

Her expression became distant and fixed. "The same thing that happened to your sister. It was a case I was working on. People didn't like it. They didn't like me. So they took out that hatred on an innocent person. You can understand why I can never...be with anyone else ever again. I can't be the cause of that...pain... that loss again." She looked directly at him. "You almost died, Jack."

"But that was not your fault. And it didn't stop me from climbing on a plane and sailing through the sky for the first time in my life."

"What about your family?"

"I came with their blessing. Especially my momma's."

She shook her head. "I went down that road once and it cost a man I loved more than anything else his life."

"Your love didn't kill Paul, Desiree. And my love for Lucy had nothing to do with her dying. Other people's *hate* did. Same thing that made that boy shoot Jerome. You know that. You've had more hate directed at you for no good reason than any human being should have to bear." He let out a long breath and said, "You gave me every chance to walk away from the case. You asked me time and again if I understood the risks."

"And your sister died. You must regret that you ever met me."

He gazed at her, his brilliant blue eyes watery but intense. "Working with you was the greatest professional honor of my life, Desiree DuBose. And getting to know you as a person…was even a greater honor."

She slowly shook her head and her eyes also teared up. "I just wish we lived in a different world."

"Well, the good news is, we can. It's what you've been fighting for all these years. Real change is built on one person at a time doing something different. Something they might have been scared to do before. Like a white lawyer who'd never thought of defending a Black man in court. Then another person and another person comes along and does something different, too. Hell, before you know it, Desiree, you've got yourself that '*United* States of America' you talk about."

Her eyes flashing with emotion she said, "You sound like you've given this a lot of thought."

"I practiced my lines the whole flight here. We made a good team before. I thought we could continue that. But I can't *make* you do anything, Desiree. Nor would I ever try." He rose to leave.

"Sit down, Jack Lee," she said firmly.

He did as she asked.

DuBose leaned close and said pointedly, "This will be far tougher than you think it will be."

"*I'm* far tougher than I thought I would be."

"Why?" she said, a sudden, desperate look in her eyes.

"I never imagined I'd have such an incentive to turn my life completely upside down—and still be looking forward to every second of doing it."

"So what now?" DuBose asked.

"Now, we get to work, Desiree," said Jack. "Together."

ACKNOWLEDGMENTS

To Michelle, for giving me the journal at Christmas many years ago in which I first started to write the novel, for being the first reader of the material, and for being so encouraging to me when I was working through the story.

To all my publishers around the world, for being so supportive of me over nearly thirty years. I couldn't do any of this without all of you.

To all the wonderful folks at the Aaron M. Priest Literary Agency, who have been with me the whole ride and who have given me great advice and wonderful friendship over many years. And especially to Aaron Priest, who has been a cherished friend, advocate, and partner from the very beginning.

To Caspian Dennis and Sandy Violette, for just being the absolute best.

To Mitch Hoffman, for pushing me harder on this book than on any other, and rightfully so.

To Professor of Law Emeritus Richard J. Bonnie, for reading an early draft of the manuscript and providing sage advice, which I followed.

To Professor of Law Emeritus Mildred W. Robinson, for

providing incredibly helpful comments and suggestions, all of which made their way into the story.

To Kristen White and Michelle Butler, for being so good at so much and keeping me on course.

And finally, to all my family and friends. Your collective impact burns brightly and powerfully within these pages. And within me.

ABOUT THE AUTHOR

DAVID BALDACCI is one of the world's bestselling and favourite thriller writers. A former trial lawyer with a keen interest in world politics, he has specialist knowledge in the US political system and intelligence services, and his first book, *Absolute Power*, became an instant international bestseller, with the movie starring Clint Eastwood a major box office hit. He has since written more than fifty bestsellers featuring, most recently, Amos Decker, Aloysius Archer, Travis Devine and Mickey Gibson. David is also the co-founder, along with his wife, of the Wish You Well Foundation, a non-profit organization dedicated to supporting literacy efforts across the US.

Trust him to take you to the action.

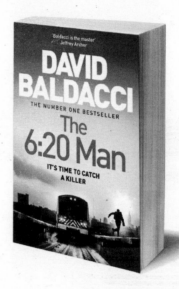
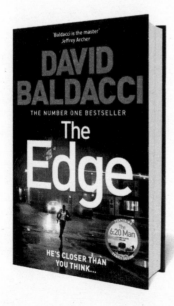

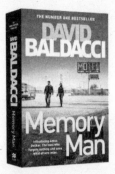
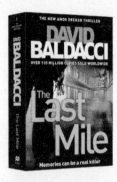
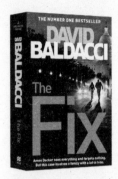
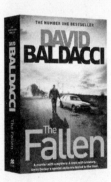
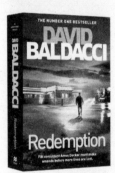
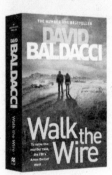
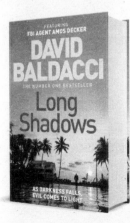

In a town full of secrets who can you trust?

Discover David Baldacci's historical crime series featuring straight-talking WWII veteran Aloysius Archer.

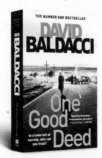 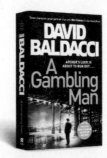 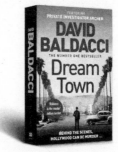

ONE GOOD DEED

Poca City, 1949. Aloysius Archer arrives in a dusty southern town looking for a fresh start. After accepting a job as a local debt collector, Archer soon finds himself as the number one suspect in a local murder. Should Archer run or fight for the truth?

A GAMBLING MAN

California, 1949. Archer is on his way to start a new job with a renowned private investigator. Arriving in a tight-lipped community rife with corruption, Archer must tackle murder, conspiracy and blackmail in a town with plenty to hide . . .

DREAM TOWN

Los Angeles, 1952. Private investigator and WWII veteran Aloysius Archer returns to solve the case of a missing screenwriter during the Golden Age of Hollywood.

You took my sister.
I've hunted you for 30 years.
Now . . . your time's up.

Discover David Baldacci's bestselling series featuring Special Agent Atlee Pine

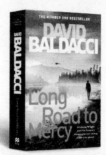

LONG ROAD TO MERCY

Thirty years since Atlee Pine's twin sister, Mercy, was abducted from the room they shared as children, Pine starts the pursuit of a lifetime to finally uncover what happened on that fateful night.

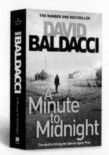

A MINUTE TO MIDNIGHT

Seeking answers in her home town, Pine's visit turns into a rollercoaster ride of murder, long-buried secrets and lies . . . and a revelation so personal that everything she once believed is fast turning to dust.

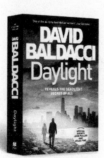

DAYLIGHT

When Pine's investigation coincides with military investigator John Puller's high-stakes case, it leads them both into a global conspiracy from which neither of them will escape unscathed.

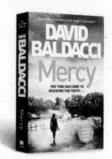

MERCY

FBI agent Atlee Pine is at the end of her long journey to discover what happened to her twin sister, Mercy, and must face one final challenge. A challenge more deadly and dangerous than she could ever have imagined.